T5-BCF-415

QUEEN
OF
BATTLE

0368-COOL

QUEEN
OF
BATTLE

John W. Cooley

Dan,
All best wishes
to a fellow author
and consultant.
Jack

0368-COOL

Copyright ©1999 by John W. Cooley.

Library of Congress Number: 98-89880
ISBN#:   Hardcover   0-7388-0313-8
                    Softcover   0-7388-0314-6

All rights reserved. No part of this book may be reproduced or transmitted in
any form or by any means, electronic or mechanical, including photocopying,
recording, or by any information storage and retrieval system, without permission
in writing from the copyright owner.

This is a work of fiction. Names, characters, places and incidents either are the
product of the author's imagination or are used fictitiously, and any resemblance
to any actual persons, living or dead, events, or locales is entirely coincidental.

This book was printed in the United States of America.

To order additional copies of this book, contact:
Xlibris Corporation   1-888-7-XLIBRIS
PO Box 2199   1-609-278-0075
Princeton, NJ 08543-2199   www.Xlibris.com
USA   Orders@Xlibris.com

CONTENTS

PREFACE 11

DECLARATION OF WAR 15

CONSCIOUS POWERS 41

DISCRETE SECRETS 74

TWISTED TRYST 108

JUMPS AND BUMPS 128

SUSPENDED AGONY 158

TARNISHED LOVE 173

HARD BARGAINING 197

COMMON GROUND 217

JUNGLE FEVER 243

BRIEFING AT CARTAGENA 254

LAMBS TO SLAUGHTER 273

FAIR MARKET VALUE 301

STAGED ASSAULT 310

SALT AND PEPPER 320

NIGHT VISION 336

HIGH-TECH JUSTICE 354

NEW HORIZONS 365

FOR MY WIFE MARIA,
A COURAGEOUS QUEEN OF BATTLE,

FOR MY CHILDREN,
JOHN AND CHRISTINA,

AND

FOR ALL OF THE MEN AND WOMEN
OF THE LONG GRAY LINE,
PAST, PRESENT, AND FUTURE

0368-COOL

Is there so great a superfluity of men fit for high duties . . . that we lose nothing by putting a ban upon one half of mankind . . . refusing beforehand to make their faculties available, however distinguished they may be?

John Stuart Mill
The Subjection of Women (1869)

PREFACE

The Story of Pallas Athena

Queen of Battle is a modern interpretation of the story of Pallas Athena from Greek mythology. Athena, Greek goddess of wisdom and war, had perfectly balanced masculine and feminine characteristics. She was both warrior and nurturer. Counterpart to the goddess Minerva in Roman mythology, she taught women the art of weaving and all other household crafts; she nurtured women during childbirth, though she, herself, was a virgin in the ancient Grecian sense that she never married. She enjoyed, however, being in the midst of male action and power, and with Nike, the goddess of victory as spiritual support, Athena led armies, but only those that fought for just causes. As a warrior, she could hurl thunderbolts and she possessed the power of prophecy. She acted as Zeus' deputy in maintaining law, order, and justice. As the patroness of art, science, and learning, she presided over all useful inventions and discoveries, and in this role, she was the supervising architect of the ship Argo and of the Wooden Horse, in which the Greeks later concealed themselves at Troy.

Athena could not tolerate disrespect. Arachne, a woman wonderfully skilled at weaving, boasted that she was better at the craft than the goddess. When Arachne wove a perfect piece of tapestry, Athena tore it to shreds. Arachne despairingly attempted suicide by hanging herself from a rafter. Athena transformed her into a spider and the rope into a cobweb, up which Arachne climbed to safety.

0368-COOL

The first battle in which Athena engaged was a crucial one.

There was a horde of giants who resented Zeus and determined to be rid of him. The giants emerged from the Underworld in a place across the sea from Mount Olympus, the home of Zeus. The giants fought with savage fury, and they might have prevailed had it not been for the wisdom and daring of the warrior goddess Athena. She was everywhere on the battle field, guiding her chariot fearlessly to where the fighting was heaviest. Athena pursued a giant named Pallas and his brother, Enceladus, a giant with a hundred arms. The two giants' combined power was nothing compared to the furious onslaught of the warrior goddess. Athena killed both giants and, in victory, added the name Pallas to her own, from then on being known as Pallas Athena.

Another explanation in mythology for the name "Pallas" Athena emerges from the circumstances surrounding the mysterious Palladium. This was a statue of the goddess Athena, which when possessed by a city, served as a pledge of safety of the place.

The origin of the Palladium stemmed from an incident in Athena's maidenhood in which she accidentally killed her dearest companion, Pallas, daughter of Triton. Athena caused a statue of the girl to be made. Afterward, Athena took on the identity of Pallas and added Pallas' name to her own—Pallas Athena. The Palladium was moved to several cities over the centuries, and its final resting place was never conclusively established.

John W. Cooley

0368-COOL

DECLARATION OF WAR

"A-layeft . . . A-layeft . . . A-layeft—rot—layeft," droned the cadet first classman, scanning ahead past Washington Monument for an appropriate point to turn his Beast Barracks platoon.

Behind him, the six-story granite rampart MacArthur Barracks loomed majestically in Gothic splendor; on his right, the Bastogne sallyport of Eisenhower Barracks opened onto Central Area, a spacious concrete courtyard where untold scores of cadets had dutifully walked their punishment tours over the nearly two hundred years of the Academy's history. On his left, the West Point Plain—a vast expanse of flat, green landscape separating rows of castlelike cadet barracks to the south and the serpentine Hudson River to the north.

Four-foot-high wooden platforms dotted the Plain, and one, sometimes two, upper-class cadets in T-shirts and gym shorts stood atop them, yelling commands into the separate seas of pallid, sweaty, scared, paunchy beings—new cadets—ardently pushing away uncooperative ground. A burnt orange July sun baked the earth beneath their T-shirted chests, teasing the scent of freshly cut grass out of the subtle mid-morning breeze.

"I don't know but I've been told," crooned the Firstie in an "achy-breaky" Country-Western voice, a lyric echoed by the deer-eyed new cadets, marching in cadence and competing with sweltering heat to carry their M14 rifles at a rigid port arms.

"This P.T. is getting old!" the Firstie intoned with mild irreverence.

After the obligatory platoon echo, the Firstie shouted, *"Column LEFT . . . HAAAAARCH,"* and resumed the "Sound off" cantata. Commanding another column left, he halted the platoon in front of the last available wooden platform. Sitting on the platform facing the platoon was a female figure, her butter blond hair pulled tightly back into a bun, her knees pulled up to her buxom, perspiring torso. Firstie Mary Kathryn McKeane,—"Kate"—peered at the motley slavelike group over her M14 rifle, held parallel to the horizon by her rigid outstretched arms.

This lone woman on a platform in the middle of the Plain. How incongruous. Famous combat heroes had trod this historic parade field in decades past as part of the "The Long Gray Line"— Eisenhower, MacArthur, Bradley, Patton, Grant. Even more famous dignitaries of their day had watched them from the reviewing stand. All dead. All men.

Kate threw back the bolt on her M14 and let it slam shut.

"Who are you?" Kate shrieked at the new plebes.

"The beasts of Sixth New Cadet Company," the recruits responded in unison.

"Why are you here?" Kate countered.

"Because we're masochists" was the pre-coached response.

"Then assume this position and hold, . . . dumbguards!!" The new cadets quickly dropped to their buttocks, pulling their knees in tight, and holding their M14s outstretched in front of them, parallel to the ground.

Kate continued to peer over her rifle, focusing now not on the grunts, but on Trophy Point in the distance, with its stately flagpole—the mast from the battleship *Maine*—flanked by a section of chain that during the Revolutionary War stretched across the Hudson River to block southward progress of British ships. Close by, the sleek, erect *Battle Monument* touted its battery of defending cannons of the artillery—the branch of the Army known as "the King of Battle".

"One,. . . . twooop,. . . . threeep. . . . fourrrrp," Kate commanded as she watched the plebes alternately raise their rifles above their heads and back to knee-level. . . .

2

In Washington D.C. on that July morning, you could have cut the humidity with a bayonet.

"Are you ready to see Commissioner Federhoff now, Mr. President," asked Tom McCafferty, President Benton's longtime friend and Chief of Staff. Somethin' about his National Drug Control Report."

"Sure, Mack," said the President. "But first, please cool this place off."

McCafferty walked to the opposite end of the office and examined the thermostat.

"It's on the coolest setting. Should I get the building engineer?"

"Yeah. Tell him he can come in during my meeting with Federhoff. I'm sure my blood'll be *boiling* by that time."

Benton lit up a cigarette and drummed his fingers on a western boot resting on his crossed leg.

"Oh, one more thing," said McCafferty.

"Yes?"

"Congresswoman Esther Grant telephoned. Said she'd like to meet with you tomorrow, if possible."

"Oh *Jesus*, what does *she* want?"

"Something about the House Armed Services Committee and women in combat."

"Not *that stuff* again! I thought that issue was a dead horse. Can't win on that one. Last time the military blasted me for weakening our defense; Lila Davis-Whitfield and her conservative groupies chided me for ignoring traditional American values. The liberal feminist groups threatened me publicly with castration for being sexist. I wish the issue would just go away."

"What should I tell her?"

"What's my schedule for tomorrow?"

"Tight as usual, but you could squeeze her in for twenty minutes, late afternoon."

"That's too bad," Benton said. "Sure I'm not gonna be out of town?"

"I'm sure. . . . One thing. Mrs. Grant *was*, as you recall, one of your staunchest supporters last election. She even gave a speech for you at the Convention."

"That's right. But I didn't ask her to do it, and I wouldn't have. Republican or not, she sure has some weird ideas—

"No question she carries a lot of liberal baggage.

"Chicago Democrat who switched parties, I recall."

"Right."

"Didn't she have trouble with the law over campaign funds while she was a Democrat?"

"I believe so. The story goes that she almost got indicted before an Irish relative stepped in and pushed the right buttons in the D.A.'s office to get it squelched."

"Irish mafia, huh?"

"Yeah."

Benton inhaled smoke deeply and then exhaled while rolling a long ash around the edge of a crystal ash tray until it disengaged. "Can't get too close to her. It'd look bad."

"Should I tell her you're too busy tomorrow."

"No. Just put something innocuous in the schedule you give the reporters—study time or something."

McCafferty nodded. "I'll get Federhoff."

As McCafferty left the Oval Office, Benton swiveled in his chair and stared at his reflection in the glass doors of his bookcase for several seconds. If he had a fetish, it was books. He collected them. Certain kinds. He owned practically every book on politics and political strategy ever printed. They included books he had collected while attending a small college in Missouri and during his years at Yale Law School; while a Missouri state legislator, state attorney general, and governor. Crammed into the several shelves of his bookcase, worn and dog-eared, the books served as his arsenal—a reservoir of weapons for political combat. Politics didn't come naturally to him. He would often come to the Oval Office late at night and skim through several books for ideas about dealing with specific problems, specific personalities. He usually found answers. And when he didn't, he at least found solace in the search. One problem, however, perpetually evaded solution: the U.S. drug problem. For months he had searched his books; for months he had turned up no new ideas. "What's *with* these figures anyhow, Vincent," Benton asked, smashing his cigarette into the ashtray and twisting it forcefully. "Look at this . . . eighteen million drug users in the U.S; three million of 'em are hard core cocaine addicts and two-and-a-half million are adolescents . . . last year alone there were twenty-five thousand drug-related murders in the U.S. . . . and we have two hundred thousand more drug damaged infants than we had when I took office a little over a year ago. . . . Rural high school seniors reported the highest annual use of crack, heroin, stimulants, barbiturates, nitrites, and PCP. . . . The influx of cocaine from Colombia has quadrupled in the past year despite Colombian National Police's seizure of over sixty-four metric tons of cocaine and the destruction of thirty-eight cocaine laboratories and fifty-eight airstrips, and the arrest of fifteen hundred drug dealers, including the notorious cartel king Raoul Bodega—an estimated two hundred and fifty million dollars in stolen property annually is attributed . . . "

"Mr. President, the numbers are dreadful. Can't deny that," Federhoff said, squirming in his chair. Did you happen to see *Base-Line* last night?"

"No, Martha and I were with the Canadian Prime Minister, until the wee hours."

"I have a videotape . . . " Federhoff said, reaching for his briefcase.

Benton's hand swept in the direction of the VCR.

Federhoff inserted the tape into a small, self-contained VCR monitor unit sitting on the President's desk. He pushed the play button, then walked around the desk and stood behind the President. After a few flickers, the tape stabilized and the graphics for the *Base-Line* program came into focus. Classical music played in

the background as the TV cameras zoomed in on veteran inter-
viewer-commentator Ed Hopkins, enthroned behind a futuristic
desk in front of a oversized map of the world. In this setting, Hopkins
had more power than the President. Hopkins knew it. He began
to speak.

> *"Good evening, ladies and gentlemen. Welcome to Base-Line. I*
> *am Ed Hopkins and tonight we will presenting some shocking*
> *information about the Benton Administration's complete inef-*
> *fectiveness in dealing with the current drug problems in the*
> *United States. With many months of experience behind it, and*
> *still riding the wave of a "law and order" reform, the Adminis-*
> *tration seems content to stand by and watch the rest of the*
> *country being engulfed by armies of illegal drug lords, drug king-*
> *pins, and drug dealers operating a billion or more dollar a year*
> *drug-distribution business. What's more, the related crimes ema-*
> *nating from this cesspool of illegal narcotics trade has infiltrated*
> *our schools, our corporations, our institutions and are ripping*
> *apart the very fabric of our society. How long can the United*
> *States citizenry wait for a solution? Our guests tonight will*
> *have answers to this question and others, but first let's take a*
> *quick look at this background piece specially produced for Base-*
> *Line by our Washington D.C. affiliate and narrated by our*
> *own Harry Copley. . . . "*

Pushing the pause button on his remote control, Benton, eyes
glazed, muttered slowly and disbelievingly, "Holy shit, Vince, this
ain't no TV program. We're watching a Presidential character assassination!!"

He hit the pause button again and riveted his attention to the
screen. Harry Copley's background piece centered on the impact
of the Colombian drug cartels on the U.S. drug scene. Copley's
voice-over of the scenes of human carnage in the streets of Medellín
and Cali, Colombia droned dramatically . . .

*"The Bodega brothers—Raoul and Hector—have a strangle-
hold on the Colombian Government and its President, Esteban
Guardina. Because of the Bodegas' awesome power and influence, garnered mostly through terrorism, fifteen hundred criminal investigators of Colombian National Police, assisted by one
hundred thirty agents of the Technical Corps of the Judicial
Police and one hundred ten agents of the Department of Ad-
ministrative Security—roughly equivalent to the FBI—have
been wholly ineffective in curtailing cocaine and heroin production. Combined U.S. interdiction efforts of the State Department, Drug Enforcement Administration, Customs Service, and the Defense Department have been equally ineffective. Most of the cocaine and heroin entering the United States
is being manufactured by cartels operated by the Bodegas in the
mountains near Medellín, Colombia in South America. Until
this supply source is extinguished, the U.S. has no hope of con-
trolling the . . . "*

Just then, a knock at the door. A portly gentleman in a blue
shirt and grey trousers carrying a small red toolbox stood in the
doorway. His first name was stitched above his breast pocket.

"Oh, Hugo," said Benton. "Thanks for coming so quickly.
Vince, this is our building engineer, Mr. Stravinsky. He'll only be
a minute. He needs to check the thermostat."

"By all means," said Federhoff wiping the perspiration from
his forehead with a cupped hand and flinging it briskly to the
floor. As the building engineer headed in the direction of the thermostat, Benton and Federhoff gazed again at the monitor.

Two of the three guests on *Base-Line*, a Democratic State Attorney General from Illinois and a Harvard expert on criminology,
spoke derisively of Benton and his Administration for what they
viewed as "bureaucratic paralysis"—a condition of indecision
spawned by the inexperience of the Administration's recent ap-
pointees. Both of these guests shared the belief that if Benton didn't
get his Administration in gear soon, the general citizenry would

suffer further, and it would be likely that Benton would not get reelected for another term. The Harvard guest pointed out. . .

> "President Guardina continues to use an ineffective 'carrot and stick' offensive against traffickers which attempts to combine strong judicial enforce- ment actions with a Presidential plea bargaining decree. But its all really just a big joke. Colombia's judicial system is still susceptible to trafficker intimidation and corruption. The recent surrender and incarceration of Raoul Bodega is just one glaring example of the farcical nature of the policy. Bodega is being kept in a location that can only be described as a country club with all the amenities that CEOs of Fortune 500 companies are accustomed to. He still has communication with the outside world and therefore is able to reign supreme over his drug kingdom. In the coming year, the Benton Administration intends in the coming year to dump thirty-six million dollars of judicial assistance money into this swirling vortex of futility. This is just plain bad U.S. policy-making. It flies in the face of the goal-oriented U.S.-Colombian Cartagena Pact of 1990 negotiated by the previous Presidential Administration."

Opposing those views were the opinions of the third guest— John Carrington, a Republican Senator from Utah. He didn't see the drug problem as bad as *Base-Line* had painted, he viewed the solution to be in the education of youth and addicts. Hopkins delighted in making a mockery of Carrington's views.

> "What faith can the American public put in the opinions of a Senator from Utah—a state that has one of the lowest percentages of illegal drug use in America?"
> "Well, your producers must have thought I had something important to say otherwise they wouldn't have invited me to appear on national television."

Benton, still seated, and Federhoff, now pacing back and forth behind the President closer to Hugo, continued to watch the video screen as Hopkins and the Senator proceeded to wrangle.

"I've got the solution, Mr. President," said Hugo.

Absorbed in the video, and thinking he was responding to Federhoff, the President said, "Yeah, what is it?"

"The mechanism is the problem—you've got to change the controls—these controls are outmoded," continued Hugo.

"You know, you're right, Vince. We need new ways to control the drug situation; new mechanisms to fight drugs, to fight crime. That's what we have to do, Vince."

"Mr. President, I didn't say anything. That was Hugo you were talking to."

"Yes, Sir," said Hugo, tapping the thermostat with the end of his screwdriver. "I'll be putting in a new control unit this afternoon." Hugo then quietly left the room.

Benton looked at Federhoff intensely, slapped his palms on the arms of his chair, and stood straight up. "That's it, Vince. We're going to declare war!"

3

Sliding her arm out from under satin sheets, Lila reached carefully across the firm pectorals of a motionless, bronzed male body to silence her clock radio's alarm. The bedroom was pitch black except for the flourescent glow of flashing numbers and letters on the clock's face, trumpeting: TUESDAY, JULY 14, 10:30 a.m. Light piano jazz lilting from the radio buffered the sudden violence of the alarm. Lila, clad only in a black lace teddy, rolled to her back, rested her right forearm on her forehead, and stared into the darkness. Thoughts of the prior evening were racing through her mind.

This wasn't the first time that Emilio had wound up in her boudoir after one of those lavish Washington D.C. receptions renowned for their sumptuous banquets, free-flowing liquor, scads of social climbers, international jet-setters, and political wannabes. He had followed her home on at least three previous occasions, and, after engaging in torrid sex, he had passed out unceremoniously, only to awaken each time a little before noon the following day. If he were anyone else, Lila would have given him the boot the first time it happened. But Emilio was different. He was a charmer, with a sprightly wit—a delicious enigma who kept Lila curious. Besides, he was a good lay, and being a middle-aged divorcee, she couldn't be too picky. Lila didn't know much about this Latin except that he was about half her age and worked as a staff assistant for the State Department. She really didn't want to know more.

Lila gently got out of bed and groped her way to the bathroom.

Closing the door behind her, she fumbled for the light switch and finally found it. In the sudden brightness, the sight of her unembellished face in the mirror was discomforting. With her forefinger she vainly attempted to stretch the furrows tight to see if they would magically disappear. They wouldn't. Years of being a socialite were beginning to take their toll. Periods between facelifts were diminishing; wrinkles now seemed to be forming overnight. She turned on the warm water, lowered her head, and began to wash her face.

It seemed like only yesterday that she was growing up as an only child in the affluent suburb of Gross Pointe, Michigan. Born into the family of auto industry blueblood Jonathan Kennert Davis, she was a product of doting nannies, Social Register friendships, multiple charm schools, and eventually Wellesley College. Her father, Hampton Davis, was a successful, multimillionaire businessman in public, but in private, a petulant philandering lush. He was too drunk to attend the ceremony honoring Lila as Detroit 1960 Debutante of the Year. Lila never forgave him for it. Her mother, from the Cochran Brewing family in Milwaukee, was an icy social climber who was conflicted about her beer heritage and her husband's alcoholism. Her mother's attempts to disguise her own Irish roots by claiming obscure family ties to old French aristocracy were roundly unsuccessful. Eventually she came to be known in social circles for the phony she was. Lila grew to distrust her as did everyone else. At an early age, Lila learned how to protect herself, to manipulate, to be wary. Because she received little parental attention when she was in her developmental years, Lila feasted on celebrity—hers and others'. Married three times, each union ended in a bitter divorce leaving Lila childless. Lila was glad she never had children. She felt she had been too traumatized by her own childhood. And besides, children would have tied her to the home and significantly interfered with her pursuit of celebrity.

Drying her face with a fluffy towel, Lila again looked at her reflection in the mirror, half-hoping that the soap and water had repaired the damage mercilessly inflicted by the passing years, the millions of counterfeit smiles, the private boozing and binging. They hadn't. She picked up her eyeliner pencil and sighed, shaking her head slightly. Maybe this would help.

Lila had lived in this upscale eighteenth-century townhouse in Georgetown for fifteen years—five years before and ten years after her divorce from her third husband, Campion Whitfield, a former ambassador to Mexico. The place, with its Martha Stewart-inspired furnishings, was geographically perfect for Lila. Three U.S. Senators, the U.S. Ambassador to Japan, the head of the Central Intelligence Agency, and a U.S. Supreme Court Justice lived on her cul-de-sac and graced her abode from time to time. In the summer, she treated her celebrity neighbors and their families to candelabra block parties, and at Christmas each year, to a Revolutionary War period holiday soirée. The celebrities always came, perhaps out of sympathy for her solo plight. Nonetheless, they reciprocated throughout the year by including her in many of their official dinners and functions around the Capitol. Lila was careful never to drink alcohol at any of them. Through these activities and her once-a-month afternoon tea parties for the celebrities' spouses, Lila stayed well connected and received all the attention she needed.

She put her eyeliner pencil back in its holder, leaning closer to the mirror to check the detail of her work. Better. Now for the makeup. Without breaking her gaze, she reached down like she had done thousands of times before, fumbled slightly for her cosmetic pad and began to perform chemical miracles on her face. Youth was seemingly restored. Maybe *this* was the real Lila.

Aside from being a celebrity by association, Lila was becoming a celebrity in her own right. For ten years, she had been an active member of the arch-conservative Women's Republican American Traditional Heritage foundation and political action committee, called WRATHPAC by its detractors. A merged offshoot of the Women's Christian Temperance Union and the Republican Women's Conservative Caucus, the organization's purpose was to promote traditional conservative values, including sobriety, no extra-marital sex, right to life, and women's role as mother and homemaker. Elected as its president a year before for a three year term, Lila had become the official spokesperson for the organization and had given several speeches at conservative Republican functions around the country. This role put her in close contact with celebrities at the highest levels of the Republican Party. She had maneuvered an introduction to President Frank Benton himself, by inviting him to speak at the organization's annual meeting in Philadelphia. Three thousand people attended from all over the country. She was blissfully up to her chin in celebrities.

Lila put the final touches on her makeup, gaining more self-confidence with every brush of her pasty flesh. Now the lipstick. She pressed the scarlet substance hard to her lips and then allowed the lips to blot themselves by placing them over one another several times. There! *Fini*! She looked searchingly into the mirror trying to detect any flaw whatsoever. Perfect! A social hypocrite and a private lush, completely disguised.

The phone in the bathroom rang low and muffled. Lila picked up the receiver quickly so as not to awaken Emilio. "Davis-Whitfield residence," Lila said in a deepened voice, and in her best stilted, British accent. She always did this to give the impression that she was wealthy enough to have European house servants and to screen out unwanted calls.

"Lila Davis-Whitfield, please," said the female voice on the other end.

"If she is on the premises, madam, who shall I say is calling?" responded Lila, maintaining the dialectic charade.

"U.S. Representative Esther Grant," replied the female voice.

"One moment, madam."

Lila was ecstatic. A real live Congresswoman calling *her*. What could she want? Lila's mind raced: "Could I have been nominated for some federal appointment? An envoy, an ambassadorship? Am I up for some award? Does she need an expert to testify before Congress?" Lila waited ten seconds and then spoke again into the phone in her normal voice without a foreign accent: "This is Lila Davis-Whitfield."

"Ms. Davis-Whitfield, this is U.S. Representative Esther Grant, Republican from Illinois. May I take a few minutes of your time?"

"Certainly. Oh, and please call me Lila."

"Same here—call me Esther. Lila, I understand that you are the current president of the Women's Republican American Traditional Heritage Foundation. Is that right?"

"Yes, it is, Esther. How may I help you."

"Well, to be honest and quite blunt about it, I'm trying to do some advance damage control. You see, hearings are being scheduled in the next few days before the House Armed Services Committee on the issue of women in combat. I want to know if your organization is going to seek to testify before the Committee, and if so, what position you are going to take on the issue? This call may seem a little unusual to you, but the Committee wants to make sure it gets balanced input on the topic."

"Well this is the first I've heard of these hearings [*The nerve of this woman!!*]. I'll have to contact my board members [*Is she trying to fix these hearings or what?*] and see what they say. I'll get back to you [*WRATHPAC has just begun to fight!*] in the next day or so. How can I reach you?

"Just call the general number at the House of Representatives, and they will connect you directly with my office. I'm looking forward to hearing from you."

After a strained but pleasant final exchange, Lila hung up. Half-stunned by the Congresswoman's ebullience, Lila wandered out of the bathroom, stumbling over Emilio's pants lying in her path. The commotion made Emilio stir slightly. He rolled over on his side. Lila froze for a second and then slowly removed her bra and panties, revealing her full-sized figure. She carefully got back into bed and placed her hand ever so gently on Emilio's muscular thigh. With her other hand, she reached over to her nightstand and bringing a silver flask back to her wax-red lips, she took a prolonged swig of vodka. Whenever he awoke, she would be ready for him.

4

The dull gray July sky made the air feel chillier than it actually was. It was winter in Colombia. A temperature of even sixty-eight degrees Fahrenheit was chilly to a Colombian. The thick-bearded, mustachioed Raoul Bodega, clad in starched jungle fatigues, had just finished brunch on the veranda of his "prison" villa overlooking Envigado, a suburb of Medellín. He was seated in a white wicker armchair, gnawing on an apple and casually reviewing faxes sent to him by his loyal lieutenant, Federico, during the preceding night. Typed in a code Raoul could easily decipher, the news was only partially heartening.

The faxes advised that the Cartel's cocaine production had substantially increased in the last four weeks due to the opening in June of fifteen more cocaine processing labs in the mountains two hundred miles north and west of Envigado. Three more captains of the National Police had been "bought" in the Cali area, substantially reducing interference with cocaine production and shipments in northern Colombia. Two judges who had imposed harsh sentences on four captured Bodega followers had been gunned down the evening before in Bogotá when they were leaving the Ministry of Justice. Plans were in the works to extort cooperation from President Guardina himself in the upcoming election year by threats to sabotage the already inadequate Colombian power generation and distribution system. That was the good news.

The bad news made Bodega writhe slightly in his chair and spit out a chunk of apple into a waste can. Bishop Pedro "The Rock" Spinoza had issued a letter from his regal headquarters in Bogotá on the preceding Friday to all Roman Catholics in Colombia. It announced from that day forward, any Catholic convicted of aiding or abetting the Bodegas in any aspect of drug production or distribution would be automatically excommunicated from the Catholic Church. Raoul mused that the edict could easily apply to thirty-five percent of the Catholic population of Colombia. Christ, the Bodegas had at least thirty priests and nine monsignors on their payroll. These clerics, in turn, put the stamp of legitimacy on his illegal drug operations in many of the indigent towns and villages all across the country. He wasn't sure how the clergy would react to that bastard prelate's edict. He knew one thing, however: it wouldn't make a rat's ass of difference to lay drug runners and dealers. They needed the money to support their families; some of them could get employment nowhere else. Many of them were addicts who needed drugs to support their habit. They were locked into the Bodegas—for life. The second bit of bad news was that President Guardina had recently announced publicly that he was going to seek additional assistance from the United States to battle the Bodega terrorists.

Giving his eyes a rest, Raoul laid the faxes down on a glass-topped table beside his wicker throne, and admired his surroundings. They were a tribute to the power he had accumulated over the past fifteen years in becoming Colombia's most influential and feared drug lord. In his ruthless pursuit of money, prestige, and power, he had personally killed or mutilated sixty-three people. His brother, Hector, had more than a hundred notches on his gun, including the brutal murder of a relative by marriage—a wayward cartel lieutenant—and his five year old son. Despite these horrible crimes, Raoul was dispatched to the lap of luxury instead of being incarcerated in one of Colombia's many maxi-mum-security dungeons. Even as a prisoner, he wielded more power than the Government itself.

Raoul was one of fifty-five prisoners being held in this mini-mum security compound. But he received special treatment. Royal treatment. His personal living quarters within the prison com-pound were an electronic marvel. A Mediterranean style office and living room sported an enormous projection TV. A high-definition television graced his lavishly appointed bedroom, off of which there was an enormous Italian marble bathroom with a jacuzzi. Raoul's communication system was state-of-the-art. At his fingertips, Raoul had two fax machines—one for receiving and one for sending—and a personal computer complete with modem and internet ac-cess. A hand-held intercom system provided him instant commu-nication with the guard desk at all times. He also had a regular telephone, a miniature cellular phone, and a telephone equipped for videoconferencing. Connected to his living quarters by an un-derground walkway was an immense building which housed the compound's formal dining room, recreation room, boardroom, indoor-outdoor swimming pool, sauna, and a library whose walls were adorned with reprints of the Bodega art collection. Raoul had access to these amenities any time of the day or night.

He could not leave the compound, however; nor could he have visitors. That was part of the deal he had cut with the Government when he surrendered. He had not seen his family, except by videotelephone, for six months. His wife, two teenage sons and five-year-old daughter lived in a penthouse condominium in Medellín. He missed them. Prostitutes provided him by the prison guards on demand did not fill the emotional void he was experiencing. He wanted out. He was waiting for just the right opportunity.

Raoul picked up the faxes again and began to read. His chair began to tremble slightly. He thought it strange. Perhaps it was laborers preparing footings for the new indoor racquetball courts under construction. The trembling increased in intensity. Raoul became concerned. He needed his intercom unit. He got up and started to walk toward his desk in the middle of the atrium-roofed office-living room. Instantaneously, the floor behind the white throne began to buckle and a huge plate glass veranda window crashed down on the throne, spreading long triangular shards of glass everywhere.

The force of the tremor caused Raoul to be thrown to the floor in front of the desk, face-up. The whole office was undulating in unempathic rhythms—the percussive expressions of an earthquake. Sirens atop high telephone poles around the compound screamed frenetically. Looking straight up at the white framed atrium, Raoul saw cracks in the tinted glass propagating slowly to form spider-web structures ready to crash at any moment.

He reached up to the corner of the desk, grasped the inter-com, and rolled across the floor toward the door. Just then, the atrium glass plummeted to the floor, shattering into a million pieces over Raoul's desk. Having maneuvered himself near the exit door, Raoul yelled into the intercom, "GET ME OUTTA HERE! PRONTO!" No reply. Books and glassware were falling from wall shelves all over the room; huge cracks were forming in all of the walls. The projection TV lay on its side, a coat rack penetrating its screen. Amidst all the commotion, Raoul heard someone at the door, trying to unlock it. A chance to escape. The compound's amenities were being destroyed; there was no reason to stay. Raoul grabbed a thick dinner napkin lying on the floor and wrapped it around the wider part of a shard of glass. The tremors were begin-ning to subside. Raoul managed to stand up by grasping an ex-posed wooden stud with his left hand. He held the covered shard in his right hand. The door opened and a guard in jungle camou-flaged fatigues and a Castro-style cap turned immediately as if to indicate that Raoul should follow. Raoul lunged at the back of the guard, thrusting his right arm over the guard's right shoulder and ripping open the guard's neck with the shard. Number sixty-four. Blood was spurting everywhere; so much so that Raoul barely managed to get the guard's pistol out of his holster and pick up the guard's uniform cap. His arms covered with blood, Raoul put the gun in his belt, the cap on his head, and ran across the long wooden front porch of the villa.

As he was running, he could see that all the buildings in the compound were in shambles. People apparently had sought shelter underground. The guard towers were still intact. But he could see no guards in them. He also noticed that a large *Araucaria* tree had fallen, crushing the satellite dish and smashing flat and extending across the twelve-foot-high chain-link electric fence as well as all three rows of concertina wire. Raoul pulled a miniature cellular phone from his breast pocket, dialed a number, and spoke a five-digit number into the receiver. He then made a mad dash toward the fallen tree, hoping that no guards would spot him, but if they did that the hat would convince them that he was one of their own. No such luck. Cracks of gunfire. Four bullets whizzed past his ears. He had been wrong about the guard towers. A guard in one of the towers was pointing a telescoped rifle at him. Then he saw the bullet-riddled bodies of three other prisoners lying near the fallen tree.

Raoul stopped in his tracks, raised his hands in the air, and surrendered. The guard yelled to Raoul, "Stay where you are!" The guard slowly descended the ladder from the tower, all the while keeping his rifle trained on Raoul. When he was about halfway down, the ladder, weakened by the earthquake, began to pull away from the tower. The guard could not prevent it. Screaming wildly, the guard stayed with the ladder as it made its wide sweep to the ground. When he hit the ground, the ladder lay on top of him. His rifle was about twenty-five feet away. Raoul walked over to him. He sensed that the guard's back was broken. Raoul pulled the pistol from his belt, trained it at the guard's forehead, three inches away. The guard said nothing; but his eyes communicated fear and a request for mercy. Raoul pulled the trigger and watched the guard exhale for the last time. The bullet had left a small neat hole. Number sixty-five.

Raoul turned toward the fallen tree, and bringing the end of the pistol barrel toward his mouth, blew away imaginary smoke. He then walked slowly toward the tree, and mounted and walked across it to reach the outside of the compound. He made his way nonchalantly to the dirt road. A jeep was waiting. A big-framed man in fatigues was sitting in the driver's seat.

"I see you received my call, Federico."

"Yes, Commandante. I've spoken to your wife. Your family is unharmed." Federico removed a long, slender wooden object from his breast pocket. It was weathered and worn. He handed it to Raoul and said, "Here, Commandante, you've probably been missing this."

Raoul's face brightened. His straight razor. Yes, he had missed it. He removed a long crumpled cigar from his pocket and quickly nipped off the end with the sharp blade of the razor.

"What about the coffin?" Raoul asked, while lighting the cigar.

"I hope you've taken good care of it."

As Raoul jumped in the front seat, Federico reached over toward the back seat and removed a poncho exposing a five-foot-long wooden coffin, with one end perched up on the side of the jeep. "I thought you might be worried about it Commandante."

"Good work, Federico. Let's get going."

The jeep sped off down the road and quickly became invisible behind a billowing cloud of dust.

5

That afternoon, Kate, in soccer gear, glanced at the clock tower in Central Area as she came trotting out of the north sallyport and headed for her room in the cadet barracks. It was four-thiry p.m. It had been a butt-buster of a day. Being the S-3 on the Battalion Staff of Beast Barracks, Kate spent a good portion of her days conducting physical training and planning military training exercises of all types for the new cadets. Today had been particularly grueling. Up at five-thirty a.m., reveille at six, breakfast at six forty-five, conducting physical training from eight-fifteen to eleven-thirty, changing uniforms and lunch, twelve to twelve forty-five p.m.; supervising drill instruction for four new cadet companies, one to two; attending a planning session for the Plebe Hike with the Battalion Tactical Officer, one-fifteen to two; making a presentation on the Honor Code in Thayer Hall Auditorium to the entire enrollment of Beast Barracks, two-fifteen to three; judging tryouts for corps squad soccer on the North Playing Field below Trophy Point, three-fifteen to four-fifteen. Dinner formation would be at five forty-five. After dinner, she had to make another presentation to three companies of new cadets on ways to prevent and treat heat exhaustion. If she kept up her current daily pace, she would soon be using this advice.

As an Army brat, Kate knew hardship. The daughter of Major General Charles McKeane, West Point Class of 1965, she had entered the Academy as a plebe three summers before. From the very beginning, she confounded expectations. She was good at beating men at their own game, both intellectually and physically, and she loved it. Her roommate, Tina Marafino, once quipped that Kate was "doing her Daddy proud." But it was more than that. She had an innate sense of duty which pervaded her very being.

That day in high school, when Kate and her classmates at the Academy of the Divine Hope in St. Louis proudly watched the Chairman of the Joint Chiefs of Staff on national news pin the first star on her father's epaulet marked the beginning. He had distinguished himself as a commander of a mechanized infantry regiment in the Persian Gulf War. The seed was planted: if he could do it, *she* could do it. Afterwards, she became obsessed with the idea of women having the opportunity for a ground combat role; to be admitted to the infantry—the "Queen of Battle." She was dedicated to making that role a reality for women, and an important step toward achieving it would be to graduate first in her class: that was her hope, her dream.

"Kate! . . . Kate McKeane!!" a voice from behind her shouted. Kate slowed to a fast walk and looked over her shoulder to see a male cadet in a sweatsuit jogging faster to catch up to her.

"Todd! Todd Gavin!! . . . How have you been?"

"Terrific, Kate," the cadet replied as they both slowed to a stroll and exchanged broad smiles as they continued talking. "I had a great summer leave. Got engaged, and everything," Todd said in slow Kentucky drawl.

"Engaged?" Kate said surprised. "Aren't you the guy who said he wasn't gonna get hitched until he was thirty and wearing Major leaves."

"Well, yeah, Kate," Todd drawled. "But that was before I met Emma Lou . . . Emma Lou Jackson from Lexington."

"Sounds like she worked pretty fast, Todd."

"She did . . . or I did. You'll get to meet her, Kate. She's coming up for Ring Weekend in September. She's a wonderful gal. Smart, gorgeous, lots of fun."

"I bet she is. I'll be looking forward to it."

"Oh, and set aside the weekend of June 17. You'll be getting a wedding invite. It'll be in Lexington. Arch of sabers and all that stuff.

"It's already on my calendar," Kate said with a wink.

Glancing down at his watch, Todd said "Gotta scoot, Kate. The company tactical officer wants to meet with me before dinner formation. I tell you—bein' a company commander in Beast Barracks is at times worse than bein' a plebe."

"Nothing could be worse than bein' a plebe, Todd."

"On second thought, you're probably right. I must have had a temporary memory lapse. . . . Oh—when you see Tina, tell her I said hello. She'll be getting an invite to the wedding, too."

"Okay, Todd. Take care of yourself," Kate said, as she watched Todd break into a jog through the west sallyport.

There would always be a special place in Kate's heart for Todd Gavin. Actually, if it weren't for Todd, Kate would have probably left West Point during her plebe Beast Barracks. As a new cadet, Kate had the misfortune of being assigned to a Beast Barracks company whose upper-class cadre quickly gained the reputation of being the toughest on female cadets. Kate and another squadmate spent every evening of their second and third weeks of Beast Barracks—between nine and ten o'clock—on clothing calls in the room of their squad leader—Dan Petrocelli. Dan was a third-generation West Pointer who relished Beast Barracks duty and thought West Point was no place for women. He liked to play a mind game with women members of his squad. He required them to report to him in as many different uniforms as possible in an hour period. Since his room was on the top floor of a division of barracks and the women's rooms were on the ground floor, they had to negotiate several flights of stairs to comply with his orders. Each time they reported to him they had to be carrying their M14 rifles at port arms and then snappily come to order arms, give him a hand rifle salute, while shouting "New cadet ready for inspection, sir".

He would subject them to a meticulous inspection, circling them like some meddlesome vulture, and shouting in their ears a litany of the most minor peccadillos. The female cadet who was second to arrive at each clothing call had to shout, "Sir, I am a lousy no good sufferin' ginch with lead in my pants. I'm not now and never will be fit for combat." The uniforms he required earlier in the hour would be the most formal—full dress-gray over white pants, full-dress hat with pompom, white cross-belts, brass breastplate, and ammo box—and then the uniform requirements would become progressively less formal. Dress gray; white shirts with gray epaulets and grey trousers; class shirts and grey trousers; fatigues; gym clothes; and finally, a cadet bathrobe only.

While they were standing at attention in bathrobes, sweat dripping off their brows, he would first order them to return to their rooms and report back in four minutes in their "birthday suits". When they dashed from his room to comply, he would command them to halt and return. He would then berate them for ten minutes for being so stupid as to follow an obviously facetious command. If they didn't dash out of the room, he would berate them for not immediately complying with his order. His intent was to break them, mentally and emotionally. Petrocelli was a master of catch 22's and his tactics almost worked on Kate. She was ready to quit. Then Todd came on the scene, like a miracle from nowhere. The lanky Kentuckian classmate, mature well beyond his eighteen years, heard through the new cadet grapevine that she was about to throw in the towel and leave West Point. Even though he was not in her platoon, one Sunday afternoon about midway through the eight weeks of Beast Barracks he sought her out and went to her room. With a great deal of concern and compassion, he convinced Kate that she had survived the worst, and that she would not have to deal with Petrocelli anymore when she was assigned to a regular-lettered company for the plebe academic year. He urged her to find humor in every challenging situation and to deflect Petrocelli's unfair criticism and gender-directed slurs. Kate felt recharged. Todd's sage advice got her over the hump of Beast. She would forever be grateful to him.

Kate entered Eisenhower Barracks, checked the bulletin board for any special announcements, and headed toward her room. Her roommate, Tina, would probably be there when she arrived.

Tina, from Hoboken, New Jersey, was in many ways Kate's opposite. The product of a lower middle class family of seven children, Tina went to West Point because it was a free education; Kate went to prepare herself to be Army Chief of Staff. Although Tina scored high in leadership, she was not on the Dean's List; Kate was a born leader and ranked second academically in her class. Tina was moody and emotional at times; Kate was solid as a rock, never crying, not even as a high school freshman at her mother's funeral. Tina liked to tease and play practical jokes; Kate couldn't take very much teasing, and she loathed practical jokes, thinking them juvenile. Tina was sexually active; Kate was a virgin following the advice of her Catholic upbringing and saving herself for her wedding night. Despite their differences, Kate and Tina had developed a close, trusting friendship. There was nothing one would not do for the other, unless it involved lying, cheating, or stealing. However, exaggerating, collaborating, and borrowing on a long term basis were, for them, always in the realm of the doable.

Kate entered the barracks, walked down the hall and into her room to find Tina lying faceup and stark naked in bed reading the *New York Times*. On an end table, a miniature television, on low volume, blinked pictures of the violent local news happenings of the day.

"For chrissakes, Tina! Getting ready for your knight in shining armor?"

"No, Kate," Tina responded casually, " . . . just the whole damned army."

Kate smiled, knowing that Tina probably meant it. "Say, Tina, I got some news. Guess who's getting married right after graduation?"

"About half the corps of cadets, 'cept you and me."

"No, I mean, *really*, Tina. Guess who."

"I give up—who?"

"Todd Gavin! I just ran into him out in Central Area."

"Unbelievable! He was Mr. Confirmed Bachelor. A great catch though."

"Well, you'll be meeting her. She's coming up Ring Weekend."

Still perusing the newspaper, Tina muttered, "Maybe she has a "hunk" for a brother she'll bring along. Southern accents really turn me on."

Kate started removing her soccer clothes and getting ready to take a shower. "What's going on in the world, Tina?"

Tina flipped the newspaper back to the front page. "Listen to this headline: *"GENERALS OPPOSE COMBAT BY WOMEN"*. Tina paused. "Go on, Tina," Kate said, untying her tennis shoes.

"Washington, July 14—Senior Army generals have forced the civilian Army Secretary to retreat from an ambitious plan to open thousands of combat positions now closed to women. At the heart of the clash is a confidential decision memorandum dated June 1 from Army Secretary John Sherrill to Defense Secretary George Masterson recommending that women be allowed to serve in the battalion headquarters of combat engineer, air defense and field artillery, and infantry units. Secretary Sherrill also urged that women be allowed to fly helicopters carrying special-operations troops and to serve as crew members of a

barrage artillery system. The memorandum reportedly made Army Chief of Staff Marlin Winterfield 'hit the roof. Throngs of other interviewed general officers expressed the belief that women fail to meet the physical requirements to serve in infantry, armor, and artillery units. The only field commander to support the recommendations of Secretary Sherrill's memorandum was Lieutenant General Winston Throckmiller, rumored to be next commanding officer of SIXCOM, the nation's drug interdiction command in the Caribbean, and Central and South America. . . . "

"Throckmiller? Is that what it says, Tina?"

"Yeah, Throckmiller."

"My dad thinks he's really a cool guy. When my Dad was a plebe, Throckmiller was his Beast Barracks cadet battalion commander. According to Dad, he has some really strong feelings about women serving in the military."

"Now it clicks," said Tina. "I remember his name from the Academy history lecture I gave last week to some new cadets. Even as a young colonel in the mid-1970s, he was pretty brash in his support of women entering the U.S. military academies. He was one of the strongest proponents. One of the arguments he used successfully then was based on women in the Israeli army. He argued to Congress that Israel was the only democracy that conscripted women into the military, and that they had done so since the State of Israel was created in 1948. His appearance before Congress was the single most important factor in opening West Point to women in 1976."

"He should have no trouble convincing Congress now that women should have broader opportunities in combat."

"Don't be too sure," Tina replied. "There are a lot of adverse forces at work now. Even more than in the 1970s. And besides, the Israeli Army argument won't work this time."

"Why not, Tina?"

"Israeli women have never been used in a combat role. But in recent years they have been trained in combat techniques and have trained male soldiers for combat duty in the West Bank and Gaza."

"Oh *that's* cool," Kate said sarcastically. "They can *train* for combat; they just can't *do* combat. How ridiculous!"

"I agree, Kate. But that's the way it is."

Kate, wearing a bathrobe, was busy looking for her shampoo and soap in her locker. Still lying on her back, Tina folded the newspaper into quarters, focusing on an obscure article on page 8. "Check this headline, Kate . . . `*Defense Department Pondering Expanded Military Anti-drug Role in Colombia.*'"

"Looks like the full-employment plan for female members of our Class," Kate dead-panned while heading out the door for the shower room down the hall.

"Dream on, prom queen," Tina jabbed.

Kate took a couple of steps out of the room, and then heard Tina call to her. "Wait, Kate, listen." Kate stepped back into the room. Tina was pointing to the miniature television in the corner. The local TV news anchor was speaking more theatrically than usual . . .

> "*This bulletin just in from the Associated Press.*
>
> *Colombian news agencies reported this afternoon that an earthquake measuring 6.5 on the Richter scale devastated large portions of the city of Medellín and caused severe destruction in surrounding communities.*
>
> *The cataclysmic event also caused severe damage to several governmental structures, including two electric power stations, and several prisons, including one near Envigado where the notorious drug lord, Raoul Bodega, was being held. Early reports indicate that Bodega has escaped. Colombia's President, Esteban Guardina, has declared a state of emergency, and has issued an official request to President Benton for financial and military assistance from the United States. We will be providing more details of this story as it develops. . . .*"

"Prom queen, huh?" Kate said, "hmmmmmphing" all the way to the showers.

CONSCIOUS POWERS

Kate alternately looked toward the wooden doors to her left across the room and then at her digital wristwatch. October 27; 9:10 a.m.. The hearing should have started ten minutes ago. Butterflies convulsed her stomach. Could she actually be here—in the hearing room of a subcommittee of the U.S. House of Representatives? Could anything she had to say be that important? It all seemed so unreal. So much had happened to her since that day last July when she dreamed about becoming First Captain of the Corps of Cadets. While she waited, Kate's mind eased into state of tangled memories.

2

The Beast Barracks detail had been more of an ordeal for her than she had expected. In early August, several female cadets in her barracks had complained to their company tactical officers about being sexually harassed by their upper-class male platoon leaders. One male platoon leader was accused of routinely referring to female new cadets as "dykes", "cunts", and "whores"; another faced charges that he bribed a particularly scrawny female cadet with "boodle"—candy, ice cream, snacks, etc.—in exchange for sex, and also extorted sex from her by requiring her to do pullups until she succumbed to his advances. Both males were given disciplinary hearings before an upper-class cadet tribunal chaired by Kate, and both denied the accusations under oath. Several males testified against them and the tribunal convicted both accused cadets of the allegations. The tribunal busted the name-caller to Private, with no opportunity for promotion during his first class year. It also gave the offender his option of a permanent demotion to Private, a "slug"—consisting of a hundred hours of walking punishment tours on Central Area—and confinement to quarters on evenings and weekends for the duration of his first class year or expulsion from the Academy. He opted to stay at West Point and take the punishment.

The victim reacted like an hysterical banshee. She immediately brought charges against her tormentor for honor violations, claiming that he had repeatedly lied to the cadet disciplinary panel when he denied the sexual misconduct under oath. A hastily formed panel of the Cadet Honor Committee, after hearing all the evidence, agreed with the victim. It found the accused guilty of violating the sacred Honor Code— "a cadet will not lie, cheat, or steal, nor tolerate those who do"—and recommended that he be "found" on honor, or in layman's terms, expelled from the Academy. An all-male review panel of regular army officers later declined to accept the recommendation on a technical ground—that the accused had not been allowed enough time by the Honor Committee panel to prepare his defense. The review panel also implied that there was some evidence that the accused was, in part, seduced by the female cadet. It ruled that the punishment earlier imposed by the disciplinary panel was sufficient to avenge the wrong. Kate was furious, as were most of the female cadets, that the all-male review panel had the audacity to conclude that the male cadet was a *victim* of female seduction. It was a man's game, played by men's rules.

All of that had occurred during the first two weeks of August. In the third week of August, Kate had been summoned to the Office of the Commandant of Cadets, Brigadier General Lance Chandler. He informed Kate that she was one of five cadets in her class being considered for the position of Cadet Brigade Commander, with the rank of First Captain. The interview went well, but not perfectly. When she left the general's office she doubted very much that she would be selected.

It certainly didn't hurt her chances, however, that Chandler had served in the 82nd Airborne Division with her father at Fort

Bragg. Nor was it a handicap that Chandler said during the interview that he thought her mother had been "the most striking example of female pulchritude that he had ever laid his eyes on." Kate remembered feeling embarrassed when Chandler made that statement. He said it with a piercing gaze that made her uncomfortable. A little later during the conversation, Chandler became somewhat somber and more measured in his speech. Looking up from some papers on his desk and over the top of his half-moon glasses, he told Kate that she had one substantial blemish on her leadership record. Kate knew what was coming. It was Buckner.

During her summer training at West Point's Camp Buckner after her Plebe Year, Kate was a squad leader in an escape and evasion exercise. One morning, about four-thirty a.m., about twenty "guerrillas", played by officers and enlisted men and women of an infantry company attached to West Point, entered her platoon barracks and ordered everyone out of bed. A couple of male cadets bolted nude out the back door of the barracks only to be stopped in their tracks by three guerrillas in black pajamas and headbands—two males and a female—armed with bayoneted AK-47 rifles. The guerrillas escorted the two Adonis-like would-be escapees into the barracks at bayonet point. They then ordered the naked duo to do fifty push-ups encircled by their platoon comrades who were directed to chant the artillery tune "The Caissons Go Rolling Along" in the background while the men's genitals were bouncing up and down on the floor. Half-shocked and bewildered, Kate caught the eye of Tina Marafino. They both knew they were not going to let this pass unavenged.

The guerrillas gave the cadets three minutes to get on any clothing they wished. They then blindfolded the cadets, cuffed their hands behind their back, and herded all thirty-six of the ragtag troop up ramps and into three uncovered deuce-and-a-half trucks. Huddled together on the bed of the trucks, most wearing only fatigue bottoms and T-shirts, some with tennis shoes, some with combat boots, and some only in shower thongs, the captive cadets trembled in the chill of the brisk morning wind. After about an hour's ride, which roller-coastered through narrow mountain backroads and treated the disoriented cadets to a gratuitous blanket of dust, the three trucks finally rolled to a stop and the back-ramps were reattached.

"Dismount, you meddling American bastards," came a loud, gruff command from the side of the trucks. Several guerrillas mounted the trucks pushing the captives toward the ramps. Some cadets stumbled, falling facedown on the ramps. Guerrillas pulled them to their feet and pushed them in the direction of a makeshift stockade. Tina resisted the pushing and bullying, and received a smack on the back of her head. Kate was pushed so hard that she lost her balance and fell, but managed to twist her body so as to land on her back just above her cuffed hands. A female guerrilla pulled Kate to her feet by grasping the chain connecting her cuffs. One of Kate's wrists began to trickle blood. Once inside the small stockade, the guerrillas uncuffed the captives and allowed them to remove their blindfolds. Kate immediately tied her blindfold around her wrist to blot the continuously seeping scarlet welts.

Within about a half-hour, the bleeding stopped. During that time, guerrillas began roughly escorting captives into several interrogation rooms off the central stockade area. They questioned the captives, one by one. The ordeal continued into the afternoon, From time to time, screams emanated from the interrogation rooms. The captives received nothing to eat; and water was only available if they crawled across the compound and begged for it. Those who refused to disclose anything to the interrogators other than their name, rank, and serial number were subjected to various kinds of moderate torture and threats of more serious torture. One captive endured water dripping on his head for six hours, and then in crazed desperation, he broke, mentally, and answered all the interrogator's questions. A female captive refused to talk until a guerrilla bent her over a table, chained her facedown, and then rubbed her genital area with a broomstick imitating rape. After she screamed the map coordinates of her parent unit, she fainted and had to be evacuated back to the West Point Hospital.

The guerrillas dealt even more harshly with more obstinate captives—males and females—who gave false answers. They were required to strip to the waist, and then blindfolded; staked to the ground, they were doused with sugar water and told that scorpions were about to be released on their bodies. If the captives still refused to tell the truth, jars filled with roaches were emptied on them. Although the roaches didn't bite or sting, the tickling sensation of insects streaking across their arms, legs, and bellies prompted their instant cooperation. They told all.

Fortunately for Kate, her squad was the last to be scheduled for interrogation. While waiting in the stockade, Kate noticed a small hole in the chicken wire which might have been made the night before by a raccoon or possum. While four of her flanker squad mates strategically positioned themselves in front of the hole, Kate, Tina, and three more of her more diminutive squad members—Charmaine Tibideau, Lori Haskel, and Sandy Rothman—squeezed through the hole and escaped. Once free, the fivesome made their way into the dense underbrush of the woodland. Within two hours, they had ploughed their way three thousand meters into the timberland of the military reservation, north of the stockade.

It began to drizzle. Before long they were caught in a torrential rainfall. Shielded somewhat by the tightly knitted branches of the overarching trees, they trudged onward. They had no idea where they were, or where they were going, but Kate thought their best bet was to find a stream or a road and follow it until they reached civilization.

With dusk approaching, Tina thought she heard something—like the whirring of a truck or a jeep engine. They moved about three hundred meters in the direction of the sound and saw a clearing. From their vantage point they could see a jeep on a narrow roadway, mired almost to its fenders in mud, its wheels spinning helplessly as its driver pushed the accelerator to the floor. Two black-pajamaed individuals were trying to rock the vehicle out of its slurried predicament. Kate immediately huddled with her squad mates and issued her plan of attack. The five cadets converged on the unsuspecting guerrillas from several directions. Preoccupied with their vehicle dilemma, the guerrillas did not notice the onslaught of Kate's assault team until it was too late. Kate, Lori, and Sandy tackled the guerrillas to the ground, rolling around in foot-deep mud, while Tina and Charmaine retrieved three sets of handcuffs from the jeep. Darkness was falling.

With all three guerrillas handcuffed, Tina snatched a flashlight from the dashboard of the jeep and shined it in the face of one of the guerrillas. A muddied female countenance glowed in the darkness. "By gosh!! Tina shrieked, "methinks we've captured the `caisson' trio." Sure enough, they had. A desire for revenge overwhelmed the cadets. They quickly led their prisoners deep into the timber, out of sight from the road, and strapped them to trees with rappelling ropes that they had found in the jeep. The guerrillas pleaded with Kate not to leave them behind to suffer the elements. Emotionless, Kate turned around abruptly and walked toward the jeep. The five cadets had no difficulty pushing the jeep out of the mire. They piled in, and with Kate driving, they slipped and slid down the road, Tina hooting and wailing all the way like a marauding Arapaho leaving a burning cavalry campsite. About 2:00 a.m., the five cadets finally made their way back to the vicinity of Camp Buckner, ditching the jeep about a half mile from the entrance, and walking through the woods back to their barracks. They showered, went to bed, and didn't report the fate of the guerrillas until noontime on that day.

When the MPs finally found the three guerrillas, they were suffering from extreme exposure. The temperature had dipped to forty-five degrees in the woods, and the rains had continued all night. They were all hospitalized. Two of them were suffering from pneumonia, but after six weeks, they were fully recovered. Kate was both hailed and assailed for her conduct. The Corps of Cadets thought Kate was a hero. She had met the enemy and conquered them. The commander of the guerrilla training company was not so pleased with her performance. He wanted Kate expelled from

West Point for committing a My Lai-like atrocity. Kate's company tactical officer, commenting in his report that Kate had "provided a terribly poor example for her subordinates," and had "used extremely poor judgment in a situation requiring more sensitive and sensible leadership," refused to impose any punishment on her other than a placing a letter of reprimand in her file. Later, he privately confided to her that the guerrilla unit had overplayed its role in the exercise and that it would be monitored in the future by representatives of West Point's full-time officer cadre. But the reprimand remained in her file, creating a stench like that of a rotting egg. Chandler smelled it. That's why the letter Kate received in the last week of August came as a complete surprise. "Dear Cadet McKeane," the letter began under the superintendent's letterhead, "I am pleased to inform you that you have been selected to be the Cadet Brigade Commander for the coming academic year . . . ." Kate was ecstatic. Tina was disappointed. She and Kate could no longer be roommates.

If August was topsy-turvy, the events of September literally swept Kate off her feet. In early September, Kate, by then a "six-striper", moved into the Brigade Commander's quarters, a private suite of rooms off Central Area. Tina, much to everyone's surprise, had been promoted to Battalion Adjutant of the Second Battalion, Second Regiment. Many thought she got the job because, though small in stature, she was spunky and had a booming voice. Some envious male cadets, however, had suggested behind her back that Tina got promoted because she was giving her lanky tactical officer head. It's a good thing that Tina never heard those snide rumors. She would have busted those cadets in the chops and probably ended up walking punishment tours.

Previously, in June, Kate and Tina had agreed to get dates and go to the September Ring Hop together. This was the autumn dinner-dance celebrating the seniors' receiving their class rings, one of the more important events of the final year at the Academy. For West Pointers, the class ring is a symbolic link between them and the "Long Gray Line"—the indispensable badge of the ever-

expanding corps of West Point "ring-knockers". There even are
traditions even connected with the *wearing* of the ring. On one
side of the ring is the distinctive class crest designed by a committee of each graduating class; on the other side is the Academy
crest, designed in 1898 by three West Point professors, consisting
of a replica of the helmet of Pallas Athena over a Greek sword,
capped by an American bald eagle carrying a scroll bearing the
motto "Duty, Honor, Country." It is customary for Firsties, until
graduation, to wear their rings so that the class crest is most easily
seen by the wearer. After graduation, the ring is traditionally reversed so that the Academy Crest is the one nearer the heart.
Tina, to use her words, "didn't give a shit which way the crests
faced". She had "more important things to worry about . . . like,
for instance, *graduating*."

In July, Tina offered to fix Kate up with a date for the Ring
Hop. Kate accepted the offer, but dubiously. Knowing Tina's bent
for promiscuity, Kate was afraid she'd get fixed up with some guy
looking for an immediate toss in the hay. Tina assured her that
wouldn't happen. On summer leave in New Jersey, Tina had met a
fellow, Mike Stanford, who was a senior at Tennessee's Vanderbilt
University. He was in the Army R.O.T.C. program, and like Tina,
he was scheduled to be commissioned a second lieutenant the following June. He was planning to go into the Army Corps of Engi-
neers. Tina had invited him to come to West Point for the Ring
Hop weekend, and he accepted. He promised to bring his classmate and R.O.T.C. buddy, Robert D. Holcroft III, to escort Kate
that weekend.

On Friday afternoon of the Ring Hop Weekend, Kate and
Tina in their black-bordered gray tunics and white trousers sat
side by side anxiously awaiting the arrival of their dates in Grant
Hall, the cadet reception hall in the east wing of Old South Barracks. Kate remembered staring, seemingly forever, at the hall's
colorful ceiling emblazoned with seals of the fifty states and at its
walls, adorned with portraits of the five-star generals of World War
II—Arnold, Bradley, Eisenhower, MacArthur, and Marshall. All

were graduates of West Point, except Marshall, who was out of Virginia Military Institute.

While Kate was engrossed in the portraits, Tina, without warning, grabbed Kate's starched white trousers in the thigh area and squealed, "Here comes Mike!!" Kate looked up to see Tina practically sprinting toward the entry hall. Tina brazenly flung her arms around the young man, hugged him, and gave him an extended kiss—recklessly risking being quilled for public display of affection, or "P.D.A." Kate sat startled, not just because of Tina's overtly affectionate behavior, but because Mike was an African-American. Kate hadn't expected this. Tina hadn't told her. Kate wasn't racially biased, but she would have preferred knowing in advance. That was just like Tina. A surprise every minute. Kate saw Mike turn around toward the doorway and apparently motion to someone to come in. Kate waited expectantly, feeling the same way she had felt as an adolescent after spinning the bottle at her first mixed-gender party. Who would he be? What would he look like? Could she spend an entire weekend with him? A Caucasian male stepped into the space framed by a Gothic archway and, smiling, held out his hand to Tina. "What a hunk," Kate had thought to herself, as she rushed over to greet him.

Ring Weekend had gone fabulously. Tina and Mike had become much closer, and Kate and Robert—he didn't like to be called Bob—seemed to hit it off well. Coming from a long line of military professionals, Robert was a bit stiff behaviorally and rather abstract verbally. He also seemed very interested in Kate, in a gentlemanly sort of way. He was immediately taken by the fact that Kate was the First Captain of the Corps and that her father was a major general. Posturing for status, he was quick to point out that his middle initial stood for Delafield, a family surname on his mother's side. One of his ancestors, Richard Delafield had been a West Point superintendent on three separate assignments. Despite his military heritage and his fine Southern upbringing, Tina sized up Robert as a social-climbing geek, and she told Kate so. As Tina put it, "Robert's so literal, if you took him down on Flirtation Walk and showed him Kissing Rock, he'd probably say 'that rock doesn't look like it's kissing to me.'" Maybe Tina was right. Maybe Robert was a brilliant dullard. But that hadn't kept Kate from writing to him every other day since Ring Weekend.

3

Kate looked at her wristwatch. Nine-thirty—they're a half hour late. This kind of tardiness could spell death on a battlefield. And this was a battle—a gender battle. It was just yesterday that General Chandler had telephoned Kate to tell her that she would be testifying before Congress today on the subject of women in combat. A recent female graduate had been scheduled to testify, but she had become ill and couldn't. The House Subcommittee's staff assistant was having trouble locating a replacement witness, and in desperation called the Commandant's office. General Chandler had been initially reluctant to dispatch a cadet on the five-hour trek to D.C., but at the Congressional staffer's insistence, he finally agreed to send Kate. He also arranged to have Captain Colin Martin, an attorney in the Judge Advocate General's Corps and West Point faculty member, to drive her to Washington in a government vehicle. Chandler told Kate that Captain Martin could brief her on the issues and help prepare her for her testimony. The Academy already had a standard written statement on the topic of women in ground combat—detailing the arguments on both sides of the issue, and Chandler promised to have the statement Faxed to the Subcommittee's staff. He had also provided a copy of it to Kate and Captain Martin.

Kate was reviewing her written statement when the large wooden doors to the conference room slowly opened. More than a dozen people poured into the front of the noisy, packed hearing room, circulating in little eddies, until they came to rest in their assigned places. Six men and one woman sat in leather chairs behind a long cherry-wood, judicial-type bench. Each person had a microphone, and behind the legislators was a row of chairs occupied by legislators' staff assistants. Each legislator had at least one assistant present. A long conference table from which the witnesses would testify was situated parallel to the court-like bench, with two chairs facing the Subcommitte and a microphone at each position. A court reporter sat to the left of the Subcommittee positioned so she had full view of the faces of all the Subcommittee members and the witnesses.

Kate studied the seven legislators as they kibitzed with one another, waiting for the chairman to sound the gavel commencing the session. Kate knew quite a bit about each of them. She had done her homework. After learning the day before that she would be testifying before the House Subcommittee on Women in Combat, she went to the library and read the biographies of the Subcommittee members. She had also spoken to her father by telephone. Charles Kennicott, Chairman of the Subcommittee, was a Democratic Congressman from Boston. He was considered a moderate and his voting on issues was not always predictable. Kate's father knew Kennicott personally. Esther Grant, the only woman on the Subcommittee, indeed the only woman on the full House Armed Services Committee, was a moderate Republican from Illinois. She was considered to be a political anomaly by many Republicans, because she was such an active proponent of the cause for women in combat. Harlan Stallwell, an ultra-conservative Republican from South Carolina, had long been on record as supporting the Army's policy excluding women from ground combat. He once was quoted in the *New York Times* as saying, "Women have a place in the bedroom and the boardroom, but the war room will remain off limits as long as I and my constituency have any say in it." Anthony Fiorelli, a moderate democrat from California, had waffled on the women in combat issue in the past, and recently he had drastically limited his public statements about the topic. Clyde Dotter was a dyed-in-the-wool conservative Republican from Montana. A true chauvinist, he recently had said on a national talk show that the nation should consider having separate military academies for women. Grandville Jones, a black moderate

Democrat from New York, was a veteran of World War II and
Korea, and was generally supportive of career advancement for
women. Leonard Goldberg, a "bleeding heart" liberal Democrat
from Pennsylvania, was an outspoken proponent of women in combat. He was notorious for raking Department of Defense officials
"over the coals" when they came to the Hill to testify on any issue.

Banging his gavel several times on a wooden block before him,
Chairman Kennicott waited for a few seconds while the loud chatter of the spectators gradually dissolved to silence. He then called
the hearing to order and began taking up some preliminary matters. He announced that the House Armed Services Subcommittee
on Women in Combat was meeting in its last day of hearings to
receive testimony from the Department of Defense and public
witnesses on the subject of the use of women in ground combat.
Three witnesses were scheduled to speak: the Army Chief of Staff
Marlin Winterfield, West Point Cadet Brigade Commander Mary
Kathryn McKeane, and Yale University Professor of Sociology Ira
Abelman. The witnesses had waived the reading of their statements into the record so as to afford more time for the
Subcommittee's questions. The Chairman expressed regret on behalf of the Subcommittee that Lila Davis-Whitfield would not be
testifying. She was present in the hearing room but had deferred
to General Winterfield in order to save the Subcommittee's time.

In his initial comments, the Chairman emphasized that there
were currently no *laws* precluding the assignment of women to
ground combat units. The Army, as a matter of *policy*, however,
prohibited the assignment of women to skills and positions that
involve "the highest probability of direct combat". He further observed that because the primary ways a person advances in a military career are actual or anticipated performance in combat, exclusion from access to combat or to combat training becomes suspect
as a career impediment. He made clear his initial hypothesis about
women in ground combat. It was not based on an extreme position. Rather, it was simply centered on the idea that women should
be provided the same opportunity as men in the military, subject

to the bottom line—the combat effectiveness of the U.S. military forces. He encouraged the Subcommittee to pay close attention to the views and recommendations of the Secretary of Defense, of senior military commanders, and particularly of junior officers and enlisted personnel, male and female, as the latter group including those whose welfare would be most directly affected by any decisions the Subcommittee made about who would serve the nation in combat. He then introduced Representative Esther Grant who had made a formal request to make some initial comments at the hearing. Esther spoke without notes.

*   *   *

GRANT: Thank you, Chairman Kennicott. I applaud you, Mr. Chairman, on the way you phrased and framed the issue before this Subcommittee today. Equity is not going to be found in extreme positions. The notion that somehow all women must be in combat or all women should be at home is simply not a tolerable juxtaposition of the issues. If we adopted the position that all women should remain at home, there would be no women in politics, in business, in sports, and certainly none in combat support missions that we witnessed in the Persian Gulf.

Technology has, in fact, revolutionized concepts of warfare. This we must keep foremost in our minds as we listen to the testimony today. Many years ago in law school, one of my professors shared a quotation which has been indelibly imprinted on my mind and which is particularly relevant here today. Justice Holmes once said that the greatest of all tragedies occurs when powers, conscious of themselves, are denied their chance. I think the purpose of this hearing is to find out whether or not, in the military services, powers conscious of themselves have been systematically denied their chance in the past, and whether that ought to be reversed or at least ameliorated for the future. I have no further comments at this time. Thank you, Mr. Chairman.

CHAIRMAN: Thank *you*, Representative Grant. Our first witness this morning is General Marlin Winterfield, Army Chief of Staff. Good morning, General. I trust you're aware of how this process works.

WINTERFIELD: (Smiling) I practically have it memorized by now, Mr. Chairman.

CHAIRMAN: Good, then let us begin the questioning.

We drew straws in our prehearing executive session, and Representative Goldberg, our esteemed colleague from Pennsylvania, won. Leonard, the witness is yours. . . . Be kind to him. (Laughter).

GOLDBERG: Thank you, Mr. Chairman. I also wish to thank you, General, for waiving the reading of your written statement. I have read it with great interest . . . and concern.

WINTERFIELD: I'm sure you have, Congressman. (Laughter).

GOLDBERG: In your statement, you identified the Army's four major categories of objections to allowing women to serve in combat. Am I correct in saying that?

WINTERFIELD: Yes, Congressman. The Army's objections may be broadly categorized as physiological, psychological, sociological, and strategic.

GOLDBERG: Good. I'll be zeroing in on the last two categories in my questioning of you this morning, General, because I think they are the most relevant to your expertise as Army Chief of Staff.

WINTERFIELD: I'm relieved to know that you think I have at least *some* expertise, Congressman. (Laughter).

GOLDBERG: Don't throw the word "relieved" around too casually, General. (Laughter). General, let me first focus on what I consider to be your philosophical objections—the so-called sociological category. This has also been referred to as the Army's protectionist philosophy, or "romantic paternalism"? My question simply is . . . what gives the Army the right to protect women from the horrors of war?

WINTERFIELD: Congressman, the Army's protectionist position

operates on at least two levels: protecting the morale of the public and of male military peers in time of war, and protecting the female combatant from herself. As to the first level, the sight of female service members arriving home in body bags would be demoralizing to a public otherwise tolerant of wartime casualties. Also exposing female soldiers to battlefield capture and the accompanying molestation, torture, or rape could have an adverse, demoralizing impact on the judgment of military commanders.

GOLDBERG: Hold on, General. Wasn't this precisely the same argument used by bigots for decades to exclude women from front-line duty in our police and fire departments across the country? Hasn't this argument largely been debunked by the empirical evidence pointing to the success of women in the crime-fighting and life-saving roles?

WINTERFIELD: With all due respect, Congressman Goldberg, wartime combat duty is a whole different ballgame from metropolitan police duty.

JONES: (Interjecting agitatedly). That depends on where you *live*, General. (Laughter).

WINTERFIELD: (Visibly unnerved) Well . . . uh . . . uh what I mean by that, Gentlemen, er . . . er . . . Lady and Gentlemen, the risks of harm, injury, or death are so much greater in a battlefield situation . . .

JONES: (Interjecting again) Did ya ever walk the streets at night in the South Bronx, General?

WINTERFIELD: (Undistracted) . . . that there really can be no comparison between the two. But if I can proceed . . .

GOLDBERG: Certainly, General.

WINTERFIELD: The protectionist objection is science-based. Anthropologists tell us that the historical practice of arming men and not women has to do with a cultural imperative—to guarantee the reproduction of society. Arming women destroys the race. Since the time of the cavemen . . . and cavewomen . . . there has existed a sexual division of labor in warfare. Men have fought offensively, "going off to war", while women have fought defensively, protecting their homes and children from attack by invaders. Many experts believe that tinkering with this natural division of labor will upset the social equilibrium and significantly disrupt reproduction and childbearing.

GOLDBERG: Come, now, General. Zoologists have long taught us that the female of the species is more dangerous than the male. You don't deny that, do you?

WINTERFIELD: No sir, . . . but the point I'm trying to make is—if women abandon their allotted tasks as wives and mothers, who can replace them? Sure, men can learn to nurture children, but they are not physically equipped to bear or breastfeed infants. Technological advances may, in the future, alter these male incapacities, but for the present, women's monopoly on reproduction remains complete.

GOLDBERG. Thank you, General—not to imply of course that I agreed with anything you said, but we must move on. In your written statement, and in your previous testimony here today, you have taken the position—which seems provocative to say the least—that women must be protected from themselves. What could you possibly mean by that?

WINTERFIELD: Simple. This is an analogy to the animal world. Evolutionary biologists have found that the female of any animal species—including the human species—may be unable to temper her brutality. It is well known that the female animal will fight to the death in defense of her young. One expert concluded that if women were authorized to engage in military ground combat, their strong child protection instincts would cause them to be more implacable and less subject to chivalrous rules used by men to mute the savagery of warfare. Women would kill too thoroughly, endanger the negotiations and posturings of armies, including truces and taking of prisoners.

GOLDBERG: Oh, so on the one hand, General, you're arguing

that women are not physically or psychologically equipped to kill, but on the other hand, that there is a danger that they will kill "*too thoroughly*".

WINTERFIELD: The army has never contended that its objections are necessarily logically consistent.

GOLDBERG: That is quite evident now, General . . . in the record. Thank you. I have previously agreed to yield the remainder of my time to my colleague from New York. . . . Representative Jones?

JONES: Mr. Chairman, just so you know, I just have one or possibly two questions, and then Representative Grant can commence her questioning on schedule.

CHAIRMAN: Fine. Please proceed.

JONES: General, I want you to know, I've been around this old world a long time. I'm 82 years young. I grew up on a plantation in Georgia. My parents were sharecroppers and worked in the fields picking cotton until the day they died. I served my country in the infantry in World War II and in the Korean Conflict. I earned three purple hearts, two bronze stars for valor, and a silver star. I'm not telling you this out of conceit, but out of pride. When I applied for the infantry in 1941 after the bombing of Pearl Harbor, I was told by your army that I was unqualified, because blacks didn't perform well in combat. They told me that I was unqualified because blacks— "Negroes" in those days—were not intelligent enough for combat. They told me I was unqualified because, in combat, blacks would break and run in time of danger. They told me that I was unqualified because Whites would not take orders from Blacks in combat. I was persistent. They eventually inducted me and assigned me to a segregated infantry unit. I eventually proved to the Army during the Normandy Invasion that I was combat qualified. In Korea, assigned to a racially integrated unit, I again proved to the army during the Pusan invasion that I was combat-qualified. What do *women* have to do, General, to prove to the army that *they* are combat qualified?

WINTERFIELD: Do you want me to answer that, Sir?

0368-COOL

JONES: . . . No, General. . . . I just want you to think about it.

CHAIRMAN: Perhaps we should take a fifteen minute recess. Everyone please be back at ten-thirty.

Kate stood up, dusted a couple pieces of lint off the front of her dress gray uniform, and looked around the hearing room. She was a picture of military rectitude. Back straight, chest out, stomach in, two gold academic stars on her collar, and six thick black stripes cascading down her coatsleeves, punctuated at the bottom by a large black star, Kate was West Point's peacock. Glancing toward the back of the hearing room, she observed men and women of the press corps milling around and chatting as if this were some kind of family reunion. A woman with a huge, wide-brimmed straw hat was, with unchecked exuberance, loudly carrying on with a reporter wearing an armband marked "ABC". Periodically, they both broke into fits of raucous laughter as if sharing stories of past experiences. Kate turned to Captain Martin and asked him if he knew who the lady was. He responded that he didn't. In a few minutes, the legislators were reassembling.

CHAIRMAN: Everyone seems to be present. I think we are ready to resume. Congresswoman Grant is next on the schedule. She is going to delve into the army's military-strategic objections. Are you ready to begin, Esther?

GRANT: Yes, Mr. Chairman. I must admit, candidly, General Winterfield, that I have a great difficulty keeping my questions within one of the four specific categories of objections that you outlined in the beginning of your testimony. I find the four categories to be, at times, overlapping and their boundaries blurred. Therefore, I ask your indulgence if I happen to stray outside the bounds of what you deem military-strategic.

WINTERFIELD: No problem, ma'am.

GRANT: General, you have been quoted in the July issue *Time* magazine as saying: "No *real* man wants a woman to do his fighting for him." First of all, General, were you accurately quoted? And if so, what did you mean by that statement?

WINTERFIELD: Well, I *did* make that statement, but as with

most press quotes, the statement was taken out of context. Here's what I meant by that. I was asked by the interviewer whether I thought women comprise the "weaker sex". I responded, "Not necessarily, but . . . " and then made the statement you quoted. I then went on to say—which was not reported—that military analysts are convinced that "reliance on women impairs readiness and the ability for rapid deployment." It is a reasonable assumption that pregnancy rate and women's family responsibilities would impede deployment in wartime and cause logistical problems.

GRANT: Do you have any empirical evidence to support those claims, General?

WINTERFIELD: Not with me, ma'am. But if I had to, I'm sure I could dig it up.

GRANT: Why don't you do that and submit it to my staff after this hearing.

WINTERFIELD: With pleasure, ma'am.

GRANT: Good. And while we're on the subject of preparedness, we'll make an even trade. I'll have my staff send you the Navy test results showing that for each four duty days lost by women, seven were lost by men.

WINTERFIELD: Being Army to the bone, ma'am, I don't really put much faith in Navy tests. (Laughter).

GRANT: (Maintaining composure) In your written statement, you also expressed concern that women's presence in combat units may cause what you termed "disproportionate U.S. losses". Would you care to expound on this?

WINTERFIELD. Certainly. The army fears, we think justifiably, that servicemen will take unnecessary risks to protect female combatants whom they perceive as vulnerable—this overlaps with the protectionist argument. Also, we fear that enemy forces may fight with greater vigor to avoid the shame of defeat by, or surrender to, women.

GRANT: But you have no proof of these claims, do you General?

WINTERFIELD: That's correct. We have no hard data to support this—but we think it is reasonable speculation.

GRANT: More reasonable than the speculation that "women are the weaker sex"?

WINTERFIELD: . . . I would have to give that some thought, ma'am. I can't comment on that.

GRANT: On another topic, General, . . . in writing, you expressed concern on behalf of the army that women in combat situations would interfere with what you refer to as "male bonding." What is "male bonding" in this context? Does it differ from "female bonding" or "male-female bonding" in combat situations?

WINTERFIELD: The bonding process, in general ma'am, requires three elements: organization for a common goal, the presence of danger, and a willingness to sacrifice. And there is . . .

GRANT: And not one of those elements is gender-specific?

WINTERFIELD: That's true. But there is some empirical evidence to suggest, ma'am, that men naturally draw together and reject females as colleagues in situations which threaten social order, such as combat. The male bonding process is linked to the presence of testosterone in men. The bonding effect is enhanced by intense levels of competition marked by extreme aggression. Because women have neither the requisite testosterone level nor the stomach for aggressive behavior, they do not bond with one another or with men in combat. The very presence of women can destroy the possibility of bonding for men and leads to psychic emasculation, stifling of masculinity, and in extreme situations, it promotes the sterilization of the whole process of combat leadership.

GRANT: But you are familiar, aren't you, with the 1977 study exploring whether the addition of women to a combat training unit caused deteriorated unit performance?

WINTERFIELD: Yes, I have read those test results.

GRANT: And what were they?

WINTERFIELD: To the best of my memory, those particular results indicated that women performed as well in the field as in garrison, and that the key to a unit's performance was not the male/female ratio, but rather the quality of its leadership. But, I hasten to add, Representative Grant, that this was an artificial, contrived combat exercise—not real combat involving real life-and-death situations.

GRANT: I see that my time is about up. I have one more area of questioning that should go quickly. Is the Army really serious about this "sex-in-the-foxhole" concern? Isn't this really an alarmist view spawned by the typical male belief—or hope—that all women are horny?

WINTERFIELD: Not at all. Not at all, madam. The Army is quite concerned about whether, in combat, sexual encounters would be prevalent in the foxhole—or anywhere else for that matter—causing a breakdown of the male *esprit de corps*. Another complicating factor would be that males could easily be in competition for the affection of the same female. This could cause all sorts of problems for the morale of the men in combat, perhaps significantly decreasing military effectiveness, at the expense of the safety of the whole combat unit. Moreover, an epidemic of venereal disease could completely wipe out a combat unit, not to mention the effect of the impact of the transmission of the AIDS virus. The trenches—for better or worse—are the last remaining stronghold of men. I suspect that many men might vacate the military arena altogether rather than share it with women.

GRANT: General, I do not find your response very convincing. Research shows that where men and woman have been assigned to mixed-gender crews at the Air Force's Minuteman intercontinental nuclear missile stations, sexual misconduct has not occurred despite the isolation and the lack of individual privacy in the deep underground rooms—comparable to foxholes—in which the two-person, twenty-four hour shifts are the norm. I still believe the army's view is colored by its exaggerated view of the women's sexual proclivities. Mr. Chairman, that's all the questions I have for now.

WINTERFIELD: Mr. Chairman, with your permission, I would

like to read into the record, President Benton's most recently
stated views on this topic.

CHAIRMAN: Be my guest.

WINTERFIELD: (Reading). *We all remember that the nation's call
to arms in the Persian Gulf was not gender specific. Of the five
hundred forty thousand troops who served in Operations Desert
Storm and Desert Shield, thirty-five thousand were women. Women
performed flight operations within the combat zone, and were involved in many support, intelligence, medical and rescue assignments that were physically demanding and carried substantial risks.
However, a decision to reverse the Army's combat exclusionary policy
based merely on the Persian Gulf experience should not be made
hastily. The answers to many difficult philosophical and practical
questions must precede this determination. On the practical side,
we must examine the physical requirements for combat roles and
design honest performance standards, not double standards, to evalu-
ate whether women can meet the demands of a variety of combat
roles. These and many other questions must be answered thoroughly
so that the United States can be certain that changes in current
policy would not occur at the expense of defense preparedness or the
safety of military personnel.*

CHAIRMAN: Thank you, General Winterfield. We'll take a brief
ten-minute recess. When we return, we will be hearing from
Cadet First Captain Kathryn McKeane from West Point. Everyone please be back at eleven fifteen.

As soon as the legislators left the hearing room, a female reporter wearing a "CBS" armband strode purposefully toward Kate.

"Isn't General Winterfield the biggest male chauvinist pig,
you've ever seen?" she asked pointedly. Kate urgently wanted to
answer "ya damned right," but a newspaper headline, "TOP WEST
POINT CADET SAYS TOP GENERAL IS PREJUDICED
AGAINST WOMEN" flashed across her mind. That wouldn't be
too peachy of a career move. Luckily, Captain Martin interceded
and politely explained to the reporter that any statement Kate

would be making would be solely confined to her testimony before the Subcommittee.

The female reporter pressed again for more information, this time directing her questions to Captain Martin. "You're a lawyer, correct sir?"

"That's right," replied the captain.

"Then can you tell me what's going to happen to the five members of West Point's football team who groped more than twenty female cadets in that pep rally crowd recently?"

"I'm sorry, ma'am, I can't speculate about that. The army's hearing process will just have to run its course."

"If I give you my telephone number here in D.C., could you keep me informed of the progress of the hearings?" the reporter urged.

"I'm afraid not, ma'am. The Academy's Office of Public Affairs handles all contacts with the press. I suggest that you contact them directly."

Visibly disappointed by her lack of success in finessing some juicy news scoops, the reporter stomped away. By the time Kate and Captain Martin had completed discussing a few items in the written statement, the Subcommittee members had re-entered the hearing room, and were taking their seats.

CHAIRMAN: The hearing is back in session. I wish to welcome our next witness, Cadet McKeane from West Point. Cadet McKeane do you have any questions before we get started?

MCKEANE: No sir, I don't. I'm ready when you are.

CHAIRMAN: Fine. . . . Incidentally, when you see your father, give him my regards. Your dad was appointed to West Point by my father when he was a Congressman back in the sixties. My father always spoke highly of your dad.

MCKEANE: Thank you, sir. I'll be sure to tell him I saw you.

CHAIRMAN: Representative Stallwell from South Carolina has a few questions for you. Are you ready, Harlan?

STALLWELL: Sure am, Chuck. Miss McKeane, if you don't un-

derstand any of my questions, please let me know, and I'll be
happy to restate or rephrase them.

MCKEANE: Yes sir.

STALLWELL: I grew up in the South surrounded by women, all
of whom were dainty, soft, retiring, unaggressive, subdued creatures of the female sex. I can't imagine any one of them worth
a damn in a combat situation. They are much more suited for
the more tedious, routine tasks that require little imagination—like knitting or quilting. Are these among the women
that the Army should send into combat?

MCKEANE: I personally don't know the women you speak of,
but the point is, not all women are cut out for combat, and
neither are all men. However, don't be too quick to disparage
women who can expertly perform tedious and routine tasks.
True heroes are not those who blaze across the horizon in a
moment of superb performance, but those who endure inter-
minably when there is no light at the end of the tunnel. A
recent study conducted at the Naval Academy revealed that in
stressful, problem-solving situations, female midshipmen have
a greater ability to see patterns, relationships, and meanings
beyond facts. They see the big picture more quickly, prefer
learning and using new skills, and are more comfortable with
the abstract and symbolic. Men, on the other hand, focus more
on the facts, attend better to details, prefer using previously
learned skills, and are more comfortable with the concrete and
practical. In actuality, men are more suited to the routine than
are women. Women, who historically have been condemned
to tedium, fortunately have had the ability to adjust.

STALLWELL: Well, I sure wouldn't want any of those blushing
violets making decisions for me on the battlefield.

MCKEANE: Some women are blushing violets because men have
denied them other alternatives. But let's get to the real issue.
Do men and women think and decide differently? The Naval
Academy study answered this question in the affirmative. Men
make decisions using an impersonal, objective approach, while

women are more likely to rely on personal, value-based components. Women take into account the personal investment of self and others while men think more in terms of consequences and cause-and-effect. This is not to say either process yields better decisions. It does suggest however, that men and women working together, can often reach more effective, well-rounded decisions. Women are not only able to collaborate with men, but they are able to compete with them as well. Competition between male and female soldiers is useful in maintaining unit effectiveness and cohesion. Male soldiers refuse to be outperformed by women and women soldiers want to prove that they can perform as well as men, thus increasing effectiveness beyond that of a single-sex group.

STALLWELL: Well, even if what you say is true, I just can't see how men—particularly older men—could take orders from a young female lieutenant on the battlefield. It just wouldn't work.

MCKEANE: Congressman, you might be surprised to learn that recent studies of *male* West Point graduates show that their weakest attribute, as rated by their Battalion Commanders, was the ability to talk with troops and to give orders. Two other low scoring areas for the male graduates were developing subordinates and concern for welfare of troops. These results corroborate other studies which show that women derive their greatest job satisfaction from working with troops, and helping them. In other words, women officers prefer the tasks which male officers are least equipped to perform.

STALLWELL: Miss McKeane, for practically every research study you describe, I can show you one that has concluded just the opposite. Isn't this really just a shell game? Women simply have not been able to prove that they can measure up to the stresses of the combat situation.

MCKEANE: That's simply the point, Congressman. They haven't been able to prove themselves because they have not been given the *opportunity* to do so. Lack of opportunity has historically caused the female sex to be subjugated to the male sex on many levels of activities. For example, a recent United Nations Report on the Status of Women has observed that women comprise approximately eighty percent of the world's population, perform sixty-six percent of the world's work, earn ten percent of the world's income, and own one percent of the world's real estate. What all this boils down to, Congressman, is that twenty percent of the world's population—men—have, as Representative Grant intimated in her opening statement, systematically denied powers conscious of themselves—women—a chance in society. And the Army's combat exclusion policy for women is just another tragic example of how powerful men perpetuate this inequity.

STALLWELL: You can't really mean that, Miss McKeane.

MCKEANE: I sure do, sir, and what's more, men putting women, without combat training, into combat situations but in non-combat roles, is a diabolic act, because it places women in real danger of bodily harm. U.S. servicewomen have been involved in recent military engagements in Panama, Honduras, Grenada, the Persian Gulf, Libya, and Haiti. Women posted to these combat zones were exposed to risks similar to their male counterparts without the same capacity of self-protection. We just want the opportunity to prove our ground combat abilities relative to men on a level playing field. What is needed is some kind of experiment—some kind of trial.

STALLWELL: Well, fortunately for all of us, except perhaps you Miss McKeane, we don't have a war right now to provide a medium for women to strut their stuff. I guess you'd be happy if we agreed to start one.

MCKEANE: Not at all, Congressman. I know women will rise to the occasion to prove themselves in combat when the situation presents itself. It has already been done in isolated instances many times in the past. Congressman, are you familiar with the Civil War story of Harriet Tubman?

STALLWELL: Yes, Ms. McKeane. But she bein' a Yankee and me

bein' from South Carolina, I always considered her "the enemy." (Laughter).

MCKEANE: And well you should Congressman. Her story is one that a Confederate would want to forget.

CHAIRMAN: I don't think any other members of the Subcommittee know about Harriet Tubman. Why don't you fill us in.

MCKEANE: I'd be happy to, sir. Harriet Tubman represents the ultimate potential of women in combat situations. Early in the Civil War, after the Federals occupied sections of the Carolina coast, Tubman left her home in Auburn, New York, in the spring of 1862 in response to a Federal request for assistance. In June of that year, she led one hundred fifty black troops in a raid up the Combahee River in South Carolina. Her objectives were to remove torpedoes in the river and to destroy bridges, railroad lines, and Confederate supplies. She and her troops succeeded in burning plantations, disrupting transportation, and freeing 756 slaves who were taken safely by gunboats to Union Lines. Throughout 1863 and 1864, Tubman accompanied Union troops on many similar raids, carrying her musket, haversack, and canteen, and sometimes wearing bloomers. Her commanding officer, General Saxton, wrote later that during these expeditions she exhibited "remarkable courage, zeal and fidelity." I say, with great confidence, that there are many Harriet Tubmans out there in this society today who can carry their muskets, haversacks, and canteens on any military combat mission that our great country decides to send us.

STALLWELL: Well, I hope they leave their bloomers at home. (Laughter). I'm afraid anything else I might say, Miss McKeane, would detract from the drama of your remarks. I wouldn't want to do that. Good luck to you, Miss McKeane. You fared well here today under some pretty severe pounding. I'm proud to know that you will soon be an officer in our Armed Forces. Mr. Chairman, that concludes my questioning.

* * *

After hearing the testimony of Professor Abelman, Chairman Kennicott adjourned the proceedings and the Subcommittee retired to Executive Session behind the massive wooden doors. The crowd inside the hearing room atomized into small clusters of people exchanging opinions about the testimony and making predictions about the most probable action the Subcommittee would take. Kate stood near a conference table, putting some documents back into her briefcase. Lila, decked out in a wide-brimmed straw hat with a conspicuous large, fake, yellow daisy in its wide black band, sashayed over behind Kate and waited for her to close her briefcase. Turning around abruptly and beginning to take a step, Kate nearly knocked Lila off balance.

"Oh, I'm sorry, ma'am," Kate said apologetically, recognizing her to be the woman she saw previously with the ABC reporter.

"Think nothing of it," Lila replied with mild sarcasm, regaining her balance and righting her straw chapeau. You definitely move like a person with a mission."

"I guess I should look before I leap more often," Kate blushingly replied.

"All is forgiven." Holding out her hand to clasp Kate's, Lila continued. "I would like to introduce myself. I am Lila Davis-Whitfield, and I am President of an organization dedicated to making society consciously aware of the true powers and abilities of women. We are looking for a national spokesperson—someone to give five or six speeches a year around the country. I was really impressed with the way you handled yourself before this Subcommittee. I think you would satisfy our needs spectacularly."

"Well first, Ma'am, I would think there are Academy regulations that would preclude my being a spokesperson for any private organization. And secondly, I have no idea what your organization's purpose and objectives are."

"Do you believe in eradicating alcoholism?" Lila queried.

"Sure," Kate replied.

"How about eliminating extramarital sex and spousal abuse?"

"I suppose so."

"How about preserving the right to life."

"Within limits, yes," responded Kate.

"Have anything against motherhood and homemaking?"

"Of course not," Kate replied. "I suppose you're going to ask me if I like apple pie next."

"No, but not a bad idea—because we're just about basic family values. You'd be perfect for us." Reaching deep into her large alligator-skin purse, Lila pulled out a slightly dog-eared business card. "Here, dear, if you're interested give me a call."

"Well, I, . . . I, . . . ," Kate stammered.

"Oh, one more thing," Lila said with a penetrating smile as her finger diddled with a with a large fake pearl on her baubled necklace. "Expect to receive twenty to thirty thousand dollars for each of your speeches. . . . Sure beats combat pay, darlin'." Lila flipped her necklace slightly, and as she sauntered away, she turned and said, "Think about it, hon. . . . Let's keep in touch." Kate stood motionless for a few seconds—as if she had been paralyzed by a scorpion's sting. Perplexity soon dissolved to realization. This woman—Lila—had come out of nowhere to *bribe* her, of all things—to offer her money to scuttle her beliefs, her values, her ideals. What scum!!

Just then, Captain Martin approached her. "Guess we'd better be heading back to the Point, Cadet McKeane."

"I'm ready when you are, sir," Kate said grabbing her briefcase and walking with him at a brisk military gait toward the hearing room door. "You won't believe what just happened to me . . . ," she whispered as the pair quick-timed down the cavelike marble hallway toward the Capitol building's exit.

4

Meanwhile, inside the Subcommittee's conference room, Chairman Kennicott had just opened the floor for discussion. Representative Goldberg, appearing both anxious and precommitted, was the first to speak. "I don't think there's much to talk about, folks.

I think we need some legislation to dynamite this archaic army policy excluding women from ground combat. I'll volunteer to have my staff draw it up. I could have a draft ready in . . . "

"Not so fast, Leonard," chirped Stallwell. "We haven't even discussed this thing or taken a vote yet. Frankly, I think the army's policy is working well. I want to hear what the others have to say, though."

"I agree with you a hundred percent," chimed Dotter. "The army's policy ain't broke—so there's no need to fix it. My mind isn't going to change on that. I'm ready to vote now. Women ain't got no place in ground . . . "

Interrupting to direct the discussion and glancing toward Representative Grant, Chairman Kennicott said softly and respectfully, "I think it would be fair to say, Esther, that your views on this are pretty evident from your questioning at the hearing. You are in favor of legislation abolishing the exclusionary policy, correct?"

"Yes, Chuck. That's my position and I'm prepared to vote now that legislation be drafted and supported by this Subcommittee."

"Chuck, I go along with Esther," added Jones.

"So it looks like," Kennicott said contemplatively, "we have three votes in favor of women in combat and two votes against. You've been awfully quiet during this ordeal today, Tony. What's your fix on this thing?"

Fiorelli, the deeply tanned Californian, grinned broadly as the attention of the other Congressmen focused on him. "I must admit, friends, that I am really torn on this issue. Being of Italian heritage, I have strong family values. And, to a great extent, I think that women's place is playin' patty-cake rather than packin' parachutes. I think I owe my success today to the special care and attention my mama provided me, while my papa was down running the restaurant seven days a week. But I recognize that not all women are the same. Some never get pregnant; some never get married—and don't want to. Some are as physically able as most men, and a few women even more so. My feeling is that if some women can do the combat thing, then let 'em do it. But I don't think we should rush to judgment on this. I think we need some sort of ground-combat experiment for women. If they can hack it fine. If they can't, then the Army policy sticks. That's my feeling about this, Chuck."

"What kind of experiment do you propose, Tony?" Dotter inquired. "Like Harlan implied at the hearing today, we can't start a war, just because a bunch of dykes want a proving ground."

"First of all, Clyde, I resent the word, `dykes,'" the Fiorelli shot back, "unless you're referring to those things that hold back water in Holland. And secondly, the truth is, we already *have* a war—a *drug* war. President Benton told the nation that last July when Federhoff's Commission issued its annual National Drug Control Report. Just last week, you know, the President sent that Defense Department contingent in here before this Subcommittee requesting additional funding for its Drug Interdiction Program in South America—particularly in Colombia, as I recall. You'll have to forgive my memory, folks—I was dozing during a good portion of their testimony. Part of the money, I believe, was to be used to send in army troops to suppress the Colombian drug lords— the Bodegas I think is the name they used. I know at one point in the hearing, we went off the record to discuss all of this because it was top secret. And, if my memory serves me correctly, the army was definitely considering a combat operation in Colombia, and we recommended approval of the funding to the full Armed Services Committee, I think. The full Committee hasn't voted on our recommendation yet as far as I know."

"Yes, that's true, Tony." Kennicott agreed.

"So where does that leave us, Tony?" Dotter asked.

"I think we have the makin's of a ground-combat experiment. We just have to let the Army know that we want to plug these two things together—that is, the Army gets the funding for the combat operation on the condition that they agree to run an experiment to test the mettle of women in combat."

"Isn't that kinda blackmail, Tony?" Stallwell asked.

"No, just business as usual," Fiorelli replied.

The seven Congressmen continued their discussion for about twenty minutes until Kennicott sprang the question: "What are we gonna name this thing?"

That spawned another fifteen-minute discussion until Fiorelli asserted, "Friends, I think I've got it. I suggest we call it the `Minerva Experiment` after the goddess of Roman mythology."

"Who, might I ask, was Minerva?" asked Dotter.

Fiorelli bubbled with the glee of a child who knew the answer to a catechism question. "It says right here in my pocket dictionary, my dear colleagues, that Minerva was the Roman virgin goddess of wisdom and art. She was the third most important divinity in Rome, joining Jupiter and Juno in a kind of trinity." Reading a few seconds to himself, he looked up and said, "What makes her particularly relevant to our combat experiment is that while she was revered by women as a patroness of domestic skills and, at the same time, worshipped by men who sought cunning, prudence, and courage in military affairs. For this reason, she was often depicted with a helmet, shield, and in plates of armor."

"Well, we have to call it somethin'," Stallwell said seeming only mildly interested. "`Minerva Experiment` is as good as anything I've heard here this afternoon. I'd just as soon put that name on it and get on with the test. There ain't no woman gonna pass it anyhow."

Sudden anger lit Esther's green eyes.

Kennicott, sensing that the discussion was winding down, said, "I think it's time to adjourn for today. I can't emphasize strongly enough how important it is that we keep the proposed `Minerva Experiment` strictly confidential. I think we have some considerable politicking to do to get the Army to join this venture. There are many people both in and out of Government who would like to deep-six this whole idea. We can't afford to have any leaks." The other six legislators nodded agreement.

Once out of the conference room, Stallwell, made animated farewell gestures to the others, then dashed to the nearest public telephone booth. He hastily dialed a number, as if he had dialed it hundreds of times before.

"Lila? This is Harlan. I saw ya t'day in the hearing room. Ya looked simply terrific! . . . Betty's down at her mother's for a couple of days. Free tonight, sweetheart? . . . Okay, I'll be over about eight o'clock. . . . You'll have dinner ready? . . . Great. . . . Sure, I'll bring some wine. How about wearing that black negligée thing I bought you?—over your black lace teddy? . . . Darlin', do *I* have some news for you. . . . Now, Lila dumplin', you're gonna have to promise not to breathe a word of this to anybody. . . .

DISCRETE SECRETS

A sleek, black Mercedes limousine roared into the circular drive in front of a honeycomb hotel edifice in Medellín Colombia and screeched to a halt near the bell captain's kiosk. The red-tuxedoed bell captain opened the rear door of the limousine and said to the sole male passenger, "Welcome to Hotel Intercontinental, señor; will you need help with your bags?"

The man ignored the question, stepped out of the limo, looked around in all directions, then walked rapidly toward the hotel's revolving front door as the limo sped away. The man was struggling to carry a large brown leather briefcase discreetly marked "top secret" securely handcuffed to his left wrist. Once inside the hotel, the man strode past the hotel check-in area and proceeded past lavish fountains, huge birdcages, and lush greenery, heading on a steadfast course toward the elevators. Five, six, seven—the floors clicked by. Soon, he arrived at the penthouse floor. Stepping out of the elevator, he observed a sign, "Presidential Suite", with an arrow pointing to the right. Twenty steps down the hall, the man approached an entranceway with double-doors ornamented with coach lights on either side. He knocked three times. The door opened.

"Emilio! . . . Welcome!" said the hulky greeter who seemed out of place, dressed in a blue pinstriped suit and red tie. "It's eight o'clock sharp. You're right on time."

"We had a good tail wind all the way from Caracas, Federico. Are the others here?"

"Yes, Emilio. They got here a half hour ago. They're looking forward to see you."

Federico, followed closely by Emilio, turned and walked

through a brightly lit foyer filled with large Italian clay vases of fresh flowers and pastel paintings in ornate brass frames displayed on the white-marble walls. A mild fragrance of fresh flowers filled the air. The foyer opened into a stark white living room with parquet floors and thirty-foot ceilings. A gaping ebony concert grand piano anchored the room's otherwise airy decor. Couches with overstuffed pillows and potted trees appeared everywhere. A black circular staircase was visible near the opposite wall leading to bilateral balconies, suitable for private meetings, or concert viewing.

Two elderly-looking gentlemen sat in separate chairs in a cozy alcove under the right balcony. Both were white-haired and bespectacled. Their faces were beardless with deep wrinkles. Both both were dressed in three-piece suits. Two Pilsner glasses half-filled with foamy beer sat on a table between the two.

Emilio didn't recognize the seated gentlemen. "Federico, I thought Raoul and Hector were going to be here," Emilio blared. Before Federico could answer, the two old men burst into loud belly laughs.

"Emilio, let me introduce Raoul and Hector Bodega," Federico said, joining in the laughter.

Emilio couldn't believe his eyes. As a child, Emilio had shined the Bodega brothers' shoes when the two visited the brothels in the back streets of Medellín. The Bodegas had taken a liking to him and later, when Emilio was a teenager, he had worked for five years as Hector's driver. When he was twenty-one, Raoul had pulled strings to get Emilio into the Colombian State Department which led to his being appointed as a staff assistant in the Colombian Embassy in Washington D.C. He knew the Bodega brothers like his own family. But the octogenarian disguises had thrown him.

Raoul and Hector stood up and both gave Emilio a macho hug. "It's been a long time, Emilio," said Hector.

"That's why I have such a large valise this trip," said Emilio pointing to the briefcase and chortling.

"Well, what are we waiting for?" Raoul said.

Federico glanced down at the briefcase and then quickly cleared the coffee table to make room for it.

Emilio squatted, placing the briefcase flat on the table with his left hand. With his right hand, he removed a set of keys from his pocket, first removing the handcuffs, and then unlocking both of the spring-loaded latches on the briefcase. He opened the brief-case slowly. Raoul, Hector, and Federico beamed. "How much is it?" Hector exclaimed.

"A cool seven million—seventy packets of one hundred, one thousand dollar bills each," Emilio replied.

Jabbing Hector's rib cage good naturedly with his elbow, Raoul said, "Nice profit, eh Hector, for three months' work?"

"Yeah, man." Hector answered. "Beats shinin' shoes with a stick, eh Emilio? Have any trouble getting it here?"

"Not a bit. Late this morning, I caught a government flight out of D.C. to Caracas. Security police never check anything on a Government flight. I flew commercial out of Caracas. When I flashed my embassy credentials at the security gate, the officers just waved me around the x-ray equipment. They even asked me if I needed help getting the briefcase to the departure waiting area. I politely declined. I got a little nervous when the police dogs fol-lowed me a few yards down the concourse, but their trainers yanked their long leashes, causing the dogs to drop my scent."

Picking up a packet of one thousand dollar bills from the brief-case, Raoul counted out ten bills and handed them to Emilio. "Here, friend, this is for your good work."

Smiling, Emilio folded the bills and put them into his pocket.

"We'll take care of everything from here, Emilio," said Raoul. "We'll get the money to Monsignor Montero. . . . Montero's still cooperating, isn't he, Federico."

"So far, so good, Commandante," Federico replied. "The Rock Spinoza hasn't gotten to him yet."

"You know, Federico, if I get the chance I'll crush that fucking bishop's balls," Raoul said with a sneer.

"I understand, Commandante. Just say the word."

Raoul continued his previous thought, "Anyway, just so you

know, Emilio, that your good work has not been in vain, Montero will be distributing these funds to the pastors of thirty-five parishes over the next several months, and the pastors will slowly deposit the proceeds into Church accounts, segregated for our use. Of course, the Church will get its usual ten percent cut. You'll get the briefcase to the good Monsignor, this evening, won't you, Federico."

"No problem, Commandante," responded Federico .

"Anything else to report before you head back?" Raoul asked Emilio.

"Well actually there is, my friends. Congress is considering an invasion of Colombia to disrupt drug cartels. Just yesterday, the legislators held final hearings on the issue of whether women should serve in ground combat."

"Yeah, so what, Emilio?" Hector asked.

"Women may be sent here to fight," replied Emilio.

"I hope they do," said Raoul. "I'd like to experiment myself—doing a few hysterectomies. Keep us informed about this."

The four men continued to talk awhile longer before Emilio left the suite. Arriving back down at the bell captain's kiosk, Emilio engaged the bell captain in vapid small talk while he awaited a limousine to take him back to the airport. "Were you in Medellín when Andres Escobar, the Colombian World Cup soccer player, was killed?"

"*Sí, señor.* That was a true tragedy. All he did was put the ball accidentally into the United States' goal. The Colombian team lost two to one. For that, someone shot him. Killed him. He wasn't a traitor or a spy, or anything. Just an athlete who made a mistake. Some Colombians think that the Bodegas were behind the killing.

"Do you know who the Bodegas are, *señor?*"

"I've heard of 'em," Emilio replied.

"The Bodegas are brutal . . . treacherous. They didn't like Colombia losing to the United States team. For them, it was an international disgrace."

"Well, here comes the car," Emilio said as the limo pulled into the hotel driveway. The red-coated captain opened the rear door of the limo, and Emilio, as he climbed into the spacious passenger area, placed a five-hundred-peso note in the captain's palm.

"*Muchas gracias, señor.*"

"*Por nada*," responded Emilio. "I'll see you in a few months."

The city lights flashed before Emilio's eyes, as the limo raced to the Medellín airport. Just twelve hours earlier, he had left the warmth of Lila's embrace. He was beginning to think about her more and more in recent weeks. What a coup she pulled, having Stallwell over for dinner the night before. In twelve hours, God willing, Emilio would be back in Lila's loving arms. He wondered what other news Lila would have for him on his return. Poor Lila. With all her projected sophistication, she was in many ways so weak, so naive, so gullible. When she spoke, she never had any idea of the breadth of her audience.

2

Kate arrived back at West Point a little before midnight on the twenty-seventh. It was raining and unseasonably cold. Captain Martin, over her objection, had done the chivalrous thing and had escorted her under his umbrella all the way back to her barracks from where he parked his car near Grant Hall. After saying good night and thanking him, Kate made her way to her living quarters—the Brigade Commander's suite.

Untypically, a lamp illuminated her desk in an otherwise dark room; a Waterford clock positioned in the middle of the desk secured a pink buck slip with something scribbled on it. Kate snatched up the buck slip and struggled to read the scribble in the shadowy environment. In shaky script, the note read: "Kate. It's *Urgent*!! I need to talk to you right away!! Tina." Kate sensed something terrible had happened to Tina. She rarely complained or asked anyone for help. Kate wasted no time. She hurriedly removed her dress hat and her caped raincoat, threw them on her bed, unzipped her dress gray jacket from the bottom, and sprinted down the long tiled hallway in the direction of Tina's room. While she ran, Kate thought of many things that might have happened to Tina. Had she been hurt practicing with the gymnastics team? Had she been caught with liquor in her room and slugged? Had she failed a test? Had she been caught in an honor violation? Knowing Tina, anything was possible.

Approaching Tina's room, Kate slowed to a fast walk and went inside. Tina lay prone across her bed on top of the covers still dressed in her usual study garb—fatigue trousers and a T-shirt, under her cadet bathrobe. There was no mistaking Tina's bathrobe. It had Army division patches sewn all over the front of it; on its back appeared a huge question mark formed by the strategic placement of large gold stars—the type which academic "hives" were authorized to wear on their dress gray collars. Her head resting on her folded arms, she appeared to be asleep. Tina's roommate, Annie Farnsworth, was snoring in another part of the room.

Kate touched Tina's arm; Tina immediately opened her eyes and sat up. Kate sat down on the bed next to her and Tina gave her a big hug and, with tears streaming from eyes cupped by heavy black circles, whispered, "Man, am I glad you're here. I was beginning to think you seduced Captain Martin in the back seat."

Pretending that she didn't hear the last comment, Kate whispered, "What's wrong, Tina?"

"You won't *believe* what happened to me today." "Try me."

"I woke up this morning nauseated—puking all over the place. Thinking I had the flu or something, I told the Cadet in Charge of Quarters that I was going on sick call over at the infirmary. Well, Doc Parmley over there checked me out, and couldn't find anything physically wrong with me. He then said that there was one more test he wanted to run on me, but I would have to go upstairs. After I took the test, I waited in his office for awhile, and then he called me in." Reaching for Kate again and putting her head on Kate's chest, Tina gushed, "Kate . . . he said I'm pregnant!!"

Kate didn't know exactly what to say. She stumbled for words, and then blurted, "Is he sure?"

"Sure, he's sure."

"Miss a period?" Kate asked sensitively.

"I can't go by that. I'm so irregular. Look a woman's either pregnant or she's not. The doctor says I'm pregnant, so I'm pregnant. And that's not all."

"What else?"

"I think Mike Stanton is the father. I didn't tell you everything about Ring Weekend. We got way beyond the kissing stage."

"What d'ya mean, you *think* Mike is the father? Could it be someone else?"

"Yeah, any one of three other cadets. One of them was a plebe in Beast Barracks. Things got kinda dull there the last couple weeks of August."

"Didn't you use any sort of protection?" Kate whispered.

"Sometimes I did, but I don't remember which times. Oh, yeah— before Doc Parmley told me I was pregnant, he asked me if I had had any unprotected sex lately. I told him "absolutely not." Actually, I wasn't sure about that answer when I gave it. I had used foam on two of the occasions, and on the other two occasions, I was so plastered, I didn't know which end was up . . . *literally.* So now I think I may have committed an honor violation by lying to Doc Parmley. What do *you* think? Should I report myself for an honor violation?"

"I can't be your conscience, Tina. But one way to look at it is that you didn't deceive anyone. Doc Parmley knew the answer to the question before he asked it. He had the test results. It was an unfair question for him to ask. You responded quickly and mechanically. You didn't harm or take advantage of anyone."

"Really think so?"

"Sure. Besides, it was a private conversation with your doctor. Captain Martin was explaining to me on the way back from D.C. that anything you say to a doctor in the course of treatment is privileged. It can't be disclosed by the doctor without the patient's permission, except in rare instances. So, if I were you, I wouldn't worry too much about the honor part of what happened."

"Maybe you're right."

"But that doesn't solve the pregnancy part, Tina."

"Maybe I should tell you the rest of the story. I really think Mike's the one who got me pregnant. We had sex on that Sunday afternoon in the sanctuary of the Cadet Chapel. I told Mike I wanted to do it in the building that housed the world's largest organ—pipe organ. He thought we'd be making history. But it looks like we made more than that. We had a bottle of scotch with us, and we were trying to suppress our moans, because of the usual procession of group tours that traipsed through the Chapel at varying intervals. We got pretty good at it. But the point is, neither of us, as I recall, had the presence of mind—nor the physical ability—to use protection. Doc Parmley told me today that if I wanted to stay at West Point, I would have to "take care of it." I took that to mean that I would have to get an abortion. So, today, when I got back from the infirmary, I called Mike.

"What??" said Kate.

"I called Mike. He, of course, was as shocked as you are. I told him the situation, and said that I was going to get an abortion right away. I guess I sounded a little angry that he had gotten me pregnant, but he reacted in a way I hadn't expected."

"How was that?"

"He told me that his father was a Methodist minister and that he had been raised to believe that abortion was morally wrong.

"Did you know that before you made the call?"

"No, Kate, I didn't. How much can ya learn about a guy in a three-day weekend, anyway?"

"Probably not a lot," Kate conceded, rolling her eyes as Tina looked downward.

"During our call, he said that there was no way that he would go along with an abortion—even if it meant that I had to leave the Academy. He also said that the fetus was much more valuable than my career."

"The *nerve* of him to say that!" Kate said, trying to comfort her. "I guess he thinks there's nothing immoral about getting a girl pregnant."

"Yeah, the shithead! He even threatened me. He said that as

the father, he had rights, and that if I didn't agree to give birth to the child and put it up for adoption, he would write a letter to the Supe and file a lawsuit against me."

"So how did the conversation end?"

"I really don't know. Everything just disintegrated. . . . I was bawling when I hung up."

"Did you say you would call him back?"

"I really don't know. Can't remember. I was confused and disoriented. I couldn't think straight."

"You seem more together, now."

"But Kate . . . what will happen if he follows through and writes a letter to the Supe, and it comes out that I really don't know who knocked me up? I might be given the choice of lying or of implicating three other male cadets. Will I get kicked out? What will my parents say about all this when they find out? What should I do? Tina asked, putting her head in her hands and sobbing.

"Let's not do anything right now. Let's see if you can get some rest tonight so we can problem-solve better tomorrow. Forget all this happened. Don't try to run through all the possible scenarios tonight. We'll tackle it together, tomorrow. I'm here for you, Tina. As always, I'm here," Kate said, gently pulling the covers over her and tucking her in.

"Thanks Kate." Tina whimpered, closing her eyes and smiling through her tears. "My gallant First Captain. My knight in shining armor."

Kate tightened her fist and gave Tina a loving tap on the chin. "Sleep well, Tiger. Let God's rain do the cryin' tonight. I'll see ya tomorrow. The sun'll be out. You'll see."

3

The television studio was abuzz, as it always was a few minutes before showtime. Makeup artists were flitting around the the three *Base-Line* guests, doing final touch-ups, primping, pampering, boldly pandering to the guests' vanity and egocentricity.

Phony smiles and exaggerated commentary on the guests' resemblance to Hollywood stars were the cosmetologists' stock-in-trade. Lila sucked up every bit of it. But she wasn't content with the facial artist's comparisons. Dispatching an artist to fetch her compact from her purse, she opened it, and looking up and down in the mirror, she fluffed her hairsprayed coiffe, and patted a single daub of powder on the tip of her nose, preempting the artist. Then closing the compact crisply, she handed the compact to the artist, conveying a Cleopatralike directive to the artist to return it to her purse. She struck a profile pose, chin slightly elevated, and waited for the countdown to airtime.

Ira Abelman, the corpulent, bearded professor from Yale University, was talking to Representative Esther Grant, in an extremely loud voice for the setting. Elitist, dogmatic, doctrinaire, Abelman was a stereotypical university professor caught up in the importance of his knowledge of a topic smaller than a pinhead. The Congresswoman had been in command yesterday at the Congressional hearing where the rules of the game were stacked against him; tonight the two of them would be playing on a level field. The debate was about to begin, and he had a lecture hall filled with an audience of millions.

Esther was listening politely to the opinionated Abelman, all the while yearning for the show to start. She had dealt with a thousand Abelmans before, but this one, from her experience at the hearing, seemed exceptionally arrogant.

Ed Hopkins, who had been made-up back stage and who up to this time had ignored everyone, walked over to his futuristic desk and motioned for everyone to be quiet. A first-class media prima donna, Hopkins said nothing to the studio guests, pompously presuming that they had been fully briefed by the studio staff. After a short sidebar with his technical director, he looked squarely into the center camera. five . . . four . . . three . . . two . . . one, rolled the countdown and on flashed the camera's red light.

"Good evening, ladies and gentlemen. Welcome to *Base-Line*," Hopkins said, transfiguring his stolid face into an unnatural beaming smile. "There are many difficult issues surrounding the matter of gender and service in ground combat. None is more difficult, however, than that concerning sex-linked or physiological differences between men and women. Tonight, we will be exploring with our guests three aspects of that issue, namely pregnancy, menstruation, and physical strength. Our guests, who are all present in our studio, are particularly qualified to address these issues. Congresswoman Esther Grant, Republican from Chicago, is a member of the House Armed Services Subcommittee on Women in Combat which conducted hearings on our topic yesterday on Capitol Hill. Lila Davis-Whitfield, is President of the Women' Republican American Traditional Heritage Foundation, headquartered here in Washington D.C. Professor Ira Abelman is a Professor of Sociology from Yale University who has published three books on the subject of women in the military service, one specifically addressing women's role in ground combat. He testified on that topic yesterday before Representative Grant's subcommittee. We asked a representative of the United States Army to be here tonight, but an army spokesperson politely declined our invitation.

"Before we get started I think we should all be on the same wavelength, definitionwise. The army defines `close combat' as `engaging an enemy with individual or crew-served weapons while being exposed to direct enemy fire, a high probability of direct physical contact with the enemy's personnel, and a substantial risk of capture.' `Direct combat' is defined as `close combat which takes place while closing with the enemy by fire, maneuver, or shock effect in order to destroy or capture him, or while repelling his assault by fire or counterattack.' With that as an introduction, I'll start the questioning with you, Congresswoman Grant, if you don't mind—and it concerns the topic of pregnancy."

"I don't mind at all, Ed."

"One basic difference between men and women is that women get pregnant and men don't."

"I can't argue with that, Ed." Esther said, with a wide smile.

Hopkins, smiling back, continued, "General Winterfield, the Army Chief of Staff, has been quoted as saying `Pregnant women holding vital combat jobs in the army would be an overwhelming hindrance to operational flexibility.' How would you respond to that?"

"Ed, General Winterfield's concern is simply a red herring. The Army's own statistics reveal that when all other factors contributing to lost time, such as alcohol abuse, drug use, desertion, AWOL, and abortion were considered along with pregnancy, the days lost for women totalled only about one-half of one percent of the total available work days, while for men the total was more than one percent. The army's position on pregnancy is grossly disingenuous."

"Ed, may I respond to that?" Lila interjected.

"Just hold your horses, madam," Hopkins replied. "I just have one follow-up question, and then I'll let you answer." Congresswoman Grant, do we know how much of military women's lost time is due to pregnancies?"

"I believe, overall, it is approximately thirty-seven percent. But realize that the *number* of pregnancies among service women is not all that high."

"Okay, Ms. Davis, your turn," said Hopkins.

"Ed, I find it utterly appalling how proponents of women in combat can manipulate the facts. Pregnancy rates among military women have been, in some years, as high as fourteen percent. The Navy provides a good example of just how prevalent the problem of pregnancy is. When the ship *Acadia* docked in San Diego recently, it had thirty-six pregnant crew members. When the *Yellowstone* docked shortly afterward, twenty of the crew were pregnant. Last week, five pregnant sailors had to be removed from the aircraft carrier *USS Eisenhower*—the first U.S. warship set to sea with women as part of the permanent crew. The Navy spokesperson defensively protested, `These women have a right to get pregnant.' Would they still have a `right' to get pregnant if the United States was at war? Regardless of whether they would or not, they

couldn't be stopped from getting pregnant. That's the point to be
made here."

"Isn't the issue also the *length* of time and the military's *cost*
related to each individual pregnancy?" Hopkins inquired.

"Absolutely, Ed. When a servicewoman gets pregnant, she is
given several options. She can resign immediately and escape from
the remainder of her enlistment, or she can have limited duty
during her pregnancy, receive full medical benefits and up to six
weeks of paid maternity leave, and promise to accept deployment
after delivery to anywhere in the world. Consider this scenario in a
combat situation: the United States spends two hundred thousand dollars educating and training a female West Point cadet to
be a combat leader; the U.S. goes to war; the West Pointer is assigned to an infantry unit on the battlefield. She would have the
option to say, 'Pardon me, fellas. I'm taking nine months off from
the foxhole in order to be pregnant, and then a couple of months
more to recuperate. You guys go ahead and do your thing, and I'll
see you back here on the front lines in about a year—that is, if the
war is still going on.' And pregnancy is only half the . . . "

"But, Ed," Esther interrupted, "the public should realize that
men have been avoiding combat duty in droves over the last century by faking disabilities and getting declared 4-F. Because women
have never been officially allowed to serve in ground combat, there
is no evidence that a female West Point graduate would do what
Ms. Davis described. Also, the average woman is pregnant for a
very small proportion of her life and some women—such as Ms.
Davis who has been carrying on tonight about the travails of pregnancy—never become pregnant. The effect of pregnancy on
women's potential battlefield performance is sheer speculation. I
think . . . "

"Congresswoman Grant," Hopkins interjected, "I know that
you have very strong feelings about the issues under discussion,
but I again politely request that you, like Ms. Davis, restrain yourself."

"Yes, Mr. Hopkins," Esther said recoiling. "I'll do my best."

"Thank you," Hopkins said, attempting to sound understanding. "Professor Abelman, you've been patiently quiet up to now. Do you have something that you would like to add to this part of the discussion?"

"Yes, Ed. I sure hope it doesn't appear to our viewers that Ms. Davis and I are ganging up on Representative Grant. But on the issue of pregnancy and combat, I must admit that I have come down solidly on the side of exclusion. Please realize that, related to the pregnancy issue, is the matter—which up to now has not been sufficiently researched—of heightened risks to the fetus of a pregnant woman in a combat zone. The possibility of increased risks of miscarriage, of a pregnant woman's need to discontinue strenuous combat duties, and of the unavailability of medical care, are real concerns affecting any military decision to admit or deny women access to combat roles.

"That's the pregnancy problem, but isn't there also a motherhood problem—who takes care of the children while the mother's away in combat," Hopkins asked.

"That's a good point Ed and one that Ms. Davis was about to make previously. With the motherhood problem, the considerations are very practical. It's just common sense that nursing mothers of six- ten- and twelve-week old babies—who may have, in addition, two and three preschool children—should not be shipped off to the combat zone. This would be contrary to combat readiness and would be in disregard of the concept of family integrity. As I pointed out in my book, *Women in Combat: The Negative Pregnant*, human experience recognizes that the mother of a six-week-old baby can never be combat ready like the father of a six-week-old baby. In concluding my comments on this topic, I ask our viewers to simply consider this question: How effectively do you think new mothers could perform their duties on the battlefield if they were yearning for their babies at home?"

"Thank you for your insights, Professor Abelman," Hopkins said. "You certainly have a way to get to the heart of the matter, and I might add, to skillfully weave in a plug for your book. Speaking of plugs, it's time to weave in a few of our own for our sponsors.

0368-COOL

When we come back . . . a look at the menstruation issue and combat. Don't go away."

While the commercials were running, Hopkins summoned his video technician and talked to him while they both looked at a sheet he was holding in hand. Professor Abelman, self-satisfied, leafed through one of his publications lying on the table in front of him. Lila looked at Esther, who was seated at the table next to her, and smiled. "I really like those earrings, Esther," Lila said in a folksy voice. "Where'd ya get them.?"

"Bloomingdale's in Chicago," Esther said, trying to maintain a dignified air, awaiting the countdown back to the program.

"Never shopped there," Lila replied. "Any bargains?"

"It's not Filene's," Esther responded mechanically, looking straight ahead.

"Are you free for brunch, the day after tomorrow?" asked Lila.

The unexpected question threw Esther into momentary confusion. "I . . . I don't know. What day *is* the day after tomorrow?"

"Sunday." Lila replied.

"I would have to th . . . think . . . "

At that instant, the large TV monitor behind the countdown. five . . . four . . . three . . . two . . . one, and the red light above the camera illuminated. An electric sign reading "ON THE AIR" in huge block letters could be seen on the back wall of the studio.

"We're back," said Hopkins, "and now we're turning our attention briefly to the relevance, if any, of the female menstrual cycle on the issue of women in combat. Ms. Davis, I'm going to put you under fire, first, on this topic.

"Doesn't bother me, Ed".

"Good," said Ed, his face slightly contorted. "Does the matter of the female menstrual cycle, in your view, present a substantial impediment to women's full assimilation into the military, including combat situations?"

"Perhaps not a *substantial* impediment, but an impediment nonetheless. You must realize that an estimated twenty to forty percent of women experience physical and mental abnormalities prior to menstruation. This malady has been labelled premenstrual stress syndrome or PMS. It has gained such recognition in recent years as a serious debilitating condition that it is being offered as a defense now in criminal cases. Admittedly, there is very little empirical data available showing the effect of PMS on women in a combat role, but it is reasonable . . . "

"Ed, I'm just going to have to interrupt here," Esther said, speaking over Lila's muffled commentary. "This is really getting ridiculous . . . even to the point of bad taste."

"Go ahead," Hopkins replied, somewhat sheepishly.

"Ms. Davis, has admitted openly that there is no data to support anything she is saying. If there is an authority on this subject, it is my husband, who has told me many times that PMS is a reason for *inclusion* of women in combat rather than *exclusion*. The bottom line is that the inconvenience of menstrual cycles will be an element of combat life the same way that most women deal with menstruation in their own lives . . . more as a nuisance than an insurmountable problem. At most, it presents issues of hygiene and possible reduced physical performance for which adjustments can easily be made by the army."

"Do you have anything to add to this topic, Professor Abelman?" Ed asked, hoping he would say no.

"Are you crazy, Ed?"

"I get the drift," Hopkins chuckled. How would you like to tackle the final issue, Professor?—physical abilities.

"Sure, Ed. Shoot."

"All right, here it is. Proponents of allowing women in ground combat argue that women should be evaluated as individuals along with men, with job assignments determined by individual merit based on gender-neutral, job-related qualifications. Under this proposal, persons who lack sufficient upper body strength—be they men or women—would be excluded from ground combat. What's wrong with this concept . . . or, what's right with it?"

"Everything is wrong with it, Ed. Currently, any male can be excluded from ground combat if he is determined to be physically incapable of engaging in it. However, women *as a class* lack upper body strength. West Point recognized this when it established physical aptitude requirements for women. Men are required to do a certain number of pull-ups to pass one of the tests; women merely have to do a flexed-arm hang for a number of seconds. Quite a difference in requirements."

Esther, cutting off Abelman, sputtered "Professor, why don't you tell our viewers the whole story—that to score the maximum on the physical aptitude test, women have to do more push-ups than men."

"Well that's true, ma'am, but if a female in combat is required to climb a fifty-foot vertical rope to lead her platoon out of danger, she may not be able to do it. Then, what?"

"A man would have the same problem, Professor."

"Would not!"

"Would so!"

"Hey, you two," Hopkins overtoned, "let's not have melée here on national television. The *American Gladiator* show we are not."

"Sorry, Ed," said Esther, "but I just want to point out that the smaller size and strength of the Viet Cong and the North Vietnamese—both men and women—who fought against the U.S. was not a detriment for them. In many instances it served as an advantage. I think we can all agree that the larger body size and strength of American men did not dictate an American military success in Vietnam. Professor Abelman, an expert in military combat, is well aware of these facts. He seems to operate on the principle that if the truth hurts, hide it."

"My dear Congresswoman," responded the professor condescendingly. "If anyone is trying to hide the truth here, it is you, not me. You raise irrelevant matters. Just because an ant can carry an object a thousand times its body weight does not mean that women should be placed in a ground combat role. West Point has made all kinds of additional modifications to its physical requirements in order to accommodate the fairer sex so that female cadets won't be quote "psychologically discouraged". A number of events in the obstacle course have been eliminated, cadets now run the course in jogging shoes instead of boots—how long would jogging shoes last on the battlefield?—a lighter rifle has been substituted, female cadets engage in hand-to-hand combat training instead of boxing, and the traditional eighteen-mile forced march carrying a heavy pack has been eliminated for the little prissies."

"Little prissies!" Esther exclaimed, almost shellshocked.

"Yes, little prissies. The female gender is systematically weakening our national defense. This is something that every American should be concerned about. The simple facts are that women are physically different—physically handicapped.

"Professor Abelman . . . Professor . . . " Esther sputtered.

Abelman, continuing unabashed: "They have forty percent more body fat than men; that's like having a man carry a seventy-pound weight. They have sixty percent the lung capacity of men; that's like having a man wear a mask to reduce air intake. They have a mechanical disadvantage in their hip structure; that's like having a man put a brace between his legs to make him walk pigeon-toed. If you handicapped men physically in that way—yes, I suppose women would have a better chance of keeping up with men on a mile run. But why should we artificially handicap men to accommodate the actual handicaps of women? Women just don't measure up physically. Men would spend half their time on the battlefield just carrying the handicapped women around on their backs."

"Professor Abelman," Esther slowly said, attempting to regain her equilibrium, "you owe every female watching this program an apology for . . . "

"Apology, ashmology," Abelman responded sarcastically. "I don't owe an apology to anyone. I was asked to come on this program to freely state my opinions. That's what I've done. I'm seriously worried about our national security. Every concession we make to women to compensate for their universally recognized lack of strength, stamina, and muscle is jeopardizing this country's ability to defend itself. All the arguments to the contrary are sheer poppycock."

"It isn't national security at all that you're worried about, Professor. What you and the rest of your arch-conservative, holier-than-thou, intolerant, bigoted, establishment types fear is not deterioration of our national defense, but rather how the assimilation of women in combat will impact on your subversive national agenda to totally eliminate gays from the military. Admit it, professor. Any concession you make for women will . . .

"Well, I'm afraid that's all the time that we have for questions and answers," Hopkins interjected, hoping to halt the escalating mudslinging colloquy. We'll will be back in a moment for a final observation from yours truly. Stay right where you are."

During the break, Lila prodded, "Esther, have you given my invitation some thought?"

Esther, wishing that Lila had given up on the idea, said with all the cordiality she could muster, "What did you have in mind?"

"How about brunch at twelve noon at my townhouse in Georgetown?"

"I have a plane to catch out of Dulles to Chicago O'Hare at three thirty in the afternoon." said Esther, hoping to deflect the brunch invitation.

"Oh, that would give us plenty of time to chat," said Lila.

"I can have my chauffeur come round to pick you up at eleven forty-five in the morning and then he could take you to the airport later. Just let me know where you want to be picked up." Lila really didn't have a chauffeur, but she knew an Italian limousine driver who would do anything for a toss in the hay with her.

Esther was curious about Lila's motivation. Curious enough to accept her invitation. The countdown to the program began. "We'll make plans after the show . . . ," said Esther, resuming an august pose.

Hopkins looked directly into the camera and launched into his final commentary. "Experts seem to agree that the roles women should play in war must be based on military standards, not solely on women's rights. The army's current position seems to be that we should err on the side of national security until such time as we have confidence that the basic mission of the army can be accomplished with significantly more female content in the active force. That argument may be true, but at some point it seems to become circular: national security *may* be weakened by women in combat roles; therefore we need to experiment with women in combat. To experiment with women in combat might risk national security; therefore, we should not experiment with women in combat. But any ordinary citizen who considers all the arguments will come to the conclusion that some kind of experiment using women in actual ground combat is needed to unravel this conundrum. We have received information today, from reliable sources, that the House Armed Services Committee is considering just that—an experiment to test the combat mettle of women. We will keep you posted on any new developments on this topic in the future. Thank you for watching *Base-Line*. And on behalf of all the people here at ABC, and at our local affiliates, we bid you all a pleasant good night."

Once off the air, Hopkins wasted no time leaving the studio. Socializing wasn't his thing. He was a totally different personality off the air than he was on the air. Only his television guests and the studio staff knew the real Ed Hopkins. It was as if he thought that being a neutral interviewer meant that he had to be independent of people. But he carried it to the extreme, almost to the point of being a recluse.

Abelman busied himself inscribing and autographing a copy of *The Negative Pregnant* for Lila, the consummate sycophant. Esther was writing out the address where the limousine driver was to pick her up the following morning. Lila, as she waited for them to finish, reflected on Esther's cheap shot on national television about Lila never being pregnant. Esther's statement was wrong, but, because of the circumstances, it was something Lila chose not to correct publicly. There would be a time and place to set the record straight.

4

Kate's prediction was right. Saturday was radiantly sunny—the perfect kind of late-October day, with trees resplendent in various shades of red and yellow; an invigorating cool breeze carrying sounds from V-shaped formations of Canadian geese commencing their annual trek south. It was the kind of West Point day one would like to hug. Heaven only knew what bitter cold the winter would bring in the next couple months to the rock-bound fortress in the Hudson Highlands.

It was eleven a.m. Kate had already made the rounds with a regimental tactical officer to spot-check a few barracks rooms in the third regiment. Being Brigade Commander, Kate was frequently excused from Saturday morning classes to tend to her barracks inspection duties. Her phone was ringing when she got back to her room. Nothing important. Just Fran Richards, a classmate, wanting to know if she wanted to go to the home football game against Wake Forest that afternoon up at Michie Stadium. Ever since plebe year, it had become a ritual, Fran and Kate going to home games together. Throughout the conversation, Kate was only half-tuned into what Fran was saying. Kate was wondering how Tina was doing. Kate hadn't seen her at breakfast formation. But maybe Tina was there and maybe Kate didn't notice her. Maybe Tina ditched breakfast. Maybe she was not feeling well enough to get out of bed. But that was unlike her. Really unlike her.

As soon as Kate hung up with Fran, Kate dialed Tina's room. No answer. Kate began to get worried. Then she dialed the infirmary. Tina hadn't been there. Next, she tried Jim Hendrix in the Barracks Police office—Tina always kibitzed with the janitors. No luck. On a whim, she dialed the hospital pharmacy. She described Tina to the pharmacist on the other end of the line. The pharmacist had seen someone meeting Tina's description a short while before and he thought he had filled a strong sedative prescription for her. The pharmacy had been extremely busy that morning and he couldn't take time to go through the paperwork to verify the name of the patient. Kate asked if Doctor Parmley had authorized the prescription and the pharmacists said that he believed that it was Parmley—but he couldn't be sure. He politely told Kate that he had ten people lined up in front of his window, and he had to get off the phone. The pharmacist gruffly said "no" when Kate squeezed in one more question seeking to find out if he knew where the person might be going after she left the pharmacy.

Kate hung up the phone, turned, and sat back on the edge of her desk. Tears began to well in her eyes. "How could they give Tina a strong sedative?" she said to herself. "Don't they know she's pregnant!!!" But Tina's *fetus* wasn't Kate's chief worry. *Tina* was. She pictured Tina curled up in a fetal position on a pile of yellow-orange leaves somewhere on Flirtation Walk with an empty prescription bottle beside her and a scribbled note which read: "Peace to all my friends: From a warmonger who lived fast, loved hard, and died young." That was like her. Really like her.

"Annie Farnsworth—Tina's roommate!" Kate thought to herself. *She* would know where Tina was! Kate blanked for a moment. Where would Annie be on Saturday morning? That was easy. Annie was a hive. She'd be in the library. Kate quickly dialed the library reference desk.

"Reference Desk. How may I help you," said a deep male voice on the other end of the line.

"Do you know Cadet Farnsworth?" Kate asked briskly.

"Look, lady, there are about four thousand cadets at West Point," the librarian responded in an angry tone of voice. "Do you expect me to know all of them by name?"

"No," said Kate also becoming a little testy. "I just asked if you knew *one* of them. She's over there a lot."

"Well, the answer still is, I don't know any cadet by the name of Farnsworth," the librarian replied sarcastically.

Kate inhaled deeply. "Sir, this may be a matter of life or death."

"Yes, madam, they all say that," the librarian responded in an affected tone. With the air of a power broker, he continued, "We don't have a paging system here, and I just don't have the time to run all over the library paging someone. Besides, it's disruptive."

Kate was about to lose it. She didn't like doing it, but she would have to bring in the heavy artillery. "Look, Mr. Librarian! . . . "

"My name is Cadwalader, madam."

" . . . Mr. Cadwalader. . . . "

"That's my first name, madam. My last name is Kappenberg."

" . . . Mr. Kappenberg, then. This is Cadet Brigade Commander McKeane you are speaking to."

"Oh, I beg your pardon madam," the voice said half apologetically. "How was I to know? I mean, really, you should identify yourself—your rank—when you first speak."

Kate was doing everything in her power to keep her rage in tow. Why shouldn't every customer of the library receive equally good service? Why should rank matter? Why should this guy be scolding her for not identifying herself? As the seconds ticked by, Kate blurted, "Mr. Kappenberg . . . "

"You can call me Kap, ma'am. Everyone else does," said the librarian trying to medicate the sting out of the conversation.

Holding a steady course, Kate retorted "Mr. Kappenberg, I want you to page Cadet Annie Farnsworth."

"Yes, ma'am. Right away."

It seemed to Kate that the librarian was gone for an infinity. Kate reflected on many fateful scenarios for Tina and none of them had happy endings. After about five minutes, Kate heard some thrashing around for the telephone as if someone were coming back on the line.

"This is Cadet Farnsworth," a voice said.

"Annie!"

"Kate?"

"Yeah, Annie, this is Kate. You can't imagine how happy I am to get a hold of you!"

"Yeah? What's up?"

"Have you seen Tina this morning?"

"Tina? Sure. Why do you ask?"

"Oh, nothing really important, but do you know where she might be right now?" Kate was trying hard not to reveal her terror about Tina being missing.

"I think Tina said she was going up to the Cadet Chapel this morning. I thought it was a little strange that she would be going to the chapel on a Saturday morning. But then she's been acting a little strange lately anyway. If she's not there, she might be over at the Weapons Room having lunch about noon. That's one of her usual hangouts on the weekend."

"Thanks, Annie," said Kate. "I'll try the chapel first. If you see Tina, please tell her I'm looking for her. I won't be heading up to the football game until about one-thirty this afternoon"

"Sure, no problem, Kate."

Kate hung up. What in the world would Tina be doing at the chapel? She *never* went to the Cadet Chapel . . . except of course to screw. Just as Kate was leaving her room to head for the chapel, the phone rang. She felt like just letting it ring. But then she had second thoughts. What if it was the Com or the Supe?

She picked up.

"Cadet First Captain McKeane," Kate said.

"Kate . . . this is Annie calling back."

"Yeah, Annie."

"There's something else strange about what Tina did lately."

"Like what?"

"When I came into the room about eight o'clock last night Tina had out a field bayonet cleaning it. Not her dull-edged *dress* bayonet but a razor-sharp *field* bayonet."

"Where'd she get a field bayonet?" Kate asked.

"I don't know where she got it. Maybe she borrowed it from a plebe. I didn't say anything to her. She was like in a trance. It was real strange. It seemed weird enough that Tina was in her room on Friday night—but seeing her sitting there cleaning equipment? That was *crazy*."

"Yeah, . . . crazy," Kate echoed, her attention trailing off.

"I don't know why I called you back to tell you this," Annie said almost embarrassedly. "I don't want you to think I am squealing on a roomie or something. But I'm concerned, Kate. Really concerned."

Kate thanked Annie for her candor and ended the conversation by assuring Annie that she would not tell Tina about Annie's disclosure. Kate then raced out of her barracks and in the direction of the Cadet Chapel.

The shortest route to the Cadet Chapel was up a zigzag rock staircase built into the granite, wooded cliffs behind Washington Hall, the cadet dining hall. Kate ran up the stairs, taking two at a time, until she became overwhelmed with exhaustion and then slowed to taking one step at a time. Two-thirds of the way up, even in the cool autumn air, she was sweating profusely. She stopped to look up. No Tina in sight. She looked down. She became dizzy momentarily from the steepness of the vertical cliff. Regaining her balance she continued to ascend. When she neared the top, she saw in the sunny distance a solitary small figure, with bushy dark hair and wearing—incongruously—an oversized cadet caped raincoat. The figure appeared as a stately monolith atop a white rock wall which jutted thirty feet vertically out of the granite to provide a majestic underpinning for the chapel's heavily turreted Gothic architecture.

Kate ran toward the figure, which was now turned slightly away, facing south and bent over, as if peering into the granite-walled abyss.

"TINA!! TINA!! DON'T! DON'T!" Kate shrieked in desperation. "DON'T DO IT!! DON'T JUMP!!"

As Kate approached within a few feet, the figure turned slowly around and said, "Tina? Who's Tina?"

"Chaplain Terronez!" Kate gasped. "I'm sorry. I mistook you for someone else. I've been looking all over for Tina Marafino. Do you know her, Chaplain?"

"No, I'm afraid I don't. But I think I know who you are. Aren't you the Cadet Brigade Commander?"

"Yes, Chaplain. I'm Kate McKeane."

"I thought so. The railroad tracks on your collar were a dead giveaway."

"Have you seen a short, dark-haired female cadet up here this morning?" Kate asked hopefully, still wondering why this guy was standing there with a cadet raincoat on.

The chaplain, pulling up the bottom of his raincoat to keep it off the ground, sensed a need to explain his garb. "Well, actually I just took a walk through the chapel before I stepped outside to get a breath of fresh air. The wind was a bit nippier than I thought, so I ducked back inside and picked up a raincoat that a cadet had left in back of the church after choir practice last night. When I came out again, I passed a young lady going into the chapel, much like you described. She may still be in there."

"Did she say anything to you, Chaplain?"

"No, except maybe 'good morning' or something. We didn't have an extended conversation, if that's what you mean."

"Thanks, Chaplain," Kate said as she darted toward the huge wooden chapel doors, and, exerting considerable effort against the wind, managed to open one of them sufficiently to squeeze her body between the door and the center post. When she was halfway through, she turned her head toward the chaplain and said smiling, "Chaplain, you really have to do something about these gates to heaven."

"Yeah. I'll get to it as soon as I find a cadet raincoat my size," the chaplain smiled back.

Once inside, Kate scanned the pews in the multiple high-arched vault of worship. The place was completely empty. No Tina in sight. Then Kate heard something. A whimpering, like a wounded puppy dog. A whimpering, magnified and echoing many times in the arched chambers. The echoing cacophony made it difficult for Kate to identify the source. Finally, Kate looked toward the front. Something moved. It was Tina! Tina was in the sanctuary! Trying not to be observed by Tina, Kate moved slowly toward an outside aisle and then shuffled quietly to the front of the chapel. Entering the sanctuary she saw a weeping Tina sitting in a pew behind the organ with her head on folded arms resting on the pew in front of her. Kate slid into Tina's pew and postured for an embrace. Startled, Tina reacted defensively by raising her hand which gripped the glistening blade of a field bayonet.

"Tina!!" Kate shouted, causing sound to resonate seemingly endlessly in the god-filled atmosphere.

Tina dropped the bayonet and engaged Kate in a fast embrace, sobbing uncontrollably.

"Kate, I almost killed you! What is wrong with me? I almost killed my best friend!" Tina wailed, barely intelligibly as she shoved her face forcefully into Kate's accommodating bosom. "There now, Tina. No harm was done," Kate consoled.

"Kate, I came up here to do harm. TO THIS GARGANTUAN ORGAN—TO THIS THING INSIDE ME—TO MYSELF. Kate, I'm out of control. Please help me."

"Tina, pull yourself together," Kate whispered pointedly. "You've been through a lot worse. Beast Barracks, the Plebe Hike, the first month of academics, physical hazing, the obstacle course. This is nothing compared to all that."

"But Kate, How do I get an abortion without anyone knowing?"

Tina said, raising her voice to the point that Kate placed her index finger to her lips to suggest that Tina converse more quietly.

"Tina, you let me handle that. Now let's get you back to the barracks. It's almost noon. How would you like to go to the game this afternoon with Fran Richards and me?"

"Let me think about it," Tina replied while picking up the bayonet from the pew. Handing it to Kate, she whispered, "Here, Kate, I won't be needing this any more."

Kate and Tina, arm in arm, walked down the center aisle toward the rear of the church. In the rear vestibule, they encountered Chaplain Terronez who was no longer sporting a friendly smile. The chaplain, sans raincoat, gave Kate a scornful look, and without saying a word, turned and walked, shaking his head, toward the sanctuary.

5

A limousine had arrived at Esther's condominium at eleven forty-five a.m. sharp, and had whisked Esther over to Lila's townhome in trendy Georgetown. As the limousine driver backed into a reserved parking space in front of the townhome, Esther, looking out the passenger side, recognized a shiny maroon 1938 Pierce Arrow as one of a collection of antique cars belonging to a justice of the Supreme Court—but she had forgotten which one. Lila was no slouch, Esther mused. The limo driver respectfully escorted Esther along the walkway between Lila's townhouse and the adjacent one belonging to the Supreme Court justice. Proceeding through an arched wrought-iron entranceway covered with blanched remnants of summer's grape and honeysuckle vines, the driver and Esther entered into a cozy garden area, with curved red-brick walkways and interspersed flower beds which must have made for a vision of glorious botanical splendor in the summertime. In the center of the garden area and at a conspicuously lower level than the extensive wooden deck attached to the main building was a screened Victorian-style white gazebo which appeared to be a perfect size for private dinner parties. Lila was standing in the doorway of the gazebo when the driver, bowing slightly in Lila's direction, announced Esther's arrival and then quickly departed.

"Esther, welcome. It was so nice of you to come," Lila said, reaching out and cordially grasping Esther's hand.

"Well, it was nice of you to invite me," Esther replied, her voice bearing a tinge of curiosity.

"I thought we'd have brunch out here in the gazebo, if it isn't too chilly," Lila suggested. "What do you think?"

Sensing the warm rays of the autumn sun on her face, Esther grinned broadly and responded, "That would be lovely."

Lila opened the screen door of the gazebo as Esther, spike-heeled and dressed in a suit with a tight skirt, began to carefully negotiate the four wooden steps up to the gazebo level. Esther having faltered slightly, Lila reached for Esther's hand and brought her back into balance. With a wink, Lila purred, "We women have to stick together." Esther smiled perfunctorily.

Lila had spent most of Saturday morning preparing for the Congresswoman's visit. There had been clutter everywhere, and she had worked a full hour just picking up things off the floor and putting them away. Actually, it wasn't the picking up that took so long—it was the deciding where to put them. Emilio's dirty underwear, for example. Her ex-husband had once told her that it took longer for her to decide where to put a bobby pin than it took Congress to decide to go to war. She had bought practically every organizer gadget in the department store catalogues, but she never used any of them. They would just take up space in her closet. And, of course, her closets and drawers in every room overflowed because she would never throw anything out.

She had even gone so far as to attend a day long "Neatnik Seminar". But even that proved useless. The psychologist giving the seminar confided to her privately that she either had an Attention Deficit Disorder or, as an adult child of an alcoholic, she was so busy being responsible for everyone else she could not accept responsibility for herself. Lila had rejected the psychologist's informal diagnosis as ridiculous and pompous. Nothing changed. But for the Congresswoman's visit, Lila had pulled out all stops trying to clean her place up. She did it, too, knowing that Esther would probably not even have time to set foot inside.

Cooking was something else. Lila was a great cook—a real artist in the kitchen. She had a sixth sense about the types and amounts of herbs and spices to mix together to create a palatable effect. This was much like her way with people. She was a singularly sloppy cook, however, leaving, for days, heaps of discarded choppings and assorted pots, pans, and dishes covered with sauces, gravies, and other food residues. She had no concept of cleaning up while cooking. It just wasn't in her. For Esther's visit, however, Lila had taken the time to clean up. Today was special. She had trotted out her best of everything—Royal Dalton china, Steuben crystal, Jensen sterling silver flatware. The centerpiece she had chosen was a richly colorful array of mums, lilies, and orchids, accented by a background of interlaced ferns. The cuisine of the day—French. Removing a bottle from a sterling silver wine chiller on a stand next to the dining table exquisitely bedecked in Irish linen and lace-edged napkins, Lila inquired, "Champagne to start, Esther?" Feigning resistance, Esther replied "If you insist." Lila poured three-quarters of a glass for Esther and a quarter of a glass for herself. For awhile, Lila kept the conversation mundane. Between sips, the two women methodically explored the weather, plans for the upcoming Thanksgiviing holidays, favorite women's stores and restaurants in D.C.. Lila then refilled Esther's empty champagne glass and immediately passed her a dish of lobster-filled crepes.

"This looks delightful, Lila. You'll have to give me the recipe."

"You'd better try it first. But I'd be happy to give you the recipe."

Taking a bite, Esther cooed, "This is absolutely delicious! Closing her eyes and savoring the taste, Esther continued more slowly, unable to avoid slurring her speech, "Mmmmmm, please . . . I want the reshipee . . . uh, recipe." Lila was artfully spinning her web.

"Okay, before you leave. I promise. Here, try some of this," Lila said while passing her a mushroom-caviar omelette.

"Thanks. Mmmmmmm, it looks equally scrumptious!"

Believing that the comfortable atmosphere and the alcohol had reduced Esther's reactive capability, Lila said sharply, "You know, Esther, you really hurt my feelings last night with your comments on the Ed Hopkins show."

Esther put down her fork and wiped her mouth with a lace napkin. "How? What do you mean, Lila?"

"You assumed that I was never pregnant. And since you were last to speak on the air, I wasn't able to set the record straight."

"So you *were* pregnant at some time in your former marriage?"

"Yes, very early in my marriage. The pregnancy wasn't planned. It was a mistake. I miscarried." Lila knew this was a blatant lie.

But she wanted to get Esther emotionally off balance before she broached the women in combat topic. Actually, Lila had become pregnant while she was single in a one-night fling. She had secretly gotten an abortion. Her mother and father never knew about it.

"Oh, I'm so very sorry, Lila. I did not know about that. I would never have said anything like that had I known. Can you ever forgive me?"

"I still wonder what my child would have been like had I not miscarried. I am still suffering the loss."

"Oh, Lila. I can't apologize enough for my insensitivity." Handing Esther the plate of omelettes, Lila said in a healing tone, "I know you wouldn't have hurt me intentionally. I accept your apology. Here, have some more to eat or you may hurt my feelings again."

While Esther was liberally dishing a portion of the omelette onto her plate, Lila decided to move in for the kill. "What do you really think about women in combat?"

Lila's question caught Esther completely off guard. Being slightly inebriated, Esther's reaction was untypically sluggish.

Buying time to respond, Esther instinctively inserted, "That's a pretty broad question, Lll . . . i . . . lla."

Lila used her fork for a moment to play with the crepes on her plate, and then cut into the crepes with the side of her fork. Raising a forkful of crepes to her mouth, she said "Well, to be more specific Esther, do you think we should really be sending young women to fight the drug war in Colombia?"

Esther had trouble swallowing her last bite. "How do you know about that?"

"Both you and I have been around long enough to know that there are no secrets in Washington. It's true isn't it? About sending women soldiers to Colombia, I mean."

"The Government's not going to send them en masse, if that's what you're asking."

"No, I wouldn't be suggesting that. But hasn't some kind of experiment been approved?"

"Not yet, exactly."

"But it's in the works, isn't it?"

"Yes, to be perfectly honest, I would have to say it's in the works." The food was beginning to counteract the disorienting effect of the champagne.

Prodding further, Lila inquired, "when do you think it will happen."

"Probably within the next year. These things always take time."

In a serious tone, Lila said, "You obviously know that I am very much against the idea of women in combat."

"I definitely gathered that from what you said on the Ed Hopkins show last night."

"No, really. I will do anything to insure that women do not have a military combat role."

"Come, now, Lila. What is wrong with an experiment? If you are right, and women cannot hack it in combat, the experiment will be your evidence. If you want to know the truth, and I must swear you to secrecy on this . . . "

"Sure, Esther."

"I don't think women will be able to hack it."

Trying not to seem overly surprised, Lila asked, "then why are you pushing the issue?"

"Because I want this issue put to rest once and for all. It's been kicking around for nearly twenty years now in Congress—ever since women were allowed to enter the military academies. And I want your support for the experiment."

This time, Lila could not camouflage her surprise. "You want *my* help? You must be kidding."

"No, I'm not kidding. I want you to publicly support the experiment. You really have nothing to lose. I estimate that there is about a ninety-five percent chance that women will fail a combat experiment. How about it? You might even be a hero in your own political circles."

"What would I have to do?"

"Simple, just hold a WRATHPAC press conference at the time

of the public announcement of the experiment and endorse the idea of an experiment."

"That's it?"

"Yes, and I can up the ante a little also."

"How's that?"

"I can get you appointed as the civilian member of the Congressional oversight committee for the experiment. You will actually go to Colombia and observe the combat operations."

This is what Lila had dreamed about—real celebrity status. She could hardly restrain her glee.

"Do we have a deal, Lila?"

"I will have to clear it with the WRATHPAC Board, but I don't think that'll be a problem." She quickly added, "But, I personally will support the idea of an experiment whether the Board does or not."

"Good. Then we have a deal."

"Yes," said Lila. "Remind me to get you that recipe before you leave."

6

Kate had taken Tina back to her room and was entering her own room when her phone began ringing. Her first reaction was that Father Terronez had squealed on her to the Com or the Supe. She hesitated slightly before picking up the receiver, trying to come up with some explanation that would preserve Tina's secret yet be truthful. Nothing came to mind. If worse came to worse, she would have to expose Tina's situation. Kate picked up the receiver and identified herself.

"Kate?" said the voice.

"Yes, sir."

"Captain Martin, here."

Kate felt a rush of relief.

"Kate, I can't talk long," he said. "I'm over at the law department grading some tests and have to leave soon to go to the game.

I just got the strangest call. It was from Chaplain Terronez. Do you know him?"

"Not really sir," said Kate. "I may have spoken to him once or so."

"Well, he seems to know you quite well. He called here a few minutes ago. He said he wanted to talk to any attorney who was here. I said I'd be glad to help him. He said that he believed the Cadet First Captain to be in serious need of legal advice."

"That *is* strange," said Kate. "Did he say why, sir"

"No. Actually, he was quite evasive. He didn't seem to know that I knew you personally, and I didn't let on that I did. He wouldn't say why he thought you needed a lawyer. He just suggested that I give you a call right away, and then he hung up. Do you have any idea what he was talking about?"

"Come to think of it, sir, there is something I need to talk to you about. Something confidential. Can we meet somewhere privately, sir?"

"Is it about your testimony yesterday?"

"No sir, it isn't. It's something else."

"Well, I'm going to the game this afternoon. How about this evening? My wife is weekending at her sister's place down in New York City. She has an important interview with an architectural firm on Monday. Would you like to come over to my quarters after dinner this evening?"

"Yes sir. That would be fine."

"Good. I'll pick you up by the east sallyport of Central Area at about seven-thirty."

"I'll be there," said Kate.

TWISTED TRYST

The football game was a catastrophe. West Point was favored, but lost to Wake Forest twenty-seven to ten. On the walk back from Michie Stadium, Tina remarked to Kate and Fran that West Point had lost because it had no bitchy women on the team. They all laughed, but they knew in their hearts there was a grain of truth in what Tina said. Before they parted company, Kate made sure that Fran would be doing something with Tina that evening. The movies, or something.

At seven-thirty p.m. sharp, Captain Martin drove up to the east sallyport in his weathered maroon Jaguar convertible with a white canvas top. Kate, in dress gray and shivering slightly in the cold October night air, was waiting on the sidewalk. Not familiar with his car, Kate bent over slightly and looked through the front passenger window to verify that it was Captain Martin. Recognizing him, she smiled, unzipped the bottom of her dress gray jacket, contorted her svelte torso like a fishhook, and slid into the deep bucket seat of the car's warm and cozy interior. With its scarred rosewood instrument panel and its frayed and discolored leather interior, car had definitely seen better days. Kate guessed the Jaguar was about eight or ten years old—probably the captain's graduation gift from law school. It had character and exuded palpable wealth. The car and the captain were a perfect fit. The scent of aftershave pervaded the Jaguar's tiny cavity.

Captain Martin cautiously pulled away from the curb and engaged Kate in small talk, casting a glance in her direction now and then as he drove. She answered his questions mechanically, desperately trying to get a handle on her feelings. Was she embarrassed about discussing Tina's problem with the captain? Was she

angry that Tina had put her in this position? Was she afraid that
the captain might expose the situation? Afraid that he may think
less of her for trying to help Tina get around the Academy rules?
Afraid that the captain—a man more than ten years her senior—
might put sexual moves on her at his quarters? Could she resist
them if he did?

In the intermittent streams of light projected by the head-
lights of oncoming vehicles, Kate could see that the captain was
dressed in civies—an ivy league look—with tailored dark green
trousers, crisp light yellow shirt, and tweed sports jacket. Kate
hadn't seen him in civies before. He wasn't wearing an ascot, but
he was the ascot type. With his wavy coal-black hair, deep-set sky-
blue eyes, and fine-chiseled facial features, and neatly trimmed
mustache, the captain resembled a movie star of early Hollywood—
a Clark Gable, an Errol Flynn.

Kate broke an uncomfortable silence. "Captain Martin?" she
began, not knowing exactly what was to follow.

"Cadet McKeane," interrupted the captain. "Why don't you
call me Colin, and I'll call you Kate—at least after duty hours—
okay?."

"Sure, Captain . . . I mean Colin," Kate replied. "Do you have
any hobbies?"

"Well, actually Kate, I do. I like to play tennis, compose music, and write articles for law journals. I'm just finishing up a very
lengthy article now on physician-assisted suicide. It's pretty legal-
istic and academic, but it's made me get in touch with a lot of my
personal values. How about you?"

"Well, yes. I like to play tennis and swim, but I don't get a lot
of time to do those things as a cadet—particularly as Cadet First
Captain."

"I can imagine."

"I'd like to know more about your article," Kate said. "I'm
afraid you'll have to take a raincheck on that," the captain said as
he turned the steering wheel sharply to the right onto an asphalt
apron and parked next to a military-style brick townhouse. A mo-

tion-activated spotlight illuminated the parking area and the side-walk leading to the front door of the house. "Here we are! The Colin Martin Manor. . . . No circular drive or anything." Opening the car door, and with a devilish flicker in his eyes, the captain continued, "That'll have to wait till I'm billing six hundred dollars per hour at one of those Wall Street law firms. But it's home for now."

Kate didn't wait to see if the captain was going to open the car door on her side. She quickly opened it and sprang from the vehicle. The temperature had fallen dramatically in the fifteen minute trip from Central Area. She noticed a few snowflakes in the air.

The captain opened the front door of the townhouse, led Kate into the living room, and turned on a lamp which added a lush glow to a motif that was distinctly Victorian, with some French overtones. The furnishings seemed a little too ornate and heavy for the room size, but they would be perfect for a Wall Street lawyer's Park Avenue apartment. Behind the fainting couch, seemingly crammed into a corner of the room, was a baby grand piano with what appeared to be compositional sketchbooks strewn haphazardly over the top. On the wall above the piano was a portrait of Mozart with an unusually playful smirk illuminating the creative corner of the captain's world.

"You really are a serious composer, aren't you?" Kate gushed. "It depends on what you call serious," the captain replied, handing Kate a bulbous glass half-filled with a caramel-colored liquid. "Here, have some brandy, it'll warm you up."

Kate accepted the snifter and, unzipping her jacket up to her midriff, sat down on the overstuffed Victorian love seat, hoping the captain would sit next to her. The captain chose a méridienne couch directly across the large butler's table from her and put his feet at an angle upon a stylishly striped stray ottoman close to an empty high-manteled brick fireplace and an apple-butter kettle full of well-seasoned firewood.

"If by `serious' you mean do I compose music for a symphony orchestra, the answer is `no'. If you mean do I really enjoy com-

posing musical ballads and jazz pieces, the answer is `yes'. When
I was in law school, I played jazz piano in a couple New York City
clubs. I even submitted a couple of my ballads to Warner Brothers
for a motion picture sound track, but nothing ever came of it. My
wife has always said I should get an agent. I probably will when I
get out of the service."

"I thought you were a lifer," Kate said playfully.

"No way. I'm just teaching law here at West Point until my
wife lands the architect job she wants in New York City. I expect
to be out of the service within a year."

Picking up his pipe and reaching for a red pouch of tobacco,
the captain asked, "Mind if I smoke?"

"Not at all," she said, quickly turning away to study the detail
of the Mozart portrait.

"You know, Kate, you look real uncomfortable in that monkey
suit. My wife has a bunch of clothes back in the bedroom that
you're free to look through."

Kate sensed something coming. The captain was the type of
guy her dad told her to be careful of. "Watch out for the handsome, quiet, well-mannered ones," her dad had warned. " They'll
get you between the sheets before you know it." Kate definitely
wanted to get out of that itchy gray uniform, but she did not want
to go past the point of no return with this guy. No harm in looking, though. And, if they ended up necking a little, so what? He
was probably lonely with his wife being out of town and all.

"You really think your wife wouldn't mind?" Kate asked.

"No problem. Just look through the closet on the left in the
back bedroom." The captain knew his wife *would* object to having
another woman root around in her closet. But, on the other hand,
she would never have to know.

Kate made her way to the back bedroom, turned on the light,
and began looking through the closet on the left. Slipping out of
her dress gray uniform, she stood in her bra and panties scanning
the rows of jumpers, pinafores, tunic dresses, crew sweaters, safari,
spencer, and bolero jackets. Slipping hangers along the metal pole

and evaluating the outfits one by one, she finally settled on a simple yoke skirt and wrap-around top which tied at the waistline and revealed just enough of the round fullness of her cleavage to tempt lust. Kate spent a few moments unfurling her bunned hair and brushing it in front of the vanity's mirror. She applied a touch of moist lipstick to her dry lips and rosied her cheeks a bit with some makeup available on the vanity.

When she returned to the living room, a fire was roaring and crackling in the fireplace, the burning hickory aroma cast a spell of instant coziness. Kate noticed that the captain now had on a cable, V-neck sweater and had moved and was sitting in the Victorian love seat she had just left, with his right arm resting along the top.

"First fire of the season," the captain said. "I didn't think you'd mind."

"I love fires," Kate replied as she felt the warmth envelope her face.

"I see you found some suitable civies." Patting the cushion of the love seat, the captain continued quietly, "Why don't you come here, Kate, and join me on the sofa. I want to tell you how proud I was of the way you handled yourself yesterday at that Congressional hearing."

Kate sat down on the edge of the love seat, half facing the captain. "Thanks, sir, I mean, Colin. I tried hard to make my points."

"And good points you have, Kate."

Kate wasn't sure how to take that remark.

"Why don't you sit back and relax, Kate. You've had a grueling past couple of days." Picking up Kate's snifter of brandy from the coffee table, the captain handed it to her and said, "Come on, gal, lighten up. No need to be so uptight."

"Maybe you're right," Kate agreed, twisting around and settling back in the love seat, lying her head back just under the captain's outstretched arm, and looking up at the ceiling. "Maybe you're right," Kate repeated as she sipped from the snifter.

"You know, I didn't learn much about you personally on our

trip to D.C. yesterday," the captain began.

"Yeah, I know. We stayed pretty focused on the Congressional hearings, as I recall. I didn't find out much about your background either."

"Mine's pretty simple. And probably boring compared to yours," the captain volunteered. "Grew up in Larchmont, New York. Dad was a banker; mom was a housewife. Have two older brothers, both married with kids. One's an accountant; the other a college professor. I went to Boston University undergrad, majored in psychology, then stayed an additional year and got a Masters in psychology. After that I went to Columbia University law school. My wife and I met in New York City when she was in architecture school and I was an intern in a small New York firm."

"How did you come to be in the Army and stationed at West Point?" Kate asked.

"It was one of those quirks of fate. In April of my senior year of law school, the army sent a JAG officer representative to the law school to recruit young law graduates. I stumbled into his interview room by mistake. I thought I was scheduled to talk to someone from the international law firm of Baker & McKenzie. Well I had shown up a day too late for that interview. The JAG officer was a real salesman. In minutes, he had convinced me that the JAG Corps was like a huge international law firm and that I could have many foreign assignments in a thirty-year career. I ranked in the upper ten percent of my class, but I didn't have any job offers. So I decided to sign up."

"Did you have any exotic assignments?" Kate asked.

"No. Really didn't get a chance to. Met my wife, Sharon, a few weeks afterward. She had to finish another two years of architecture school in New York City. We dated a few months and when I graduated from law school, she had an uncle who was an army colonel stationed in the Pentagon pull a few strings and get me assigned as an instructor here at West Point. That way we could stay pretty close to each other. It was the first time any one was assigned to West Point's law department right out of law school.

First time, too, they ever had a law instructor with a psychology degree. That was eight years ago. And I'm still here.

"When did you get married?" Kate inquired.

"Three years ago."

"Long engagement, huh?"

"Yeah, you could say that. After finishing school, Sharon started as a novice architect in a small New York architectural firm. After a couple of years she moved to a mid-sized firm. She's gone to New York City a couple of days a week. But a lot of her work can be done here at home. Her office here is completely computerized—modem and everything. Now she's seeking a partnership in a huge firm, and I think she has a good shot at it."

"That could change your life drastically, don't you think, Colin?"

"Yes and no. We don't have any children; and don't intend to have any. So children won't be a problem. We'll be moving to New York City when I get out of the service, so our life may actually be simplified. I may be kidding myself that I can land a job at a Wall Street law firm. I don't know. But one way or another I'm sure I'll be able to find a job as a lawyer in New York City—even if its for the State or City government. Don't get me wrong . . . I've enjoyed my law experiences in the military. It's just time to move on."

The captain's life story had lasted longer than he'd expected, and Kate had been sipping all the while. Taking the snifter from Kate's hands, he said, "Here let me freshen this a little bit."

"Okay, but less than half full this time."

Kate watched the captain as he got up and, carrying both snifters, made his way over to the built-in wet bar on the other side of the room. In her imagination, she undressed him as he walked, visualizing his firm round buttocks and muscular thighs.

She raised her hand to her wrap-around top and opened it slightly to expose more of her bosom.

"Twist of lemon?" the captain asked from across the room.

"Sure, why not," replied Kate.

"Want anything to eat?"

"No, thanks. . . . To be honest, I pigged out on Baked Alaska in the dining hall tonight. I couldn't handle any more food." The captain returned with two snifters half full and handed one of them to Kate, which Kate accepted without comment. Sitting down next to her again on the love seat, the captain said, "Now let's hear about *your* life, young lady" clearly communicating that he wanted to hear more than just a biographical sketch. The captain gave no indication that he was admiring the expanded view of Kate's supple breasts, rising and falling rhythmically with each breath she took.

"We're not finished with your story yet, Colin."

"What do you mean?" Colin asked in a quizzical tone.

"What's the story on the baby Jaguar?"

"Oh, that," the captain said with a smirk. My parents gave me the Jaguar when I graduated from law school. It was kind of a joke. My parents inscribed in the card that came with it, `A Jag for a JAG . . . officer.' A pretty expensive joke now that I think about it. I've never been able to save enough money to maintain it the way it should be. When I get a job in the real world, I plan to get a replacement . . . but probably not the first year."

Kate leaned lightly into the captain and tilted her head toward his. "My life story is somewhat less serene than yours," she said. "My family situation was much less stable."

"How so?"

"I forget whether I told you that my Dad is a West Point grad—Class of '65."

"Yes, I knew that. Maybe General Chandler told me. . . . I think he's a general, too—a brigadier, I believe."

"No, major general. He got his second star last year. . . . He's a great Dad, Colin—but growing up as an Army brat had some drawbacks for me . . . and my sister."

"You have a sister?"

"Yes, my sister—Karen—is five years older."

"She in the military too?"

"No, she lives in St. Louis."

"Married, with kids and all that?"

"No, she lives in a communal home run by the Mothers of the Divine Hope. . . . She's mentally ill. Manic depressive with schizoid tendencies. She was diagnosed in high school—went through a nervous breakdown. My mother died a year after Karen was diagnosed. . . . I went to live with my aunt—my mom's sister's family—in St. Louis. My dad thought it would be best because he was moving around so much. He came to see me and my sister once every . . . "

"Whoa, Kate, slow down a little," said the captain. "Let's back up a second. Your sister was diagnosed mentally ill and your mother died a year later?"

"Yes. There was no connection. My mother died of breast cancer. When they discovered she had it, the cancer had already metastasized. My father was devastated. He had depended on my mother for so much. There he was—45 years old, a colonel in the Army, a widower with a mentally ill teenage daughter and another daughter—motherless—in junior high school. He was forced to choose between a promising military career and retirement. He chose his career. I could never fault him for that."

Kate's voice cracked when she made the last remark.

"So you went to live with your aunt?" the captain asked.

"Yeah, she lived in St. Louis—where my mother was from. She was married with two boys—one in eighth grade, one in sixth. I was in seventh grade. My aunt always wanted a daughter. And I was it."

"Was she nice to you?"

"Yes, she was, and so were the boys. The boys included me in all their activities. I played neighborhood basketball, soccer, and even football with them and their friends—I mean tackle football too, not just flag football. Went to summer camp with them too. They always made me feel accepted—one of the boys."

"Did you see your dad much during those years?"

"My dad came to visit me at least twice a year—usually once in the summer and once at Christmastime. He always seemed pleased that I was doing boy things. I sensed that he always wanted a son. And looking back, I guess, to him, I was the next best thing. Dad was my inspiration. I mean, he could do everything, and do it well. I guess I wanted to be just like him. I idolized him . . . and still do."

"Were you physically attracted to any of those boys when you were growing up?" the captain asked. "I mean most girls get crushes on guys in those middle school years."

"No, Colin. I tried not to let my emotions get in the way. To be one of them, I had to deal with them as peers. Oh once, I guess in eighth grade, I had feelings for a guy—Randy McDermott—a guy not in my circle of friends. I even remember one day when I was at summer camp and out in the woods by myself, I carved a heart on the side of a maple tree and inscribed Randy's and my initials inside. But that was as far as the romance got. He never knew that I had any special feelings for him. I guess you could say he was my secret love. Until this moment."

"Did you have any other heartthrobs in high school or anything?"

"Not really. I went to Divine Hope Academy for girls. Spent most of my time getting A's and playing sports. I didn't have time for romance. My goal was to get into West Point.

My Dad said he could arrange for me to get a Congressional appointment if I had the grades and the athletic ability. I did, and he followed through."

"And your sister—did you see her much during high school?"

"Just once, by myself. I remember taking three buses on a blizzard of a Valentine's Day to get to the convent. I wanted to give Karen a little gift that I had made especially for her. It was a needlepoint—a yellow butterfly on a light blue background. Karen loved butterflies. The wings sort of formed a Valentine's heart. I thought it would cheer her up. I guess I really wasn't aware of the severity of her mental illness. When I got there, one of the nuns told me that Karen was hallucinating, and that it would not be a good idea for me to see her in that state. She took the wrapped box from me and promised me she'd give it to Karen when she came back to reality. I left without seeing her. I don't know if Karen ever received the gift. She never acknowledged it in any way."

"Is that the only time you went to the convent to see Karen?" the captain asked.

"The only other times were when Dad came to town. She and I just didn't have much in common. She had psychotic breaks periodically when she went off her lithium and prozac. She was horribly overweight—she got up to two hundred fifty pounds at one point. She's down to two hundred now. She does terribly inappropriate and embarrassing things in social situations. I feel sorry for her. But I can't do anything about it."

"What about your success. Does Karen resent it?"

Biting her quivering lower lip to hold back tears, Kate stalled answering the question. "No . . . I don't think so. And that's part of the problem."

"What do you mean?"

"She writes to me at least twice a week, telling me about her grandiose plans to get elected to Congress and change the way society deals with the mentally disabled. She has begged to come visit me here at West Point several times. She thinks I have some pull, or something, in getting her elected to Congress. She's linked my Congressional appointment to some supposed influence I have in politics. When she learns that I testified before Congress yesterday, I know I'll be getting an avalanche of mail from her."

"How do you respond to the letters."

"I don't."

"You don't?"

"Well, I wrote back to her a couple of times when I was a plebe. But I couldn't get this idea out her head that I have some sort of political influence. She's obsessive about this. I just gave up. I just send her birthday and holiday cards with short notes. My dad apparently told her she could come here for my graduation in June. I don't want her to come, Colin. This is *my* graduation. *I* should be able to decide who comes to it! "

Tears began streaming down Kate's cheeks.

"You feel guilty about all this, don't you, Kate?"

With that, Kate burst into tears and, turning toward the captain, put her arms around his neck, buried her head in the softness of his sweatered chest and cried. Hard.

"There, there, Kate," said the captain, rubbing her back gently. "Everything is going to be okay. It'll all work out just fine."

The captain put his arms around her and held her tightly and silently for several minutes. He felt aroused sexually. She was vulnerable and he knew it.

Sobbing, Kate continued. "I keep thinking back to the time when Karen was okay. When we were young and played "King of the Hill" with the boys on that construction site near our house. There were these huge mounds of dirt and the boys would always be on top first and we would join hands, and rush them, and force them off the top. Victorious, Karen and I would cheer and laugh and give each other a high-five. When we turned around, we would see they had scampered to another hill, taunting us—defying us to another challenge, which, hand in hand, we gleefully undertook. Those were some of the happiest moments of my life, Colin. Those are my happiest memories of being with Karen."

With her head still on his chest, Kate said "Crying like this— you must think I'm a real wimp."

"Not at all. It's obvious that you have some emotions that you've repressed for a long time. I noticed you didn't tell me much about your mother."

"There's not much to tell. I really never knew her. She was orphaned as a child and raised in a Divine Hope convent. She was cold and detached toward me. A stern disciplinarian. I don't remember her ever giving me a hug. She was incapable of expressing love— although I sensed that deep down she really cared for Karen and me. I think she was angry that my father was gone all the time—hardship tours, to Korea, Vietnam, Panama. . . ." Kate paused, thinking. "It was almost as if she wanted to punish him by dying of cancer."

"That's quite profound."

"Yeah, . . . I guess I really never thought much about all this before. After my mother died, I learned from my aunt that my mother had a deathbed chat with some Divine Hope nuns at the hospital. My mother was concerned that my father would not take responsibility for raising us girls, and the nuns apparently promised her that they would take care of us if it became necessary. When Karen had the nervous breakdown a year later, the nuns took her in and cared for her at no expense to my dad. Of course, my dad paid my tuition for school, but the nuns kept their word to my mother and took responsibility for Karen."

"It sounds like you have a great deal of respect for the nuns."

"Now that I think about all this, I have to admit I have mixed feelings. They've taken good care of Karen. But because of the nuns, I grew up without my real father. They let him off the hook. So I guess I'm grateful and resentful of them at the same time. . . . And then there was that day in the shower room."

"Where? At school?"

Kate paused and looked down, the brandy stealing her inhibition.

"Yeah," Kate said finally. "I was in first year high school. It was springtime, and I was showering after a couple hours of playing field hockey. I was the last one in the showers because I had to unwrap my ankle which had been sprained slightly. I was there in the shower room by myself—taking a shower, probably longer than usual, and really enjoying lathering all over and feeling the warm water cascading down my nude body. Then I sensed a presence. . . . I felt someone watching me. You know what I mean, Colin?"

"Sure, I can relate to that."

"There she was . . . Sister Josephina, . . . my homeroom teacher, standing there, staring at me while I moved a bar of soap gently over the front of me, creating mounds of white lather. She kept staring at me for what seemed an eternity. Then I finally broke the silence and asked her if she wanted something. She asked me if I needed to have my back scrubbed, since no one else was there to do it for me."

"What did you say?"

"Because I was very young and naive, I didn't question her motives. I thought she was being helpful. So I said okay."

"What happened?"

"Well, she took the soap and rubbed it all over my wet back for a few seconds. But she didn't stop there. Standing behind me, with both arms she reached around me to my chest, and began lathering the front of me ever so gently. Then she asked me to turn around, and for the next few minutes, all the while staring into my eyes, she lathered my private parts, telling me how important it was for good health to keep my private parts extra clean."

"Didn't you try to stop her?"

"I felt powerless, Colin. Remember, this person was my homeroom teacher. She also was superior in rank to all my other teachers. I couldn't cross her. She could make it very hard for me in the classroom. My grades could suffer."

"Yes, but she was taking advantage of you—sexually abusing you."

"I realize that now. But I didn't realize it at the time. I was confused. I just thought she was being helpful. Besides, when my mother was alive, she used to do the same thing—I mean she would clean my private parts with soap and tell me she didn't mind helping me keep that part of my body extremely clean.

Because it was so important. I remember her always using the words 'the female scourge'. At the time I didn't know what she was talking about."

"And your mother grew up in a convent, right?"

"Yes, and only recently I've begun to put two and two together. She was trying to tell me about menstruation, but didn't know how. I didn't have my first period until after she died."

"Are you sure that's the total explanation?"

"No, . . . I'm not absolutely sure. You see, my mother did something else when I was growing up. She always had me sleep with her when my dad was away on his hardship tours. Karen had to sleep with her too until Karen had her first period—and then it was like she was banished from my mother's bedroom. I only recently realized this. I don't know if Karen ever really knew why my mother ostracized her. But the break was abrupt. My mother would rarely talk to Karen—and was never civil to her—after Karen was in about the seventh grade."

"But, you kept sleeping with your mother after Karen was, as you say, banished?"

"Yes. I really didn't have a choice. I mean, my mother was in charge. I had no power in the situation. She made me feel that it was my responsibility to take my father's place."

"In bed?"

"Yes, I was daddy's substitute in her mind. And I was ex-pected to do some of the things that daddy did to her to make her feel, as she would say, pampered and loved. But I didn't know this was wrong, because I had no measuring stick for this. This was the only family experience I had ever had, Colin. I thought all kids slept with their mothers when their fathers were away. I thought all kids pinchhit for their fathers like this. How was I to know differently?"

"You weren't able to, Kate. Don't be so hard on yourself."

"And, when Sister Josephina told me in the shower room that if I ever wanted to have a private shower in her room I was wel-come, I thought she was just being nice."

Kate sat straight up and, looking directly in Colin's eyes, said, "How could I have been so stupid, Colin?"

"You weren't stupid. You just didn't have enough life experi-ences at the time to enable you to understand the actual situation. There's no need to feel guilty about any of that. Be thankful that you are beginning to unravel all this so soon."

Kate stood up and walked over to the fireplace, as if to get some room to think. Only red-hot embers remained from the once raging inferno. "Mind if I stoke this thing up a bit?"

"Don't mind at all." The captain began repacking and light-ing his pipe.

Using large metal tongs, Kate laid three medium-sized logs on the hearth on top of the glowing embers. Soon the logs caught fire and the foot-high flames were dancing once again.

Standing in front of the fireplace, seemingly hypnotized by the infernal ballet, Kate said, "I don't feel as guilty about this as I feel afraid."

"What do you mean by that?"

"Afraid for Karen. Think about it, Colin. She's been in the clutches of those nuns for about eight years now. Heaven only knows what they've done to her over the years. How they might have abused her. And I'm powerless to do anything about it."

"Oh that's all speculation. Speculation can drive you insane if you let it."

Turning away from the fire and walking back and sitting down again next to Colin, Kate sighed, "I guess you're right. I suppose one crazy person in a family is enough, huh?"

They exchanged a brief smile.

"Not to change the subject, or anything, but I think you said on the phone you had something you wanted to talk to me about tonight, right? " the captain inquired.

"Yes, I do," replied Kate. "But first, I want to know more about your article."

"My *article*. Why that?"

"I'm just interested, that's all," Kate said while sitting on the edge of the loveseat, arms rigid with her hands on her thighs. "Are you for or against physician-assisted suicide?"

"Well that question doesn't have an easy answer. I would have to say that I am not *for* physician-assisted suicide . . . "

Kate's heart sank.

" . . . categorically."

"Categorically?" Kate inquired.

"Yes, categorically. What I mean is, I am not for physician-assisted suicide in every situation where a person wants to take his or her own life. Rather, I am for it in situations narrowly prescribed by law, where the person is mentally competent, has an indisputable terminal illness or health condition, and wants to die."

0368-COOL

"So you're for the right to choose."

"Well, I suppose you could say that, but within narrowly defined boundaries. Say, all this is a bit esoteric, isn't it?"

Ignoring the captain's last comment, Kate queried, "Do you
feel the same way about abortion?" Kate picked up her snifter of
brandy.

"Abortion? What do you mean?"

"I mean are you *for* abortion in the same way?"

"If you're asking me if I am *personally* in favor of abortion, I
would have to say no. It's against my religion—I am a Catholic.
But the courts have already said that women have a right to have
an abortion in certain defined circumstances. As a lawyer I must
respect that. I am not about to impose my own notions of moral-
ity on anyone. How did we get on this topic, anyway, Kate?"

Sitting back now and gazing at the ceiling, Kate asked, "Are
you my lawyer, Colin?"

"Well, in a certain respect, I guess so."

Running her middle finger continuously around the top edge
of the brandy snifter, Kate continued, "Then everything I tell you
will be kept confidential, right?"

"Not exactly."

"That's what you said last night."

"Not so fast. If you tell me, for example, that you are about to
commit a crime and I genuinely believe you are going to commit
it, then if I could not talk you out of it or stop you, I would have
to report the matter to the authorities."

"So, short of telling you that I am about to commit a crime,
everything I tell you is secret, right?"

"Okay, Kate, what gives? Are you in trouble? Do you need a
lawyer? What is it that Father Terronez knows that I don't know?"

Kate put down the snifter, moved closer to the captain, pressed
her body against his, gazed up into his deep blue eyes, laid her
arm gently across his chest and whispered, "Colin, my best friend
Tina is pregnant and needs an abortion."

The captain, looking searchingly into Kate's eyes. "Tina's a cadet, I presume."

"Yes, she's a cadet, Colin. But I'm afraid she won't be one for long if anyone finds out about this."

"I would agree with that. Who's the guy?"

"Some whacko ROTC cadet from Vanderbilt who's threatening to go to the Supe if Tina doesn't carry the fetus to term."

"Is he really serious about that?"

"Yes."

"Well, he has a lot to lose, too, doesn't he?"

"Like what? Do you think they would really kick a guy out of an ROTC program just because he got some girl knocked up? It'll never happen, Colin"

"Maybe you're right about that. . . . What else can you tell me about this guy?"

"His father is a Methodist minister who's a staunch anti-abortionist."

"Great!"

"Great?"

"This is the whacko's Achilles' heel. Just get me the guy's telephone number at Vanderbilt. I'll take care of the rest."

"Okay, I'll get you that tomorrow. But what about the abortion? Tina has no money—she can't let her family know. Even if she did, they couldn't afford it."

"Don't worry about that either. You know my wife's sister—the one she's visiting this weekend?"

"Yes."

"She's an internist at Mount Sinai Hospital. She can arrange for the abortion."

"At no expense? Because if it costs something, I can find plenty of female cadets to donate to the cause."

"I don't think that'll be necessary. My wife's sister, by the way, is a raving feminist—a femi-Nazi, no less. I'm sure she will see to it that everything is taken care of secretly and without charge. Trust me."

Kate could not restrain an instinctive impulse to give the captain a kiss on his cheek. As soon as she did, she reached for the cocktail napkin beside her brandy snifter, wiped the lipstick imprint from is face, and said, "Oh, I'm sorry . . . I guess I got carried away."

"No need to apologize, Kate." Smiling, he added, "What's a kiss between friends?"

For a second, Kate felt an incredible urge to wrap her legs around Colin's body and let him bury his genitals in her velvety virginity.

She and the captain spent another hour or so discussing politics, religion, and sex without actually sampling any of it. The captain spent much of the time extolling the qualities of his wife and how happily married he was. At eleven o'clock, the captain noted it was time to get Kate back to the barracks. In the back bedroom, Kate put her hair back up into a bun, got back into her itchy gray uniform, and the two of them went outside.

The snow was falling furiously now and the ground was covered with a thick downy blanket. It took several minutes for the captain to scrape the snow and ice off the windows while Kate got the car heater adjusted inside. Soon they were on their way and eventually they arrived at the east sallyport. Kate yearned to enfold the captain—this *deus ex machina*—in a rapturous embrace and give him a warmly passionate goodnight kiss. It never happened. After pulling the Jaguar up to the curb, the captain turned to Kate, gently clasped her hand in both of his and said, "Don't worry about Tina. Everything will work out. Get some rest."

Emerging from the tiny sports car, Kate gave the captain a smart half-salute and smiled broadly. "G'night, captain," she said. He saluted back, grinned, and then piloted his feathery snowball through the rapidly descending white curtains of snowflakes and out of Kate's sight.

For a few seconds, Kate stared at the deep tire tracks left by Colin's car in the snow. She was alone . . . again. She felt confused and dazed. Had she just discovered the premier "officer and *gentleman*" or did Colin simply find her unattractive? She sensed she was losing confidence in her femininity. Were soldiering and femininity mutually exclusive? Was she also losing control of her emotions? She had never cried at West Point before—not like she did with the captain tonight. Was she kidding herself that she could handle ground combat? These questions frightened her.

She slowly turned around and started for the sallyport entrance. Rivulets of tears on her face were turning crystalline in the arcticlike wind. Stopping just before she reached the entrance, Kate looked down at the snow-laden top of a low stone wall and childishly drew a large heart in the snow with her gloved hand, inscribing KM + CM inside. No sooner had she had drawn it, she passed her glove through it several times and obliterated it. She then turned and passed through the sallyport into the glistening, trackless marshmallow world of central area, thinking as she walked of what might have been, had she been older or Colin younger, and had fate intertwined their destinies.

JUMPS AND BUMPS

"SHIT!!" Tina cried, as she slammed butt-first into a pebbly berm and then bounded high into the air only to be saved from serious injury by two strips of canvas attached to her chest harness and to a pulley rolling on an overhead steel cable. This—her first exit from the thirty-four-foot tower—was a real bummer. She had already forgotten what the training sergeant had said seconds before—"keep your eyes open, face the berm, and pull up slightly on the risers."

"GET YOUR FAT ASS BACK TO THIS EARTH!!" growled a crusty staff sergeant. Clad in heavily starched fatigues and a shiny black helmet liner, he stood off to the side of the berm. For a few seconds, he watched Tina bouncing uncontrollably up and down like a paddle ball some distance from him on the far side of the berm. Then, in a thick South Carolina accent, the "Black Hat" finished his thought: "THIS AIN'T NO BUNGEE JUMPIN' OUTFIT!! THIS IS THE UNITED STATES ARMY'S JUMP SCHOOL!!" Tina's bouncing slowed to a stop as the pulley slid her back over the top of the berm. Then the sergeant barked, "WHEN YOU GET THAT HARNESS OFF, PEA BRAIN, REPORT TO ME ON THE DOUBLE!!"

"AIRBORNE! SERGEANT," Tina yelled back mechanically. She knew saying "Yes, Sergeant," would get her an even greater penalty.

Her feet finally dangling over the berm's terra firma again, Tina popped the release button on the center of her chest harness, and the harness fell away from her and hung suspended from the overhead cable. Tina ran as fast as she could to where the Black Hat was standing.

"Cadet Marafino reporting as ordered, Sergeant," Tina said breathlessly.

"MARAFINO? IS THAT A SPIC OR A WOP NAME?" the Black Hat bellowed.

"It's Italian, Sergeant."

"PASTA PACKER, EH?"

"Airborne! Sergeant."

"FISHEATER, TOO, I BET."

"Airborne! Sergeant."

"OBVIOUSLY A TENDER GENDER, RIGHT?"

"Airborne! Sergeant."

"SO YOU'RE A PASTA-PACKIN', FISH-EATIN', TENDER GENDER, SPASTIC WEST POINT CADET, AREN'T YOU?"

"Airborne! Sergeant."

"AND WHAT DOES THAT MAKE YOU?"

"Lower than whale shit! Sergeant."

"GOOD! DROP DOWN AND GIVE ME TWENTY-FIVE AND THEN HIGHTAIL IT BACK TO THE TOWER!! I'LL BE WATCHING FOR YOU ON YOUR NEXT JUMP."

Tina dropped immediately to the prone position and started doing push-ups.

"DO 'EM LIKE A MAN, PROM QUEEN. GET OFF THOSE KNEES!! START OVER!!" commanded the Sergeant. Four male airborne trainees moving by on the overhead cable were still laughing at the sight of Tina doing push-ups on her knees.

The Black Hat yelled to them, "THIS AIN'T NO COMEDY CLUB, BUCKAROOS. WHEN YOU FOUR GET BACK TO EARTH, DROP AND GIVE ME FIFTEEN. COUNT 'EM OUT LOUD!"

"AIRBORNE, SERGEANT!" they responded in unison.

Meanwhile, Tina was doing her push-up penance directly in front of the Black Hat. "Call me anything, but don't call me prom queen," Tina thought to herself. What a hell of a way for a West Point senior to be spending Christmas leave. Jump school at Fort Benning, Georgia.

2

If Tina was able to survive the last two months, she could survive anything. In early November she had taken a long weekend leave, and Captain Martin's wife, Sharon, had driven her down to New York City on a Friday to meet with Sharon's sister, the internist. It was decided that Tina should have the abortion immediately. Sharon's sister arranged for the abortion to be performed after hours that Friday evening at a local clinic. On Saturday and Sunday she recuperated at Sharon's sister's apartment, and then Sharon had driven her back to West Point, arriving before call to quarters on Sunday night. On her return, Tina was greeted by about ten phone messages from Mike Stanton. She really didn't feel up to speaking to him. She called Sharon to get some advice. It was a good thing she did. Apparently, over the weekend, Captain Martin had phoned Mike Stanton at Vanderbilt, identified himself as a lawyer, and told him that if he put any more pressure on Tina about going to the Supe or about not having an abortion, he was going to let Mike's father—the minister—know that he had gotten some girl pregnant. Captain Martin had tracked down Mike's minister father and when he spoke to Mike on the telephone, he recited Mike's father's telephone number as proof that he could contact him at any time. Mike quickly got the picture. Captain Martin also told Mike that he was going to pass along the minister's telephone number to Tina. That's apparently what had precipitated Mike's numerous telephone calls to Tina over the weekend. Buoyed by this information, Tina returned Mike's call. She told him that she had already had gotten an abortion. He did not object. He just made her promise that she would not tell his father about what had happened.

That first week after the abortion, Tina took it as easy as possible. She went to class, but was excused from physical education classes because of strong pain-killers she had been prescribed. By the end of November, she was pretty well back to normal physically and emotionally; in the meantime, miraculously she had been able to maintain her grade-point average. Kate and her other friends made sure she got extra tutoring during those few weeks. Then, during the first week of December—right before the written final reviews—Kate sprang a bomb of a surprise on her. "How would you like to be famous?" she remembered Kate asking her. Tina should have foreseen that fame seldom comes easy. And it didn't. Kate had received word through General Chandler, Commandant of Cadets, that she had been selected for the *Minerva Experiment*, if she wanted to participate. Obviously, there was nothing she wanted more. The Com also gave her the opportunity to pick four other female classmates to join her in training for the assignment. Kate's first thought was the foursome that had "beat" the escape and evasion game with her at Camp Buckner. As the Com had explained, part of the training would be attending Airborne School at Fort Benning over Christmas leave. Later, after graduation, they would all attend Ranger training at Benning. Before talking to Tina, Kate had approached the other three Buckner-mates—Charmaine, Sandy, and Lori—with the invitation. They were ecstatic and were on board right away. Tina balked at the idea initially. But when Tina learned of the others' acceptance and realized that—with the abortion and all—she really didn't want to be at home with her parents over the holidays, she decided to join them. She really had no idea of what was in store for her at Airborne School.

In mid-December Tina, Kate, and the other three female cadets had received orders sending them to a special session of the Basic Airborne Course at the U.S. Infantry Center at Fort Benning Georgia from December 27 to January 18. They would have to miss the first few days of class of the new semester, but they didn't mind. They were hyped for the adventure—the challenge of learning the basics of jumping out of "a perfectly good airplane" as the Army's pamphlet had described it. They were confident they could take Airborne School by storm. After all, they had survived Beast Barracks and Plebe Year. What could be worse? The news about hair didn't stop them, though it did dampen their spirits slightly.

All five females would have to have their hair shorn shorter than a pixiecut to go through the paratrooper training. They hoped that their hair would be grown out by graduation—but Kate's wearing her hair in a bun again by that time seemed like a long shot.

"Fort" Benning was not exactly what the five cadets had pictured. They had romanticized it as a stockade-type structure typical of the Old West, and it was nothing of the sort. What they found when their bus passed through the gate of the "Home of the Infantry" on December 26, was nothing short of a modern small town, with all the same types of services and conveniences. The bus made two stops along Sigerfoos Road and Vibbert Ave. Then, as the bus traveled down Edward Street, Charmaine—in her strong New Orleans accent—began reading aloud from a promotional pamphlet on Benning she had brought with her from West Point.

"I bet you guys didn't know this," Charmaine began:

Henry Lewis Benning, for whom the Fort was named, saw careers as a soldier, attorney, politician, and Justice of the Georgia Supreme Court. A native Georgian, Benning's professional career began in Columbus in 1835 when he set up residence and began practicing law. At the age of 39, two years after an unsuccessful campaign for Congress, Benning was elected associate justice of the Georgia Supreme Court. He was the youngest man to ever to hold that office at the time. Benning was a staunch advocate of States Rights and took a prominent part in the conventions concerning secession prior to the Civil War. With the start of the Civil War, Benning recruited men to form the 17th Regiment of Georgia volunteers. During the first year and a half of the war, he fought with General Robert E. Lee, and attained the rank of brigadier general. After the war, Benning returned to his law practice in Columbus. He died in 1875 at the age of 61."

"No, I guess I didn't know that," Tina mocked. "But the question is, Charmaine, did I really *need* to know it?"

"Well, maybe you *need* to know this, Tina," Charmaine retorted.

"The Fort is located in the lower Piedmont Region of Central Georgia and Alabama, six miles southeast of Columbus, Georgia and its sister city, Phenix City, Alabama, across the Chattahoochee River. Its 285 square miles of river valley terraces and rolling terrain and its moderate climate are well-suited for infantry training and support missions engaged in by more than 20,000 troops and officers."

"Come on, Charmaine," Tina urged. "Get more relevant." As the bus turned right onto Marchant Street and passed by three impressively tall red-and-white jump towers on their left, Charmaine continued the travelogue.

"The area bounded by Marchant and Burr Streets, is used by the 1st Battalion, 507th Parachute Infantry Regiment to train volunteers in the techniques of military parachuting. The three towers, 250 feet tall, are used to familiarize airborne trainees with the sensation of descending under a canopy and were originally built for the 1939 World's Fair in New York."

At that moment, the bus came to a halt and the driver announced, "Last stop . . . Building 2748, the Queen of Battle's Airborne School . . . Many are called, but few are chosen. . . . Good luck." The five cadets and twelve other enlisted men filed out of the bus and claimed their baggage from the underside storage bins. The bus driver waved to the group as he drove away.

A staff sergeant in camouflage fatigues stood on the sidewalk in front of the entrance to Building 2748. "Welcome to Airborne School," he said in a loud voice to the seventeen new arrivals standing in a semicircle around him. "For the next three weeks you will have no rank—you will all be *students.* Before we go inside, I want to make sure you have the following items available and ready for inspection: fifteen copies of your orders and/or DA Form 1610 with fund site; Physical Examination Standard Form 88 with Block

5 indicating that the purpose of the examination was for airborne training and with Block 77 indicating that you are qualified for airborne training; and a DA Form 705—a valid Army Physical Readiness Test Score Card showing that you took the test within the timeframe required by DA Pam 351-4."

The five cadets went through their baggage and found the required documents. Two of the enlisted men were missing some of the papers and were told to report to another building. The staff sergeant then led the fifteen remaining students inside. After passing out a sheet of paper to each student which explained some of the Airborne School requirements, he told them to read the sheets while they were waiting to be processed. Kate began reading some of the uniform requirements:

Boots: They must be highly polished (not to be confused with spit shine) and free of all dirt and sawdust including around the soles and tongue. They will be laced up before entering the training area.

Dog Tags: One long chain and one short chain interlaced together, with one tag per chain allowed.

One key, and any medical alert tag, and barracks pass are allowed.

Jewelry: No jewelry will be worn in the training area.

A designated student may carry a watch but may not wear it.

Headgear: Only a serviceable parachutist helmet will be allowed in the training area.

Females: Makeup will not be worn in the training area. Hair will be secured by hairnets only. No metal or plastic pins or barrettes will be allowed.

Tina got Kate's attention, pointed to the last statement on Kate's sheet, and smiled. It read:

You are trained by the same squad leader, section sergeant, and platoon sergeant throughout all phases of training—from in-processing to graduation. Your leader trains you as though you will go to war as a member of his unit tomorrow.

"Nothing like a little drama to stir up some passion for our mission," teased Tina.

"Yeah," replied Kate. "I'm surprised they're not playing the `Star-Spangled Banner' in the background as we in-process."

In about thirty minutes, all fifteen students had been pro-cessed and were seated in a holding room awaiting further instruc-tions. The staff sergeant came in and announced barracks and mess hall assignments. The five females were assigned to one barracks building, which would house no other occupants. They would be eating their meals in the Rhineland Regimental Mess along with the other Airborne students. The sergeant told them that supper would be served at 1800 hours and that it was optional for them to attend. However, an Airborne School orientation would be con-ducted at the Main Post Theater at seven-thirty p.m. All students were required to attend.

At seven-thirty on that first evening, the five cadets and ninety-one enlisted men and women found their way to the Main Post Theater. Master Sergeant Shirley Davidson gave a forty-five-minute talk on what the Airborne students could expect over the next few weeks. The sergeant, a tall African-American female sporting a brown Canadian Mounty-type hat and clad in crisp fatigues. With a chest full of ribbons and airborne jump wings over her left breast pocket, she paced back and forth on the stage while she talked, occasionally striking a black swagger stick on the side of her leg when she wanted to emphasize a point. Although a twenty-five year veteran of the military service, her excellent physical condi-tion and smooth, tight facial skin made her appear thirty years old at most. Through a fire-and-brimstone-like sermon—one that she had obviously given innumerable times before—she painted a fairly dismal picture for the students.

The three-week course, she explained, was divided into three segments—Ground Week, Tower Week, and Jump Week. The first two weeks would be heavily laden with physical training. That meant that early each morning, the students would have an hour of calisthenics and a three-mile run. The students would do more push-ups in those two weeks than they had done in their previous life. By the end of the two weeks, each student would be expected to be able to do fifty push-ups at one time. Some would be able to do a hundred. It was routine to see students dropping to do push-ups throughout the training day for even the most minor infractions of the rules—intentional or unintentional. Ten push-ups was the standard penalty, but the students would be expected to do more than the number ordered by a sergeant just to demonstrate that they were dedicated to the cause of Airborne preparedness. During Ground Week, in thirty-three hours of instruction, the students would learn the basics of exiting an aircraft, donning and adjusting a parachute harness, and doing parachute landing falls— PLFs, as she called them. They would have five hours training at the mock door for exiting, twelve hours on the mock (thirty-four-foot) tower gaining confidence to step out into space and slide down a slightly inclined cable to a berm, and fourteen hours practicing parachute landing falls from four-foot platforms. The next week, Tower Week, they would be practicing guided descents from the two-hundred-fifty-foot parachute towers they had seen previously that day from the bus windows. They would also spend more time at the mock door and the thirty-four-foot tower, this time practicing mass exits. The most dreaded part of Tower Week— at least for the males—would be the suspended harness, also called 'suspended agony', and the swing-landing trainer, the latter conducted together with a movie-set wind machine to teach recovery after landing in windy conditions. During this second week, the trainees would also learn how to deal with various types of parachute and equipment malfunctions.

Finally, in Jump Week, the trainees would experience five static line, as opposed to freefall, parachute jumps. Two of these jumps would be from a height of twelve hundred fifty feet, two from fifteen hundred, and one from two thousand. Three jumps would be made with a standard T-10B parachute introduced in the 1950s. The T-

10B, with its thirty-five-foot canopy would be equipped with an anti-inversion net skirt and ejector-snap quick releases. Two jumps would be made with the MC1-1B steerable parachute. One night jump and two with equipment would be included in the training. At the conclusion of her sermon, Master Sergeant Davidson asked if there were any questions. Her tone of voice implied that she expected none. There were none.

She continued, "If you think you won't be able to hack it here, you probably won't," said Davidson. "If you want to get out of Airborne School, the time to do it is now." She looked around for a few seconds. There were no takers. Looking over toward Kate and the other four cadets, she bellowed, "We don't tolerate no pussies in this outfit either. You all remember that."

The scuttlebutt Kate and Tina had heard in the mess hall at dinner that first evening was that Davidson's nickname was "Hardtack." Apparently someone had referred to her as "tough as nails" when she was going through Jump School. That description was modified to "Hard*tack*" by some cynical male member of the training cadre and for some reason the nickname stuck. After hearing her presentation, Kate and Tina were more than just a little convinced that the moniker fit her perfectly.

Hardtack, so the story went, had been an NCO in the Quartermaster Corps during Desert Storm in the gulf war. A twelve-truck supply convoy she was part of was surrounded by a platoon of five Iraqi tanks and brought to a halt in the middle of the desert, miles from any friendly units. The first round of tank fire blew up a deuce and a half and the convoy commander's jeep. Pieces of four human bodies were scattered among the twisted, burning segments of vehicle hulks. Hardtack, second in command, saw there was nothing that could be done for the commander and the other three victims. By radio, she immediately gave an order for the remaining trucks to form an expanded circle—like circling conestogas during an Indian attack. But there was one difference, she ordered the drivers to keep the trucks moving in the circle at erratic rates of speed, making it difficult for the tanks to get a "bead" on any single truck. This tactic threw off the tank gunners so much that the first three rounds fired were way long and ineffective. Meanwhile, Hardtack took advantage of the gunners' spasms to call in jet air strikes on the tanks. Within seconds, the jets had swooped down and dropped their payloads on the defenseless, now retreating, tanks. Several members of the tank crews scurried, completely afire, from the tanks and rolled around in the sand trying to extinguish the flames without success. Soon the fire had reduced the burning Iraqi soldiers to small piles of dark ashes lying in the dunes. The entire crews of three of the tanks were all killed in the air strike. Four crew members from the other two tanks were injured, but managed to climb out of the tanks with their hands raised high into the air in surrender. Hardtack took them as prisoners and led the convoy on to complete the resupply mission. For her quick thinking and courage, she received a letter of commendation from her brigade commander. No medals though. She was not in a combat unit. This had caused Hardtack unrequited bitterness, and she had been quite vocal about it to her commanders. In an effort to quiet her, the Army offered to send her to Airborne training at Fort Benning, which she accepted. She aced the training, but since she couldn't be assigned to an airborne combat unit, she opted to stay in Airborne School as a trainer. She'd probably be an Airborne trainer until she retired. She was still bitter about the combat thing—very bitter. And the bitterness sometimes came out sideways in her treatment of the Airborne trainees. In Kate and Tina and their three classmates, she saw hope. Hope for women; hope for the Army. But Hardtack didn't play favorites. That just wasn't her style.

3

Except for Tina's berm smash-up, Ground Week was fairly uneventful for the five female cadets. The weather cooperated fully, with temperatures in the mid-fifties and sunny, blue skies. The women were in good physical shape, so the physical training gave them no problem. After thirty-one hours of doing parachute landing falls, of mock door and thirty-four-foot tower training they were ready for something a little more challenging—the two-hundred-fifty-foot Tower, or free tower.

On Tuesday morning of Tower Week, Charmaine and Kate were assigned to go with the first platoon to receive training on the high tower. They were filling the slots of two male enlistees who had dropped out of training during Ground Week. As their platoon jogged along Burr Road, Kate stole a glance at four trainees of another platoon getting extra instruction in the suspended harness. They were red-faced and obviously feeling a tremendous amount of discomfort in the genital area as they hung suspended and practiced emergency parachute landings. Kate recognized them as the four trainees that had laughed at Tina that day doing pushups near the thirty-four-foot tower the week before. She burst into laughter and quickly converted the laugh to a cough. What goes 'round, comes 'round, she thought.

Soon, Kate's platoon trotted onto the free tower field. There stood the three red-and-white two-hundred-fifty-foot steel towers, each having four steel projections on top with separate cone-like parachute receptacles. Each tower resembled the Erector-set structures she used to build with her male cousins when they were all growing up together—even down to the two-story house-like structure inside their base and the step ladder extending from the base clear to the top. As she jogged with the others, Kate felt strong gusts of wind against her face. The wind was strong, but apparently not exceeding twelve miles per hour—the maximum allowable safety limit for the high tower training.

When the four-squad platoon arrived at the base of Tower One, two squads separated from the platoon and double-timed over to Tower Two. Kate and Charmaine went with the Tower Two group. When their squads arrived at base of Tower Two, Hardtack was there to greet them, along with four other training NCOs. Impeccably uniformed and black helmeted, Hardtack was strutting her stuff. Walking back and forth in front of the two rows of trainees, and looking each trainee in the eyes, she said nothing for three or four minutes. Then she stopped, dead center, faced the trainees and said, "If I teach you nothing else today, my young fledglings, I will teach you to concentrate on your mission. If you become distracted or panic when you are descending from the Tower you could end up buying the farm. You got a lot invested in this training already. No use throwing it all away. Understand?"

"AIRBORNE! SERGEANT," the squads wailed in chorus.

"Good. I need four volunteers."

Ten seconds passed without a response. "I SAID I NEED FOUR VOLUNTEERS THIS MORNING, MY LITTLE PARAKEETS!" crowed Hardtack, this time much louder.

At least eight trainees raised their hands this time, including Charmaine who was in the front row, and Kate, in the rear row. Hardtack tapped the shoulder of three male trainees and Charmaine. "You're the first four on the Tower this morning. You'll be the examples for the others. Go with Sergeant Cranston and he'll explain what you have to do. Move out, soldiers." The four double-timed off with one of the training NCOs. Then Hardtack shouted to the remaining trainees, "THE REST OF YOU FLEDG-LINGS ASSUME THE LEANING REST POSITION AND GIVE ME YOUR UNDIVIDED ATTENTION!"

Kate and the others immediately dropped to a push-up posi-tion—their bodies inclined rigidly between their locked arms and the toes of their feet. Kate questioned the logic of being required to as-sume this strained position and then being asked to pay attention. But then again, she questioned the logic of a lot of things about Jump School. The three-mile run every morning; the harsh verbal treat-ment by the NCOs; the incessant push-ups; the fourteen hours of PLFs. All of this seemed hardly necessary to teach a soldier equipped with a parachute to exit a sky-borne airplane. Civilians learning the more difficult free-fall parachuting don't have to go through all this crap. Why should soldiers? Anyway, Kate held the leaning rest posi-tion in the back row for about five minutes while Hardtack explained how they were to get into the parachute harness for their first tower jump, and what they were to do during their descent. Kate was get-ting angrier with each passing second. Her arm and thigh muscles being stressed to their limit, she wasn't paying much attention to what Hardtack was saying. Pebbles were grinding into the palms of her gloveless hands, and, even in the fifty-degree temperature, sweat was streaming down her brow and cheeks. Finally, she slowly lowered her knees to the ground.

"MCKEANE!" roared Hardtack. "JUST WHAT ON GOD'S GREEN EARTH DO YOU THINK YOU ARE DOING? LOOKS LIKE YOU ARE DISOBEYING A DIRECT ORDER."

"No, Sergeant!" Kate replied sheepishly, raising her knees off the ground and her bottom back into rigid incline.

"YOU KEEP THOSE KNEES OFF THE GROUND! UNDERSTAND, MCKEANE?"

"Airborne! Sergeant," Kate replied.

"NOW YOU DO 20 PUSH-UPS AND SAY YOU'RE SORRY TO YOUR FELLOW PARAKEETS AS YOU DO EACH ONE," Hardtack blustered.

Kate complied, doing the twenty push-ups and yelling "I'm sorry" as she struggled to do each one. Her initially stiff form slowly transformed into a moving sine-wave near the end. "YOU DO PUSH-UPS LIKE A GREEN RECRUIT, MCKEANE. ARE YOU SURE YOU'RE READY FOR AIRBORNE SCHOOL?"

"Airborne! Sergeant." Kate responded, holding a leaning rest position as steadily as she could.

"ALL RIGHT, EVERYONE ON YOUR FEET AND STAND AT EASE!" commanded Hardtack. The sixteen or so trainees jumped to an upright position, put their legs a shoulder's width apart, and rested their clasped hands on their buttocks. Returning to a normal tone of voice, Hardtack continued. "Keep your eyes focused, my parakeets, on those four parachutes with bodies dangling from them now being hoisted by cable to the top of Tower Two. You'll be doin' the same thing in a few short minutes. This is pretty close to the real thing. When you step out of that aircraft next week, you'll be only five to eight times as high as Tower Two. Today is a good chance to see what it's like to do a PLF with an open canopy and a brisk wind. Remember to hit, shift, and rotate, before you make that first body contact with the ground."

Kate watched as the first parachutist was released from one of the cone-like receptacles at the top of the tower. The parachutist floated down uneventfully, drifting away from the tower, and executing a fairly decent PLF about a hundred yards from where Kate was at the base of the tower. Kate and the others waited several minutes for the second parachutist to be released. Hardtack told the group that the training officer in charge was probably checking the wind conditions. A few seconds after that explanation, the second parachutist was released. Within a second or two after the release, a windshear suddenly developed and Kate could see that a powerful high-altitude crosswind was forcing the parachutist rapidly toward the steel structure of the tower. The parachutist was in a frenzy, pulling the risers in several different directions, to steer clear of the tower. The canopy began to rotate out of control as it descended. Then Kate heard a female's scream.

"CHARMAINE! CHARMAINE!" Kate yelled. "PULL RIGHT! PULL RIGHT!"

Hardtack pointed to the distressed parachutist and screamed to Kate, "WHO IS THAT?"

"TIBIDEAU, SERGEANT! TIBIDEAU!" Kate shrieked.

Before Hardtack could say anything, the parachutist was propelled headlong into a steel cross member of the structure; the parachute ruffled slightly as the parachutist tried frantically to hold onto the tower. Her grip slipped and she free-fell thirty feet before enough air was caught again in the canopy to break her fall. By this time she was unconscious, and as the parachute descended, more slowly now in the lower altitude calm air, her head and torso made contact several times with steel members. When Charmaine finally hit the ground, twenty yards from Kate, she lay in a heap with part of the parachute covering her body completely, as if in a funeral shroud.

Kate ran to the large white canopy, now billowing slightly, in the mild gusts of ground wind. Meanwhile, Hardtack radioed for an ambulance and then ran toward Kate, while telling the others in the platoon to stay back and out of the way. Kate rummaged through the white silk, now partially blood-stained, searching for Charmaine. When Kate found her, she almost wished she hadn't. Blood was streaming down Charmaine's face from a three-inch gash in the top of her head and blood was oozing from her mouth. Her right arm had a compound fracture, exposing an inch or two of shattered bone. Several of her teeth were missing and she was not breathing. Kate dropped to her knees, stuck her finger in Charmaine's mouth to clear away any wind-pipe obstruction, and then immediately began to apply mouth-to-mouth resuscitation. By then, Hardtack was beside Kate, assisting her with alternating CPR chest pressure.

Charmaine began breathing again, sporadically at first. "Good Job, McKeane," Hardtack said. "You're definitely ready for Airborne School."

"Thanks, Sergeant," Kate said between mouth-to-mouth applications.

Within thirty seconds, the medics arrived on the scene and, sirens blaring and red lights flashing, whisked Charmaine off to the Fort Benning Hospital. Charmaine was gone. Gone from Airborne School; gone from the *Minerva Experiment*. So quickly, so completely, and with such finality.

It was not until late the next day that Kate and the others learned that Charmaine had, in Hardtack's words, "bought the farm". She had died on the operating table at the Post Hospital. She was being shipped back to her home town for burial, and there would be a thorough military investigation of the incident, but that's all they knew. They were completely devastated—particularly Kate who had left the Tower area thinking she had saved Charmaine's life. It was a stark lesson in life . . . and death . . . which they did not expect to receive in Jump School. The loss of Charmaine affected each of the women deeply, but just as the loss of a comrade in combat cannot be allowed to deter a unit's mission, the women could not let the death of a close friend interfere with the completion of their training. It was a matter of reason over emotion. They could show no weakness. They had to go on with Tower Week. There was no time for grieving. They were on a mission and their objective was in sight.

4

On Sunday night before the beginning of Jump Week, Kate and Tina were sitting on their bunk beds in their barracks. Tina was shining her jump boots and getting her pack ready for the equipment jumps later in the week. Kate was writing a letter to Robert Holcroft. She received a letter from him every other day without fail; but Kate could not keep up with that schedule in getting her letters off to him. She thought of him constantly since Ring Weekend, and even more so during Jump School. Thoughts of him helped her get through the worst of it. She was disappointed that she wasn't able to be with him at Christmastime, but she was looking forward to seeing him over Spring Leave at his parents home in Arlington, Virginia. They would have to be just pen pals until then.

In the alcove across the center aisle, Lori and Sandy were playing a game of Scrabble and had planned to wait till later in the evening to get ready for the equipment jump. A single knock was heard at the door. They all knew what that meant.

Kate snapped to attention and gave the command "Tensch Hut!" The other three women sprang to their feet, backs straight, arms at their sides, and looking straight ahead at the wall opposite the door.

"At ease, soldiers," came a deep stern voice from behind them. They then heard what sounded like two quick swats to the side of a pants leg. It was Hardtack.

The veteran master sergeant walked slowly around them to a point where she could be seen by all four women. Looking down at the Scrabble board, she asked, "Well what do we have here, soldiers? The intellectual approach to Jump Week?"

"No, Sergeant," Kate replied in defense of her barracks mates.

"I guess some of us just want to get our minds off of stepping out of that airplane for the first time."

"The more you take your mind off your mission, McKeane," said Hardtack, "the more you'll follow the way of Tibideau, your absent cohort. She allowed herself to get panicked—and got herself killed. Is that what you want to happen to you?"

"No, Sergeant," Kate responded, her eyes moistening at the mention of Charmaine's ill fate.

"Well, I guess you're wonderin' why I'm here," Hardtack said as she began pacing around the room appearing to be half-inspecting, half-musing.

After an awkward silence, Tina said, "Airborne, sergeant!" which produced a smirk on the faces of the other three women.

Even Hardtack smiled ever so slightly.

"Well I'm here," said Hardtack, "to have a heart-to-heart chat. When I said `at ease' while ago, I really meant it. I want you to share with me any of your apprehensions about the coming week. Even about an Army career. Neither you four nor I may ever have this chance again. Do we understand each other?"

Still suspicious, they all nodded yes.

Sensing their incredulity, Hardtack sat down on a footlocker in the center aisle and, motioning toward their bunks, said, "Please, all of you, sit down and be comfortable." Putting her swagger stick on the floor, and bending to place her forearms on her thighs with her hands clasped in front of her, Hardtack continued now in a whisper, "The conversation we are about to have never happened. If you say it did, I will deny it."

Kate looked at Tina and then looked back toward Hardtack.

In a tranquilizing voice, Hardtack said, "Now what *are* your concerns, *ladies*," conveying genuine interest in them as soul-mates in a man's army.

Lori spoke up first. "Sergeant, I really have to admit that I'm scared to death about jumping out of that airplane tomorrow. I even prayed for bad weather last night . . . hoping that the C-140s would be grounded?"

"Are you naturally afraid of heights, Haskel? I mean, are you afraid to fly in a commercial airplane?" asked Hardtack.

"No. I've never been afraid to fly. It's just jumping out a plane's side door that bothers me."

"Hmmmmm," Hardtack replied, gaining some time to think. Did you have any problems with the thirty-four-foot or the two-hundred-fifty-foot towers?"

"No, not a bit. But there I could *see* all the mechanisms—the cables, the pulleys, the straps, and on the two-hundred-fifty-foot tower—the parachutes. But it's different in an airplane where all you can see is the snaplink you are sliding along a shoulder-high cable when you're shuffling to the door. You can't see the parachute; it's in a pack on your back. You don't even know if a parachute's inside; you never met the person who packed it; what if the person made a mistake?"

"But Haskel . . . " Hardtack attempted weakly.

"And then," Lori continued, "I think about what the ground looks like from fifteen hundred feet up—the trees, the lakes, and everything—zipping by. How do I know for sure that the static line won't break; or that my chute won't malfunction and get me all tangled up? How do I know I'm going to land on solid ground—that I won't get caught up in a tree or won't fall into a lake and drown, or something . . . and then I wonder if all this fear is just hormonal, or gender-related, or something, and that maybe I shouldn't be here in . . . ."

"Haskel!" This time Hardtack spoke louder and got her attention. "What you're worried about are the same things that every trainee worries about—male or female. I had these same fears during my Jump Week."

"You did?" Lori said, sounding surprised.

"Sure, and every man I've trained has too. They just won't admit it to one another. But I can see it in their faces. That ashen, despondent look when they shuffle toward me the instant before they jump into that wall of rushing air. I've never seen one smile. No one smiles when he's thinking about death."

"Do you ever have serious injuries around here?" Lori asked. "You know, the strange thing is, Haskel, there are very few injuries in Airborne training," said Hardtack. "Oh there might be a sprained ankle or wrenched back now and then during Ground Week or Tower Week. But there is rarely an injury during Jump Week. This is probably because people's fear makes them concentrate harder."

"But I've heard a couple horror stories," Sandy spoke up.

"You mean about the parachutist whose chute only partially opens and then he fast-drops on the canopy of another student below, collapsing that student's chute?" asked Hardtack.

"Yeah, that's one of 'em," replied Sandy.

"That's probably happened only a couple times in the whole history of Benning's Jump School, and even when it happened, there were no permanent injuries. Most of what you've heard is Airborne folklore, passed from one Airborne class to another, and usually blown completely out of proportion."

"That's good to know," said Sandy as she began putting the Scrabble game pieces back into the box. "But I still don't have grasp of what it's gonna be like standing in that stick of parachutists lined up waiting to jump from a plane traveling several hundred miles an hour. I mean, we've done all this mock door stuff. But what is it really like standing in that line of parachutists getting ready to go out the door?"

"Don't worry about it, Rothman," said Hardtack. It will all come automatic to you *because* of your ground training. Before the aircraft gets to the drop zone, you will be hooking up your static line snaphook to the overhead anchorline cable and checking the person in front of you to make sure the static line is not twisted or caught on anything and properly attached to the anchor line cable.

"What if you're the last person in the stick of parachutists? Does anybody check your equipment?" asked Lori.

"Sure," said Hardtack. "A training NCO will inspect the static line hook-up for the last person in line."

"Boy, I hope I'm the last person in the stick," piped up Tina. "I'm not sure I want a scared, sleepy student checking my static line."

"Well, Marafino," said Hardtack, "I wouldn't be too worried about that. There is a double check—particularly for your first jump tomorrow afternoon. The first jump is a "tap out". This means you will grasp a bight—a fold—of the static line about six inches down from the overhead anchor line cable and shuffle straight forward to the training sergeant facing you at the door. When you get to the training sergeant, he or she will direct you to assume a door position—which you've rehearsed in ground training count-less times. The sergeant will have an opportunity to check your static line before tapping you out of the aircraft. So there are really two checks of your equipment before you exit the door."

"I suppose that sometimes students need more than a `tap' to get them out of the aircraft, right?" Tina asked smiling.

"Sometimes," said Hardtack. "I've seen my share of students who froze at the door. But after they were given some friendly assistance by a sergeant on that first jump, they had no problem with subsequent jumps."

"What is it like falling through the air for the first time," Sandy asked.

"Wonderful!" said Hardtack.

"Wonderful?" asked Sandy. "Are you kidding?"

"No, I'm not kidding," said Hardtack. "It's exhilarating. It's about the closest thing to sex without actually doing it." Looking around at the four and seeing a couple of puzzled looks, Hardtack continued, smiling, "Perhaps, for some of you that example doesn't mean very much. But take my word for it. The tension and release that occurs when you are dropping through the air and counting to four thousand until that canopy opens, and then the visual and physical experience of floating slowly down through the air creates a sensation of true pleasure. It's very difficult to describe in words. But you'll know what I mean after your first jump."

"And if the canopy isn't open after that four thousand count?" asked Lori.

"Well then, you may have to make a difficult choice," said

Hardtack. "Your question highlights some important points for you all to keep in mind when you're jumping out of that aircraft. First, keep your eyes open and do the four thousand count at normal cadence—don't rush it. Keep your right hand over the ripcord grip on your reserve chute resting on your chest. If after four thousand, you do not feel the force of that canopy opening, look toward where the parachute should be. If it is twisted on itself or only partially opened, then you have to decide whether to pull the ripcord on your reserve chute."

"They don't teach much about the reserve chute in Jump School, *do* they?" asked Tina.

"No, that's right, Marafino," replied Hardtack. "Because the reserve is rarely used, there is very little training about it. You won't have a scheduled training jump with your reserve. But if you have to use it, realize that after you pull the ripcord, you will have to manually pull the reserve out of its case and feed it out in front of you, so that it can catch the air. It's really important to throw the reserve out away from you so that when it fills with air, it won't become tangled in your partially opened main chute. Don't be too worried about the reserve chute. There's less than one-half of one percent chance that you'll have to use it."

"Then let's review the procedure for landing on the ground," said Kate. "That's the part I fear the most—especially if there's a wind."

Hardtack looked around at the four women. Their attention was glued on her. "Let's go over the procedures together," she said. "First, when you're preparing to land, check the direction of drift and slip in the opposite direction, i.e. move so you are facing into the wind. What's next, Tina?"

"Hold the risers firmly against the chest and press the elbows against the body."

"Good, Marafino. . . . Haskel, what else?"

"Keep your head erect and your eyes on the horizon."

"Fine. Rothman?"

"Keep your legs straight and knees unlocked."

"Okay, one more, McKeane. What is it?"

"Keep your feet and knees together, and the balls of the feet pointed slightly toward the ground," said Kate.

"Fine, and why do you do that, McKeane?" asked Hardtack.

"To get you prepared for the parachute landing fall," Kate responded.

"That's right," said Hardtack. "And the PLF is the most important part of the whole jump sequence. More students get hurt doing PLFs than anything else. It's because they just don't think when they're about to make contact with the ground."

Jumping up on one of the footlockers, Hardtack said, "Look, there's nothing to it. You just have to remember to execute the sequence of movements." Jumping down from the footlocker, Hardtack continued to talk and to demonstrate at the same time. "As the balls of your feet strike the ground, first lower the chin to the chest tensing your neck. Then, bring your hands up in front of your head, elbows in front of your chest, and continue to grasp the risers. Bend and twist your torso sharply to the left or right depending on the wind conditions, causing the body to form an arc." After falling to the ground while executing a PLF, Hardtack quickly stood back upright again; pointing to various parts of her body, she said "And then make contact with the ground with your five points of contact—balls of your feet, calf, thigh, buttocks, and push-up muscle on the side of your torso—and then to avoid being dragged by the wind, immediately activate the canopy release assembly."

Appearing as if a lightbulb went on over her head, Tina said "You mean there's a *reason* why we do all those push-ups in Jump School."

"Yes, there really is," replied Hardtack. "The purpose is to build up that muscle which serves as the last point of contact in your PLF."

"Hmmm. Maybe I shouldn't have cussed out those training sergeants so much under my breath," Tina confessed.

Hardtack smiled. "Maybe we should make that clearer in the beginning of our training in the future."

"Yeah, . . . maybe," Tina smiled back.

Hardtack picked up her swagger stick and started toward the door of the barracks, and then turned around. "Well, that just about does it for the extra instruction, unless you have any more questions."

Kate looked at the others as if obtaining permission to broaden the field of questions. "I guess, sergeant, we'll never have an opportunity like this again. I mean, you being a woman and having been in combat and everything. We'd like to know more about what it's like to be a woman in real combat—not just training situations. I mean, like can you give us some tips or things we should know about?"

Hardtack walked back toward them. Multiple thoughts whirled in her mind. Since day one, she had known they were a special group—part of a combat experiment. It's hard to keep something like that secret in the Army. But she had never let them know that she knew. Nor would she. On the training fields she had treated them as she did their male counterparts. Never showing them favoritism, and if anything, making it tougher on them. They had to be tough. Maybe twice as tough as the men. It's always been that way. Women have to prove themselves once, and then they must prove themselves time and again. Not only in the Army, but in all professions, women first have to prove themselves to have the intellect and the physical ability to accomplish the assigned task. But the physical ability part has to be proved over and over, in case the first proof was a fluke, or in case the physical ability might dissipate faster than it does in men. It's all part of the stereotype of women as being physically inferior to men—physically handicapped."

"Like what?" Hardtack asked.

Like the impact of the obvious plumbing and chemical differences between men and women," Tina interposed.

"Are you talking about menstruation, menopause, and things like that," Hardtack clarified.

"Well, yeah," said Tina, "I mean, all we hear and read about is that women can't be in combat because of the effects of premenstrual syndrome and all that, and because they turn into bawling incompetents or screaming meemees during menopause. Have you seen any of that—particularly in the Desert Storm operation?"

"Frankly, no," replied Hardtack. "Menstrual problems, as I'm sure you're well aware, are individual among women. Some women have no problems whatsoever; others have cramping and related conditions that literally put them to bed for a few days each month. But from puberty, most women know the physical effects of their menstrual cycles and most know what to do to minimize their problems. But to answer your question specifically, Marafino, I saw no women causing a failure of mission because of menstrual cycles. Those who had menstrual difficulties were put in very low-risk combat positions. It just wasn't a problem. They didn't want to be in combat, and the Army didn't want them there either. Actually, what I saw was that some of the men had periodic problems with prostate infections and recurrent venereal disease, which had to be treated and often took them out of their combat assignments for days and weeks at a time."

"What about menopause—what effect, if any, did it have on the combat mission?" asked Kate, trying to be sensitive to Hardtack's more advanced years.

Hardtack, walked over to the footlocker and sat down again. "That's a different story, McKeane," Hardtack said, now appearing more sullen. "I'm forty-seven . . . I know that may surprise you . . . and I started experiencing the first signs of menopause—perimenopause—near the end of my tour of duty in Desert Storm. I didn't know at first what had come over me. I started to get mild hot flashes and cycles that were shorter with heavy flows of blood. I also had some exaggerated mood swings and interruption of sleep. I was ignorant about what was causing such things. But an Army doctor steered me to some books and pamphlets on menopause. She suggested that I would be a good candidate for hormone replacement therapy, since I did not have cystic breasts and there was no history of breast cancer in my family. She also said the treatment would decelerate bone loss and decrease my risk of coronary artery disease. Actually, . . . I feel weird sharing all these highly personal things with you. But I wish someone would have told me about this when I was your age and just entering military service."

"Why?" asked Kate. "If you had known, would you not have enlisted?"

"No," said Hardtack. "I still would have enlisted—I had to. I wanted to get away from the sharecroppin' life of my parents and grandparents; I couldn't find a job in town. Jobs were scarce generally and even scarcer for a twenty-one-year-old black girl. Didn't have a boyfriend. Never had one to this day. No, I just wish I would've known. I'm just not the rip-snortin' carefree soldier I used to be. I now know I have some limitations."

"Yes, but isn't that true of everyone over forty—male or female?" asked Kate.

"Well, I suppose so," replied Hardtack.

"And the hormone therapy—it worked, didn't it?" interjected Tina.

"Yes, pretty well," said Hardtack.

"Then, what are you so concerned about?" asked Tina.

"I'm just angry that I can't be who I am without the chemicals. I'm just angry that I'm a fake."

Kate saw a tear glisten in the corner of Hardtack's eye. Changing the subject, Kate said in a cheery tone, "Well, Sergeant, we needn't take up any more of your valuable time. Besides, we'd better hop into the rack and get some shut-eye if we're going to pop those chutes tomorrow."

Hardtack attempted a smile, quickly stood up in a rigidly erect position, kept her eyes straight ahead, and again made her way to the door. Opening the door, she continued to talk facing the outside, "I trust I will see you all at Lawson Airfield tomorrow morning bright and early," as she swatted her swagger stick against her pantleg. Closing the door firmly behind her, Hardtack heard a rousing chorus of "AIRBORNE! SERGEANT."

5

Lori's prayers had worked. The next morning—Monday—Kate
awoke to the sounds of rain pounding against her barracks window and of wind whistling through the downspout of the World
War II relic of a building. It was doubtful that the first jump
would occur that day. Instead they'd probably have a lecture session, watch a couple World War II documentaries of airborne operations, and prepare for a jump on Tuesday. That would also mean
that graduation would be on Saturday instead of Friday. At ten-
thirty that morning, Kate and company got the official word that
Lawson Airfield was socked in and that all jumps that day were
canceled. Consequently, they would have to suffer through one
more day and one more night of hyperanxiety.

The next morning the sky was overcast with clouds and the
wind was out of the northwest at less than five miles per hour.
Perfect jump weather. Kate's platoon was seated on the grass beside the runway, listening to Hardtack wind up a last minute review of some of the jump basics.

Standing on the edge of the runway, silhouetted against a background of a huge camouflage-patterned aircraft, Hardtack concluded
her briefing with a few points about the aircraft itself. "And finally,
my parakeets, this airplane you see directly behind me is a Lockheed
C-130 Hercules—the Army's workhorse—the primary transport of
the 82nd Airborne Division for more than a quarter of a century and
a prime mover of troops and equipment during the Vietnam War as
well as the Desert Storm operation. It is able to carry sixty-four fully
equipped paratroopers, who can exit the rear of the aircraft in two
columns, or forty-four thousand pounds of equipment. This aircraft
has a range of four thousand four hundred sixty nautical miles, and
with aerial refueling, it can drop paratroopers anywhere in the world
they might be needed. The C-130 can take off from unpaved runways
as short as two thousand feet, and it can . . ."

Kate was beginning to tune Hardtack out. She couldn't understand why all this detailed minutia was necessary. But every

military training session she ever sat through had it. The numbers, the statistics, the maximum effectives, the minimum effectives. Kate wanted to get on with the jump.

Pointing to another large aircraft on another runway, Hardtack continued, " . . . and in conclusion, that aircraft on Runway Three is a Lockheed C-141 Starlifter. The Starlifter can carry one hundred twenty-three fully equipped paratroopers who can jump from two doors at the aft end of the cabin. Those of you who join airborne infantry units after this training will do your jumping from that aircraft. The females in this group don't have to worry about ever bein' inside a Starlifter."

Kate resented that last comment. Although it was probably true, it was cruel. She passed it off as Hardtack's anger coming out sideways.

"Are there any questions before we board the aircraft?" Hardtack asked the group.

There was no response.

"All right, parakeets, it's time to spread your wings and get ready to leave the nest. Give me two files right here in front of me."

Kate and a male trainee ran to stand at the head of the two-file column in front of Hardtack. Kate wanted to get this over with fast.

"FORWARD, . . . HARCH," commanded Hardtack. Hardtack marched the two sticks of parachutists toward the gaping opening of the rear of the aircraft and up the equipment ramps. Four other training NCOs were already inside. The two sticks continued to march toward the cabin of the aircraft and then were given the command to sit down. In response, they sat along the two walls of the aircraft facing inward and strapped themselves in for takeoff.

Soon the Hercules' engines began revving up; within seconds it was taxiing down the runway for takeoff. Kate was sitting on the starboard side of the plane, and the force of the takeoff pushed Kate hard to her left against an enlisted man—Corporal

Henderson—who was in turn canted to the left against his neighbor. Kate smiled an apology to Henderson, and he smiled forgiveness in return. In seconds, the plane climbed to twelve hundred fifty feet and leveled off.

While the parachutists were still seated, Hardtack left her seat on the front cabin wall and moved passed the stick of parachutists on the starboard side of the plane. Another NCO mirrored Hardtack's movement on the port side. Two other NCOs stood up at the cabin side of each stick.

The two sidedoors at the rear of the aircraft were opened by Hardtack and the other NCO. Hardtack and the NCO turned and looked toward the front of the aircraft. Kate then realized that she would be last out of the aircraft. She had momentarily forgotten about the "first-in, last-out" concept.

Hardtack gave the command as loud as she could above the propeller noise, "STAND UP, HOOK UP, AND SHUFFLE TO THE DOOR." Kate had practiced this so often she could do it in her sleep. She and the others immediately unbelted themselves, stood up, hooked their static line snaphook to the anchor line cable, turned toward the aft of the aircraft, took a bight of static line with the hand toward the middle of the aircraft, and shuffled toward the door. Hardtack then gave the command, "PERFORM YOUR BUDDY CHECK." Each parachutist in the stick checked the equipment and static line snaphook of the person in front of him and gave a pat on the shoulder to indicate that the everything was okay. The NCO standing behind Kate checked her off and gave her a pat.

The stick was beginning to move forward, Kate knew the jumps had started. As she moved closer to the door, she heard screams of "GERONIMO!" as the fledgling parachutists left the plane for the first time. Henderson faced Hardtack, turned left, took up a door position. Hardtack tapped his shoulder. The wind whipping his static line, he froze. "JUMP HENDERSON!" Hardtack shouted at the same time tapping his shoulder. Still, Henderson did not move.

Hardtack moved behind Henderson, and with both hands, Hardtack gave him a strong steady push out the door. If she would have waited much longer he would have missed the Drop Zone. He gave a frightful scream as he plummeted away from the aircraft. Hardtack waited in the door to watch his chute open without incident. She turned back and nodded to Kate to take up a door position. Kate smiled and moved to the door, prepared to jump. Hardtack tapped her shoulder and Kate was out the door.

"THOUSAND ONE, THOUSAND TWO, THOUSAND THREE, THOUSAND FOUR" Kate counted to herself as she fell, keeping a tight body position and trying to keep her eyes open in the torrent of wind. Then she felt that marvelous, expected, forceful jerk. She looked up and saw a huge white canopy fully deployed. What a lovely sight, she thought to herself. She wanted to relax, but she knew she couldn't. The hard part was yet to come—hitting the ground.

In a few short minutes, Kate could see activity on the ground in the Drop Zone. Unfortunately for her, because Henderson took so long to get out the door, there was a good chance she would be in a forest outside the landing area if she didn't take some corrective action fast. To her front, she could now clearly see some of her stickmates in the Drop Zone, some of them doing PLFS, some of them releasing their parachutes and gathering them up, others heading for the deuce-and-a-half trucks for the trip back to Lawson Field for a debriefing.

The trees were getting closer and closer. For a second she pictured herself impaled like a Christmas tree angel on top of one of them. Luckily the wind had shifted, producing strong pressure against her back, so she reached high up with her hands and brought two fistfuls of risers back toward her chest. That action increased her speed in the direction of the Drop Zone and she slid across the treetops at the Drop Zone's edge with only a few yards of elevation to spare. Now the ground was coming up fast and she was approaching it with a brisk wind at her back. She pulled down hard on the left risers to rotate slightly to the left. She went over the PLF sequence a couple of times in her mind, and waited for her toes to hit the ground. When they did, she shifted and rotated her body, made contact with the ground with the five points of contact, and immediately stood up. A perfect PLF.

SUSPENDED AGONY

Kate, Tina, and their other two classmates made it through the rest of Jump Week literally with flying colors. Tina had only a slight problem with the equipment jump when her quick-release mechanism didn't work properly and she was wind-dragged and tumbled for about twenty yards across the Drop Zone before two of her stick-mates came to her rescue. She walked away with no serious injuries.

Everyone was looking forward to graduation on Saturday, especially Kate and Tina. Classmate Todd Gavin and his fiancé, Emma Lou, were coming down from Lexington for the graduation ceremony. Todd too was getting a late start on his last semester at West Point so that he could give some recruiting talks to students at some Lexington high schools. Todd thought it was neat that he and Emma Lou would be staying at the "Gavin" Visitors' Apartments at Benning. Kate had made the arrangements.

Kate was excited about seeing her good friend Todd again. She had truly missed his congenial ways and spritely sense of humor. Robert had written Kate about possibly coming down to Benning from Nashville for her Airborne School graduation, but before Christmas he had gotten the flu for a few days and missed a couple of his exams. They were rescheduled for the Monday after Kate's graduation. Since he had to study over the graduation weekend, he wasn't able to come to Benning. Kate was disappointed, but she understood.

That Saturday, after the Airborne School graduation ceremony, the new paratroopers were leaving the theater with their friends and families. Kate took Tina, Todd and Emma Lou aside to talk privately in the foyer.

"We have to do some celebratin' tonight," Kate said excitedly.

"That's puttin' mildly," Todd drawled. "You don't think Emma Lou and me came all the way down here from Lexington just to see a few chicks get their wings pinned on, do you?"

"Don't mind him, Kate " said Emma Lou. "That's just his Kentucky blarney workin' overtime."

"Yeah," chimed Tina. "Todd's a wingless ground-pounder—a `leg'. He's just jealous of us high-flyin' storm troopers. Why he'll never be able to hold a candle . . . "

"Leg, hell," said Todd. "Leg man, maybe."

"Guys always have to bring sex into it, don't they Todd?" Tina said kiddingly.

"Hey, you two." Kate interrupted. "Cut the chatter. We really need to decide what to do tonight. Tina and I haven't been off Post since we got here. Any ideas, Todd?"

"Well, driving through Columbus we saw a few . . . "

Just at that moment, Sergeant Davidson entered the foyer through the swinging doors from the theater.

Kate called to her. "Sergeant Davidson? Can we ask you something?"

"Sure. What is it?"

"We first want to thank you personally for your support through all this. . . . But, additionally, we have a question."

"Shoot."

"Do you have a suggestion where we could go tonight to really celebrate?" Kate asked.

"You mean to really raise hell, hang one on, and not have the MPs on your back?" the sergeant replied with a smirk.

"Yeah, that's exactly what I mean, Sergeant."

"Well, I know this joint in Phenix City. It's really hard to find—not on the beaten track. Lots of Airborne grads celebrate there. The owner—Charlie Steiner—is a retired military man, an Airborne grad himself who served for ten years in the 82nd Airborne Division.

"Sounds great! How do we get there?"

"Well, once you get to Columbus on U.S. Two-eighty bypass and cross the Chattahoochee, exit right at Ingersoll Drive and go north until you reach Crawford; turn right; then continue until Seventh Ave; left on Seventh which turns into Summerville road across the railroad tracks; follow Summerville road north to Twenty-sixth Street; turn right and then immediately after the gas station, turn into the alley and you can park in the back. The name of the place is Charlie's Bull Pen—sort of a sports bar feel to it." Taking a pen out of her pocket, the sergeant continued, "if you want me to draw you a map, I'd be . . . "

"No, that's okay," replied Kate. I gotta better idea. Why don't you come with us."

"Me? You want me—a sergeant—to go carousing with you— you cadets from West Point?"

"Sure—you deserve a night out on the town."

Flattered, Hardtack looked down at the floor and then directly at Kate and said, "Well, if you insist."

"We insist," Tina piped in.

"I have to warn, you, though," Hardtack said. "This place sometimes can get pretty wild on a Saturday night."

"I think we can handle it," Tina shot back. "We're Airborne, Sergeant."

"Yeah, but remember, you're not made of steel," said Hardtack, "even though you might think so. I guess we ought to decide what we're going to wear and when we are going to leave."

"Well, we grads are going to be wearing our uniforms—dress gray—and sport these new wings," Tina said looking at Kate as if to speak for her.

"Then I'll get into my greens," Hardtack said, looking at Kate and Tina. "We paratroopers have to stick together."

"Uh, uh, just so you know," said Todd. "Emma Lou and I will be going in civvies. Emma Lou doesn't have a uniform and I'm on a vacation from uniforms."

"No problem," said Kate. "You two will be able to blend in

with the local riffraff.

"What do you say we leave from Kate and Tina's barracks at about seven," said Todd. "I'll drive. I drove my parents' Jimmy down. It should hold everybody. Maybe dinner at the Black Angus and then on to Charlie's Bull Pen. I'll make reservations for seven-thirty. Sound okay?"

Everyone nodded agreement and then departed the theater.

No one ever left the Black Angus hungry. Located on the outskirts of Columbus, the restaurant was famous for its reasonably priced twenty-ounce steaks with all the trimmings, and on this Saturday night it certainly lived up to its reputation for the five revelers. There was an old saying around Benning that the fifteen pounds trainees lost during the three weeks of Airborne School could be gained back in just one meal at the Black Angus. When they had finished their meal, the saying seemed to hold true. When they were walking out of the restaurant, they all were complaining how stuffed they were. They all piled in Todd's Jimmy and off they went to Charlie's Bull Pen.

By the time they got to the bar, it was ten o'clock. As soon as they put foot in the dimly lit parking lot behind the bar they were greeted with a strong smell of hickory smoked barbecue and loud, foot-stompin' country western music. Most of the vehicles in the parking lot were highly polished pick-up trucks, some customized with oversized wheels and extended cabs. The rear windows of most of the them had rifle racks holding one or more rifles and shotguns. Large spongy sets of dice hung uniformly on strings from inside rearview mirrors. A neon sign extended the full length of the hip-roofed structure, and since the sign faced the front, it was difficult to read. But one thing was for sure. It didn't read "Charlie's Bull Pen."

After a few seconds, Todd deciphered aloud: "Jesse's Vigilante Outpost". Are you sure this is the right place, Sarge?"

"Yeah, it's been a year or so since I've been here. But this *is* the place. No question. I remember the "Mullanphy" sign on the junk yard fence over there. Charlie must have changed to a western theme to attract more business."

"Okay, if you say so," Todd said, surveying the ominous surroundings while hearing several dogs barking behind the high wooden fence of the adjacent junk yard. Leaving their hats and overcoats inside, they all exited the Jimmy and started walking toward the back of the Outpost. Todd, as usual, handed his keys to Emma Lou, saying, "Here, keep these in your purse. I just hate bulgy pockets."

The back door of the Outpost was covered from top to bottom with a huge poster of Garth Brooks in a cowboy hat imprinted with an American flag design. Garth was pointing at each observer and the inscription read in large red-white-and blue letters, "I WANT YOU!!" Holding open the door for the others, Todd made some pun about "drafting us to drink their draught". When she passed by him, Kate groaned at his pun and caught up with Hardtack who was leading the procession down a dark narrow hallway, lined on each side with smelly restrooms.

From the hallway Hardtack could see neon beer signs on posts throughout a large smoke-filled room with a massive square-shaped columned wood bar at one end of the room and a stage at the other end; a five piece country-western band accompanied a female singer wailing the lyrics of a country ballad.

"I'm tired of picking up the pieces
Of my heart when you go berserk.
I used to wait by the window, but
Now I hate it when you come home from work."

Waitresses in tight jean shorts, cowboy boots, and loose- fitting low-cut Mexican-style tops served working-class male customers seated and standing three deep around the bar, keeping three busty "Daisy Mae" bartenders busy. The dance floor, in the middle of the room, was overflowing with couples in Western garb, hanging on each achy-breaky word and on each other, some because they were too drunk to stand up on their own. Several patrons were playing pool at the six pool tables on one side of the dance floor, and patrons occupied most of checkerboard oil-clothed tables on the other side.

When Hardtack got to the entrance of the barroom, a bulky bouncer, bearded and wearing Western clothes and a ten-gallon white hat, stepped in front of her and said, "Darlin', these here folks you're brangin' with ya are gunna need some ID to get past this here point." Kate and the others accordion-bumped in the hallway behind Hardtack.

From the rear of the human caravan, Todd quipped "Better get your tail lights fixed, Sarge!"

Hardtack turned around, and loud enough to be heard above the din of hillbilly music, and the hoopin' and hollerin' around the bar, yelled, half-facetiously, to the others, "Prepare to present ID's!"

Kate, Todd, and Emma Lou, dug into their pockets and got out their driver's licenses. Tina pulled out a West Point library card with her photograph on it, and brazenly flashed it to the bouncer as she paraded by him. In the dull lighting, the bouncer did not question it.

As Todd, Emma Lou, and the close-cropped trio of women passed into the barroom, the bouncer yelled to Hardtack, "Sarge, I wanna give you fair warnin'. You're comin' in here at your own risk. Charlie don't own this place no more. These here rednecks don't like soldiers—'specially female ones. They don't like what the soldiers have done to this town." Hardtack didn't respond, but when she looked around, it was unsettling that she was the only black person in the place.

At that moment one of the cute scantily clad waitresses came up to Hardtack, smiled, and said, "I got a table for your group. This way."

The waitress led the five past the bar. Practically every man's head turned to appraise the entourage. Winks, smiles, and nods punctuated the men's slurred conversations. One of the men, con-

siderably overweight, jowly, and shirtless in denim bib overalls
and a black cowboy hat, poked his friend in the ribs with his
elbow when he saw them coming and said, "Boy, are we gonna
have some fun t'night."

When Hardtack and the others filed passed the bar, the fat
one called to her, "Hey missy, we don't 'low no poontang in here.
Specially no military poontang." The other men around the bar
laughed heartily. Hardtack ignored them and continued to follow
the waitress to an empty table for six on the other side of the room.

When they were all seated, Todd said, "How about a couple
pitchers of beer for starters?" Everyone agreed and the waitress
nodded and began to walk away. Todd called to her, "And don't
forget to bring a big bowl of pretzels. We don't want to get our
thirst quenched too quick tonight." The waitress smiled and gave
him the "okay" sign with her fingers.

Kate and Tina talked to Emma Lou about what it was like
growing up in Lexington, Kentucky, as Hardtack kept Todd busy
telling him a few war stories about Desert Storm. In a few minutes
the band began playing an old Hank Williams' number—"Your
Cheatin' Heart." Todd politely interrupted one of Hardtack's war
stories and said, "Care to dance? This is one of my mother's favorite tunes." Hardtack graciously accepted but stressed that the foxtrot
wasn't her forte. As they made their way to the dance floor, Todd
made some quip about Hardtack's foxtrot problem was that she
was most likely a better leader than a follower. He told her he'd
foller her anywhere . . . he didn't care.

On reaching the dance floor, about fifteen couples were already dancing. The pair began to slow dance, awkwardly at first,
to the female singer's mournful strains,

> *Your cheatin' heart*
> *Will make you weep,*
> *You'll cry and cry,*
> *And try to sleep.*
> *But sleep won't come . . .*

The more Todd and his partner danced, the more synchronized they became. Todd made smooth turns and Hardtack, her body pressed close to his, followed as if they were one. Being caught up in the music, Todd didn't notice that, one by one, the other couples were leaving the dance floor.

Soon he and Hardtack were moving in ever widening circular patterns around the dance floor while the patrons watched. In his peripheral vision, Todd noticed the jowly man in the bib overalls and black hat walk to the edge of the dance floor, face the band, and move his horizontally held hand across his flabby neck. The singer stopped singing in the middle of the phrase; the band trailed off into a disjointed closure, then fell silent. The patrons, just stood around watching, staring at the two figures on the dance floor. Feeling uneasy and embarrassed, Todd took Hardtack by the hand and led her back to the table where Kate and the others were still conversing. As soon as the pair reached the table and sat down, the band started playing again and couples began returning to the dance floor.

A waitress, different from the previous one, came toward their table carrying a tray with two pitchers of beer and several beer steins. Todd asked, "Excuse me, miss, who is that guy over there in the black hat?"

"Oh, that's Glen Shelby," said the waitress. "He comes here three or four nights a week and brings six or seven of his truck drivers with him. He owns a big grain storage company here in town. Everybody around here knows him. Brings a lot of business into this place."

"I see," said Todd. "Is the owner here tonight?"

"Jesse?"

"I guess, if that's who owns this place."

"Naw. Jesse had to go to Atlanta this weekend. His mother's sick in a nursing home there. He should be back on Monday, though, if you want to see him."

"No, that's okay," said Todd. "Who's in charge here t'night, then."

"You're lookin' at her, sir. I'm Jesse's daughter-in-law. Anythin' I can do for y'all?"

"No, . . . I guess not," replied Todd. "But there is one thing you can tell me."

"Yassir?"

"Does the band always stop playing like that in the middle of songs?"

"Well, no sir." Then bending over toward Todd and cupping her hand on the side of her mouth she added, "Only when there's a nigger on the dance floor." With that, she walked away from their table and headed toward a table of six patrons just being seated.

"Hey, aren't those pitchers ours?" Todd called to the waitress.

"No sir. Didn't they tell you? You're sitting at one of our non-alcoholic tables. Glen reminded me. I'll get you some water right away."

Todd was steamed. Kate and the others had not yet completely comprehended what was happening. He looked across the dance floor toward the pool tables and watched the black hat weaving between the dancers and coming toward Todd's side of the bar-room. Within seconds the black-hatted man—Shelby—emerged from the dancers and walked toward Todd.

"Pardner, you just don't get it, do you," Shelby said angrily to Todd, still seated. "Just what does it take to convince you that you and your military lesbos aren't welcome 'roun these parts?"

Todd immediately stood up, towering several inches over the middle-aged heckler.

"You're not tryin' to threaten me, now are you young feller?" Shelby said looking up at Todd. Todd said nothing. Kate and the others stopped talking, sensing that something was happening. Shelby turned to his right and motioned to the bulky bouncer now standing near the bar. "Rex," he yelled. "I think I'm gunna be needin' a little assistance over here."

The bouncer plodded over toward them and asked, "What kin

I do for ye, Mr. Shelby?"

"These folks here, Rex, need some help findin' the back door. Musta drunk too much, or somethin'. They're gettin' a little sassy. Know what ah-mean?."

"No problem, Mr. Shelby. I'll take care of 'em."

"Hey wait, fellas," said Todd. "All we want is to sip a few brews and dance a little bit. We don't want any trouble."

"You've danced and drunk too much, already," Shelby said sarcastically. "Rex, I'd be much obliged if you'd show 'em the door."

"Sure, Mr. Shelby," replied the bouncer grabbing Todd by the left arm and shoving him hard in the direction of the dance floor. Todd was caught completely by surprise. Before Todd could recover his balance, the bouncer lunged toward him and gave him a body block propelling Todd chest-first onto the dance floor amid several dancers.

"Look, Rex," shouted Shelby. "Now he's interferin' with the line dance. Isn't that a cryin' shame?"

Doing their natural forward, backward, and sideways progressive movements, Todd was kicked and stomped on by several of the male line dancers. At first, the kicks and stomps seemed accidental. But when they continued, Todd became convinced that they were being intentionally inflicted. Somehow, Todd managed to roll off the dance floor. Out of range of the foot-pummelers, Todd sprang to his feet, arms bruised, bleeding at the mouth, and completely enraged.

"My boys gave ye a little tour of the inside of a combine, did they, young feller," Shelby said sarcastically, scowling at Todd. "Aint you had enough yet?"

Dazed and barely holding a caveman stance a couple feet from Shelby, Todd pulled his right arm back and attempted to land a blow on his chin. So slow was Todd's movement that Shelby stepped out of the way in time to see Todd's body move past him and fall spread-eagle on a table of startled patrons. Todd's face landed in a large basket of pretzels.

Smiling, Shelby turned toward Todd helplessly scrambling to

right himself from the tabletop, and with hands on his hips said, "See, young feller, how hospitable we are here. We didn't forget your pretzels." Then, frowning and looking around at his truck drivers, Shelby continued, "It looks like we're just gunna haf t'lynch him." Shelby pointed to a square beam over the dance floor that had a thick hemp rope and noose hanging from it. "Boys," he said. "Form your posse."

Things had happened so quickly Kate and the others at the table hadn't had time to react. Several people had walked between them and Shelby, blocking their view of the dance floor. They stood up, but the swarm of people still obscured their view. The noise of the music, yelling patrons, and stomping dancers was deafening.

Suddenly, the four women saw Todd's body being hoisted up above the heads of the people in front of them toward the wooden beam, twenty-five feet overhead. The noose had been placed under Todd's arms and tightened, and he appeared limp, perhaps unconscious. The line dancers had stopped in their tracks, but the band still blared.

"Holy crap!" Kate exclaimed. "This place is outta control. We gotta do something fast. Come with me, Tina." Moving away from the table and looking back, Kate screamed, "Sarge—you and Emma Lou get the Jimmy started. We'll be out there soon!"

While Kate and Tina were trying to get through the human cordon in front of the dance floor, Shelby was looking up at Todd, the top of whose head was now touching the wooden beam, saying, "Pardner, I bet you don't know what falls outta the sky. Tell him boys!"

"BIRD SHIT AND PARATROOPERS!" the men shouted.

Still looking up at Todd, Shelby yelled "Which one are you, pardner?" The crowd roared with laughter.

Todd didn't respond. It didn't seem funny to him that he wasn't a paratrooper either.

Popping out of the sidelines, Kate and Tina unzipped their dress gray jackets. Tina ran toward Shelby, stopped half-way, and went into a step-stool position directly under a wagon wheel light hanging from a twenty-foot chain from the barn-like roof. Kate ran as fast as she could, placed her foot on Tina's back, and reached up and grabbed the wagon wheel light with both hands. Swinging through the air, yelling "REMEMBER CHARMAINE", she planted both of her shoes forcefully in the center of Shelby's back. The impact whiplashed his head backward, but his body, still powered by the battering ram force of the gray-coated duo, moved in the direction of the pool tables. Shelby's groin area made contact with the edge of the center pool table and his head slammed down hard on the felt-covered slate. The crowd of men and women line dancers moved into the poolroom to watch what they thought would be turning into a wrestling match. The men were shouting, "Get up Glen! Stomp those lesbos!" Some of the women were cheering for Kate and Tina, giving each other "high fives" and urging Tina to "Kick him in the balls!"

Meanwhile, Hardtack and Emma Lou were running down the narrow back hallway toward the parking lot. Emma Lou struggled momentarily to find her keys, and then jumped in the Jimmy, and revved up the engine. From outside the Jimmy, Hardtack hand-signaled to Emma Lou that she was going back inside.

When she got to the entrance to the barroom, Hardtack looked toward the poolroom and saw that Kate was lying, back down, on the pool table and Shelby was using a pool cue across her neck to choke her. Tina, armed with a pool cue, jumped on top of an adjacent pool table and holding tightly onto the slender end of the cue with both hands, took a high block-chopping downward swing at Shelby's black hat. He immediately released pressure on the cue he was using to choke Kate. Stunned and shaking his head briskly from side to side, he raised his chest up slightly and collapsed almost immediately, bouncing off the pool table and onto the sawdust floor.

Meanwhile, Hardtack ran toward the piling around which was tied the rope holding Todd in suspended agony. Todd was semi-conscious, but he managed to give her a high sign as she untied the rope and guided his descent to the floor. Hardtack fireman-carried Todd to the dark, rear hallway and told him that he would have to make it back to the Jimmy on his own. Todd said he thought he could. Hardtack then moved back to the poolroom area to help extricate Kate and Tina. As she scurried, Hardtack wondered why the police hadn't arrived yet, then realized that it was probably because Jesse hadn't paid his police "protection" money yet this month—with his mother sick and all. Tavern shakedowns were pretty common in the Columbus area.

By now, Kate and Tina were standing on top of the same pool table swinging pool cues at six or so of Shelby's "boys" trying to keep them at bay. Approaching the bar, Hardtack grabbed a bartender's apron from the top of a bar stool and headed toward the two pool tables closest to her. She stuffed more than a dozen pool balls into the deep-pockets of the apron and went back toward the narrow hallway again to gain some distance from the crowd. Then, taking aim at Shelby's "boys" she began to propel pool balls in their direction. Her first shot was a direct hit, striking one of the unsuspecting bullies in the ear, putting him out of action as he fell to the ground holding the side of his head, moaning, and rolling around on the floor under the feet of his compatriots. Hardtack fired two more pool balls at the "boys". One missed its mark and went crashing through a side window of the pool room; the other caught another bully in the chest and knocked him backward, numbed, into the crowd of spectators.

Hardtack's "artillery" was exactly what Kate and Tina needed to distract their enemy. The crowd having cleared away from the pool table, Kate and Tina, still holding pool cues, simultaneously did a "hit, shift, and rotate" from the table and over Shelby's motionless torso, and raced in tandem toward Hardtack standing near the dark hallway. "Did we win?" Kate yelled to Hardtack, kiddingly, as she ran past her and entered the dark hallway with Tina following close behind. "You'll have to bring up the rear, Sarge!"

Just as she said that, the door to the men's room opened, blocking the constricted passageway completely. It then slammed shut to expose an even more formidable obstruction . . . Rex in his ten-gallon hat. He had apparently been in the men's room during the whole poolroom skirmish.

"And just where do you two lesbos think you're goin'?" said the bouncer, realizing that he had just upset their escape plan.

Slowly walking backward in step with Tina, Kate said to the bouncer, "Where are we *goin'*, caveman? We're just *goin'* to give lil-o-you a crash course in astronomy."

"Astronomy?" said the bouncer.

"Yeah, astronomy," said Kate. By then, Kate and Tina had backed their way into the barroom. Tina, her pool cue at port arms, watched the stunned crowd still milling around over by the pool tables trying to give comfort to the wounded.

"Lock and load!" Kate screamed to Hardtack as she reached with both hands into Hardtack's deep apron pockets to grasp several pool balls. Hardtack knew exactly what to do. Kate stepped a few more feet into the barroom and then began hurling pool balls with all her might down the barrel-like dark hallway. Hardtack followed her at a fast clip with a second barrage, hurling several more pool balls at the massive, screaming figure which had moved backward and up against the door at the opposite end. He eventually fell backward and out the doorway onto the parking lot, his ten-gallon hat sliding along the pavement well beyond some parked pick-up trucks. Kate and Hardtack ran down the hallway and out to the parking lot and continued to pelt him with pool balls at close range. The bouncer got up, and apparently seeing the prophesied stars, stumbled and fell several more times until, once upright, he finally gained enough momentum to carry him out of the parking lot and down the alley behind the junkyard as fast as his aching legs could carry him. No doubt he had been exposed to about as much astronomy as he wanted for one night.

Kate, Tina, and Hardtack jumped into the Jimmy with Emma Lou and Todd. While Emma Lou was screeching the Jimmy backward, smashing flat the bouncer's ten-gallon hat. Todd, still groggy, made some comment about it being "the first time he had ever seen a bouncer bounced." Emma Lou quickly shifted into first gear, squealing the tires and laying rubber the length of the parking lot. The Jimmy was down the alley and onto the main thoroughfare before several of Shelby's bullies fanned out of the bar into the parking lot to get a license number.

Police sirens could be heard in the distance and the junkyard dogs were by now barking more fiercely than ever.

TARNISHED LOVE

On the far east side of the West Point Plain, beginning near Cullum Memorial Hall, is a pathway which winds alongside and just above the level of the Hudson River, ultimately opening at its north end onto the graceful terraces of Trophy Point. Off limits to all but cadets and their dates, Flirtation Walk or "Flirty", as the pathway is sometimes called, offers a cool shady trail through charming riverside woodland in the spring, summer, and fall, ideal for intimate romantic liaisons. In those seasons, it is not uncommon on weekends to see numerous pairs of upper-class cadets and their dates strolling along Cullum Road toward the southernmost entrance to Flirty, the cadet in each pair carrying a case for a laptop computer. Uninformed observers of this scene never completely comprehend it. They accept this case-carrying phenomenon as the Academy's chic new "corporate look". The cadets, however, have a singular mission in mind—finding a secluded comfortable spot on Flirty, taking a blanket out of their case, and having wholly uninhibited, raucous, rapturous sex the rest of the afternoon. Sometimes they accomplish their mission, sometimes they fall short of their attempts. This is what Flirty is like on weekends "in season".

In winter, Flirty changes character. It's like a cemetery after dark—quiet, ominous, and desolate. Its grayness is even more hauntingly lonely than the perennial gray of the stern granite cliffs and the stoic stone buildings embedded like gravestones in the institutional panorama. In the dead of winter, there are no sparrows dancing and chirping on low tree branches, no playful squirrels stealing bread crusts from box lunches of preoccupied lovers, no itinerant monarch butterflies perched on shoots of high grass, slowly fanning their giant wings in the late afternoon sun. Just grayness—with occasional splotches of snow—and quiet. That's Flirty in winter. Kate often went there on Sunday afternoons to escape the pressures of academics and for a respite from the demands of cadet life in general. That's where she was headed on the last Sunday in February. Stuffed in the pockets of her short overcoat were a romance novel she had started reading on the trip back from Fort Benning, a Walkman, her favorite Mozart cassette, and a recent, yet unopened, letter from Robert. Walking east on the sidewalk along Cullum Road, as it had been her custom since Plebe Year, Kate stopped in front of the entrance to the USMA Library nestled between the academic buildings, Bartlett and Thayer Halls, and gazed for several seconds at the figure projecting from the relief in the military gothic turret. She then followed the curve left as the road turned north toward the Officers' Club and Cullum Hall. The backstops of Doubleday Field, named after Major General Abner Doubleday, alumnus of the Class of 1842 and inventor of baseball, loomed on her left under low clouds in an eerily leaden February sky. Whenever Kate made this trek, she was reminded that every monument and building at West Point was named after some famous military *man*. Sylvanus Thayer, considered "The Father of the Military Academy, had been its superintendent from 1817 to 1833. Colonel Bartlett was a Professor of Natural and Experimental Philosophy from 1836 to 1871. G.W. Cullum was a Major General, Class of 1833. The MacArthur, Eisenhower, Sherman, Lee, and Grant Barracks. The Taylor, Grant, Mahan, Washington and Eisenhower Halls. The eleven major monuments located on and around the Plain. All men. There was one exception—and this one exception lent special significance to Kate's Sunday afternoon excursions. The exception was the eighteen-foot statue in the relief of the USMA library. The statue of the Greek goddess, Athena, the mythological protectress of heroes, the brave, and the valorous. Athena's right arm stretched skyward, her left resting upon her shield, suggested to Kate a goddess who spread globally her supreme wisdom of the industries of peace and the arts of war. Kate knew the helmet in the relief was that of

Pallas, daughter of Triton and Athena's dearest companion—the same helmet emblazoned on West Point's historic coat of arms and cut in stone over the entrance to Thayer Hall. This constituted the sum total of West Point's recognition of woman's role in combat. And all of it was based on pure myth. Kate felt that some recognition of a female role model was better than none; but, deep down, she interpreted all this, rightly or wrongly, as the Academy's derision and mockery of women—a cruel lie perpetrated over the decades since the founding of the Academy in 1802. What military women needed, Kate felt, was for women to prove the accuracy of the Athena model in combat. Kate yearned for the coming of that day.

Proceeding north on Cullum Road, Kate finally arrived at the entrance to the museumlike Cullum Hall, adorned with four stately white Grecian columns and two mammoth black steel doors. The lower floor had a lounge which, in former years, was for the exclusive use of plebes and their visitors. In recent years, the Cadet Hostess maintained her office in the building and it had been open to all cadets and their guests. On really cold Sundays, like this one, she often stopped here at Cullum Hall first to read for a while and to warm up prior to embarking on the ritual Flirty odyssey. It was a wonderfully quiet place to relax. Too staid and mustily historic for most cadets to hang out, it was, for Kate, a unique island of serenity located just far enough from the swirling vortex of cadet life. Kate was hoping that Brad Hunterford would be there that day. He usually was.

With her shoulder, Kate strained to open one of the heavy steel doors, struggling against the vacuum created by a fierce winter wind on the outside and the building's natural draft on the inside. Squeezing through the opening, Kate couldn't keep the door from slamming shut, which startled her red-sashed classmate, Allison Mumford, serving an otherwise sleepy tour of guard duty that day.

"Kate!" said the guard. "I didn't expect to see you here. This place is an absolute ghosttown, today."

0368-COOL

"This is a regular hangout for me on Sundays, Allison," said Kate.

"Well, make yourself at home," Allison said matter-of-factly, refocusing on the textbook she was reading before Kate distracted her. "It's just me, you, the piano player, and some other recluse." Kate could hear Brad's piano music in the background: she recognized the melody as Chopin's *Nocturne in E-flat*. Brad could play anything. Classical pieces, standards, movie themes, jazz. Anything—and he rarely needed sheet music. All from memory. Kate had tried on a past Sunday to stump him with requests for a couple Mozart sonatas, but to her surprise, he knew them and played them flawlessly for her. He was a yearling—a sophomore—who had turned down a scholarship offer from the Juliard School of Music to accept an appointment to West Point. Near the top of his class academically—a "Star Man"—, he was an extremely talented musician who, many thought, had chosen the wrong career path by opting for the military.

Kate looked around the sitting room. Portraits of distinguished and deceased officers of West Point lined the walls. Winners of the Medal of Honor, graduates killed during World War II, former Academy superintendents, permanent professors of the Military Academy, and others ascribed to be the "memorable" members of the "Long Gray Line." Kate thought this gallery to be elitist, but the snobbishness was somewhat offset by plaques, commemorating the more bourgeois grads, hanging on the walls of the second-floor formal ballroom. Inscriptions of famous American battles—Antietam, Cedar Creek, Little Big Horn—could be seen in foot-high letters just beneath the key-cut molding around the ballroom's ceiling. This was the famous ceiling having three hundred forty lights—a number that every Plebe had to know if asked by an upperclassman.

Kate walked toward the concert grand piano and Brad smiled broadly as she approached. He was a nice guy. She often thought it would be neat to get Captain Martin and Brad together at a piano and watch the two artists collaborate and explore each other's talents.

Continuing to play, but more softly, Brad said, "Well, if it isn't my faithful following of one. Gonna try to stump me again, Kate? What will it be? Mozart? Beethoven? Bach? Bachrach?" Brad was always down to earth and friendly. He never let Kate's rank get in the way. Kate liked that about him.

"I'm gonna let you off the hook today, Brad," Kate said returning the smile. I just want to listen and enjoy."

"Well, I'll have an audience of two, for a change. See, over there." Brad nodded his head. "That's my uncle Steve. Please go introduce yourself."

Kate turned around and saw, across the room, a handsome gentleman, gray-haired in his late fifties, sitting in a comfortable sofa and reading.

Kate walked over to him and, holding out her hand, said, "Hello, I'm Kate McKeane—one of your nephew's most ardent fans. Really, he should be a pianist with a symphony orchestra."

The gentleman put his book down on the sofa and stood to greet Kate. "That's very nice of you to say," he said, shaking her hand gently. "I'm Steven Hunterford, Brad's uncle. I'm just here for the weekend."

"Oh? said Kate. "Where are you from?"

"Cambridge . . . ."

"Cambridge, England? Never met anyone from there."

"No, I'm afraid not, Ms. McKeane . . . "

"Please call me Kate."

"Sure, Kate. No, I'm from Cambridge, Massachusetts. I head up the Department of Classical Studies at Harvard University. I've been a tenured faculty member there about twenty-three years. My specific area of study is Greek and Roman mythology."

"Really?" Kate said surprised. "That's an interest of mine, too. I had a course on Greek mythology in high school and loved it. By now, though, I've probably forgotten three-quarters of what I learned."

"Well, that's easy to do. There are so many characters, and the stories are so complex and interconnected. Even after writing eight

books on Greek legends, I still get the characters mixed up sometimes."

"You're just being modest, professor."

"No, not modest, Kate, just *honest*," said the professor. Won't
you sit down and join me for a few minutes?" Teasingly he added,
"I would sure like to find out how a young lady goes about getting
all those stripes on her sleeve."

As they both sat down, Kate grinned and said, "Maybe for a
few minutes, professor, but I can't stay too long. I *would* like to
know more about your work, though. I'm particularly interested
in the story of Pallas Athena. I know a little about her because, as
a plebe, we had to know the origin of West Point's coat of arms.
But I don't know the full story."

"Yes, I noticed the images of Athena and Pallas Athena's helmet in the stonework of the library and Thayer Hall when Brad
and I walked over here this afternoon. I thought that was quite
interesting. I hadn't known before then of the classical Greek influence on the Academy's heraldry."

"I guess what I'm not clear about is why Athena is called Pallas
Athena," said Kate. Brad had since shifted music selections and
was now playing Mozart's *Rondo Alla Turca*, a favorite of Kate's, in
the background. She looked Brad's way, smiled and nodded ap-
preciation.

"That'll be easy," said the professor, "but the more interesting
story is the one about the Palladium. There's still and unsolved
mystery surrounding it."

"The Palladium—isn't that a metal?"

"Yes, actually it is," said the professor chuckling slightly.

"It's a tarnish-resistant metallic element that occurs naturally
with platinum. But that's not the palladium I'm talking about.
The one I'm talking about is a statue—a statue of Pallas Athena,
several thousands of years old."

"Does it still exist?"

"Maybe. In some part of the world. But let me tell you the
entire story, and then you decide."

"As I'm sure you're aware from your plebe year, that according to Greek legend, Athena's warlike attributes were geared more to protectiveness than to aggression."

"Yes," said Kate, "and as I recall, her principal role was the strengthening of the state from within and the civilization of its people. And I think she is said to have invented several things."

"That's right. Athena was quite creative. Supposedly, she invented the plough, the rake, the bridle, numbers, the chariot, and navigation. She also invented the trumpet, the flute, and domestic arts such as weaving. Athena was almost entirely a benevolent goddess and a virgin. She had very few selfish motives, and for the most part was totally ethical. She seldom did anything spiteful, and if someone incurred her wrath and received punishment, he or she usually more than deserved it. It is said that she used disguises to accomplish her ends. She was balanced in the sense that she could perform functions of both warrior and nurturer.

"Wasn't Athena involved some way in the Trojan War, professor?"

"Quite true. The idea for the Greeks using the wooden horse in the Trojan War is attributed to her. She was also instrumental in the demise of Hector, son of Priam—the King of Troy—by impersonating Deiphobus, the brother of Hector, and urging Hector to face Achilles who killed Hector and dragged Hector's body behind his chariot to the ships. Achilles then went . . . "

"Excuse me, professor, but how does Pallas fit into all of this?" Kate interjected.

"Well, that gets us to the topic of the Palladium," responded the professor. A substantial part of the mythology of Athena has to do with the mysterious Palladium, a statue of the goddess. If possessed by a city, the statue supposedly served as a kind of pledge of safety for the place, and therefore it was always kept in a highly secret location to prevent its theft by an enemy. Apparently, the origin of the Palladium, stemmed from the incident in Athena's girlhood in which she accidentally killed her dearest companion, Pallas, daughter of Triton. Athena caused a statue of the girl to be made. Afterward, Athena took on the identity of Pallas and added Pallas' name to her own—Pallas Athena—and the statue came to be her image as well as that of Pallas."

"Does anyone know what the statue looked like—I mean, was it like the statue in the library's relief?" asked Kate.

"Well, actually, the Palladium is described in some accounts. It was said to measure three cubits, about 54 inches, in height. The legs of the female figure are supposedly together; its right hand holds a spear, and its left, a spindle and distaff."

"Professor, you talk about the statue as if it currently exists," said Kate. "Does it? I mean is it in some museum some place?"

"That's where the story gets interesting. According to legend, the Palladium remained at Troy until Odysseus and Diomedes carried it away, though skeptics contend that that statue was a copy. They might have been justified in their beliefs because it is likely that something, like the Palladium, guaranteeing the city's security would have been carefully guarded and would have provided the mold for numerous decoys. Various stories emerged about the real Palladium's eventual resting place. After Troy, Athens and Argos claimed it, as did Rome, Lavinium, Luceria, and Siris. Aeneas, a prince of Troy whose descendants eventually founded Rome, was said to have brought the real Palladium from Troy to Italy.

"So is the Palladium in Italy?"

"No, it's not quite that simple. Experts now believe that the original Palladium is somewhere in South America."

" Why South America?"

"A quirk of history. Recently discovered documents of the Spanish royalty reveal that Columbus' voyage wasn't funded out of the goodness of Queen Isabella's heart. Columbus had to put up collateral. And that apparently consisted of a solid gold statue of a Greek goddess, believed to be the original Pallas Athena."

"But how did it get to South America?" Kate asked.

"That happened some years later, in 1546, during the reign of Charles the First, King of Spain. The Spanish conquistador, Francisco de Orellana, returned to Spain in 1842, after assisting Pizarro in an Ecuadorean expedition. He told stories of being separated from Pizarro, navigating what is now called the Amazon River, and finding a band of female Indian warriors, which he called the Amazons after the Greek legend in an area that is now a small portion of southeastern Colombia, bounded by Brazil and Peru.

"Didn't the Amazons, in Greek legend, fight on the side of the Trojans during the Trojan War," asked Kate.

"Yes," said the professor, "and they are said to have had the unusual custom of removing their right breasts in order to handle a bow more easily. In fact, the ancient Greek translation of the word "amazon" was "without breast". But, I guess that's neither here nor there."

"So what happened after Orellana got back to Spain?"

"Charles the First was so intrigued by Orellana's story that he granted Orellana a governorship in South America of what was to be called New Andalusia and commissioned him to found towns and colonize along the Amazon's right bank. Those recently discovered documents I mentioned seemingly imply that Charles also presented Orellana with the golden statue of Pallas Athena as the symbol of values around which the new colony was built and by which it would be protected."

"And where is New Andalusia today?" Kate inquired.

"Well, really nowhere. When Orellana's expedition arrived at the Amazon's Delta, the main channel could not be found. Eventually, Orellana's party disintegrated and he died, soon after, of illness and grief."

"And the Palladium? What happened to it?"

"No one knows. There are many Latin American fables concerning the mystery of its whereabouts. It's believed to be somewhere in South America. Some say Brazil; some say Ecuador; and still others say Colombia. But no one really knows, except the person possessing it. And, then again, maybe no one possesses it."

"Why is that?"

"Because if the legend is true, possessing it would be very dangerous. In ancient times, to touch the statue was forbidden. It is said that

Ilus, King of Troy, once rushed in to rescue the statue during a fire, and was struck temporarily blind. So it's not something you'd want to display in your TV room and dust occasionally."

"And I suppose it's very valuable."

"Very, very valuable. Its historic significance makes it worth millions, and then the fact that it is solid, untarnishable gold— well, you get the picture."

Brad was now playing Bachrach's "What the World Needs Now Is Love Sweet Love" and smiling a mischievous smile.

"That's my cue to get movin'," said Kate to the professor. "Brad's completed the musical circle." Standing up and shaking the professor's hand, she continued, "It's really been great visiting with you, professor, and I hope you enjoy the rest of your stay at West Point. Thanks for the crash course in mythology."

"It was my pleasure, Kate." replied the professor. "You still owe me a story about how a young lady gets all those stripes on her arm."

"I'll send you a copy of it when it appears in the *New York Times*," Kate replied with a wink.

Kate waved goodbye to Brad, gave a thumbs-up to Allison as she passed by, and, after struggling momentarily to open the huge steel door, thrust herself outside in the cold air once again. The wind had died down considerably.

Kate made her way down the steep embankment just north of Cullum Hall, avoiding slippery splotches of snow, to arrive at the famous pathway of flirtation. Putting on her Walkman headphones, she began listening to a Mozart symphony. She first passed by a little sheltered plateau below Cullum Hall called Kosciuszko's Garden, an unassuming rock garden constructed by the Polish patriot during moments of recreation when assigned to oversee the erection of the original fortifications of West Point in 1778. Proceeding on her walk, Kate encountered other points of histori- cal significance—the site of the old Chain Battery, where the chain stretched across the Hudson River during the Revolutionary War was anchored—the lighthouse at Gee's Point near the site of the Lantern Battery—a view of Constitution Island in the middle of the Hudson which had been integrated into the defense of West Point during that war.

When she reached Kissing Rock—a enormous moss-covered overhanging boulder—Kate paused for awhile and sought shelter from the cold under its cantilevered mantle. She then pulled from her pocket the envelope containing the letter she received from Robert on the previous day. As usual, Kate sniffed the envelope briefly before she opened it, enjoying the subtle vestiges of fragrance of Robert's aftershave lotion. It always gave her a slight high and had the added benefit of seemingly injecting some humanness and warmth to Robert's oversized penmanship and haughty, stilted writing style. The letter began:

> *My Dearest Kathryn,*
>
> *I hope this epistle finds you happy and in good health.*
>
> *I can't wait till I see you in next month in Alexandria—the perfect place for me to rendezvous with a modern-day Greek goddess. My parents are looking forward to meeting you with great anticipation. They've planned all sorts of activities and a couple of parties for us. They seem to want to really "show you off." I told them we're getting a little serious—hope you don't mind. My mom wants to share with you some of her famous family cooking recipes.*
>
> *Be prepared! It wouldn't be a good idea to mention that you want to be an infantry officer someday. My parents are quite conservative and that wouldn't fly too well with them. I'll write again soon, sweetheart. Till then, be assured that I continue you to love you with all my heart.*
>
> *Affectionately,*
> *Robert*
>
> *P.S. Thought you might be interested to know that part of the time we will be spending together coincides with*

*Quinquatrus, the March 19-23 festival of the Roman
goddess, Minerva.*

Kate folded the letter and put it back into her pocket, stunned
by its presumptuousness. "Affectatiously" would have been a much
more accurate closing. She was incensed that Robert had *presumed*
she wanted to spend most of the weekend in the company of his
parents. Not only that, but he had also *presumed* that it was okay
to tell them that she and Robert were "serious". Kate wasn't sure
whether she was serious about Robert. She liked him, but getting
married to him had never even crossed her mind—not right away
anyhow. Recipes? Cripes! Can't mention the infantry? Bullfeathers!
And what was all this stuff about her being some kind of goddess?
Could it be that Robert was on some kind of enfatuation trip? She
didn't like the sound of this at all. He was coming on way too
strong. This was all happening way too fast.

Kate continued her walk along Flirty, her anger building with
each step, and she eventually arrived at Trophy Point. She walked
up the low stone steps to Battle Monument and read the inscription at its base, "to the *men and officers* of the Regular Army killed
in the Civil War." She then looked up to the top of the memorial
to see the winged statue representing "Fame" standing on top of
the column, and she recalled the words of General MacArthur's
1962 Farewell Address to the Academy which she memorized as a
plebe: Duty, honor, country "create in your heart the sense of
wonder, the unfailing hope of what next, and the joy and inspiration of life. They teach you in this way to be an *officer and a
gentleman*." Leaving the monument and walking south on Thayer
Road toward Eisenhower Barracks she looked to her left across
Doubleday Field to behold the library and the imposing statue of
Athena. It was in this image, and this image alone, that Kate sensed
the "unfailing hope of what next."

2

Alexandria Virginia is an historic city located across the Potomac River, slightly south of the center of Washington D.C. In the 1740s, a group of English and Scottish merchants established a tobacco warehouse there, and by seventeen years later the tiny settlement was a prospering commercial center. It was then that the surveyor John West, Jr., and his young assistant, George Washington, planned streets and eighty-four-acre lots in this settlement soon to become known as Alexandria. Men of noble lineage erected handsome townhouses on the lots and they soon brought a lively and cosmopolitan air to the city with their Federal architecture, parties, balls, and horse racing. George Washington eventually located his home at Mount Vernon, about nine miles south of Alexandria and just a few miles east of what is now Fort Belvoir, Virginia, the home of the Army's Engineer Corps. Not forty miles southwest from Alexandria is the town of Fredericksburg, where four major Civil War engagements—the heaviest most concentrated military fighting ever seen on this continent—were fought between December, 1862 and May, 1864. Because Alexandria had been safely behind Union lines and even occupied by Union forces, it escaped the devastation which befell many Southern towns like Fredericksburg. Kate was looking forward to soaking up some of this history during her visit with Robert and his parents over spring leave. She also was looking forward to being with her father for a few hours on Sunday afternoon before returning to West Point. He had invited her to be with him at a combined-services Pentagon reception for top-level officers on the President's yacht for the first sailing of the season.

Kate arrived at Dulles airport in D.C. on Saturday afternoon and Robert was at the gate area to greet her. After a warm embrace, Robert asked Kate for her airline ticket and handed it to a young man in a burgundy sportcoat and gray pants. He then whisked Kate off to his family's waiting limousine. "Don't worry about your luggage," he said. "My dad's personal valet will fetch it from the carousel and bring it by the house later."

Conversation on the way to the Holcrofts centered mostly on
Kate's father. Robert wanted to know all about his years at West
Point, his assignments, how he moved up the ranks, his political
connections, his present ambitions. Kate had trouble answering
many of his questions. The fact was that she really didn't know her
father very well. Robert naturally felt that Kate was being evasive,
coy, maybe even protective. Nonetheless he kept pressing her for
information. While they spoke, Kate looked past Robert out the
car window and her eye caught the image of a stately chateau,
with four stone chimneys, standing on a grassy knoll surrounded
by a low stone wall and tall pine trees.

"Gosh, that's a beautiful estate," said Kate.

"Keep your eye on it, Kate, said Robert. "That's where we're
headed. That's home."

Soon the limousine rolled up and stopped in front of the French
country manor, and three servants were there to greet them. Robert hopped out of the back of the limo and said to a tuxedoed
gentlemen, "Bentley, please announce our arrival." The gentleman
went inside the manor. Kate stood in awe of the two chateaulike
coach houses on either side of the main manor and the glass-roofed
plant conservatory encircled by the driveway.

Pointing to the conservatory, Robert said, "I hope you like
plants, Kate. My mom's nuts about 'em. Gets in flower competi-
tions, that sort of thing. My dad just humors her. And over there,"
Robert continued, pointing to a quaint outbuilding with a gasoline pump beside it, "that's all that interests my father. Oil. Oil
and oil companies. He owns one." Kate didn't respond. She just
looked around, trying to absorb it all.

Kate's first meeting with Robert's parents in their lavish Louis
XIV style parlor was tense and awkward. Although Roberts' parents were cordial enough, Kate sensed that they weren't altogether
pleased that Robert had chosen to bring someone home who was
other than a blueblood; who was, perhaps, a boorish outsider. At
times, she wished she were on a tour of Fort Belvoir rather than
sharing time with the Holcrofts. Unlike Robert, they were not at

all impressed that Kate's father was a general. Even though Mrs. Holcroft was a Delafield, surprisingly, she was not enthralled with her family's military lineage. She had married into money—oil money—and preferred to forget her family ties to the military. The military, to the Holcrofts, was riffraff, and they did not completely understand, nor approve of, Robert's participating in ROTC. They hoped he would grow out of it.

While Robert chatted with his father about fox hunting, Robert's mother grilled Kate about genealogy. Apparently, Robert's mother not only liked flowers, she also was enthralled with trees - family trees. She could trace Mr. Holcroft's back to the pilgrims who landed at Plymouth Rock. Kate had to admit that she was third generation Irish, her great-grandparents having fled Ireland during the great potato famine. Not exactly landed gentry, Mrs. Holcroft concluded.

It wasn't that the Holcrofts didn't go out of their way to show Kate and Robert a good time. They did. The grand reception held in their home in Robert and Kate's honor; the night at the ballet; the tour of Mount Vernon; the trip to the Smithsonian; even the sharing of the Holcrofts' traditional recipes. The Holcrofts orchestrated all of this. But Kate knew they didn't have their hearts in it.

Everything came to a head on the evening before Robert and Kate were to leave. At dinner with Robert and his parents that evening in their formal dining room, Kate mentioned, rather offhandedly, that women should have a role in ground combat. Mrs. Holcroft became volcanic, saying things like "her grandchildren would never have a mother who'd leave them to go kill people," and "mothers and marauding don't mix." Mr. Holcroft was less impassioned, but it was clear that he didn't approve of the idea either. Robert remained silent, leaving Kate to fight her own battles. That, Kate resented.

At breakfast the next morning, the Holcrofts were civil to Kate, but not warm and friendly. She spent the rest of the morning walking around the grounds with Robert talking about everything except their future together. Robert tried to talk about graduation a couple times, but Kate immediately changed the subject. Shortly after noon, the valet put Robert's and Kate's luggage in the limousine and took off for the airport to drop off Robert. The driver was to drop Kate by the President's yacht afterward. The Holcrofts had waved goodbye. But no one shed any tears.

3

After dropping Robert off at the airport, the Holcrofts' limousine returned to Alexandria with Kate as its only passenger. As she rode alone, her thoughts turned to her father whom she would be seeing in a very few minutes. General McKeane had been an army brat and had lived all over the world. His father, now deceased, had worked his way up from private to sergeant major, and was assigned to the Pentagon in Washington D.C. as the senior enlisted noncommissioned officer for the joint chiefs of staff when he retired. His mother had been a doting army wife, of another generation, who unquestioningly did whatever her husband and the army told her to do. General McKeane's parents had moved twenty-seven times throughout his father's military career and they were proud of it. They really never had roots anywhere, and neither did General McKeane. That may explain why General McKeane took all his hardship tours and absences from his family in stride. It may also explain why he expected that his family should accept his absences as part of the military culture. Whatever the reasons, Kate was conflicted over her father's success in the military and her desire to know him better.

Kate remembered one occasion when her father visited her after her mother died. It was right before Christmas. He came to the Divine Hope school to see her, and at the request of one of the nuns, he gave a short talk to her class about the military. She could never forget how he stood next to the Christmas tree in the classroom, and using several of the tree ornaments as props, described in excruciating detail several of the major battles he fought in while assigned to an infantry company in South Vietnam.

He just didn't get it. He didn't realize how embarrassing it was for Kate to hear her father tell gruesome war stories to a classroom full of her girlfriends. Not only that, but he did this while standing next to baby Jesus in a manger scene and under a large sign above the blackboard which read "Peace on Earth to Men of Good Will." He was simply oblivious—wholly insensitive—to peoples' feelings, to relationships, to situations. All that was important to him was the military and all its trappings.

Eventually, the Holcrofts' limousine pulled onto a street which paralleled and rose above the level of the Alexandria city wharf. Kate looked out the window and was spellbound. The President's yacht—*The Phoenix*—was not the Chris Craft motorized launch she had imagined, but rather it approached the scale of a small ocean-going liner. It seemed so vast, so majestic. Multitiered, with extensive deck areas in staggered iteration on each level, the vessel was a paradigm of the geometrician's art. Numerous shiny brass portholes formed a fashionable necklace around the ship's hull, while gossamer fingers of milk-white smoke curled capriciously skyward from the centered blue stack. A bird-shaped swimming pool located aft, in front of a helicopter landing platform, grayish marble in color, conveyed the distinct impression of the legendary phoenix rising from its own ashes. The yacht's towering size and the long line of uniformed people and their guests moving up the articulated gangplank in spurts were indications that the vessel could easily handle a reception of two hundred people.

Kate, dressed in a chic navy blue suit and heels, got out of the limo, thanked the driver, and walked toward the gangplank. Her dad had asked her to be in uniform. She thought that too embarrassing. Too many questions. Too much hullaballoo. Too many sotto voce judgments. Kate didn't need any more of that. She looked around for her father, but didn't see him. Maybe he was already aboard.

As the line moved up the gangplank toward the head of the receiving line, she conversed with a marine colonel and his wife trying all the while to keep her identity secret. Too much to explain. Finally she reached the receiving line. And there he was. In the flesh. Her nemesis. General Winterfield, the Army Chief of Staff, shaking hands, smiling, and mechanically passing each shaken hand off to the next dignitary in line. When the general's aide asked her name, Kate impulsively said "Kathryn Galway", using her mother's surname. When her name was announced and Kate and Winterfield came face to face, the General said, quizzically, "You look very familiar, my dear. Have we met somewhere before?" Kate said something to the effect that it might have been in Washington and then, smiling, moved quickly to shake the next hand in line. The General's eyes trailed her and glazed over as if his memory were working overtime.

Kate walked around the vessel for awhile, trying to spot her father and avoiding conversations with the guests, except to say hello and to smile shyly. Seemingly from nowhere erupted a loud clattering, drowning out the clusters of conversation on the deck and causing guests to look toward the rear of the ship. The President's helicopter was preparing to land. Kate watched as the chopper hovered like a dragonfly at a pond's edge, gauging the appropriate moment to drop onto a lily pad. Within seconds the whirring craft sat down on the helipad, the rotors slowing to a stop. Several Marine Corps captains helped the chopper's passengers step down to the pad and then onto the rear deck of the yacht, while a small Marine Corps drum and bugle ensemble played "Hail to the Chief". Kate watched as President Benton and his wife paraded the top-deck amid swarms of high-ranking subordinates executing their sharpest salutes. Two blasts of a foghorn, and the vessel shoved off, quickly making its way to the center of the Potomac. Gulls trailed for a short time and faded away as the yacht picked up speed.

Dead set on getting a closer look at the President, Kate inconspicuously maneuvered herself into his amoeba-like entourage. With the intense military presence, only two secret service agents accompanied the President, and Kate soon found herself swept inside the ship's dining room along with the undulating, chatty crowd. Like uniformed vultures, paunchy colonels escorting stocky red-faced spouses, encircled the two long tables resplendent with intricate ice carvings and sumptuous foods. Soft bossa nova rhythms backdropped haunting Jobim melodies as a small army of cocktail waitresses, in French maid garb, insinuated the buzzing throng offering fluted glassfuls of French champagne. Kate took a glass of champagne and politely negotiated through arms and elbows toward the small circle now forming around President and Mrs. Benton.

Almost in earshot of the President's clique, Kate stopped abruptly.

"Cadet McKeane!" Kate heard someone say from behind. "Aren't you Cadet McKeane?"

Kate turned around slowly, crushed that her cover had been blown. A middle-aged woman with a glass of champagne in one hand, smiled approvingly and held out her hand to Kate. "Remember me?"

"Representative Grant!" Kate yelped, clasping her hand and trying to appear under control.

"Look, Marlin," the Congresswoman said, tapping the back of the blue-uniformed gentleman standing near her. "It's Cadet McKeane."

The gentleman turned around and looked at Kate. . . . "McKeane? I thought it was Galway," Winterfield said. "I never forget a pretty name."

Blushing, Kate said the first thing that came to her mind. "The name belongs to my mother; I just borrow it on special occasions." She quickly added, "I didn't expect to see you two being so nice to each other."

"Oh, you mean that Congressional hearing stuff," said the General. "How we behave for public consumption is quite different from how we behave privately. Actually, Representative Grant is a superb bridge player. Believe me. I know from experience. Loves the intellectual combat." Smiling, the general excused himself and turned back to his cluster.

"Oh, Marlin's just putting me on," said Esther motioning for a waitress to fill her champagne glass. "He's one of the best bridge players around. But I have to admit, it's fun to beat the generals once in awhile." Her tight grin fading to seriousness, she asked, "And what's happening with you these days? I saw your father briefly in the Captain's guest lounge a while ago. He didn't mention that you were going to be here."

"Maybe he thought I didn't show up. He's expecting me to be in uniform. I thought I'd surprise him in civvies."

"Good luck. From what I know, he doesn't take to surprises too well. . . . Have you heard what's happening with the Experiment? The Minerva thing?"

"Not really. Not the details, anyway," replied Kate.

Moving closer to Kate, Esther whispered, "It'll be Throckmiller. Marlin will be disappointed. He wants some sexist machoman. I have the fix in at the highest levels. Marlin doesn't know it. Throckmiller will command the operation. Just remember, you heard it here first. You're bound to secrecy, young lady, until then."

"Yes ma'am. Bound to secrecy," Kate whispered back.

"The army's going to need a name for the overall operation," said Esther. "Any ideas?"

Kate thought for a moment. "How about `Operation Athena?'"

"Has a nice ring," said Esther. "I'll make sure it gets on the list. Oh, by the way, I'm going to be at West Point for your graduation ceremony," said Esther. The President wants some female involvement there. Real smart man. I want to get a picture of you and your Dad with that diploma. Don't let me forget."

"I'll try not to."

"I must circulate a bit," said Esther touching Kate's hand. "Ta, ta."

Kate spoke to a few of the officers' wives for a while and President-watched. Then she went searching for her father again. She finally spotted him across the mid-deck, in dress blues with a chest full of medals. He was gesturing animatedly to a group of about six people, obviously in the midst of telling one of his famous Irish jokes. He was a master of brogue and blarney, attributes of charm that were in part responsible for his meteoric rise through the ranks. As she approached, she could hear him delivering a well timed punch line, " . . . and when the jury acquitted O'Riley of bank robbery, he jumped right up and asked the judge, `well noo, yure honor, does thut mean I con keep the mooney?'" The small audience laughed uproariously, as much at the naive expression on the general's face as at his words. Before the laughter had completely subsided, Kate put her hand on her father's elbow. When he turned around, she said with unmistakable directness, "Dad I need to talk to you. It's getting late. . . . The ship will dock in twenty minutes. I have to talk to you . . . in private."

General McKeane reacted immediately, politely excusing himself and his daughter from the cluster of rapt guests, which, after their departure, quickly disintegrated into dyads of conversation.

As the pair walked along the deck, the general, looking straight ahead; said to Kate tensely, "What's so important this instant that you feel compelled to tear me away from my colleagues? And why are you dressed in civvies? You're a West Point soldier not an Ivy League coed."

Kate, astounded by this reaction, replied, "Dad, I haven't seen you in six months. Why didn't you search me out in this crowd? The least you can do is give me a few minutes of your time." Then raising her voice angrily, she added, "Well, then again, why should I expect more? You haven't given me more than a few minutes of your time in the last twenty years."

An admiral, dressed in a white uniform and gold shoulderboards, his spouse on his arm, passed by and looked back when they heard Kate's last comment.

"Control yourself, young lady," said the general still looking straight ahead and speaking tightlipped. "Remember, *you* chose the military path. I didn't force you. You've got to be able to make it on your own. When you're in the military, there's not a lot of time for pampering."

"Pampering! Dad, I don't want pampering!" Kate rasped. "How

could you say such a thing?"

"How are your grades this semester?" the general asked, attempting to change the subject and to quiet her.

"Good, they're good. But, Dad, pampering is not the question. I just want you to take some interest in me as a person," Kate said escalating her voice level.

Another couple passed them, and looked back frowning.

"Here we are," said the general, attempting to sound matter-of-fact to passers-by, as he opened a door for Kate. "Here's the Captain's guest lounge. We can talk here for awhile."

After they entered, the general motioned for Kate to sit down on the cushioned sofa and he sat next to her. "Now, young lady," he said. "You're unusually uptight. What's the problem?"

Kate felt the need to back into the real topic. "Robert is part of it. I've decided this weekend to dump him."

"Dump him? From your letters, I gathered you two were an item."

"That's before I realized how selfishly ambitious he is."

"How so?"

"He doesn't want me for me. He wants me for what our contacts can get him. Tina was right about that. It just took me a lot longer to see his true colors. And his parents. They're absolute snobs. I just can't stand them."

"So, how are you going to break the news to him? He'll probably want to come to your graduation, won't he?"

"I've already done it."

"You don't waste time, do you?"

"We had a heart-to-heart on the way to the airport in the back of his parents' limousine. He seemed totally surprised and shattered. He asked me to think about it some more."

"Will you?"

"No, it's over. It can't be fixed. But that's not my real purpose in wanting to talk to you."

"Then what is?"

"Something you mentioned before."

"What?"

"Who's coming to graduation."

"What do you mean?"

"*Karen*, Dad. That's what I mean. I don't want Karen at my graduation."

"But she's your sister—your only sister. And she's begged me to let her come. As a father, how can I tell her no?"

"It's *my* graduation. Not yours. And certainly not hers!"

"What does that have to do with it?"

"Why do you even care if she comes or not, Dad? You've never cared much about her before. One or two visits a year. Why the big change of heart now when I'm graduating."

"She'll feel hurt if she can't come."

"I'll be super-embarrassed if she *does* come. What if she does something really inappropriate? What if she goes off her medication and behaves psychotically? Will we hospitalize her in the middle of my graduation?"

"Well, I guess . . . "

"And her weight, Dad. Her weight. The press will be there taking pictures of the lady brigade commander and her family. I can see the caption now on the front page of the *New York Times*, 'The general, the cadet first captain, and . . . . . .' You fill in the blank. Get the picture, Dad?"

"Yes, Kate, I get the picture. But it doesn't bother me. You spoke of Robert being selfish awhile ago. But doesn't that label fit you equally? Karen is your sister. You owe it to her."

"I owe her nothing, Dad. But *you* do. You're the one who left her down there in St. Louis with those perverted nuns."

"Kate! Stop it! You shouldn't talk like that."

The yacht's horn sounded. The vessel had docked and the gangplank was being lowered.

"I must leave, Kate. Must say good-bye to my colleagues."

"I'll think about what you said. But I can't promise anything."

Reaching into his pants pocket, he pulled out a twenty dollar bill and handed it to Kate. "Here's cab fare to the airport." Kissing

Kate lightly on the cheek, he added, "Think about what I said—about being selfish."

"I will, Dad. . . . I will."

HARD BARGAINING

Emilio flashed his U.S. State Department credentials toward the security guards and walked stridently up the circular drive toward the West Wing of the White House that Wednesday morning, a saddlebag brief case in one hand and a long black umbrella in the other. D.C. in April—cherry blossoms and birdsongs, the perennial spring backdrop for Congressional wrangling amidst a witch's cauldron of unpredictable weather. Weather much like the Colombian Andes. Predictably unpredictable—a familiar climate in which Emilio thrived. Emilio . . . and his umbrella.

Damned tired. Any man would be. Spending the night "fucking Lila's brains out". Insatiable. That was Lila. He wondered how she survived when he wasn't there. He was kidding himself. He knew, but he was in denial. She fucked everybody. But all he could think of was the way she was purring when he left her an hour before.

On the previous afternoon, Emilio had received an urgent call from a Presidential staffer to attend an emergency White House meeting. The meeting concerned South America, and the staffer thought that Emilio's knowledge of the intricate military structure of various South American governments would add a helpful dimension to the discussion. No question, South America was a hotbed of conflict. Just a month previously, Peruvian President Furomonte reported that two Russian-built Peruvian Sukois war planes and an American-built A-37 fighter were shot down by Ecuadorean anti-aircraft fire in a seventeen-day skirmish over a disputed border zone. The dispute was over territory along an unmarked forty-eight-mile stretch of the one-thousand-mile border set by the 1942 Rio de Janeiro Protocol. Thirty-six Peruvians had been reported killed in the recent border dispute, and sixty others were wounded. Ecuadorean casualties were estimated to be much higher. Prior to working for the State Department of his native Colombia, Emilio had spent time in the State Departments of both Peru and Ecuador as a research fellow in the early years of his diplomatic career. He wasn't sure whether the meeting this morning concerned these recent Peru-Ecuadorean skirmishes or not. Just a guess.

Everyone was already there when Emilio arrived at nine a.m. sharp in the large conference room off the Oval Office. To Emilio, the room looked more like a formal dining room than a conference room. In the center of a seemingly endless expanse of shiny hardwood floors was a ten-by-twenty-foot square Oriental rug, deep red and navy blue in color, with a highly intricate patterned border. Centered on the rug under a tiered crystal chandelier, ornamented with twenty-five tall electrified candles, was a long wooden banquet table which could accommodate ten people comfortably. The chairs barely fit on the Oriental rug when people sat around the table. President Benton sat at the head of the banquet table with his back to a fireplace that had a five-foot high cream-colored wood mantle. On top of the mantle stood a large golden statue of a seated Minerva with a small clock embedded in the shield on which her arm was resting. The "Minerva Clock" was one of several ordered from France in 1817 by President James Monroe who required that all statues in the White House be fully clothed. At each end of the mantle were matching candalabras. On either side of the fireplace stood a credenza with two-foot-high Oriental vases. Three-foot-high, gold-bordered oval mirrors adorned the walls over each credenza.

Amid the chatter of seated dignitaries, Emilio approached the one empty chair at the far left end of the table from President Benton, and stood behind it sheepishly, hoping the chair count had been accurate. The last thing Emilio wanted was to be conspicuous.

"Right on the button," President Benton said to Chester

Trumble, First Deputy Secretary of State, sitting immediately to his left.

"Mr. President?" replied Trumble, not understanding what Benton was referring to.

"Your assistant—He's right on time. Now we can get started."

"Oh yes, Emilio—Emilio Gutierrez. He's quite dependable, Mr. President," Trumble said, beaming.

"Won't you sit down and join us Emilio?" Benton said motioning to the empty chair on the left side of the opposite end of the table.

"Thank you, Mr. President," Emilio said, scooting out the chair and placing his briefcase and umbrella on the floor beside it. He sat down and finally looked around the table. Emilio was shocked to see who was sitting on the opposite side of the table immediately to the right of the President. Why hadn't he been told? How could he have not known? Esteban Guardina. The President of Colombia. It was Emilio's business to know. It must have been a top-top-secret visit. If he had been around the office more and not romancing Lila so much, maybe he would have known. So be it. He was at this meeting. That's what counted. Raoul would be proud of him.

Guardina stared at Emilio as if looking straight through him. No gesture; coldly, with no emotion. He then continued conversing with President Benton. Guardina appeared to have aged noticeably beyond his seventy years since Emilio had last seen him in Bogotá at a State Department meeting the previous summer. He looked tired and haggard. He gave the appearance of an old man who was succumbing to the pressures of years of political and personal strife. No wonder. Guardina for years had been wedged between his desire for a democratic government, the desires of others for a dictatorship, and the voracious appetite of the drug lords for boundless power. Deep down, Guardina knew that true democracy in Colombia was an elusive goal.

For literally decades, the Colombian government had endured the stresses of left-wing guerrilla forces on the one hand, and the right-wing drug lords on the other. For the most part, these left-wing and right-wing factions were bitter enemies. The guerrillas—the Revolutionary Armed Forces of Colombia (FARC), the National Liberation Army (ELN), the Popular Liberation Army (EPL), and M-19 rebels—had staged a thirty-year struggle, fueled by a Marxist ideology which was responsible for killing over seventy thousand people and for forcing one hundred fifty thousand more to move from violence-riddled regions. The guerrillas supported themselves through extortions and kidnappings, flitting through the jungles with near-impunity and occasionally aligning themselves whenever convenient with the nation's more notorious drug traffickers. More often, however, the drug lords financed right-wing death squads to murder suspected guerrillas and their followers.

While the Colombian government was absorbed in its war against the Medellín cartel and other drug barons, the guerrilla groups pressed their seemingly endless conflict by destroying more than a million barrels of oil and continually blowing up pipelines, power stations, and refineries. Eventually, however, the guerrilla groups were no longer caught up in schemes to change the state. What they came to want was legitimized power—more equal distribution of wealth, economically and politically. They seemed willing to do anything to get it. In 1980, the notorious M-19 rebels took over the Embassy of the Dominican Republic and held twenty diplomats hostage, including the U.S. Ambassador, for two months. Five years later, M-19 guerrillas stormed the Palace of Justice in Bogotá and held it during a two-day battle. When the dust cleared, one hundred five people were dead, including eleven Supreme Court Justices. Shortly after that, the drug lords—prodded on by Raoul Bodega—attempted to take advantage of the shell-shocked Colombian Government by stepping up their own terrorist efforts. In December 1989, Pedro Gonzalo, a leading member of the Medellín cartel, was killed in an encounter with government security forces. Violence again escalated.

In February 1990, at Cartagena, the Presidents of Colombia,

Peru, Bolivia, and the United States entered into a joint strategy on drug control. This milestone quickly crumbled in importance with the assassination in March and April, respectively, of Felipe Santiago, the presidential candidate of Union Patriotica (UP, the political wing of FARC) and Tomás Pintero, the M-19 candidate. Telephone transmissions intercepted by government forces indicated that Raoul Bodega had masterminded both assassinations. Guardina was first elected to the presidency in May 1992, gaining forty-seven percent of the vote. The M-19 candidate and Bodega-sympathizer, Paulo Salceda, polled thirteen percent to earn an unexpected third place in the election.

On assuming office, Guardina pledged to the Colombian people that he would not rest until he had "surgically removed Bodega and the insidious narco-cancer he has inflicted on this country." But even so, Guardina still looked the other way. He knew that many of Colombia's police were on the Bodegas' payroll, but he did nothing about it. The drug cartels had also used more than a hundred American companies to launder in excess of three billion in cash a year. The last thing Guardina wanted to do was interfere with the U.S. corporate presence in Colombia. He accepted the situation as business as usual. He also knew that the Catholic Church was involved in a massive drug money-laundering network. But the Catholic Church was off limits. Questioning the Church's authority could produce a widespread popular backlash against the government. He wanted assistance from the United States, but he didn't want to become dependent upon the gringos. He would accept the gringos' technology and military weaponry. But he didn't want them—especially the military—on his soil. They'd take over—just like in Vietnam. CIA power meddlers had already orchestrated a condition of chronic imbalance in the Colombian governmental structure. The U.S. was not to be trusted. Undeniably, Guardina was living a life of conflicted feelings, multiple personalities, and appeasing lies. Yes, he was old beyond his years.

Emilio continued to survey the attendees. On the opposite

side of the table, next to President Guardina, sat General Winterfield, the Army Chief of Staff, and next to him, Colonel James Miller, the Pentagon's expert on SIXCOM, the Army's Central and South American Command. Senator John Carrington, a moderate Republican from Utah and member of the Senate Armed Services Committee sat directly across from Emilio. To Emilio's immediate right was Congresswoman Esther Grant. Between Esther and Trumble—Emilio's boss—was Vincent Federhoff, the national drug czar. Senator Carrington nodded a good morning to Emilio and smiled. Emilio returned the gesture.

President Benton said, "Good morning, everyone" and all eyes shifted toward him. "My house staff will be serving rolls and coffee in a few minutes, but I thought we'd get an early start out of respect for all your busy schedules."

"Yeah—my city tour starts at ten-thirty," quipped Guardina. Smiling, Benton continued. "This meeting has been arranged on short notice at the request of our good friend, President Guardina of Colombia. Since he can best explain his position, I think I'll turn the meeting directly over to him."

"Thank you, President Benton," said Guardina. "It was so gracious of all of you to accept President Benton's invitation to attend this breakfast meeting. I'll get right to the point. The people of Colombia are in dire straits. In recent months, several of our oil refineries have burned and two of our major electrical power generating stations have been incapacitated by a devastating earthquake. Water supplies are also being threatened. We have an enormous need for U.S. technology grants, construction materials, and equipment. We also need military arms and armaments of all types to equip our governmental police in securing the construction projects, during and after the actual building takes place. We would consider all this a loan and we . . . "

"Excuse me, President Guardina," said Trumble, "but this seems like a familiar refrain. Didn't the U.S. give literally a barnful of similar aid to Colombia just two years ago?"

"Two years ago?"

"Yes, sir," replied Trumble in an irritated tone. "Emilio," Trumble said looking toward the end of the table, "pass me my Colombia portfolio."

All eyes shifted to Emilio as he reached down with his left hand, flipping open the flap on his briefcase and pulling out a thick portfolio as quickly as he could. Emilio heard something plop on the floor. He ignored it and passed the thick folder immediately to Esther, who in turn passed it to Federhoff, and then to Trumble. Emilio saw Esther looking toward him with raised eyebrows as if to peer over his shoulder to see what might have fallen. She couldn't see anything, but she felt certain something hit the floor. Emilio waited until Esther was again looking toward Trumble, then turned his head slightly to the left so that his peripheral vision could behold the object which had escaped from his briefcase. He saw it. A clear plastic bag of coke. Lila must've stuffed it in his briefcase before he left. There it was—in all its fuckin' splendor on the shiny hardwood floor a foot behind his chair. Talk about fuckin' conspicuous. He had to stay cool.

While Emilio had his head turned toward the little bag, Esther caught a glimpse of it too, but said nothing. She knew exactly what it was, exactly. She would file this happening away. It could be worth a lot to her.

Just then, over Carrington's shoulder, Emilio saw a male waiter thrust open a swinging door from the kitchen area and walk singlemindedly toward Emilio's end of the table carrying in each hand a doilied, sterling silver tray stacked with sweet rolls. The waiter sat one tray down at Emilio's end and then walked behind Emilio's chair with the other tray, eventually arriving at the President's end of the table. He sat the second tray down and went around the table on the side opposite Emilio and strutted back to the kitchen. Emilio looked to his left again to catch a glimpse of the plastic bag. The bag was gone! Emilio panicked. Coffee was coming any minute.

Trumble was droning away in the background, reading out loud from the Colombia portfolio the details of the millions of dollars in economic and military aid the U.S. had given to that country over the past few years. Emilio quietly slid his chair backward and crossed one leg over the other as if to get more comfortable. He looked along the floor to his right. There the bag was, still intact, behind Federhoff, the drug czar. The waiter must have kicked it along the floor without noticing it. He heard Guardina acknowledge receiving the U.S. aid, but contending that the money and equipment had been used to fight the war against the drug lords. Trumble countered with facts and figures showing that over the past two years the flow of cocaine and heroin into the United States from Colombia had increased, not decreased.

While Guardina was for the moment holding everyone's attention, Emilio, his eyes fixed in Guardina's direction, slid down in his chair, reached down with his right hand and began feeling around for his umbrella. Grasping the pointed end, he slowly swung the curved wooden handle of the umbrella and thrust its long slender stalk as far as he could behind Esther's chair. Too short. Two fucking inches too short. Emilio looked back toward Carrington who was still intently watching Guardina and trying desperately to understand his broken English. With dismay, Emilio noticed the waiter back-butting the swinging door open again and entering the room, this time carrying silver coffee pots in each hand. He glanced again at the plastic bag on the floor behind Federhoff as the waiter came toward the opposite side of the table and filled Carrington's cup first. The waiter then proceeded to pour coffee for each person across the table from Emilio until he came to the President. "I'll take herbal tea," Benton said to the waiter. And then to the others, he added smiling, "even Presidents have prostates." The waiter told the President he would be back with tea in a minute.

As the waiter rounded the bend toward Emilio's side of the table, Trumble waved him on indicating he didn't want any coffee. Federhoff abruptly pushed his chair back to make access easier to his cup. In doing so, he had created a temporary sanctuary under his chair for the small plastic bag of white powder. The waiter walked around Federhoff's chair, and Esther requested tea. When the waiter got to Emilio, the young Colombian was shaking as though he had already had several cups of coffee. The waiter asked Emilio if he was feeling alright. Emilio nodded "yes" and gestured for his cup to be filled and asked for the waiter to leave a pot on the table. He looked back toward Federhoff. Federhoff had scooted his chair back in, and the bag was again in plain view.

"... well, it's pretty obvious to me, President Guardina," Emilio heard Trumble saying, "that your government has been unsuccessful in solving the drug traffic problem with all the economic and military assistance we've already given you, so why should we ... "

President Benton thought the discussion was getting a little prickly, and as if all this had not been orchestrated in advance, he said in a conciliatory voice, "Now, now, Chuck. The past is the past. What we need to do this morning is concentrate on the future. That's in all our best interests."

"I agree, Mr. President," said Trumble, "but we can all learn from the past, too."

"True enough, but the key here is to look for opportunities for joint gain," said Benton. "For example," the President continued, trying to make his words seem spontaneous, as he now looked toward President Guardina. "Our South American friends in Colombia need help restoring their oil refineries, water treatment, and electric power facilities. We have a need to stop the flow of drugs into the United States from Colombia. Why can't we provide the economic aid for the water and energy projects and simultaneously put some of our fully-equipped military ground troops into Colombia and fight these drug lords to the finish? That way, when the reconstruction is complete, the drug problem will be solved also." Looking toward Winterfield, Benton said, "Is that proposal feasible from the Army's viewpoint, Marlin?"

Guardina's face was pallid.

"The Army, Mr. President, would have no problem putting troops in there on the ground." Catching his aide's eye for reassur-

ance, Winterfield continued, "We'd, of course, need some time
to plan the operation. But we could do it. It'd be similar to Vietnam, except this time we'd be going in with the blessing of the
governmental power structure."

Annoyed, Esther quickly rejoined, "Marlin, please don't speak
of such an operation in the same breath with Vietnam . . . unless
you want to have the whole thing scuttled in Congress."

"No, you're absolutely right, Esther," replied Winterfield.

"That was foolish of me. You won't hear me say anything like
that again. But I think you get my point."

"Yes, I get your point, General" said Senator Carrington. "But
Esther's right. Not only Congress—but also the press corps—would
have a heyday with your Vietnam comparison. It's like bidding on
your weakest suit in a hand of bridge. Certain disaster."

Guardina got the point. The Army considered a Colombian
operation like another Vietnam. They weren't even trying to hide
it. It was there right in the open.

General Winterfield turned his head abruptly toward Benton.
"Mr. President, to answer your question succinctly," said
Winterfield, exhibiting mild irritation at the legislators' interrup-
tion, "a ground operation in Colombia would be quite feasible."

"Well then," said Benton turning to President Guardina, "I
guess we need to hear from you, sir."

At that moment, a waiter carrying a tray with two teapots
entered the room and made his way directly toward President
Benton. The waiter sat one of the teapots down near Benton's cup
and proceeded to go around the table in Emilio's direction. Only
Emilio watched him. Only he saw the whole sordid event. Before
the waiter could get to Esther with the other teapot, his feet flew
straight up in the air and he had landed on his back as the tray and
teapot crashed to the floor. Esther muttered something like "I didn't
need that cup of tea anyway," as Emilio rushed to pick up the
slightly shaken but mostly embarrassed waiter. Dropping to his
hands and knees for a few seconds and frantically inspecting—
unsuccessfully—the immediate floor area for the whereabouts of

that little bag, Emilio sprang upright and remarked, quite authoritatively, that an invisible puddle of water on the slick floor probably had caused the accident. The conferees nodded acceptance, expressed their concern for the waiter, and returned to their discussion. The waiter made his way back to the kitchen, rubbing his hind end and limping slightly as he walked. Emilio, as inconspicuously as possible, scrutinized the shiny floor within his range of vision. The bag was again nowhere in sight. President Guardina was presenting every argument he could think of as to why U.S. ground combat troops would not be effective in the Colombian jungles and highlands. Too hot, too cold, too wet, too many diseases, too many dangerous animals, reptiles, and insects; the drug lords were too ruthless, too elusive, too resourceful, and on and on.

The other conferees listened to him respectfully and when he stopped talking, President Benton said to Winterfield, "What do you think, General?"

"Adversity never stopped the U.S. military before. Battle of the Bulge, Remagen, Iwo Jima, Normandy, Guam, the Philippines. We thrive on adversity."

"I would have to agree," said Benton. Then looking at Guardina, he said thoughtfully, "Esteban, we're ready to send our troops to Colombia—despite all the challenges that will confront them. We are prepared to give you the technological and economic aid you seek in addition. What do you say?"

"We do not need U.S. soldiers getting killed in our drug war," said Guardina pointedly.

Federhoff, quiet till now, finally spoke his mind. "President Guardina, don't you understand? The drug war is ours, equally or more so than yours. We are accumulating tens of thousand of new drug addicts a year. Our prisons are overcrowded with drug users and people who rob and steal to feed their habit. Violence is rampant. Our children are dying in the streets from drug-related causes everyday. It's not enough to tell us that you are working on the problem at its source. The Colombian cocaine and heroin source continues to flow like a rampaging river. We are the ones who are drowning at this end. We are the ones who have the ability and the motivation to dam up this thing at its source. To plug it once and for all—or at least, try to. If you don't allow us to do that, we'll simply drown and decompose into nothingness."

Federhoff was surprised with the drama of his own words, but not moreso than Guardina himself. "I hear what you're saying, Mr. Federhoff. We're a proud people. It's difficult for us to admit we cannot solve our own problems—especially the problem of the powerful drug lords—the Bodegas and others. If it must come to the point that we can't have U.S. economic aid without inviting U.S. combat troops on our soil, then so be it. We've no place else to go for economic aid. We've tried. We've been rejected at every turn. As much as I'm aware that our people will welcome U.S. economic aid, I'm sure they will resent U.S. military presence in Colombia. I can say that categorically. You should know that, President Benton. You should know that."

Reaching out his hand toward Guardina, Benton said, "So do we have a deal, Esteban?"

"Yes, Frank, we have a deal," Guardina said shaking Benton's hand vigorously.

"Good," said Benton, "as General Winterfield said before, it will take some time to plan the operation. The target date to put troops on the ground in Colombia will be sometime next fall. There should be no problem with Congress voting the aid package for Colombia, particularly if the legislators know that we will have a good shot at reducing the enormous expense attending the illegal drug culture in this country. We'll keep you informed, President Guardina, of our progress on the aid and the estimated time of arrival of the troops."

Emilio was shocked that Guardina had caved in so easily. He would have to get word to Raoul about this right away. But first he would have to do something about that damned plastic bag. The meeting was beginning to break up, but people were still seated and talking at the table. Federhoff stood up first, shook hands with both Presidents and the other dignitaries, and started to walk away from the table. Emilio took this opportunity to follow him out and get a bird's eye look at where the bag had ended up. Federhoff, with Emilio trailing, was just rounding the end of the table near President Benton. Emilio spotted the bag on the floor, three feet behind Benton's chair. Federhoff, who had turned back toward the still seated Trumble and was shaking his hand, had not seen the bag. Emilio walked up to Federhoff and shook his hand and complimented him on the "speech that had turned the tide" in the negotiation. Flustered, Federhoff thanked Emilio and began to back up in preparation to turn and be on his way to his next meeting. Two steps back and squuuiish.

Federhoff looked down, picked up the bag, and said "Hmmmm, what's this?"

Without hesitating, Emilio said, "Oh, that probably belongs to the waiter who fell while ago. Powdered milk for the coffee. Some people prefer it, you know." Taking the bag from Federhoff's hand, Emilio said, "Don't worry Mr. Federhoff, I'll make sure it gets back to him."

Federhoff replied, "That's very kind of you," and as he left, he said over his shoulder to Emilio, "it's great working with such dedicated people."

2

That evening, soothing strains of violin sounds filled the White House East Room, as President and Mrs. Benton and President Guardina disbanded the receiving line in the cross-hall of the White House and made their entrance through tall ivory French doors opening into a sea of people milling around in formalwear. Although not large by European palace standards, the ballroom of the White House was enormous by American standards when built. Traditionally identified with momentous news briefings, bill signings, and black tie evenings with dazzling entertainment, the East Room was considered to be the nation's "audience room" and had long been a repository of priceless artwork. Perhaps the single object in the White House with the greatest aura—the Gilbert Stuart portrait of George Washington—decorated the east wall of the room. This, flanked by other outstanding portraits including those of Martha Washington, painted by Eliphalet Andrews, and of Theodore Roosevelt by John Singer Sargent, gave the room a museum feel. Three immense chandeliers, lined north to south in the center of the room and each made up of more than six thousand pieces of cut Bohemian glass, presented a powerful impression. The elegant, natural wood grand piano case resting on a pedestal of three golden eagles, a breathtakingly lovely piece of art, was said by President Truman to have had the most wonderful sounds of any piano he had ever heard.

All day long the President's staff had toiled frenetically to throw together an "emergency" reception for the President of Colombia. Staffers had made over two hundred direct calls and had developed a guest list of about a hundred and twenty-five people. The morning conferees were in attendance with the exception of Federhoff and Senator Carrington. General Throckmiller and General McKeane were there, as was Lila Davis-Whitfield. Lila had received word from Emilio about the reception and had twisted the arm of a White House insider to get invited. This is one affair she didn't want to miss.

Guests moved quickly to get out of the way as President and Mrs. Benton and their entourage slowly entered the room. President Benton looked around at some of the guests and spotted several military officers in dress blues talking in a group with Esther Grant. Excusing himself from Mrs. Benton, the President said to Guardina, "Come here, Esteban. I want to introduce someone to you." Mrs. Benton was already busy talking away with Elizabeth Courtney, the editor in chief of *Vogue*.

Generals Winterfield, Throckmiller, and McKeane were listening to Esther telling war stories about her last election campaign in Illinois when the two Presidents approached the group. "If I might interrupt," said President Benton.

"Certainly, Mr. President," said Esther, sounding a bit up-staged.

"President Guardina," Benton said, turning to the Colombian Chief Executive, "I know you shook hands with these folks a while ago in the receiving line—and two of them you met this morn-ing—, but something I didn't tell you about one of them, I want to tell you now."

"I hope it's not about bad breath," quipped Guardina. "Not even your best friends will tell you, you know."

"No, it's not that," chuckled Benton. "I just want you to know that today I signed the order appointing General Throckmiller as Commander in Chief of SIXCOM effective May 1. He will be personally responsible for Operation Athena—the special anti-car-tel campaign I authorized today. I have a feeling you two are going to get to know each other a lot better over the next year or so."

Esther beamed.

President Guardina smiled and shook the general's hand as Esther watched General Winterfield's jaw drop. Apparently Benton had not consulted Winterfield before making the appointment. Benton had simply exercised his prerogative as Commander in Chief of the U.S. Armed Forces; he was a good enough politician to know that his choice would have the total support of the Con-gress and, just as importantly, the press—even though the mili-tary establishment would have favored a more hard-liner.

General Throckmiller was everything one would imagine a gen-eral to be: a William Westmoreland clone, with steely blue eyes, silver-gray hair, and a jutting, uncompromising chin which seemed to imbue everything he said with an air of decisiveness and cred-ibility. "Throck," as he was called by his military colleagues, had graduated from West Point in 1962 as Cadet Brigade Commander and at the top of his class academically. Because of the timing of his graduation from West Point, he had missed service in the Ko-rean conflict, but he had made up for it by heroic duty as a battal-ion commander in the 101st Airborne Division in Vietnam. One Associated Press version of his Vietnam exploits described the early-

promoted Lieutenant Colonel's "selfless involvement" in personally directing the rescue of one of his infantry platoons which had
been surrounded by a company of North Vietnamese regulars. On
learning of his unit's predicament, he quickly had ordered eight
choppers to action. He rode in the lead chopper to supervise the
rescue. When the pilot of the lead chopper was critically wounded
by enemy fire and disabled, and having, himself, suffered a grazing wound to the shoulder, he piloted the lead chopper and continued to direct the firepower of all of the choppers on the enemy.
Keeping two choppers in the air to provide cover, he led the other
six choppers into a clearing, and, amid a barrage of enemy fire,
managed to evacuate to safety twenty-five of his troops, many of
whom were seriously injured. For this, he had been awarded the
Purple Heart and the Congressional Medal of Honor. In the Desert
Storm action of 1991, he had been one of General Norman
Schwartzkopf's principal advisors. Even his envious detractors would
have to admit he had all the requisite ability to assume the post of
Commander in Chief of SIXCOM.

President Guardina stayed with the group talking to Throckmiller
and the others as President Benton circulated among the crowd of
guests, shaking hands and casually talking to everyone, as if he were at
an ice cream social in someone's backyard. Eventually, Winterfield
left the group to find his aide, Colonel Miller, and General McKeane
took Throckmiller aside for a few minutes to tell him about Kate's
progress at West Point. President Guardina and Esther were conversing, when Lila walked up to them.

"I hope I'm not butting in," Lila said meekly.

"Of course not, Lila," said Esther. "You've met President
Guardina, haven't you?"

"Well, just in the receiving line. But a man this handsome I
want to know more about."

"You're putting this old man on," blushed Guardina.

"Not in the least," replied Lila. "I use handsome as a measure
of all your qualities. Not only your face."

"You are more than kind, ah, ah . . . Ms . . . " attempted

Guardina.

"Whitfield . . . Davis-Whitfield," interjected Esther. "She's one of Washington's "real people", not one of us government clones. "Just call me Lila, President Guardina." Everyone else does.

"Lila, may I have a waiter get you a drink?" asked Guardina.

"No, sir. I don't drink alcohol. Bad for the figure. I'm not thirsty either, but thanks"

Esther was baffled at Lila's response. Lila had gotten practically snockered that October afternoon in her backyard gazebo. Who was she trying to fool anyway? Esther decided to let it pass.

Esther looked out toward the dance floor and saw President and Mrs. Benton dancing the first dance, signaling that all the guests were now free to join in. She also saw Emilio walking across the dance floor toward her. When he approached, Esther said to Guardina and Lila, "Excuse me, but I would like you to meet a young gentleman whom I met this morning. This fine young man is Emilio Gutierrez who is from Colombia and works for the State Department."

Guardina replied curtly, "We've met," and nodded unenthusiastically, looking from side to side.

"I don't think I've had the pleasure," gushed Lila. "Was that *Emilio?*"

"Yes, ma'am . . . Emilio. Emilio Gutierrez. But don't try to remember the last name."

Guardina looked back toward the group. "Is that because it changes too often?" Guardina said blandly, little disguising his contempt.

Sensing the uneasiness of the situation, Esther said to Emilio, "I would be honored if you would have this dance with me."

"My pleasure, madam," Emilio replied, quickly engaging her in a few swirls toward the main dance floor.

Lila looked at Guardina expectantly. "How 'bout it Mr. President? I never danced with a President before." Of course, she knew well that she had danced with President Benton at the WRATHPAC convention in Philadelphia.

"Well, okay Lila, if you don't mind dancing with an old man."

When Lila and Guardina arrived on the main dance floor, the band was playing "Tea for Two" cha cha. She could see that Guardina loved the Latin music and rhythms. His face immediately lit up and he quickly engaged the cha cha step pattern, rolling his arms one over the other, and then reversing the rolls. She mirrored his movements. Within a few minutes, the orchestra slowed the tempo way down and played an old Cole Porter standard, "Night and Day." As Lila and her "catch" slow danced in a tight body position, Guardina whispered in her ear, "You know, Lila, you are a very nice person . . . a beautiful person."

"Why thank you, Mr. President."

"Esteban—call me Esteban. And I don't like to see nice people get hurt."

"I'm not sure I follow," whispered Lila.

"Emilio—you know that man named Emilio you met a few minutes ago?"

"Yes."

"Stay away from him."

"Why?"

"He's trouble."

"How so?"

"He's in with cartels."

"What's that?" Lila asked, feigning naivete.

"Colombian drug cartels—the Bodegas."

"Is it a family?"

"You could say that. A powerful enough family that the U.S. Army is going to send troops to my country to wipe them out."

"So what does Emilio have to do with all this?"

"He's a principal courier of drugs and information for the Bodegas."

"Why are you telling me all this?"

"You're not part of the government. If I exposed Emilio to U.S. officials, the Bodegas would have me killed tomorrow. Take my word for it. Emilio's a rat and a womanizer. He'll hurt you."

Meanwhile, Emilio and Esther were doing the fox trot half-time and conversing. Midway through their conversation, Esther said to him bluntly, "I saw what happened today."

"What do you mean?"

"At the meeting this morning . . . "

"Yes?"

"I saw the little white bag."

"So—it was a bag of powdered creamer."

"But it didn't come from the waiter's tray, it came from your briefcase."

"How do you know that?"

"Because I saw the bag on the floor before the waiter ever came near the table."

"Well, powdered creamer could have come from my briefcase."

"It could have, but it didn't. I also liked your little umbrella routine. Now that was cute."

"Uh, uh, my umbrella? . . . "

"And convincing Federhoff that the coke was powdered creamer—that was down right classic."

"But it *was* creamer," replied Emilio meekly.

"Cut the chit chat, Emilio. How much are you willing to pay me to keep our little secret?" she whispered.

"Is this blackmail, madam?"

"Let's just call it a contribution to my campaign fund."

"And what if I refuse to pay."

"You won't, Emilio. You're too smart."

Emilio thought for a few seconds and then blurted, "How about twenty-five thousand?"

Esther smiled and looked him squarely in the eyes. "Triple that in cash and we have a deal."

"When?"

"As soon as you can get it to me. I have no qualms about taking money from drug dealers."

"But madam, what makes you think I'm a drug dealer."

Esther laughed out loud. "Remember, it's our little secret."

Sensing they had moved toward Guardina and Lila, Esther tapped President Guardina on the shoulder and motioned for him to switch partners. Esther danced away with Guardina, leaving Emilio and Lila staring at each other.

"Care to dance, Mr. Gutierrez?" asked Lila. Emilio smiled and pulled her into his chest, whisking her across the dance floor to the melody of "Dancing in the Dark."

Emilio hoped that Esther would keep their little secret. *He* certainly would.

As they danced, Lila slipped Emilio a key to her townhouse. She needed to take good care of her new discovery. To win the Minerva game, she'd have to play her cards very methodically. Very methodically, indeed. With Emilio's help.

COMMON GROUND

By late May, Federhoff's Drug Commission had issued its annual report. As the White House staff expected, the drug scene had worsened domestically. Drug-related crime and youth drug use had increased considerably. Colombia was still the primary drug source and the Bodegas were still systematically keeping the drugs flowing into the U.S. Benton's re-election campaign having begun to rev up, Operation Athena provided the perfectly timed antidote to the negative information in the report. Not by accident, Benton arranged that the Drug Report be released on the same day that Congress officially approved Operation Athena and publicly announced the sending of U.S. troops to Colombia to wipe out the drug cartels.

The Minerva Experiment had been downplayed in most press accounts of Operation Athena, as premature. The *Washington Post*, however, quoted some chest-pounding Congressional leaders as taking credit for initiating it. Women selected for the "grand experiment", as the article referred to it, had to be army officers and had to complete special Airborne and Ranger training. The article emphasized that "no artificial standards" would be imposed for the participating women, and it quoted Lila on behalf of WRATHPAC as "supporting the Experiment in concept." It also identified the members of the Experiment's oversight subcommittee as Esther, Lila, and Senator Carrington. Throckmiller's name was not mentioned; nor was a timetable for the Operation suggested. The Pentagon was playing close to the vest regarding the details of the prospective Colombian campaign.

At West Point, Kate's class was surviving the stresses and strains of Graduation Week, enduring one military and social activity after another. The Graduation Parade and Hop had been held, the plebes had been officially "recognized" by the upperclassmen, and Kate and Tina were counting down the hours to the commencement exercise. Kate was to be valedictorian and was putting the final touches on her speech for tomorrow—Saturday, June 3. Esther would be giving the commencement address. General McKeane would be arriving this evening. On Saturday afternoon there would be a reception in the Superintendent's garden for all graduating cadets and their families. Everything was moving like clockwork.

Kate's father was due to arrive at seven p.m. at the home of General Chandler, the Commandant of Cadets, her father's colleague at Fort Bragg, North Carolina during the early days of his career. General and Mrs. Chandler had invited General McKeane to stay at their quarters over Graduation Weekend. They had also planned a reception and buffet dinner for him when he arrived and arranged to have classmates of General McKeane—stationed at West Point—to be there. Esther Grant and Kate were also on the guest list.

At six fifty p.m. Kate, in dress whites, walked from her barracks toward the commandant's home located near the northwest corner of the Plain directly across from Thayer Monument. On her right, she watched shadows of Gothic structures cut prismic stencils on the Plain as the sun was retreating behind impregnable mountains of granite. Sounds of the Hellcats' drums and bugles punctuated the cool evening air, prompting Kate to stop and salute as she watched the American flag being lowered on Trophy Point. A crack of echoing cannon fire solemnly reverberated the Academy's mission, while the pungent sulphur smell wafting in the breeze a few seconds later captured the horrid reality of war.

When the flag detail had completed the ceremony and began marching to a rousing military drum beat, Kate resumed walking, instinctively in cadence, toward the Com's house. When she reached the north end of MacArthur Barracks, she could see in the shadowy distance a military sedan turning off Washington Road, coming toward her, but stopping in front of the Com's house. The driver emerged from the car, opened each of the back doors, opened the trunk, and began removing luggage. A uniformed officer got out of the car on the rear driver's side, putting on his hat with scrambled-egg visor at the same time. Kate wondered if that was her dad. Then she noticed another figure, a woman in what looked like a flowered dress, getting out the rear passenger side of the sedan. That couldn't be dad, she concluded. He doesn't have a wife, much less a pregnant wife. She kept walking toward the Com's house and observed the pair being greeted and let in the front door. In a few minutes, she arrived at the front door and rang the doorbell. The door opened.

It was her father. He smiled at the sight of her, but said nothing. He was not one to show elation in public. Kate said the first thing that sprang to mind. "When did you get here?"

General McKeane stepped out on the porch with Kate, closing the door partially behind him. "Just arrived. Just before you rang the bell. How's my favorite First Captain," he said, giving Kate perfunctory hug. She sensed a defensiveness in his voice. "It's not a public display of affection violation, you know, to hug one's own daughter," he added.

Kate sensed more defensiveness. "Who's that woman who came in with you?" Kate asked.

"Oh," said General McKeane. "It's a surprise. Here, I want you to come on in and meet her." General McKeane took his daughter by the arm and helped her over the threshold and inside the Commandant's house. General Chandler's aide-de-camp and several guests, including Esther, stepped out of the way to expose the back of the woman in the brightly flowered dress. "Kate, here is someone you should know," General McKeane said. The woman turned around. "Kate, meet your sister Karen."

For a few seconds, Kate was speechless. Her father had tricked her. She hated him for it. Master of deceit. She had asked him not to. He didn't tell her he would. He didn't tell her he wouldn't. Kate felt her world collapsing around her. Her classmates wouldn't understand. They would be judgmental. So would the officer cadre. So would the press. Her future—certain doom.

0368-COOL

Without saying another word, Kate walked directly to the other side of the room and struck up a conversation with one of her classmates. For the next half hour, she made a determined effort to avoid both her father and her sister. Out of the corner of her eye, however, she was keeping track of what her sister was doing. What she saw worried her. Karen was making continuous trips to the bowl of spiked punch. Karen was never one to hold her liquor well. Besides, she was taking several prescribed medications.

Karen, as she became more and more intoxicated, began marching around the room singing "On Brave Old Army Team" and saluting every person in military uniform. Kate was mortified.

General McKeane immediately took Karen aside to quiet her. Kate, red-faced, walked past Karen as if she didn't exist. Her father looked up and Kate beamed a laser stare into his eyes designed to burn his soul. Esther was watching. She instantly read the situation and followed Kate to the far side of the adjoining unoccupied dining room where the punch bowl was located. Kate was standing next to the punch bowl looking out the window into the backyard, still fuming, but trying to get her emotions under control and wondering what she would do next.

Esther waited a few minutes before approaching Kate. She filled a cup with punch, and, saying nothing, offered it to Kate. When Kate looked toward her, she observed pain in Kate's eyes. Kate accepted the cup and looked out the window again.

Stripped naked. That's how Kate felt. Embarrassed that Esther now knew the family secret.

"Thanks for the punch," Kate said still gazing at the back yard. "Please forgive my curtness. I'm just trying to deal with my shock. I didn't expect my sister to be here."

"I know. You didn't disguise your feelings very well. You feel trapped, don't you."

"Very."

Kate took a sip of punch and glanced out the window into the Com's backyard. "I don't believe it! I don't believe it!" Kate thought to herself. There was Karen, in full view of anyone who cared to look, out in the backyard squatting and doing her duty in the Com's flowerbed. She apparently hadn't enough patience to wait in line to use the bathroom.

Esther, preoccupied filling her punch glass, didn't notice what was occurring in the backyard. Kate moved toward the center of the room, luring Esther away from the window to a position where Esther's back was toward it. Kate continued making small talk with Esther, and at the same time, stealing peeks at Karen through the window. Luckily, the guests in the room were too busily engaged in conversations to notice what was happening outside.

Over Esther's shoulder, Kate could see that Karen was no longer squatting. She was now picking the Commandant's flowers and frolicking in a series of circular dance movements, strewing petals in all directions over the Commandant's lawn.

Kate had had it. She excused herself abruptly, telling Esther that she had another engagement and that she would see her tomorrow.

Esther, somewhat bewildered, watched as Kate struggled to forge her way through the clusters of guests and proceed directly out the front door without saying a word to anyone.

2

The graduation exercise commenced promptly at ten o'clock at Michie Stadium the next morning. After the incident at the Commandant's home the evening before, Esther had spent considerable time back in her room at the Thayer Hotel modifying her commencement address to focus on the topic of compassion—an attribute she believed each West Point graduate should work hard to develop. During her address on Saturday morning, she hit hard on the compassion point, and she talked a lot about the "gray area" and the ethics of the real world. "Rarely is anything in life wholly black or wholly white; wholly right or wholly wrong," she said in her prepared speech. Much of this went right over the heads of her uninitiated, self-righteous audience. But at least she said it.

As for her part, Kate played off some of Esther's ideas in her valedictory speech and also noted that the army's system precluded her—First Captain and first in her class academically—from entering the combat arm of her choice—the infantry. The branch in which she was commissioned—Military Intelligence—was her third choice after infantry and armor. In her speech, Kate strongly made the point that there would be no career equality in the military until the army extended to women the opportunity to serve in ground combat. "Until the glass ceiling of branch restriction was broken," she argued, "women would be excluded from serving in the highest positions of responsibility in the army." She received a standing ovation from the cadet corps when she made that statement. General McKeane stood and applauded also, but the other general officers had remained seated because of the political sensitivity of the matter.

After the last-ranked graduate received her diploma, the entire class rose, and on a signal from Kate, the graduates threw their white hats high into the air. They were no longer cadets. They were all now second lieutenants in the United States Army.

The ceremony having concluded, Kate, her father, and Esther posed for pictures outside the stadium gates. Most of the major newspapers TV networks from around the country were there, practically in a state of frenzy to get Kate's story on the airwaves and in print. Karen wasn't there. She was at the Commandant's house recuperating from her bout with alcohol on the prior evening. After the photo session, Kate told General McKeane that she was very tired and needed rest and that she would see him at the Superintendent's reception that afternoon.

3

Kate arrived at the Superintendent's garden, a stone's throw from the Douglas MacArthur Memorial, at three-thirty that afternoon.

The reception had begun about a half hour before she arrived. The first to greet her was Tina and her family, visiting from Hoboken. Tina, effervescent as usual, held up an early edition of the Sunday *New York Times*. Appearing on the front page was a picture of Kate in full dress uniform—gray, gold-buttoned coat over white, starched skirt—grinning widely and holding her rolled diploma in one hand and giving a "thumbs up" with the other.

The story noted that she ranked first in her class both academically and militarily—a first in the nearly two hundred year history of the Academy—and that she had been selected for participation in the Minerva Experiment, was airborne qualified, and would soon be heading for Ranger School.

"Congratulations!" Tina cried. "I could be the one in that picture, if I only had another four years to prove myself!"

Kate laughed with Tina and hugged her, talked for a few minutes with Tina's mother and father, and then went over toward the long receiving line to see if her dad was there. Sure enough, there he was, standing ramrod between the Superintendent and the Commandant and their wives, greeting the newly commissioned officers and their families. Looking toward the south end of the garden, Kate noticed Esther and Karen, seated on a bench facing MacArthur Barracks, conversing intimately. Esther happened to look back and see Kate. She excused herself, and came over to where Kate was standing.

Esther was quite direct. "Your sister is very sorry for the way she behaved last evening," she said. She wanted me to tell you that."

"So? Saying one's sorry doesn't erase the embarrassment."

"She's not asking for your forgiveness, Kate."

"Then what does she want from me? I just wish she'd leave me alone and stay out of my life."

"Maybe she should tell you herself."

"No, I don't want to talk to her."

"Kate, you must make the best of this. Every family has something."

"Yes, but why was I stuck with Karen?"

"Do you think Karen chose to be the way she is?"

"No, but . . ."

"You could be Karen."

"Yes, but . . ."

"Where's your compassion?"

"You don't understand."

"Kate, I understand perfectly. I have a mentally retarded younger brother. He has Downe's syndrome. I try to include him in my life as much as possible. He lives . . ."

"I'm sorry. I didn't know."

" . . . in Chicago. His positive attitude has been an inspiration to me."

"I feel so confused."

"Confusion, Kate, is the first step to a solution."

"But I don't know what to do; I'm cornered."

"Then there's only one thing to do, isn't there?"

"Take the high road; do what's gallant."

"What does that mean?"

"I suggest you share your feelings with Karen."

"I can't do that."

"You really have no choice. You'll look like—pardon the French—an ass, otherwise. Do it for appearances, if for nothing else.

Kate turned around, startled to see Karen standing a few feet away.

"Kate," Karen said. " I have something for you. I hope you like it."

Karen bent over and took from her shabby leather purse a box wrapped in the cartoon section of a newspaper. Fluffing up the white silk bow stuck to the newspaper, she handed it to Kate "Here, Sis," she said. "I want you to have this for your graduation."

Ambivalently Kate took the gift and removed the wrapping, being careful not to disturb the bow. She opened the box and slowly pushed back the tissue paper. There it was, perhaps slightly more faded, perhaps a little more tattered than when she'd last seen it. The figure in the framed needlepoint was still pretty much as she remembered it. A heart-shaped yellow butterfly on a light blue background. But something was different. Something had been added. Haphazardly configured above the butterfly in a squiggly arch-shape appeared five handstitched white words. "ALWAYS LISTEN WITH YOUR HEART".

Kate looked away from the needlepoint and raised her hand to her face to shield her reaction. Sadness engulfed Kate. Karen's amateurish handiwork—those few simple words—spoke tomes about Kate's own internal frustration. So incisive, yet so appropriate. Kate could only think of the times in high school she wanted to visit Karen, but didn't; all the letters she wrote during Plebe year to Karen, and never mailed; all of Karen's phone calls she never returned; all of the stacks of letters from Karen she never read. All of the anger she had toward her dead mother for causing Karen's mental problems and for dying. All of the guilt she carried around for abandoning Karen after her mother's death. All of the anger she kept inside about her Dad's abandoning both of them. All of these feelings and memories surfaced instantly when Kate read those five words.

Wiping tears from her cheeks, Kate reached toward Karen, embraced her, and whispered quietly, "I'm sorry, Karen." Confused, Karen asked, "Why are you crying, Sis? I thought you would like my gift."

"Oh, I do. These are tears of joy. . . . Maybe it's hard to tell the difference. One thing's for sure, Karen."

Their eyes interlocked searchingly.

Kate broke the gaze and looked at the floor, waiting a few moments until she was able to form words again. Re-engaging Karen's eyes, Kate whispered, "I promise to listen with my heart from now on."

Taking Karen's hand, Kate and her sister walked back into the central garden area where they joined several other of Kate's classmates and their families who had arrived in the meantime. Esther looked on with satisfaction as Kate introduced Karen to several of the new arrivals. In a few short minutes, Kate had emotionally matured years, and Esther was pleased with the transformation.

4

Splendid. That's how Kate wanted to remember Graduation Weekend. Her reunion with Karen marked the beginning of a new, close sibling relationship, displaying a nobler dimension of her character. Also, Karen and Esther seemed to hit it off quite well. Karen discovered that she didn't have to be elected to Congress to advance the interests of the mentally ill. She had a voice through Esther, and Esther promised to introduce some bills based on some of her ideas. They exchanged addresses.

The day after graduation, Kate clipped out the *New York Times* article and sent it to Professor Hunterford—Brad's uncle—whom she had met that February Sunday afternoon in Cullum Hall. A few weeks before, the professor had been kind enough to send her, through Brad, a gold "good luck" charm for a graduation gift in the semblance of Pallas Athena. Kate kept it with her constantly. She had it on her key chain two days after graduation, when she and Tina left the academy in Tina's "pre-owned" red Corvette convertible headed for Lexington to attend Todd and Emma Lou's wedding. They planned to do some sightseeing on the way.

It was early Friday afternoon, when they started south out of Paris, Kentucky toward Lexington on Route 68, along Paris Pike. The wedding was to be on the following day. While riding along, Kate was lost in thought about the conversation she had with Todd when they spoke at the Graduation Hop. He had described Lexington as a gracious city, located in central Kentucky and steeped in a tradition of tobacco and thoroughbreds. Romantic antebellum mansions, he had said, graced the city's center and the rich bluegrass countryside. Hometown of Henry Clay and Mary Todd Lincoln, it was renowned, worldwide, for its horse events, parks, farms, and its annual festival of bluegrass music.

After a couple hours on the road, Kate took the wheel while

Tina dozed. Mesmerized by the expressway monotony, Kate day-dreamed, reflecting back on her relationship with her mother, try-ing to recollect any good memories of the short time they had together. She could remember only one occasion on which her mother had revealed any positive emotion whatsoever. It was when Kate was in about sixth grade. It was a sunny Saturday, about noontime. Her mother was in the kitchen doing the dishes; her father was away as usual on one of his many hardship tours to the Far East. Kate entered the room looking for a school notebook and noticed her mother looking out the kitchen window and smiling. Kate thought something was happening outside the window and approached her. Kate remembered asking what she was smiling at, and her mother told her it was nothing . . . she was just thinking about her wedding day. Kate pressed her to tell more, and finally her mother sat down with her and told her all about it. She ges-tured enthusiastically, her face filled with glee, as she conveyed the details of her elaborate wedding at the Cadet Chapel at West Point, complete with an arch of sabers and, afterwards, a wonderful re-ception and dance at a country club in Newburgh, a town a few miles up the Hudson from the Point. She was careful to point out that the McKeanes picked up the tab for all this because she had no living parents and only a handful of relatives, none of whom could attend. Kate could remember how her mother's eyes wid-ened in joy as she described how handsome and debonair her bride-groom looked that day. It was clear to Kate that her mother's wed-ding day was the highpoint of her mother's life. Nothing before or after could compare. It was that one island of happiness in a life otherwise filled with, loneliness, discipline, and self-sacrifice. When Kate asked what made her think of her wedding day, her mother admitted matter-of-factly that it was her wedding anniversary, then returned to doing the dishes. Kate knew that her father had for-gotten to write or call. He never remembered anniversaries or birth-days. Something else was always too important.

As the red convertible sped down the highway, Kate was ut-terly captivated by the incomparable resplendence of the rolling fields of blue-green grass polysected by four-board white fences stretching beyond sight, corraling premier herds of handsome thoroughbreds and colts. Gainesway, Walmac, Tree Haven, and Fairway—charming horse farms with graceful equestrian outbuildings—lined the welcome corridor that eventually delivered Kate and Tina to the Lexington city limits.

Tina drove awhile around the downtown area taking in the sights of Victorian Square before heading out Highway 27 to the Hilton Suites of Lexington Green where Todd had arranged for out-of -town wedding guests to stay. Todd's dad, a prominent Lexington surgeon, was picking up the tab for the wedding and the guests' expenses. Tina thought it was cool for Todd's dad to do that, especially since Emma Lou's parents had limited finances. Kate and Tina tooled around downtown that night, hit a couple bars, saw Todd and Emma Lou briefly, and turned in early. They had to get their beauty sleep and get gussied up in preparation for the wedding the next morning.

The next day, Kate and Tina donned their dress blue uniforms, and headed for the wedding site in the red Corvette. The wedding and reception were to be held at eleven a.m.on the grounds of White Hall, the beautifully restored Italianate mansion of Cassius Marcellus Clay, located about twenty miles south of Lexington. Clay (1810-1903), an outspoken abolitionist and minister to Russia, had settled in the Lexington area and had built the mansion, unique for its day, complete with central heating and indoor plumbing. Situated on a sprawling estate, the three-story grand dwelling with Palladian facades sternly dominated the hushed countryside. By ten-thirty a.m., the Corvette was making its way up the long road leading to the mansion from the main road.

Kate and Tina joined Todd and Emma Lou's families and friends as well as the other West Point classmates who had gathered outside the mansion. The ceremony was to be held in a small grove of trees a few hundred yards from the mansion; the reception would be held in a large red, white, and blue tent erected for the occasion. A few minutes after a young officer handed Kate and Tina swords and sheaths, four black hansom cabs, each pulled by two French coach horses, arrived in front of the mansion. The driver of Todd and Emma Lou's carriage, dressed in a blue military uniform, stood at the top rear of the cab. As soon as the horses stopped, he saluted a tall, dark-haired uniformed officer who gave a series of commands, causing Todd's West Point classmates to form an arch of sabers as the married-couple-to-be exited the carriage and walked toward the grove of trees. The other couples in the wedding party followed, the ground-length pastel-colored dresses of the bridesmaids billowing in the breeze. After a very brief ceremony officiated by an Army chaplain, the party began.

Inside the tent, a quartet was playing a mixture of tunes including light jazz, country rock, and bluegrass while the wedding party took their places at the head table. Todd and Emma Lou sat in the center and kissed when the guests struck their wine glasses with their spoons. After several clatterings of glasses, the best man, a strikingly handsome dark-haired, blue-eyed officer approached the microphone. When he began speaking, Kate became hypnotized.

"Ladies and Gentlemen," he said. "For those here who don't know me, I am Captain Bryan Flanagan. I graduated from West Point a couple of years ago, and I have the special privilege of being Todd's cousin and the best man of the newlyweds. I also have the honor of making the first toast to the new couple. I thought long and hard about what I should say. I first considered telling you about the time when Todd and I were kids in third grade and Todd dressed up like a small gorilla to scare his teacher by jumping out of classroom supply closet. Instead he was picked up by Lexington's animal control department before he even got to school."

The crowd laughed politely.

"I was going to tell that story, but then I decided against it. Then I considered telling you about the time in high school when Emma Lou was letting her Saturday afternoon date out the back door of her home at the same time that Todd—her Saturday evening date—got tired of waiting for Emma Lou to answer the front door bell and walked around to her back yard. I was going to tell you how Emma Lou handled that situation, but I decided against it. One thing's for sure—whatever she said to Todd didn't put the kibosh on the marriage vows they took today."

The crowd again laughed. Kate was finding Bryan charming.

"What I *did* decide to do today was to share with you the "The Legend of Benny Havens' Well" and a marriage toast to the newlyweds. Here goes."

Without notes, Bryan continued speaking:

THE LEGEND OF BENNY HAVENS' WELL

In the early eighteen hundreds, so the legend goes, cadets of West Point, isolated for four years in the rockbound fortress in the Hudson River, needed an outlet, from time to time, for their enthusiasm and high spirits. While, officially, in those early years of the Academy, there was no free time for recreation, cadets found ways to play pranks and to outwit authority. Many became quite adept at stealing off post in the middle of the night, and making their way to Benny Havens' Tavern in Buttermilk Falls. There, Mrs. Havens would have waiting for them roasts and fowl turning on spits, pots of soup, and freshly baked pies. Mr. Havens served them up kegs of his own special brew and kept a watchful eye out for Academy officers so he could warn cadets of their approach. Benny Havens befriended cadets for more than fifty years. Edgar Allan Poe, a misfit in his brief stint as a West Point cadet, once referred to Benny as "the only congenial soul in this God-forsaken place." But aside from his hospitality, Benny Havens is equally remembered for the magical well behind his establishment next to the chicken coop. According to legend, when West Pointer took a wife after graduation, the marriage partner who drank first of the well's waters would "rule the roost" in the marriage. It is this legend of a West Pointer, put to verse, that I now share:

BENNY HAVENS' WELL

One day a young lieutenant,
    disheveled and distraught,
Came into Benny Havens',
    a-smiling he was not.
Benny gently said to him
    wha tis the matter, son?
Set me up an ale, he said,
    then pour another one.

Ye know that well behind yer place,
    he said to Benny straight.
Sure, said Benny with a wink,
    the water there is great!

It's more than great, it's magic sir,
    if you're the first to drink.
But if your bride partakes it first,
    she'll change the way you think.

Today I took my wedding vows,
    in the chapel on the Post.
I planned to come straight to the well,
    and have me solo toast.

Me bride, she did me in good man,
    she bade them not to tell.
She said her vows, and then produced
    a bottle from the well.

She drank it deep and with a smile,
    she passed it on to me.
As if to say that she's in charge for
    all eternity.

> *"Don't be too quick" said Benny now,*
>   *to judge the outcome yet.*
> *The rooster never counts the eggs,*
>   *until the hen has set.*

Picking up a bottle of champagne and handing it to the newly weds, Bryan recited the final stanzas of the poem:

> *I gave the bottle to your bride,*
>   *with nothing from the well.*
> *She said the things she wants of you,*
>   *are things I do not sell.*

> *Hope and love and trust and care*
>   *are things you'll each impart.*
> *Go tell her, son, that I said this,*
>   *and say it with your heart.*

"And now all of the West Point graduates and I would like to recite a special happiness toast to Todd and Emma Lou," said Bryan. Todd's fourteen classmates in attendance stood up. Bryan recited the first line, and each of Todd's classmates recited a line in sequence, Tina and Kate reciting the last two lines in unison:

> TRAVEL LIGHT IN LIFE,
> TAKE ONLY WHAT YOU NEED:
> THE LOVE THAT YOU HAVE PROMISED ONE AN-
>   OTHER TODAY;
> THE STRENGTH AND WARMTH AND VALUES OF
>   YOUR FAMILIES;
> THE FRIENDSHIP AND SUPPORT THAT ALL OF US
>   GATHERED
> OFFER TO YOU TODAY AND ALWAYS.
> TAKE SIMPLE PLEASURES:
> ENOUGH TO EAT;

ENOUGH TO WEAR;
ENOUGH TRUST, FOR JEALOUSY IS A TERRIBLE
    THING;
ENOUGH PATIENCE, FOR ANGER IS A TERRIBLE
    THING;
ENOUGH GENEROSITY, FOR SELFISHNESS IS A
    TERRIBLE THING;
ENOUGH CHEERFULNESS, FOR UNHAPPINESS IS
    A TERRIBLE THING;
BUT BE SURE TO TAKE MORE THAN ENOUGH
    TO DRINK,
FOR THIRST IS A GOD-AWFUL THING.

Then, the fifteen toasters raised their champagne glasses and shouted in unison:

*TO LIEUTENANT AND MRS. TODD
AND EMMA LOU GAVIN!*

Other toasts followed from family members, and eventually the bride and groom danced the first dance. Then the party really got underway. Kate was determined to find out more about Bryan. Was he single? Engaged? Where was he stationed? She knew he was in the infantry from the powder blue background on his epaulets and the crossed rifles on his lapels. Kate didn't want to seem too interested though. She might scare him away. She would have to play this one a bit cool. Though not too cool or he wouldn't notice her. She saw him standing and talking with Todd and Emma Lou on the dance floor and she walked toward them.

"Oh, Bryan," Todd said as Kate was passing by. "Have you met Kate McKeane?" Kate was relieved; she couldn't have planned it better.

"I don't think I've had the pleasure," responded Bryan.

"I really enjoyed the legend and the toast," Kate bubbled. "You really have a way with words."

"That comes from my Mom's side of the family—the Gavins. Todd suffers from the same gift of blarney," Bryan smiled, giving Todd a gentle elbowing. While the cousins exchanged a couple more verbal parries, Kate noted Bryan wasn't wearing a wedding ring. "Hey, Kate," said Todd. "You free tomorrow to go out to my folks' cottage on the Kentucky River? You can ride horses, swim, take hikes,—whatever you want to do. Emma Lou and I will be on our way to Jamaica, but my brother Seth is organizing it, along with Bryan here. Six of our classmates are going. Interested?"

"Well, I . . . "

"Oh, why not, Kate," said Bryan.

"Okay—you'll have to give us directions. Is Tina going do you know?"

"Don't think so, Kate," replied Todd. "Said something about needing time to recuperate. I think she really plans to hang one on this afternoon and tonight."

"Won't be anything new," Kate murmured.

"Tell ya what," Bryan blurted. "What if I pick you up at the Hilton at ten tomorrow morning? Deal, Kate?"

"Deal," Kate said shaking Bryan's hand once as if locking in a contract.

"Oh, wear jeans and some hiking shoes. And don't forget your bathing suit. I want to show you some fun swimming holes and caves along the river—places Todd and I hung out when we were kids."

"You mean when Todd wasn't in his gorilla suit," Kate winked toward Todd.

"Yeah, Kate," Bryan smiled. "You got it."

5

Todd's parents' weekend cottage was located on a twenty acre farm off Stony Run Road along the Kentucky River, thirty miles southeast of town. Bryan picked Kate up at the hotel as planned but he listened to radio sports news for most of the drive to the farm.

When Bryan and Kate arrived there at about eleven on Sunday morning, a friendly collie bounced around them when they got out of the car and didn't settle down until Bryan gave him a dog biscuit and told him quite firmly to sit. Apparently, Kate's other classmates had already arrived and Seth had steered them toward the activities of the day. A few were riding horses, some were off on the hiking trails through the bluffs overlooking the river, and some were swinging on a spare tire and dropping into the river from a promontory at a swimming hole just below the cottage. There was a lot of whooping and hollering going on at the swimming hole. "Come on, Kate," said Bryan. "Let's grab the rowboat and go downstream aways. I got lots to show you."

Bryan led Kate through a wide squeaky gate of a four-board white fence and out toward a massive white barn topped by a brass horse-shaped weather vane and two tall lightning rods at either end. A few thoroughbreds grazing in the barn lot neighed quietly, just enough to let the outsiders know that they were encroaching upon their turf. Kate tried to pet one, and it backed slowly away. Sparrows engaged in dogfights over the barn roof, while the aroma of freshly mown alfalfa on an adjoining farm wafted pleasingly in the breeze.

"Grow up in Kentucky?" Kate asked as they walked beyond the barn. "You don't seem to have any accent."

As he walked, Bryan picked up a fist-sized rock and threw it over toward the fence line. "Born here, and moved when I was two years old," said Bryan. "Raised in Colorado—near Telluride. Came back here almost every summer and hung out with Todd and Seth mostly here on the farm. We had a great time. I can remember this one summer we got this old Model T Ford running and we—look out for that sinkhole, Kate. Between the limestone and the groundhogs, the fields around here are like Swiss cheese."

Kate jumped over a hole which could have easily swallowed her leg up to her knee. "About the Model T?" she asked interestedly.

"Oh, that was just an example of the fun. We were about ten years old. Eventually, Seth lost control of it and rammed it into a tree down by the Ritter's property line over there. We never got it started again. Mr. Gavin had to scrap it. . . . Shame. A real shame. It'd be worth something today."

"What got you interested in West Point?" Kate asked trying to get him to talk about more current matters.

Helping Kate down the steep embankment toward a small wooden dock area, Bryan replied, "Nothing—you see I really didn't want to go to West Point. I wanted to go to the Air Force Academy right there in Colorado. But my Congressman only had an appointment open to West Point the year I graduated from high school. He said I could go to the Air Force Academy if I waited a year. But I didn't want to do that."

"And so you went to West Point."

"Yeah, begrudgingly"

"Then what?"

"Graduated and went to Airborne and Ranger Schools. I maxed Ranger School so well that the commanding officer asked the Pentagon to keep me on as a trainer. . . . Here, Kate, I'll hold the rowboat while you climb in. . . . Yeah, that's where I'm stationed now. Been there about two years."

Sitting down in the aluminum boat, Kate had to take the risk. "Get married after graduation?"

Bryan laughed. "Are you kidding Kate? I basically went straight to Ranger School and stayed there. It's like giving a young officer an unconditional pass to bachelorhood. I go for months sometime, without even seeing a female. You can't meet the woman of your dreams as a Ranger lane grader—except maybe in your dreams."

As they floated with the current, Bryan pointed to a rock formation on the other side of the river and said, "See that large round opening at water level in the side of the limestone strata, Kate?"

"Yeah."

"That's what me and Todd call the "Powervac". There is a huge whirlpool inside that opening that sucks downward anything that comes near it. An underground cave filled with water runs for about six hundred yards downriver where it empties back out into the main river. Enormous tree trunks have been swept through there and spit out below. No people have drowned here because most everyone in these parts knows about it. About five years ago though, an inquisitive colt wandered away from its mother, found its way in there and got sucked the whole length of the cave. It didn't survive. By the time it had reached the exit downstream, its sides had been ripped open by the hardened, diverticulated inner surface of the limestone bowel. The colt didn't have a chance. It wasn't pretty."

"And you *swim* in this river?" Kate asked disbelievingly.

"Yeah, but you have to choose your spots. Over there on the other side of the river is probably the best swimming hole on the river. But I don't go there anymore."

"Why not?"

"Lost a dog there once."

"A dog?"

"Yeah. About ten years ago. Ol' Shep and I were down here by ourselves one sunny summer afternoon in the rowboat and I rowed in to that little lagoon over there. I tied up the rowboat, and Shep, feisty as usual, jumped in the water, swam around, and wanted to play. I had a red rubber ball that he liked to retrieve, so I threw it out into the river a couple of times and he swam out and brought it back. Then I threw it over near the bank and the ball was bobbing up and down under some branches and brush by the lagoon's edge. Shep swam after it. I dove in the water and swam toward Shep because I wasn't sure he would be able to get the ball out of the brush. When I got about twenty feet from him, he let out a yelp from under the brush and started thrashing around and rolling over and over. Then I saw them—there must have been fifty of them. A nest of water moccasins. They chewed him up. Massive doses of their deadly poison went through his veins, and he was dead in a few seconds. I sensed I couldn't help him, so I swam away fast. After climbing back in the rowboat, I watched the snakes radiate away from Shep's lifeless carcass."

"That could have been you floating there lifeless, Bryan."

"That's right. I think about that a lot. . . . Oh, there it is Kate, ahead. See the hooked sandbar near the side of the river down there? It forms the nicest little swimming hole in this part of the river. No brush, no snakes, water's clear. There's even a rope hanging from a high branch of an oak tree. Great for swinging and dropping."

Kate was not very excited about going swimming after hearing Bryan's stories, but it didn't seem as though she had much choice. Bryan turned the boat in the direction of the sandbar and began to row vigorously. When he got close to the sandbar, he gave three powerful pulls on the oars and beached the boat firmly. He then jumped out and assisted Kate onto the sandbar.

"This *is* beautiful, Bryan," Kate said looking around at the snow white sand and at the weeping willow trees lining the bank of the river across the small lagoon. Kate took off her blouse and jeans to expose a skimpy black bikini bathing suit.

Meanwhile, Bryan stripped to his swim shorts and took a couple of beach towels out of a waterproof bag he had removed from the boat and spread them out on the sand, side by side. With his palms up, he gestured in the direction of the towels, and said, "Be my guest, Kate. Your choice."

Kate walked toward the towel with the huge Ranger logo across it, leaving the one with a Colorado ski slope theme for Bryan. They both laid back on the towels, clasping their hands under the their heads and gazing up at the cloud-spattered blue sky. Without any lead-in, Kate asked directly, "Bryan, what do you think about women in combat?"

"I can take it or leave it."

"No, really, Bryan. You know about the Minerva Experiment, don't you?"

"Just what I've read in the newspapers."

"Well, do you think women will be able to hack it in Colombia?"

"You know, I really haven't given it much thought. My gut feeling is that if the military machine ain't broke, don't fix it."

"Then, you don't think women can hack it."

"I didn't say that."

"But that's what you implied."

"I'm sorry if you took . . . "

"How else could one take it?"

"Look, to me, it's just a matter of where there's a choice between so-called career equality for women and this nation's combat readiness, the latter always wins."

"But that assumes those things are mutually exclusive—that they both can't exist at the same time."

"Well, I suppose you're right about that. I think there could be some common ground."

"And what might that be,?"

"I guess it might be letting women serve in ground combat who prove themselves equally able as men—if they can meet the same standards. But really, all this doesn't interest me one way or the other. I'm just a soldier, and a soldier just follows orders."

"Well, this interests me quite a lot, Bryan."

"That's quite evident."

"You see, I'm one of the Minerva participants."

"You are? Well, in that case, it interests me a lot too."

Bryan sensed that his last remark was not all that credible.

Kate felt the need to change the subject. Sitting up, inhaling deeply, and looking around at the pristine sand, lazy lagoon, and empathic weeping willows, Kate sighed, "You know, Bryan, this really is a special place."

"Well, let's try it then," Bryan said, as he teasingly picked Kate up kicking and screaming and carried her toward the crystal clear ten-foot deep swimming hole. On the third swing, he released her and watched her splash and frolic in the water.

"It's *cold* in here, Bryan. Wait till I get my hands on you," Kate added playfully as she swam toward the lagoon's edge to get back onto the warm sand.

As Kate crawled back on the sandbar, Bryan dived into the lagoon headlong, swimming as fast as he could to the river's bank, where a thick rope was hanging from a huge oak tree which arched over the lagoon.

Kate went back to her beach towel and stretched out on her back, soaking up the sun's warm rays.

"Hey Kate!" Bryan yelled from across the lagoon.

Kate propped herself up on her elbows.

"Watch this!"

Bryan scaled the embankment dragging along the ground the massive knot at the rope's end. When he got to the top of the embankment, he walked a few more feet away from the river and turned around. He then ran as fast as he could toward the river, hanging tightly to the rope as he cleared the bank, and slipping slowly down the rope until his feet touched the massive knot. Three times he swung back and forth about fifteen feet above the lagoon while the human pendulum slowed.

"Here goes nothing, Kate!" Bryan yelled, letting go of the rope with the timing of a bombardier. Bryan bullseyed the lagoon, plunging to the bottom, resurfacing after a few seconds.

"Not bad, for a man," teased Kate.

"I suppose you could do better," Bryan said breathily as he struggled to tread water.

"No doubt, Tarzan," Kate said smiling.

"Then be my guest, Jane."

Kate jumped up, dived into the lagoon, and swam to the opposite shore. She climbed the embankment and, once on top, she grabbed hold of a small guide rope and pulled the thick swinging rope toward her. The thick rope in her hand, she walked away from the river twice as far as Bryan had walked. She then turned toward the river and, holding the rope tightly, sprinted as fast as she could off the end of the embankment. In midair, she slipped down and standing on the massive knot, she swung way out past the sandbar above the rapidly moving river. When she was suspended horizontally, she heard a loud pop and felt herself being propelled downward toward the river. A large tree limb, with the thick rope attached, crashed into the lagoon and came close to striking Bryan, while Kate plunged helplessly into the river whose brisk current banged her into several protruding rocks as it whisked her downstream.

"Kate!" Bryan yelled as he forcefully pushed the rowboat into the fast-moving water. "Kate—don't panic! I'm coming!"

Kate heard nothing. The rushing water swallowed other sounds. She was now only semi-conscious, bobbing along like a rag doll in the rushing water.

Looking downstream from the rowboat, Bryan saw something that caused his stomach to knot. A large whirlpool—and Kate was heading right for it. He'd never seen it before. Must have formed in the last few months. Bryan rowed faster. Maybe the rock ahead would stop her. No, . . . she bounced around it. The log in the river. That would hang her up. . . . Yes! The log stopped her. Bryan came within a few feet of Kate, grabbed for her, and missed. She slowly slipped around the log, and continued to float downstream. She would soon be at the outer reaches of the whirlpool's sucking vortex—and there would be no saving her then.

Bryan looked frantically around the rowboat for any thing that might help him. Nothing. No innertube, no life jacket, no rope. It was the boat and him. He had to think fast. The boat picked up speed as the current propelled it within twenty-five yards of the outer edge of the vortex—enough speed that its streamlined hull allowed it to come even with and pass Kate's half-submerged, motionless body Bryan jumped from the boat, clutching onto Kate, and tried unsuccessfully to swim against the current. The boat entered the vortex, and Bryan, his eyes directed upstream, waited for the inevitable. He waited to begin feeling that increasingly strong sucking sensation on his body. He prayed that death would be swift. He waited and waited. It seemed like an eternity. Nothing. He turned around in the water and looked downstream. The whirlpool had disappeared. Like a miracle, it had disappeared.

Then he realized that the boat had plugged the underground

cave. He began to cry. He couldn't stop. Sobbing, he swam toward the flat river bank, pulling Kate along with him.

When he got Kate onto the sandy bank, she began to regain consciousness. She coughed a few times and spit up water. "How'd I do?" Kate gasped.

Bryan stroked her cheek a couple times and tenderly kissed her on her lips.

"Not bad, Kate. Not bad, at all."

JUNGLE FEVER

"Skeeters. That's what Tina called them. They could bite through flak jackets. Immune to repellent. That's what Tina used to say about the mosquitoes in Ranger School. Tina's gone now. Maybe forever."

Kate laid down her pen, closed her diary and stared out the front opening of her pup tent into the darkness. The swamp critters were making all kinds of weird sounds. Maybe they were mourning the loss of Tina. It had been three weeks since she had left. Critical. Near death. Still in intensive care. That was the latest report. The Ranger training sergeant said it was Tina's fault. But nobody's that stupid. Not Tina, anyway. And about the death. Maybe it happened for the best. If death can ever be justified.

During the first week of July, Kate, Tina, Sandy, and Lori had reported to the nine-week Ranger School Course at Fort Benning, and on arrival, the Ranger Battalion S-1 assigned Kate and Sandy to one training platoon, and Tina and Lori to another. The first eighteen days of training—the Benning phase—were particularly grueling. Awakened sometimes at two-thirty a.m to begin the training day, they doubletimed everywhere they went, and like Jump School, they constantly complied with orders to do pushups for any minor infraction of the rules. In this first phase, the young women—along with the male trainees—underwent training in hand-to-hand and pugil-stick combat, map reading and land navigation, demolitions, calling in artillery fire support, reconnaissance, and combat patroling. Tina referred to the training exercises variously as "beavershit patrols," "kneeknockers," and "shinbusters". She thought it was a waste of time, and was fairly vocal about it. Eventually, she was disciplined during one night patrol. After-

JOHN W. COOLEY

wards, she laughed about it because she thought her infraction had been so minor. She didn't understand why the cadre couldn't find humor in it. During night patrols, the trainees walked single file through the wooded training areas to their objective. Each trainee had phosphorescent tape on the back of his or her fatigue cap so they could follow one another. Tina delighted in removing her hat and placing it in the fork of a tree as she passed by, and then listening for the rest of the column accordion-crash into the tree behind her. The third time she did it, the commotion attracted the attention of the NCO lane grader. He wasn't amused. The rest was history. Despite Tina's shenanigans, by the end of the first phase, the four young women were skilled in forty-three separate combat tasks and were participating in five-mile runs daily.

After the Benning phase, the women went into the mountain phase of the training. For this, they were trucked to Dahlonoga, Georgia for seventeen days of military mountaineering skills, including rappeling, rock climbing, and building rope bridges. The high point of this training was rappeling down a two-hundred-foot cliff. That's where Tina met her fate. On that cliff.

Kate could not be sure how it had happened. She had not been there and thus had to rely on others' accounts. It had been raining that day, and the Ranger trainees had been sitting around in their ponchos in the gray, misty atmosphere waiting for their turn to rappel down the cliff. Tina had complained about nausea and stomach pains and had even vomited a few times waiting to rappel. She had asked permission of the training NCO to leave the mountain and go to the infirmary, but he had denied the request, noting that she would have to start Ranger School over if she didn't do the two-hundred-foot rappel. Looking back, in light of what happened, it probably would have been better for her to start Ranger School over.

The training cadre should have known better. Just last February, three officers and one NCO died of hypothermia in Ranger training in a swamp near Eglin Air Force Base. One of the second lieutenants had been the president of his West Point class. Kate had heard of him, but she didn't know him personally. Now Tina. And before, Charmaine. It shouldn't have happened. None of it should have happened.

But it did. Witnesses said the rain had stopped, and Tina had already negotiated her way down the escarpment once using the seat hip rappel. They had some training time left and the NCOs wanted a few trainees to do a hasty rappel, a more difficult, scary maneuver, particularly down a two-hundred-foot cliff. They asked for volunteers. No one volunteered. Tina—the female—was singled out. She resisted. She said she was sick. They called her a wimp; then they ordered her to do it. Tina knew the procedure—she had memorized it from the Ranger Handbook:

> *(6) Hasty rappel.*
> *(a) Face sideways to anchor.*
> *(b) Place rappel rope across the back.*
> *(c) The hand nearest the anchor is the guide hand;*
>   *the downhill hand is used to brake.*
> *(d) Descend sideways, full sole, body is almost*
>   *perpendicular to rock.*
> *(e) To stop, bring brake hand in front of body and*
>   *turn facing anchor point.*

But *knowing* the procedure wasn't enough. Tina had gone over the rock stiff-legged and had gotten to the point where she was standing full-sole, perpendicular to the vertical escarpment, rope over her back, left gloved hand up toward the anchor, and right gloved brake hand down the ravine. She started to move down the rock very slowly. Bringing her brake hand in front of her body, she turned toward the cliff every few feet and stopped for a few seconds. The training sergeant leaned over the top of the cliff and started yelling at her. At least, that's what the witnesses had said. He told her she was supposed to be doing a *hasty* rappel, not a *pasty* one—to get the glue off her feet and get down that rock. She put her brake hand down toward the ravine, and that's when it happened. The rope began slipping through her brake hand, and her foot caught in a crevice, causing her to turn upside down. Her body banged into the cliff, and she lost her grip. The wet rope began to slide through her hands, faster and faster. With the speed of slippage, there was no hope of braking. She plummeted down the cliff, only the friction of the gloves against the rope impeding, however slight, her descent. Two NCOs at the base of the cliff tried to break her fall with their own bodies, but with little success. The medics carted her away unconscious with internal injuries, multiple fractures, and worst of all, paralyzed from the waist down. The NCO at the top of the cliff said it was her error. If she had followed "the specs" and not panicked, it wouldn't have happened. That's what he told the investigators.

Tina didn't die at the base of the cliff. Neither did the NCOs who tried to break her fall. But someone did. Tina was pregnant. Again.

Kate didn't know who the father was. It wasn't really important. He probably would never know he had even been a father. Kate was angry, though, and hurt. Tina had said nothing to her about the pregnancy, either in Lexington or during the Benning phase. Probably too embarrassed. Kate was most angry, though, at the system. The system that stole Tina from her. A system that stole Tina's dream.

Kate brushed a couple mosquitoes from her arm, turned off her flashlight, and gently laid her head back on her rolled poncho. Tomorrow would begin her last week in the jungle phase—her last week in Ranger School. She could still blow it—Ranger School, the Minerva Experiment, her career, everything. Sleep didn't come easy.

2

The jungle phase of Ranger School is the toughest of all. In that phase, the Ranger candidates undergo a series of twenty-one-hour training days and are put through small boat operations, stream crossings, platoon swamp operations, counter guerrilla operations, and helicopter rappeling. They learn some advanced survival skills; they also become acquainted with some of the pervasive dangers of living in jungle and swamp terrain.

The training for Operation Athena, however, went beyond the traditional topics. The trainees were introduced to the kissing beetle, a poisonous insect prevalent in South and Central America, that carries Chagas disease and prefers to bite its victims on the face. At night it crawls out of its hiding place in an adobe wall or thatched roof and searches for a meal of human blood. It usually bites its victim near the eyes, first injecting an anesthetic to ensure the victim doesn't awaken. Like a vampire, the beetle drinks blood until it is gorged. And then, before crawling away, it defecates in the tiny wound, leaving behind in the victim's blood, deadly and untreatable protozoa that can kill—though sometimes not until twenty years later. Strangely, the bite is completely painless, and normally there are no immediate symptoms. Victims usually have no symptoms at all until the day they mysteriously collapse with heart failure.

Another "bug" that Rangers are taught to avoid is a micro-organism that causes the flesh-eating disease—necrotizing fascitis. A mild case of chicken pox can transform into the disease. It sometimes begins by showing signs of an abdomen that is red and tender to the touch. A couple days later, a ten-inch by ten-inch blistering black hole forms and spreads where the flesh-eating bacteria damages underlying tissue. It causes a loss of the skin lining of the abdomen and the stomach. The bacteria is believed to be a modified version of a virulent form of strep that caused life-threatening cases of scarlet fever in the 1800s. Others believe that it is an aggressive form of the streptococcal bacteria that has been causing strep throat and scarlet fever for thousands of years. Once in the body, the infection can spread, killing body tissue at a rate of up to an inch an hour.

Kate ruminated about these things that night as she stumbled through the thick mangrove swamps in the Florida bayou near Eglin.

She didn't know why she was having these thoughts. The face of that training NCO just kept popping back into her mind. He was almost diabolic in his teaching of these horrible things. It was as if he wished that some trainees would fall victim to these killer organisms so that he would have something to talk about at his next lecture. He probably didn't wish that; but it sure seemed like it. There was no question that he had relished telling stories about Ranger trainees who had surrendered parts of their legs at night to alligators in the mangrove. With every step, Kate's leg came in contact with an underwater root, creating the sensation that she was stepping on a gator. If she stepped on a loose limb, and it splashed up out of the water, she thought it was the tail of a gator coming at her. She was petrified. Sandy, her Ranger buddy, was behind her. If it wasn't for Sandy's presence and support, Kate might not have taken another step.

She tried to get her mind off these things by picturing Bryan. She had seen Bryan only once during the Benning phase. He was her squad's lane grader for a night combat patrol and he had been kind of stand-offish, not wanting the other squad members to know that he and Kate knew each other. He was afraid of showing favoritism that might reflect adversely on her. Ranger School is very competitive; if a trainee had complained that Kate was getting special treatment, she might have been booted out—or put back a class. She also had to worry about charges of fraternizing with superior officers. Kate definitely didn't want that.

She had also seen Bryan once again in the jungle phase. On the third day into the training, Bryan had sought her squad out while they were building a rope bridge across a stream. He had some bad news for her. He asked for help with a special reconnaissance mission, and of course Kate volunteered. When they were some distance from the rope bridge site, he told her that Lori had to be evacuated from Eglin. She had developed a high fever and a rash. Kate thought right away it was that flesh-eating disease, but Bryan assured her it was not. The doctors didn't know exactly what it was, but they thought she would have a full recovery. But one thing was for certain; Lori was eliminated from the Minerva Experiment.

As she sloshed through the mangroves, a thought flashed across Kate's mind. Could there be some kind of conspiracy going on here? First, Charmaine, battered to death against the jump tower; then Tina, falling from the cliff and left in critical condition; then Lori, with the fever and all. Not to mention Kate's own close brush with death on the Kentucky River. Could someone be masterminding a plot to thwart the Minerva Experiment? Paranoia was closing in.

A couple hours passed, and Kate's squad made some headway toward the edge of the swamp. Still walking through water, and occasionally stepping into holes of water up to her neck, Kate was holding up pretty well—with Sandy's help. Trying to keep rifles dry seemed futile, and the swamp water seemed a lot colder than the air, but that was an illusion. So were the vines that hung low from the trees and glanced off bare arms. In the darkness they felt like snakes—the snakes that Kate had seen in the Benning phase. The ones they had to cook and eat that night on the long range patrol or eat nothing at all. As they trudged on, a pink haze descended and the sun emerged to paint bright patches in the cage-like mesh of the timbered swamp. Kate heard the uniform clapping of chopper rotors in the distance—the chopper that was to extract Kate and her squadmates from this swamp and insert them within the hour—by rappelling—into an even more inhospitable one. The swamp where the four soldiers had died from exposure.

Thoughts of the "caisson trio" from Camp Buckner flitted across Kate's mind. Now she could empathize with their plight in being left to endure elements strapped to that tree for twenty-four hours. For the first time, she felt remorse for what she had done to them. She felt a strong need to convey her feelings to them. Wimpy; a Ranger wouldn't do that. She felt confused . . . and tired. Hunger gnawed her to distraction.

After a few hundred yards more of slogging, the squad came to a small clearing of solid ground. The emboldened sun had, by

250 JOHN W. COOLEY

now, exposed itself fully above the horizon, and even at that early hour, its light was warm and comforting like a mother attending to a waking child. The Huey had already landed, and the sun rays bathing the polished exterior made it sparkle. It seemed out of place in a combat setting—even a hypothetical one. The lane grader sergeant gave the signal for the squad to board the chopper. Despite their exhausted condition, the trainees quickly took their positions and the chopper roared away with its rotor at steep tilt. Within twenty minutes, the Huey was hovering fifty feet above a tiny clearing carved in dense jungle-like terrain. Two ropes dropped from both sides of the chopper, and Kate's squadmates began to rappel down them into the thicket's chasm. Into hell—another two days and nights of it.

Kate stepped to the door, her M16 rifle slung over her back. She bent over and reached for one of the ropes with her gloved hands and looked down into the chasm. She froze. Fear gripped her very soul. She could not take hold of the rope. The lane grader shouted at her to "move out." She did not react. Thoughts of Tina plunging down the two-hundred-foot cliff consumed her. More thoughts of a conspiracy whirled through her mind. The lane grader again shouted at her. She straightened up and, in the deafening roar of the rotors, shook her head "no" to the lane grader and withdrew to a webbed seat inside the chopper. The lane grader pursued her, pointed to the Ranger tab on his upper sleeve, and yelled something as loud as he could at her. Because of the din, she couldn't understand it, but she sensed it was insulting. Maybe even obscene. Something about never getting a Ranger tab. She just sat there in a trance. After trying once more to get her attention, the lane grader signaled the pilot to head back to the combat base.

Back at base camp, Kate remained in a trancelike state and cried intermittently most of the day. She refused medical attention and asked to be left alone. She had one request. She wanted to see Bryan. At dusk, Bryan arrived by jeep and took her, on foot, far into the thicket where they could be alone.

Bryan spread out his poncho on the damp ground and invited Kate to sit down with him. He asked straightforwardly, "What is wrong with you, Kate? What happened out there? I just got bits and pieces from the NCO. You balked or something."

"I can't explain it," Kate replied, trying to get next to her feelings. "I simply can't explain it. When I was in the Huey and looked down into that hole in the jungle, I felt repulsed. Like someone or something was telling me something bad was about to happen to me. Like I would never come out of that hole alive. A premonition . . . I couldn't move."

"You've had premonitions before, right?"

"Yeah."

"Did they always prove true?"

"No, not always. But things have happened. Recently."

"Like what?"

"Tina's fall; and other things."

"Yes?"

"Charmaine—and Lori."

"Yeah, so what."

"Bryan . . . I think there's a conspiracy against us."

"Against whom?"

"The women in the Experiment."

"Come on, get serious."

"I'm serious. For some reason, I keep thinking of that lizard of a woman I met in Washington the day of my Congressional testimony. Lila Davis, or something. I never told you about her. But she's evil. I just feel it."

"And, so you think she's orchestrating . . . "

"There's also something else I never told you, Bryan. About my sister. She's paranoid and schizoid."

"Yes, so . . . "

"So I'm paranoid about being paranoid. Could that happen to me? I mean about what happened to my sister? Living in a home for the mentally ill. I've thought about that all day."

"I think you're making tremendous leaps of logic. Look, the

explanation is simple. The night swamp training has different effects on different people. You just have let yourself get painted into a corner by all the potential dangers. You have let it overwhelm you. It's really not that bad at all. Many people experience the same fears as you did during this training. You'll survive it."

"Thanks for your confidence in me, but . . . "

"No buts, Kate. You can make it. You've made it so far through Ranger School. You're right at the end. Sandy—your ranger buddy—will be there to pull you through. You know you can rely on her."

"She's probably wondering right now about . . . "

"One valuable lesson my Beast Barracks squad leader taught me I recommend to you—take one day at a time; if that's overwhelming, one hour at a time; if that's too much, one minute, and so on. The point is you can survive anything if you break it down into its survivable pieces. This has nothing to do with male or female. When you're in that swamp, just put one foot in front of the other. And soon the training will be over."

Kate looked into Bryan's deep blue eyes and reflected for a moment on similar advice given her by Todd Gavin back in Beast Barracks. She knew it; she just had failed to apply it. She also knew that she was becoming intensely attracted to Bryan. The soft sound of Bryan's voice induced her return to reality.

"Guess there's only one way I can prove my absolute faith in you," Bryan whispered as he began unbuttoning and removing his fatigue shirt.

Kate was startled. She saw him pull a knife from his front pants pocket and, as he sat next to her, pull the fatigue shirt over his groin area.

"This thing means nothing to me, if you don't have one too."

With that, Bryan slashed the threads holding the Ranger tab to his upper shirtsleeve and removed the tab. Handing it to Kate, he said warmly, "You earned this token of my trust by getting this far. Return it to me when you get your own, Kate."

Kate inched her warm, moist lips toward Bryan's and closed

her eyes, wagering humiliation that his would be there to receive them. They were and more. Their lips plied feverishly against each other for seconds and then opened, flowerlike, their tongues probing the innerreaches of ecstasy. He held her tenderly in his arms and slowly laid her back on the poncho. Without protest, he sought the buttons of her fatigue shirt, one by one. Moonlight rippled off her ivory breasts, as his hands roamed magically over them. Her nipples firmed instantly and her back arched, anxious to receive him. Soon it was flesh against flesh; man against woman.

0368-COOL

BRIEFING AT CARTAGENA

President Guardina sat expressionless, gazing pensively through the vertical slit-window of his medieval-style office in the fortress San Felipe de Borajas. He was waiting for General Throckmiller and the others to arrive on this November day for the VIP briefing on the plan to raid Bodega's hideout.

"Beautiful Cartagena!" he thought to himself. He was enjoying a variegated tapestry of red-tiled roofs, white balconies, and makeshift wooden sales stalls staffed by sleepy-eyed *mercantes*. Watching these businessmen play mind games with smug American tourists was always entertaining. He reveled in the Americans' gullibility.

He shifted his gaze for a moment to the plaza area. He knew that the panorama he was enjoying would change significantly over the next several days. Soon, vast throngs of people would be filling the maze of narrow streets and the expansive Plaza Bolivar, with its famous namesake giant statue of "The Liberator" to celebrate Cartagena Independence Day. A colorful, carnival atmosphere would shortly permeate the city, culminating in the crowning of Miss Colombia. As President, he would be expected to take part in the crowning and make the customary patriotic speech. "This year," Guardina mused, "Independence Day will have special meaning."

A sudden knock at the door brought President Guardina back to reality. "Are you ready for us, Mr. President?" uttered a voice through the door.

"Certainly," Guardina said as he arose and walked briskly to meet fifteen or so military officials and government dignitaries now filing into the room. Esther, Lila, Emilio, and Senator Carrington were among them.

As she glanced around the room, Lila's face displayed a blend of curiosity and envy. She felt a rush of power just being in the presence of the Colombian President again.

Smiling hospitably, Guardina circled the group, mixing handshakes with verbal pleasantries, and then led them to a, high-ceilinged conference room adjacent to his office. The large room, looked more like a posh parlor than a place for a business meeting. A faint musty odor filled the air and conjured up visions of pirates and swashbucklers.

Gradually, the members of the entourage chose their seats, Lila and Esther almost vanished from sight in their overstuffed chairs. All eyes turned toward President Guardina who was standing in front of a projection screen at the end of the dimly lit room. His short stature, bald head, and corpulent physique made him into an Elmer Fudd lookalike. When he spoke, everyone anticipated humor, though he did not always expect to evoke it.

"I hope you find this meeting room satisfactory," said the President in mildly broken English. "It served as Simon Bolivar's war room during the Magdalena Campaign of 1811. Some people say his ghost is still here. I hope it is." Pausing, he dead-panned, "We need all the help we can get."

As a wave of muffled laughter traversed the room, Lieutenant General Throckmiller, Commander-in-Chief of SIXCOM, rose from his chair and moved slowly toward President Guardina. He shook Guardina's hand firmly, and, with an engagingly sincere smile, said pointedly, "I'm here to help, too, Mr. President."

"Good, General" Guardina replied with an impish grin. "You can begin by helping me get this damned overhead projector working. I'm all thumbs when it comes to this hi-tech stuff."

" Uh, uh, Mr. President, . . . " General Throckmiller began respectfully, "it might help if we plugged it in."

"*Hay carumba!*" Guardina roared with playful sarcasm. "You Yankees really *are* ingenious."

Colonel Steuben, one of the general's aides, obsequiously moved behind the screen and plugged in the projector. "Mission accomplished, sir!" he said to the general in a tone inviting a compliment. None came.

"Ladies and gentlemen," said President Guardina, his face just visible above the top of the podium and his hands tightly clutching its sides, "I welcome you all to the beautiful island fortress of Cartagena. First I must apologize for the hoarseness of my voice. I've been trying to fend off a touch of the flu for the past few days. We are assembled here today, as you know, for a very important purpose. Drug cartels, under the overall leadership of Raoul Bodega and operating in Medellín, Cali, Barranquilla, and Bogota, have practically brought this country to its knees, economically, politically, and sociologically." Guardina paused and then intoned, "It is difficult, at times—even for the President—to know who is in charge of the government." Guardina broke into a full grin and his audience chuckled. "Kidding aside," Guardina continued, "the drug kingpins' covert influence in the government, in the political parties, and in the police and military organizations has been so pervasive that the distinction between good and bad, between right and wrong, has frequently disappeared."

"For the Colombian people, the situation has been hopelessly confusing, and, sometimes mercilessly unjust. People with a civic conscience who have reported cartel members to the police authorities have found, much to their chagrin, that the police to whom they spoke were cartel sympathizers and, in some cases, actual cartel members. Consequently, police frequently did not act on the reports; in other situations, the police committed heinous atrocities against the reporting persons or members of their families."

"In many ways, our government is paralyzed. The Bodegas are totally ruthless. Responsibility for the Intercontinental Aviation jet crash recently, which left over a hundred people dead and a nine-year-old child as the sole survivor, has now been traced conclusively to the Bodegas. They wiped out all those innocent people because a warring drug lord from the Cali cartel was on that flight. It is our hope that, with the type of U.S. military combat assistance that will be described here today, we will stop this senseless blood-letting and wrest our governmental power from the grip of these drug villains and return it to the citizens of Colombia once and for all. Having made these short introductory remarks, I am now pleased and privileged to present to you, Lieutenant General Winston Throckmiller, who will, I am sure, superbly serve as our master of ceremonies for our briefing this afternoon. General Throckmiller?"

Throckmiller approached the podium while contemplating what his opening remarks would be. He was still trying to sizeup Guardina. When he met him previously in Washington, he seemed both businesslike and affable. Today Guardina was acting differently. It was difficult to know when to take the President seriously.

As Throckmiller stepped toward the podium, the diminutive Guardina faced him, pulled a short, black comb from his trouser pocket with his left hand, placed it directly under his nose, while simultaneously clicking his heels together loudly, and, without uttering a sound, thrust his right arm in the air in the infamous Hitler-style salute. Guardina then executed an abrupt about face and goose-stepped to the largest of the overstuffed chairs next to his chief of staff. Throckmiller strained to appear composed. He had never experienced this kind of conduct from a high public official. Good-natured laughter signaled that the audience was enjoying the President's performance.

Emilio, watching the others' sycophantic behavior, was not at all amused. He knew another not-so-pretty-side of President Guardina. He recognized Guardina's present behavior for what it was: a mocking burlesque through which Guardina was trying to vent some of his long and deeply held animosity toward the United States.

In the late 1930s and during World War II, Guardina was engaged in extremist right-wing politics in Colombia. He was a Nazi sympathizer and, after the War, he was instrumental in arranging the safe passage of several accused Nazi war criminals to South America. Some of them were assassinated shortly after their arrival. Guardina, privately, had always blamed the United States' Central Intelligence Agency for these murders, but he had no proof of it. Only in the mid-seventies did Guardina begin to shed his Fascist tendencies and to become more moderate, politically. This was in part because the Colombian people no longer wanted anything to do with dictatorships. Also, it was in Guardina's health interests to do so. The rapidly forming drug cartels, under the leadership of "young buck" drug lords like Raoul Bodega and his brother Hector, did not tolerate extreme right wing or extreme left wing politicians. Many of the extremists were tortured, maimed, or killed by conscienceless, faceless renegades using the most abhorrent methods imaginable. Learning of these atrocities and liking life a lot, Guardina had lithely moved more toward the center, politically, and had succeeded in avoiding the Bodega brothers' wrath. The only thing that Guardina despised and distrusted more than the United States was the Bodega clan. Emilio knew. . . . Yes, Emilio knew Guardina well.

Taking Guardina's unusual behavior in stride, General Throckmiller began his presentation. "Thank you, President Guardina, for your introductory remarks. They have put our reason for being here today very clearly into perspective. Before we begin the detailed portion of the briefing, I would like to acknowledge the presence of several dignitaries of both Colombia and the United States. First, I would like to acknowledge General Oscar Rojillo, the President's Chief of Staff and the Minister of National Defense." Throckmiller paused while Rojillo smiled, moved his head from side to side, and bowed ever so slightly in a rocking motion, seeming all the time to enjoy the recognition. "Also present," Throckmiller continued, "are Jose Validato, Colombia's Minister of the Interior, Fernando Virgadamo, Colombia's Minister of Mines and Energy, and Luis Ramirez, Colombia's Minister of Foreign Affairs." Throckmiller again paused while the two men, smiling and raising their hands, identified themselves for the group.

Throckmiller continued, "I can tell you, President Guardina, how impressed we are that such high-ranking members of your cabinet are present here. It clearly communicates your country's dedication to the success of the military operation that we are about to describe. We are also fortunate to have with us today, U.S. Congresswoman Esther Grant; U.S. Senator John Carrington; Ms. Lila Davis-Whitfield, President of the Women's Republican American Traditional Heritage Foundation; and Mr. Emilio Gutierrez, a Chief Staff Assistant at the Colombian Embassy in the United States."

Allowing a few seconds for them to identify themselves, Throckmiller continued. "We are honored to have these four Government servants, handpicked by the U.S. Congress to act as observers for "Operation Athena".

Throckmiller continued, "Before we get to Colonel's Steuben's part of the briefing, I need to make you all aware of a recent development involving the Bodegas. Raoul Bodega's brother, Hector, was captured three days ago by the Colombian police in a shootout in the Tequendama Hotel in Bogotá. Hector was wounded in capture, though the seriousness of his condition was not disclosed. I can tell you now that Hector's wounds were not life-threatening. During the capture, he received a gunshot wound to his shoulder and was struck repeatedly on the head and the back with a police nightstick. His present prognosis is very good; but he will be experiencing significant pain for some time."

"This description of his condition is, of course, top secret. Also top secret is his present location. He is currently being detained in a holding area on the first floor of this very fortress. He is expected to be kept here for approximately one more week. Then he will be moved to another secure location yet to be identified.

"How was it, General, that Hector was able to be captured?" interjected Minister Virgadamo.

Throckmiller's face turned to gray and his eyes filled with uncharacteristic disgust. "It's not a very pleasant story, but to understand the nature of the beasts we are dealing with, you should know the background of the capture. Hector's wife, Maria, has a cousin named Sofia Cordova. Sofia's husband, Pablo Cordova, was for many years one of Hector's lieutenants in the drug cartels. About a year ago, Pablo decided to form his own cartel and, essentially, to compete with the Bodega brothers."

"Outraged, apparently, Raoul and Hector decided to have him executed. They arranged for him to be ambushed when he was driving his jeep near Barranquilla on the mountain roads between the campesinos that he managed in his newly formed cartel. What the Bodega brothers didn't count on was that Pablo's five-year-old son would be with him. But they didn't let that interfere with their plan."

"Pablo's head and torso were found on the roadside, with four limbs still missing to this day. His son's bashed and battered body was found at the foot of a cliff. The boy's body was missing its right arm. Sticking out of Pablo's mouth was his son's blood-drenched arm with the hand clenching a note which read "*Un hombre no viva de pan, solamente*"—"Man does not live by bread, alone." The note was signed, "*Afectuosamente* (fondly), Raoul and Hector."

"Needless to say, Pablo's wife went hysterical when she learned of the massacre of her husband and child. She wanted immediate vengeance. Through her cousin, Maria Bodega, she had learned previously that Hector frequented the Tequendama Hotel in Bogota. She had also known that, for about two years, the Bodega brothers had been operating their cartels from hideouts located in abandoned gold mines in the Envigado area and from the active Cosquez and Muzo emerald mines located north of Bogota. She didn't know exactly when Hector would be at the hotel in Bogota or where, precisely, the abandoned gold mines were located, but she knew that the information would aid the police investigation of the Bodega brothers. It did."

"Colombian police staked out the Tequendama Hotel and caught Hector completely by surprise. The police also alerted the Ministers of Defense and Interior; and a joint Colombian-American military reconnaissance team was assembled."

"Police raided the Cosquez and Muzo emerald mines and found no Bodega followers. Shortly afterwards, four of the abandoned gold mines, approximately thirty-five miles west and north of Envigado, were identified as possible Bodega hideouts. Two weeks ago, a U.S. Ranger platoon which was part of the reconnaissance team spotted Raoul Bodega and some of his cohorts in the vicinity of one of the gold mines."

"They observed activities at that site for about three days and estimated that the Bodegas had the equivalent of about a reinforced battalion of guerrilla forces in the area. Apparently these guerrillas had been trained by Hector during Raoul's imprisonment. During the day, these guerrillas worked as laborers in the campesinos. At night they took up weapons and went on clandestine missions of terror establishing their control of the small villages in the vicinity. In compliance with its orders, the reconnaissance team took no direct action against Bodega's forces." "There was only one skirmish in which a platoon-sized guerrilla force happened on to a squad-sized U. S. Ranger patrol at dawn—coincidentally on the same day Hector was captured in Bogota. The patrol, with the help of a quick-thinking patrol leader and some fast-acting helicopter assistance, was evacuated safely while inflicting several casualties on the guerrilla platoon. The perceived substantial buildup and increased activity of the Bodegas' guerrilla forces precipitated the present interest in a direct combat, search and destroy type operation in the area of the goldmines. Thus, the birth of the concept of Operation Athena, officially approved by the two Presidents yesterday."

"Oh, I should add one somewhat positive footnote to all this. Sofia Cordova, who provided the material information which led to Hector's capture, will be receiving the equivalent of three-and-a-half American dollars in the near future. The American Government offered a bounty of two million dollars for information leading to Hector's capture and the Colombian government had a million dollar price tag on his head. Similar amounts are being offered for information or activities leading to Raoul's capture. Of course, bounties cannot be paid to professionals like U.S. and Colombian military or police personnel. I hope this answers your question, Minister Virgadamo."

"Quite satisfactorily," General.

"Good. Then we should move on to Colonel Steuben's presentation." Throckmiller glanced to his right and nodded to Steuben who was poised to assume the spotlight.

Steuben, a man in his late forties with a shaved head and Santini-like bearing, strode toward the podium. He exuded confidence. Beneath his seemingly impenetrable veneer, however, resided an angry, contemptuous, conflicted psyche. He was a graduate of the Virginia Military Institute. No small accomplishment. When he entered on active duty as a second lieutenant, he initially thought himself to be inferior to West Point graduates. He soon learned differently. Over the years, he was promoted quickly in the military because of his deep-seated desire to outdo West Pointers, whom he subconsciously despised. In many ways, Steuben thought West Pointers were stupid—naive, narrow-minded, and hypermechanistic. He learned how to use their stupidity to his advantage.

In his view, West Pointers were successful in their jobs because of the strong-willed, resourceful, ambitious women that they married and because of the "West Point Protection Association"—West Pointers for West Pointers. The WPPA was sort of a Pentagon-controlled West Point mafia which guaranteed timely promotions and select military assignments for their own. Steuben was unaware of the influence of the WPPA until after he had been in the service for about five years. He was turned down by the Pentagon on two service assignments which he had requested as a captain—one assignment to the 82nd Airborne Division and one to the 101st Airborne Division. The pentagon slotted two West Point "ring-knockers" in those positions. He had no actual proof of West Point favoritism, but it sure smelled like it to him.

A year later he received an assignment to the 82nd Airborne Division, but he still had a bitter, "second best" taste in his mouth. Recognizing the power of the WPPA, he decided to collaborate, not compete. He manipulated himself into key "second best" advisory roles where he could play upon the West Pointers' vulnerability to adulation. He had served as briefing officer for two other general officers prior to General Throckmiller. He massaged their egos well enough to land a job with Throckmiller during the Desert Storm campaign.

He hated doing what he was doing. It was like constantly giving blowjobs. He often suffered a bulemic urge to vomit. But at the same time he liked being within that small circle of military power at the top of the military pyramid—even if he was really only a flunkie without any hope of ever becoming a general officer.

Steuben had rehearsed this briefing for a couple of hours. He felt well prepared, perhaps over-prepared. He was under strict orders from Throckmiller not to mention that Operation Athena had a secondary purpose of testing the combat mettle of military women. Throckmiller felt that it was not necessary to remind President Guardina that the U.S. was using females for the first time to fight Colombia's battles.

Steuben began speaking with meticulous precision. "Ladies and gentlemen, in the next ten minutes or so, I am going to briefly describe the tactical situation concerning Operation Athena and answer any questions you may have regarding it."

He flashed on the screen his first transparency consisting of a map of the Envigado area showing the locations of four abandoned gold mines, in a crescent configuration, labeled A,B,C, and D with four broad-brush, arc-shaped arrows pointed toward each of the letters. Removing a shiny, telescopic-type metal pointer from his pocket, he extended it smartly to its full 30-inch length. He pointed to the Letter "A" projected on the screen and continued speaking.

"This is our primary target. Reliable intelligence information leads us to believe that Raoul Bodega has located his principal operations center here. However, we also know that Bodega moves, from time to time, to locations "B", "C", and "D" which are at distances of about one, two, and three miles, respectively, from location A. About one mile separates the four mines from each other."

"Our overall mission in this operation is to capture Raoul

Bodega alive. Thus, we are going to move ground troops against all four locations simultaneously. Four Ranger companies will individually attack each of the four abandoned mines at a predetermined date and time. Two Ranger companies will be held in reserve about six miles south of the location "A" and will be choppered in as needed. Four helicopter gunships will provide cover for each of the advancing Ranger companies at each of the four objectives. We will also soften up the four targets a few minutes before the attacks with synchronized precision bombing executed by low-flying, stealth fighter-bombers. The 15th Air Squadron on the aircraft carrier . . . ."

"If I might interrupt, Colonel Steuben?"

"No problem, Minister Rojillo."

"Please clarify how you intend to capture Bodega alive if you are going to bomb the hell out of the mines before the Rangers move in."

"I was going to cover that later, came the reply, but I will be happy to provide the explanation now. The fighter pilots will receive a detailed briefing on the carrier *Enterprise* just prior to take-off. It will be impressed upon them that the nature of their mission is *not* to collapse the bunkers and to inflict casualties, but rather to create clearings in the jungle on the Rangers' approach routes to their four objectives. I should add that the fighter-bombers will be making only one bombing run on each of the locations. Intelligence indicates that the four locations are equipped with quad-fifty anti-aircraft guns, but are not routinely manned. The jet airstrikes must be accurate on the first go-round, because a second fly-over would spell certain disaster for these jet-jockies. Surprise and precision bombing are the keys to a successful air mission here. This is similar to . . . ."

"Colonel, I would like to point out something here."

"Be my guest, Minister Virgadamo."

"As Minister of Mines and Energy, I am very well acquainted with the nature of the four mines that you have described as military objectives here. About ten years ago, I was part of an expedition to explore these abandoned, Government-owned mines to determine whether they would useful to the Government of Colombia for any purpose. They had been abandoned approximately one hundred years ago. We had no idea what we would discover inside them. But we were well aware of the saying ` *La curiosidád mató el gato.*' Over a ten month period our eight-man expedition toured the innards of these four mines. What we found was astounding. Even though the mine entrances were separated by some miles on the surface, what we found under the ground was an interconnecting web of tunnels. It was not clear to us who had dug this labyrinth of interconnections, why they had dug them, or when they had been dug."

"In the report we eventually submitted to the Ministry of Mines and Energy, we noted this unusual discovery and our recommendation was that the mines be used as an underground control center for government operations in the event of a nuclear attack or some other kind of cataclysmic event. A bill was introduced into the Colombian legislature to appropriate funds to develop such government emergency operations center, and it was soundly defeated. Within two years, our expedition's report and all papers related to the legislation had mysteriously disappeared. The purge was so thorough that no member of the expedition team could even document that he had been a member of it. I want to emphasize this also. About at this same time, millions of dollars worth of computer equipment, communications equipment, high-tech military weapons, including heat-seeking missiles, and strangely, one thousand U.S.-manufactured tactical nuclear artillery projectiles, were discovered missing. A half-hearted investigation was undertaken by the Government and was concluded unsuccessfully within about three months. The Government reported publicly that the investigation determined that the stolen equipment and material had been taken out of the country and perhaps out of South America and that further investigation would be futile and ineffectual. I point out these facts only to underscore the dangers which might accompany the operation you've described."

"No, you are quite right, Minister Virgadamo. We are well

aware of the potential danger you have just described. We have simply concluded that the importance of our mission outweighs the dangers."

"But what if those bombs land on some of those nuclear projectiles?" asked President Guardina. "Is it possible that we could have a nuclear holocaust in the city of Medellín?"

"Well, Mr. President, we don't see that as a reasonable possibility. First, we have no information that any of the nuclear projectiles are still in this country. But even if they are and assuming that Raoul has them in his possession, we think that it is highly unlikely that they would be stored outside the entrances to the mines. It is far more likely that they are secreted away in the underground labyrinth."

"Secondly, even if they were outside the mine entrances, because of the design of the detonating devices on these projectiles, nuclear fission could not be activated by the concussion of exploding bombs. The only exception to this would be, of course, a direct hit. We think this possibility is so remote as to be discounted. But even assuming a direct hit, these nuclear projectiles are of a very low yield—approximately five thousandths of a megaton. Remember, these are *tactical* nuclear weapons, designed for battlefield use by being propelled from eight-inch howitzers, which are tracked vehicles. The zone of destruction of one of the nuclear projectiles is approximately fifteen hundred meters in diameter."

"Fallout and residual radiation do pose problems after detonation, but their effects can be controlled through appropriate warnings, protective clothing, and other precautions. We will be prepared to distribute to the troops and civilians in surrounding villages, the appropriate protective clothing and equipment immediately upon learning of a nuclear blast. We are also prepared to effect mass helicopter evacuation of all military and civilian personnel in the area, should that become necessary. But, again, let me emphasize that we estimate the probability of a nuclear blast is less than one thousandth of one percent. Probability theorists would . . .

"I am not concerned with what the probability theorists think,

Colonel Steuben," Guardina said agitatedly. "I'm concerned with the health and safety of my citizens. The theorists were wrong about Pearl Harbor, the *Titanic*, and the dissolution of the U.S.S.R. One nuclear blast could not only cause death and injuries to our people, but it could also have international diplomatic implications. We could be embarrassed in the world community and could be viewed as "nuclear nutcakes" who should be carefully watched and controlled. We definitely don't want that."

Throckmiller interrupted. "With all due respect, Mr. President," I think that you are exaggerating the situation well beyond the realm of reason. If you are having second thoughts about Operation Athena, then perhaps you may want to discuss the matter with President Benton, and we can postpone these present plans until after you have had that opportunity. The point is that, militarily, we cannot conduct Operation Athena without the bombings. Without the initial sorties, we would subject our ground troops to a high risk of annihilation, particularly considering the terrain in the area of the mines."

"No, General, postponing Operation Athena will not be necessary. I guess my Latin hyperanxiety is getting the best of me. As you can appreciate, presidents *do* have to worry about these kinds of things."

"I can certainly understand that, Mr. President. Perhaps Colonel Steuben should resume."

Guardina nodded agreement; Steuben began again. "General Throckmiller alluded to something which perhaps I should go into a little more: the terrain. The area of the Andean Ridge in which these mines are located is an extremely treacherous region. Mountains reach heights of six thousand five hundred feet. Thick jungle foliage on the lower portions of the mountains and in the lowlands generally restricts movement and there are few paved roads. While the temperature hovers around seventy degrees Fahrenheit in this region most of the year, heavy rains, usually totaling about fifty-six inches annually, regularly convert the few existing dirt roads into impassable quagmires. The month of November is no exception. Steep cliffs, unexpected ravines, high waterfalls, and channel-cutting streams are prevalent in the area." "Animals, reptiles, and water creatures are in prolific abundance. Some of the species are quite dangerous to humans. For example, piranhas are known to gather in shoals and prey upon any living things, including large mammals, and occasionally humans. Electric eels, some measuring up to six feet in length, patrol the wider tributaries and prey on their enemies by inflicting electric shocks. Anacondas, constrictor-type water snakes, live in the rivers of the area and can attain a length of up to thirty feet. Many species of venomous snakes, including the coral snake, can be found in the surrounding rivers and streams. In some respects, the region of Operation Athena is a military tactician's nightmare. In others, it represents a challenge which pushes the envelope of a soldier's endurance and ingenuity. It is not surprising that the Bodega brothers chose this terrain to locate their operations center. It has natural defenses of almost unparalleled advantage." "Colonel Steuben," Minister Virgadamo murmured, in measured speech, half angrily, half ominously. "Don't forget the caiman—"

"The what?"

"The caiman—that sneaky, perfidious crocodile. One of the members of our mine-exploring expedition lost his arm to one of those abominable creatures when he was relaxing and sunning in what he thought was a placid cove off one of the streams about a half-mile from mine area. It was a grotesque sight. The screaming; the screeching; the blood everywhere. They are not to be trusted."

"That's one I overlooked. Thanks for reminding me. Actually, the joint reconnaissance team reported spotting several Caiman in the vicinity of the mines. The Rangers will be given specific warnings about them."

Steuben quickly flashed another transparency on the screen to draw attention away from his oversight. He was supposed to be perfect. He wondered what Throckmiller was thinking now. Would Throckmiller needle him later about it? He had needled him before. But on those occasions Steuben felt he had deserved the needling.

Besides, it had helped him become more perfect. Throckmiller had always told him that the goal of a good briefing officer was "superfection"—a word that Throckmiller took pride in coining. Pointing to the screen, Steuben began speaking at an accelerated rate of speed. "This chart shows the numerical composition, armaments, and technical equipment of the air and ground forces which will be used in this operation. Note that each Ranger on the ground will be equipped with a device that emits a radio signal. This will assist the chopper pilots and other ground troops in locating individual Rangers who might get separated from their main units during a firefight. This device will also help unit commanders to keep track of or locate his or her . . . " Steuben bit his lip. God! More ammunition for Throckmiller " . . . eh, ah, correction, *his* soldiers should the fighting move into the maze of tunnels in the mines. We don't expect to . . . "

This was a good time, Lila thought, to put Steuben on the spot. "Colonel Steuben," she blurted out in her nasally high-pitched aristocratic tone, "I have a question," her voice dropping to a lower, self-righteous level.

"Yes, Ms. Davis-Whitfield?"

She continued with an authoritative air. "My question is really basic. I am no military strategist, but common sense tells me that maybe the underlying premise to this whole operation should be questioned. Maybe we don't need to *execute* the operation at all. Wouldn't it make much more sense simply to surround these four objectives with troops and then give Raoul Bodega an ultimatum to surrender or suffer the consequences. Under those circumstances it seems to me highly unlikely that Bodega would stand and fight—with the most elite of the U.S. military fighting men staring at him." Now, Lila was biting her lip. "Bodega would, I think, most likely surrender. Also, a related question is, how do you expect to succeed against Bodega, should he retreat into the tunnel maze? Wouldn't you be likely to 'shoot yourself in the foot' if you tried to chase Bodega and his desperados through those dark, uncharted passageways?"

"Your questions are right on the mark, ma'am," Steuben responded politely. He wondered to himself why this *American* bitch was attempting to criticize this *American* plan in front of the Colombian dignitaries. The thought briefly crossed his mind that maybe she was out to get him, personally. She was bitchy enough. "In designing this operation, I assure you that we have considered both of your questions. As to the ultimatum suggestion, this technique has been attempted unsuccessfully many times in the past by Colombian police and military in situations involving both of the Bodegas. In all of those situations, the Bodegas feigned cooperation, sought time to consider terms of the surrender, and in the meantime, called in reserve guerrilla forces inflicting tremendous casualties on the police and the military. The Bodegas fight like rats when cornered. We have concluded that the ultimatum technique will not work in this situation."

"As to your second question, as I was about to explain before, we do not expect Raoul and his comrades to retreat into the mines. It would be like retreating into a brick wall. He would be faced with the same combat limitations which would face us fighting through the dark passageways. His only advantage would be that he might know the twists and turns of the tunnels better than we would. However, we would have the advantage of chemicals, such as tear gas, to flush them out of their rat-holes."

Throckmiller flinched slightly, adding "All of the Rangers, of course, will be provided with gas masks and protective gear for chemical warfare."

"Thank you, General, for pointing that out," Steuben said respectfully. "I hope this satisfies your concerns, ma'am."

Of course, it doesn't, Lila thought to herself. "Perfectly, Colonel," Lila said in a satisfied tone.

"Well that completes the briefing for this afternoon, unless there are any remaining questions," Steuben declared. Pausing slightly, he continued. "Fine, since there are no more questions, I will turn the podium back to General Throckmiller."

Guardina piped up, "When is all this to take place, Colonel."

"Perhaps, I should answer that question," General Throckmiller interposed. "The specific date and time of the initiation of Operation Athena has not yet been determined. It will depend on further intelligence information and, quite frankly, the weather. We wouldn't want to kick off this operation in the middle of a tropical rainstorm. The most I can tell you is that the operation will probably occur within the next week. You will be kept constantly informed, President Guardina, of the tactical situation and you will be given at least twelve hours notice of the scheduled time of attack."

"Thank you, General," said Guardina. "I guess many of you would like to get back to your hotels and get freshened up for the State dinner this evening. We will be meeting in the banquet room of the Cartagena Hilton Hotel at seven-thirty p.m. You don't have to worry about security . . . ."

While Guardina was talking, Esther leaned over to Emilio and whispered. "Where's my contribution? It's been more than six months."

"Soon, madam, soon," Emilio whispered back.

"You have forty-eight hours," she said in a voice that meant business. "After that, I'll take pleasure in exposing you."

Guardina continued in the background, " . . . Both General Throckmiller and I have arranged for an elite, joint security contingent for the entire evening, and for individual escorts back to your hotel rooms if you so desire. This is not done to scare you, of course. Actually, we have not had much terrorism lately in Cartagena. The extra security will be present only to provide you with absolute peace of mind. We hope to treat you to a memorable evening, capped by some of the top-name musical and dance entertainment in Colombia. We look forward to seeing you all there."

The group began to move toward the outer chamber. At the door, Lila paused and turned once more to capture the ambiance of the sumptuous, historical setting. She then turned, looked intensely at Emilio, and smiled a feline smile. Stone-faced, he abruptly turned his head, and they all moved out of the antechamber.

Guardina closed the door behind them and slowly ambled

toward his easy chair beside the vertical slit-window. Seemingly exhausted, he plopped himself down as if to acknowledge a well-deserved rest, once again looking out at the panorama he had admired earlier that day, and perhaps a thousand times before.

The sun was much lower now, allowing the fortress to cast an irregular shadow over the marketplace. The *mercantes* were readying to close their shops for the day, only to repeat the same cycle tomorrow, ad infinitum. Guardina's gaze settled on one of the sales stalls. An American woman—one that he had noticed earlier in the day—was haggling with one of the male *mercantes*. She held a large wooden carving in her left hand while talking, raising and lowering her right hand. He was shaking his head, all the while smiling and looking at his watch. Then, he spoke to the lady and pointed to a sales stall some distance from him, on the same side of thoroughfare. The lady shopper slowly moved out of the stall in the direction toward which the *mercante* had pointed, as his assistant began to close down the wooden awnings.

The *mercante* left through the rear door of his stall, taking an inferior, but similar-looking large wooden figurine with him, and walked very briskly down the alley toward the rear of the sales stall to which he had pointed. He entered the distant sales stall, stayed for about fifteen seconds, then exited and returned to his sales stall along the alley, counting money as he walked. Guardina watched the lady enter the distant sales stall from the thoroughfare side. In about thirty seconds, she emerged from the distant sales stall carrying a large wooden figurine and smiling broadly—in her haste, perfectly oblivious to the inferior quality of her purchase.

"Stupid, greedy *Americanos*!" Guardina muttered to himself.

LAMBS TO SLAUGHTER

In his cavernous hideout northwest of Envigado, Raoul Bodega bit down tightly on an unlit cigar while reading a two-day old newspaper. In 30-point type the headline blared: "CAPTURE OF HECTOR BODEGA SOUNDS DEATH KNELL FOR CARTELS". Raoul was in no mood for bad news. Everything seemed to be going wrong for him. The Government police had captured his brother Hector in Bogotá and were daily putting pressure on his cocaine operations in Medellín. Rumors were spreading among his men that the U.S. military was about to step up operations against the Bodega cartels. Raoul had generally discounted these rumors, believing them to be inspired by the Government to discourage cartel activity during the Independence Day celebration.

One of his lieutenants burst into the room, seemingly quite agitated. "Commandante, you need to take a look at this!"

Swinging around in his executive's chair, Raoul held out his hand to receive a tattered communiqué. "What is it?"

"I'm not exactly sure," the lieutenant nervously muttered, "but I knew you would want to see it right away."

Raoul grabbed the communiqué and while reading it stroked his beard inquisitively.

Raoul, mi amigo,

U.S. military to conduct operations against your hideout in the next few days. Be prepared for air and ground attack. Their mission is to capture you alive. Take all necessary precautions. They mean business! Best personal regards. Emilio.

"American Swine!!" Raoul bellowed. "Who do they think they are! This is *my* territory! Where did you get this?"

"It was passed to one of our lieutenants in Cartagena. We have no reason to believe that it's not authentic."

Enraged, Raoul stammered, "Get me . . . get me . . . Frrr . . . Federico!"

The lieutenant quickly departed. After a few minutes, Federico Alvarez, a huge mass of lumbering manhood moving with a noticeable limp, trudged into the room. "You called, Commandante?"

"*Yes*, I called. Have you seen this?" extending the document to Federico.

Federico read the document, his eyes widening in disbelief.

"How did they locate our hideout?"

"That's immaterial," Raoul said with clenched teeth and a piercing gaze which virtually immobilized Federico. "The question is *what* are we going to do about it?"

Federico was Raoul's most valued strategist and loyal advisor. Once when a small police patrol staged an ambush of a truck convoy carrying a load of coca, Federico had saved Raoul's life, or so thought Raoul. Federico was driving the point vehicle, a jeep, and Raoul was his passenger. When the first shots rang out, Federico intentionally swerved the jeep into a ditch and yelled to Raoul to get down behind it. Just as the words escaped his mouth, Federico looked up and saw a police sniper in a banana tree taking a bead on Raoul. Federico dived headlong toward Raoul, as if to tackle him, pushing Raoul out of the bullet's path. The bullet instead penetrated Federico's left hip, causing permanent damage. After a short firefight, Raoul's 50-caliber machine gunner on the rear truck in the convoy proved most persuasive. The police patrol was routed and it quickly faded away into the dense jungle foliage. Raoul was forever grateful to Federico and rewarded him by making him his top lieutenant. Federico had proved that he would do anything for Raoul, . . . anything.

Federico groped for a response to Raoul's pointed question. "We have to beat them to the punch, Commandante. No question, we have to beat them to the punch."

Throwing his cigar butt toward an ashtray and narrowly missing it, Raoul inquired impatiently, "Well what do you have in mind, Federico?"

Federico turned away from Raoul and walked pensively around the room for a few moments. He slowly turned and faced Raoul and intoned slowly and demonically, "Murder and mayhem." Then he added in a slow, deliberate monotone, "We must eliminate the reason for the Americanos' presence here. We must dispose of Guardina."

Raoul was incredulous. "How do you propose to do that?"

"In a public execution, Commandante."

"Yeah, but where and when?"

"In the Cartagena Citycenter on the day after tomorrow when Guardina gives his annual Independence Day speech. Guardina's assassination will also provide the perfect distraction while we effect Hector's escape from the fortress."

Realizing that Federico had factored Hector's rescue into the plan, Raoul smiled broadly. "Brilliant, Federico! How ironic both to liberate our country from Guardina and to liberate Hector on Independence Day! But what do we do about the U.S. raid on our hideout?"

"Simple, Commandante, we let them raid."

"We let them raid?"

"Yes, but there will be nothing to raid. We will move our equipment and munitions into one of the side tunnels and seal it off. Then we will booby-trap the four mine entrance locations and, from afar, wreak havoc on the advancing Americanos."

"What do you mean by "from afar?"

"We will secrete you and Hector to friendly cartels in Peru. I will take our men to our alternate hideout near Barranquilla and wait out the storm. When the U.S. commanders realize the folly of their attempts to capture the Bodegas, they will eventually withdraw their troops from Colombia. We will then return to Envigado and resume our cartel operations."

"Excellent plan, Federico, but we will need to work out the

details of Guardina's assassination and Hector's rescue. I want our best men assigned to this operation."

"Don't worry, Commandante, everything will come off like clockwork. I will brief you on the details this afternoon."

Federico gave a perfunctory hand salute and left the room like a man with a mission, slightly dragging his left foot.

Raoul removed a huge Cuban cigar from his breast pocket, slowly peeled off the cellophane, and with a penknife, cut off the tip of the cigar with the precision of an executioner. He then licked the cigar all over, clamping it snugly between his teeth, and lit it. As he watched the wafts of smoke circle away from him, he visualized, contentedly, American forces in retreat.

2

Independence Day dawned gloriously when President Guardina awoke to the sound of pigeons' flapping their wings outside the shuttered window of his citadel bedroom. Most Cartagenans thought the pigeons were a nuisance and despised them. Guardina didn't. He thought the pigeons were one of the true assets of the island city. He considered them to be his friends. They were interesting to watch and not unreasonably demanding. The time he spent with them served as a balm for the loneliness of his job. And heaven knows that his job, which often entailed making unpopular executive and military decisions, was a lonely one.

The President got up out of bed and shuffled toward the shuttered window. He shivered slightly. The bright sunlight had disguised the much chillier temperature of the air. Peering through the slits he caught a glimpse of a pair of cooing gray birds perched precariously some distance from him down the granite ledge. The morning wind ruffled their steel-gray coats, forming collars of undisciplined feathers under their beaks.

Careful not to disturb his feathered friends, he gently unlatched the shutters and slowly drew them back. He knew what they wanted. On a table next to the window he always kept a small round tin of bird seed. As he opened the tin and poured a small amount of seed into his hand, he watched the two birds walk along the ledge toward him, bobbing their heads repeatedly. When they arrived in front of the opened window, they began pecking their bills on the ledge, as if asking for breakfast. Guardina smiled. "*Buenos dias, mis amigos,*" Guardina whispered while sprinkling some seed on the ledge. He knew that the food would temper their natural skittishness. He prepared to talk to them, as usual, in his normal tone of voice. "What do you think of this wonderful day?", he attempted. But he could not get his voice to go above a raspy whisper. Guardina cleared his throat, and tried again. Even less sound emerged on the second go-round.

Laryngitis! What a heck of a day to have laryngitis! Guardina thought to himself. At the same time, he began to feel chills again and realized he was feverish. By the time the pigeons had finished their breakfast, Guardina was on the telephone to his staff's doctor, who was always on immediate call to respond to the President's health needs.

"Dr. Mendoza, please," Guardina whispered into the telephone.

"Speaking, Mr. President. Are you okay? You sound like you feel terrible. How may I help you?"

"You can help me by curing this damn laryngitis by noontime, doctor." Guardina was barely able to force the words out through his windpipe.

"I'm afraid that will be impossible, Mr. President. There is practically an epidemic of the flu and laryngitis going around here in Cartagena. Laryngitis typically lasts for two days and sometimes longer. The only way to cure the condition is bed rest and plenty of fluids. Do you have a fever, presently?"

"I feel, feverish, yes, but I have not yet taken my temperature," Guardina whispered.

"Well, I'll come to your room in a few minutes and bring some medication to control the fever. However, I suggest that you cancel all your Independence Day activities. You are going to feel worse before you feel better."

Whispering, "Doctor, before you come, please call General

Rojillo, my Chief of Staff, and advise him of the situation. He will have to handle the Miss Colombia crowning ceremony and read my speech to the people."

"I will be happy to take care of that, Mr. President. I will see you in a few minutes."

3

The sky was cloudless and the sun was unusually bright for a November day, but the wind from the north was brisk, making the air chilly and the water choppy. A small motorized dinghy carrying six of Raoul's guerrillas wended its way, meticulously, through a maze of coral formations as it approached the wharf near the city's center. For the six men, disguised as fishermen, the view of the fortress and the Citycenter was spectacular at high noon. Colombian and Cartagenan flags were flying everywhere, and the bells of the many churches of the city were clanging in a spritely cacophony. Swarms of people could be seen in Plaza Bolivar around the speaker's platform; rivulets of Cartagenans were visibly emptying into the plaza from many of the side streets. Excitement filled the air in anticipation of the President's crowning of Miss Colombia, scheduled for 1:00 o'clock.

As the dinghy came alongside the wharf, one of the guerrillas carrying a rope jumped onto the wooden walkway and tied the boat securely, front and back, to two posts. The other five quickly disembarked. The six men huddled, synchronized their wristwatches, and split into two teams, four walking toward the fortress, and two toward the plaza. Of the two, one was carrying a black cloth bag. They blended in well with the other groups of fishermen coming and going in the vicinity of the wharf.

Federico had given detailed instructions to them during the course of a lengthy briefing the previous evening. A pair of guerrillas was responsible for the assassination of President Guardina, while, simultaneously, the other four were to effect Hector's escape from the fortress. In a van that would be parked for them near the Plaza Bolivar, the pair was to take off their fisherman's clothes under which they wore priests' robes. They were then to proceed to the plaza, one of them carrying sticks of dynamite and a timing device concealed in the black cloth bag. One of the pair—the sapper-priest—was to gain access to the speaker's platform about fifteen minutes prior to the crowning on the pretext that the President's chief of staff had asked him to bless the Miss Colombia crown. The black bag containing the explosives would be set under the podium, timed to go off in forty-five minutes. That would give time for the ceremony to begin, Miss Colombia to be crowned and leave the platform, and President Guardina to be about ten minutes into his speech, before the big bang. The other member of the pair—the observer-priest—would blend in with the crowd as an observer.

Similarly, the foursome, after leaving the wharf, was to enter a separate van which would transport them to near the entrance of the fortress where Hector was being detained. They were to take off their outer layer of clothing to expose police uniforms which they were wearing underneath. They were not to leave the van nor begin their rescue effort until exactly seven minutes after they heard a loud explosion in the plaza. The explosion would signal the destruction of the speaker's platform along with Guardina and the members of his staff. Federico had told them in the briefing that Raoul wanted to receive a report from the pair of guerrillas that "they saw bits and pieces of President Guardina flying through the air." Such a report would give Raoul great pleasure.

The explosion would cause mayhem in the plaza and, within five to seven minutes, sirens would be blasting, and police would be called from the fortress by the droves, greatly reducing the security around Hector. That's when the foursome would make its move and rush the prisoner detention area on the first floor of the fortress. Hector, through a security guard informant, would be advised in advance of the impending rescue operation and would assist in it. After the assassination and rescue, the two teams and Hector would rendezvous at a van located near the citadel detention center and be transported to a helipad where two choppers would be waiting to airlift them back to a prearranged meeting place in the mountains southwest of Envigado. Raoul and an entourage of his followers would be waiting there to welcome his brother. The plan seemed failsafe.

The two guerrillas, Julio and Carlos, dressed as priests emerged from the sliding side door of a black van parked about a block from the plaza now teeming with citizenry. They were a handsome pair of bachelors in their mid-forties—soldiers of fortune deeply committed to the Bodegas' objectives. As they entered the plaza, Julio, carrying the cloth bag with the explosives, whispered to Carlos, "The time now is twelve forty-five p.m. You wait here at the outskirts of the crowd and I will go 'bless the crown.'"

Julio, bobbing back and forth like a duck, began to push his way through the crowd, all the while looking back at Carlos and smiling his cynical smile, and tugging at his too-snugly-fitting Roman collar. The dynamite was set to go at one thirty-five p.m. Julio had estimated that it would take him five minutes to reach the speaker's platform. But the crowd, packed shoulder to shoulder, was much more grid-locked than he had anticipated. Already he had spent five minutes wedging his way through the throng, but he was less than half-way to the speaker's platform. He was beginning to worry whether he would get there in time to bless the crown and deposit the cloth bag. Many people, seeing his Roman collar, tried to accommodate Julio's forward progress, respectfully attempting to part the sea of humanity, but with little success. Finally, a distraught and frustrated Julio shouted, "In the name of the Lord, please stand aside so that the crown can be blessed."

Julio's prayer was answered. A towering hulk of Cartagenan manhood came up behind Julio and said, "Father, you look like a man who needs a ride." With that, the Goliathan figure, a large, shiny gold, earring glimmering in his right ear, swooped up the diminutive Julio and sat him on his shoulders. Julio gripped the black cloth bag tightly against his cassock. As if Moses had commanded the parting of the seas, the people found new directions in which to move in order to avoid being trampled by Goliath with the ravenlike figure perched on his shoulders. Within five minutes, Goliath had made his way through the crowd and had gently removed Julio from his shoulders and stood him near the steps leading to the speaker's platform. As quickly as he had appeared, the Goliathan figure turned and made his way back through the first few rows of the crowd to rejoin his corpulent, animated wife. *"Gracias, mi amigo.* May God bless you," Julio shouted to the hulk disappearing into the crowd. Turning to ascend the stairs to the speaker's platform, Julio glanced at his wristwatch. Twelve fifty-six, he thought to himself. Not much time to spare.

From the rear of the crowd, Carlos had been watching Julio's excursion atop the waves of celebrating Cartagenans and was relieved to see Julio finally ascend to the speaker's platform. Carlos could plainly see Julio, holding the black cloth bag, bend down behind the podium. When Julio stood upright again, Carlos no longer could see a black bag in his hands. The explosives were in place.

Julio turned and spoke to one of the President's female staff members. She pointed to a large silver box sitting on a table near the podium. Julio and the staffer then walked toward the silver box, and the staffer opened the lid of the box while Julio made the sign of the cross over the box's contents. Carlos looked at his wristwatch. The time now was exactly one p.m.

Julio was pleased with how efficiently things were going. He thanked the female staffer and turned around to start back down the stairs. His downward motion was blocked by a tall gentleman in a dark, pinstriped suit and four burly military officers ascending the stairs together behind him. Julio stepped out of their way on the top stair. As the tall man in civilian attire passed Julio, he stopped briefly and said, "Father, it is a Godsend that you happen to be here. The Presidential staff chaplain just telephoned to say that he was caught, inextricably, in traffic and would not be here in time to lead the invocation. Would you be so kind as to take his place?"

Julio's face turned ashen. Every passing second seemed like an hour to him. How could he say no? What excuse could he give? No weddings or funerals were ever scheduled on Independence Day. No masses were ever scheduled for mid-afternoon. He finally thought of something. Clearing his throat, he began to say, "Well, er . . . "

Just then the female staffer came closer to the duo. "Father . . . I didn't catch your last name," she said to Julio with a warm smile.

Julio inserted the first name which came to his mind, "Cantado. . . . Father Cantado."

"Father Cantado," she asked, "you know General Rojillo, correct? The blessing of the crown. You know, right, Father?"

"Well, yes and no," Julio nervously responded, trying to steer a middle course.

"Then, Father, I would like formally to introduce you to President Guardina's Chief of Staff, General Oscar Rojillo. General Rojillo, Father Cantado."

"It is a pleasure to meet you, Father," General Rojillo said in a gracious voice.

"Likewise, General," Julio responded, finding it somewhat difficult to reconcile why this "general" was dressed as a civilian.

"I hope you can do this small favor for us, in a few minutes," General Rojillo continued.

"Well, I, . . . I, . . . I do have to make my rounds at St. Theresa's Hospital in a few minutes."

"Please, Father, do us this favor," the female staffer chimed.

"If you insist. . . . When do you want me to say the prayer? Immediately? At the beginning of the ceremony? Julio asked with ill-concealed anticipation. The time was ticking away. Looking at his watch, Julio saw that the time was now seven minutes after one. The crowd began chanting, "We want the President, we want the President."

The chief of staff responded hurriedly. "Well, Father, the tradition is to first have Miss Colombia crowned, then an invocation by the new Miss Colombia, then the priest's invocation, and then the President's speech."

"Okay," said Julio. "I'll stay, but I will have to leave immediately after I give the invocation."

"Fine," responded General Rojillo. "Let's get started."

The female staffer interrupting, "Oh, there is one final thing you should know, General. We also received word that the limousine carrying three visiting U. S. dignitaries has also been held up in traffic."

"Well, we will just have to proceed without them," General Rojillo sighed in a disappointed tone. He then looked over the staffer's shoulder and smiled in the direction of two other people on the platform he wished to greet.

Julio watched the general walk across the platform toward a beautiful, blond-haired young lady dressed in a pink-and-white flowered dress. Next to her stood another strikingly beautiful lady with long, flowing, black hair wearing a blue dress trimmed in silver. Julio wondered how he could have missed noticing these two beauties previously. He watched Rojillo smile, shake their hands, and engage in an exchange of apparent pleasantries. Why was he dallying so! Finally, after a few minutes, Rojillo made his way to the podium. Julio could see that Rojillo was stepping on the corner of the black cloth bag with the toe of his left shoe. The time now was twelve minutes after one. Members of the crowd were frantically chanting for the President at the top of their lungs.

It took three intonations of "*Señoras y Señores*" before General Rojillo could reduce the noise level of the crowd to the point that he could begin speaking. "We are here today," he began, "to celebrate the independence of our great country and the crowning of the new Miss Colombia. As you know, the tradition is that the current Miss Colombia together with the President of Colombia, jointly crown the new Miss Colombia after which the President gives his Independence Day speech. With respect to that tradition, I have some good news and some bad news. First the bad news. President Guardina is ill with the flu and laryngitis and he is under doctor's orders to stay in bed." Julio's face froze in shock. "Therefore, I will be assisting in the crowning of the new Miss Colombia. Of course, that is *good* news for *me*." The crowd erupted in laughter and it took awhile for the noise to subside to a speakable level. (Time: 1:17). "The good news for *you*," General Rojillo continued, "is that *I* will be reading President Guardina's prepared speech, without any of the usual side trips to nostalgia, so it should be much *shorter*." The crowd again broke into laughter mixed with cheers and whistles for a while and the din eventually subsided. "Without further ado, we will now proceed with the crowning of the NEW . . . MISS . . . COLOMBIA!!" (Time: 1:20).

The two beauties, waving their right hands and looking left to right and back again toward all parts of the crowd, walked forward in tandem from the rear of the platform, amidst the roar of the citizenry and the blare of a small *mariachi* band. General Rojillo tried but could not silence the crowd. Spirals of confetti were being showered onto the stage. The lady in the pink-and-white dress raised an ornately jeweled crown high above her head for all to see. The crowd roared again at even a higher pitch.

Rojillo tried again, "SENORAS AND SENORES, MAY I HAVE YOUR ATTENTION . . . PLEASE." He repeated it into the microphone two more times. (Time: 1:24). Finally, he turned to the lady in pink and white, and said, "Let's go ahead with it." They each held a side of the crown and placed it gently on the head of the lady in blue and silver. General Rojillo intoned into the microphone, "MARIA ELISA FORTUNADO, I CROWN YOU THE NEW MISS COLOMBIA. MAY YOU WEAR THIS CROWN WITH GREAT PRIDE AND IN GOOD HEALTH FOR THE COMING YEAR."

Julio looked down at the black cloth bag. General Rojillo now had his left foot squarely placed in the center of the bag keeping his weight on his right leg. The crowd was applauding and cheering even louder. (Time: 1:26). Practically shouting into the microphone, Rojillo said "Now we will hear the invocation of the new Miss Colombia."

The Cartagenans quickly grew quiet and bowed their heads, almost in unison. General Rojillo adjusted the microphone to Miss Colombia's height as she approached the podium.

"My fellow Cartagenans," Miss Colombia began. "Today we ask the Lord God, our Father, to bless our great country and our island fortress, and to make them safe places within which to live. We ask deliverance from the heinous cartel operators, the Bodegas and the others, . . . " (Time: 1:28).

A goddamned political speech! Julio thought to himself as the new Miss Colombia droned on. This could last forever. Why is she talking about her upbringing in destitution and squalor in some small village near Bogota? Who cares if she is a 'rags-to-riches' beauty? She still is a bitch! Okay, so she is the only female member of four generations of her family who completed high school. Who cares? (Time: 1:30). So her brother *is* a Franciscan priest and two of her sisters work in convents in Medellín. Does that make this political speech an invocation? Where's the prayer? Where's the punch line? (Time: 1:31). God!!!! Four minutes to blast-off."

Speaking with a detectably phony religious-patriotic quiver in her voice, the new Miss Colombia continued, " . . . And finally, I would like to ask the Lord our God to assist me in spreading good will throughout our great country during the coming year. I promise to be a faithful representative of our proud people. Thank you very much for being here today." (Time: 1:32).

As the new Miss Colombia walked away from the podium, General Rojillo motioned to Julio to step forward. Julio froze for a few seconds, thinking of what tack to take as the seconds ticked away. He had no guilt or remorse for what was about to happen. The two Miss Colombias were simply Guardina's political mouthpieces; General Rojillo and the four burly military officers were Guardina's marionettes; the affable female staffer was a disposable commodity. (Time: 1:33). Julio had a choice. He could either save himself by leaving the platform or obscure the trail to the Bodegas by being a martyr for the Bodega cause. He stepped to the microphone and adjusted it to his height. (Time: 1:34).

0368-COOL

The wind whipping his coal black hair, Julio spoke solemnly into the microphone, " . . . All of us were like lost sheep, each of us going his own way. And the Lord made the punishment fall on him, the punishment all of us deserved."

General Rojillo, with a wrinkled brow, looked toward the two Miss Colombias, who returned a perplexed stare, trying to make sense of what the priest was saying.

Julio continued, methodically, "He was treated harshly, but endured it humbly; He never said a word." As if each utterance were time-measured, Julio raised his eyes slowly upwards toward the blue November sky, and reaching up, he grasped and slowly pulled off his Roman collar, while dramatically intoning, "Like . . . a lamb . . . about to be . . . slaughtered . . . Isaiah, . . . 53: . . . 6-7." Julio's chin suddenly crashed to his chest. He gritted his teeth and closed his eyes tightly. . . . (Time: 1:35).

4

Carlos, two hundred yards away, was stunned into a state of shock. The entire speaker's platform was disintegrating amid a bright yellow-orange flash and charcoal-colored smoke; burning bits of timber and body parts were catapulted high into the air and landed randomly on the terrified spectators. A shock wave accompanied by a piercing sound reached Carlos, causing him and others around him to plummet to the ground, covering their heads with their arms, frightened and wondering as to when the next explosion would occur as the seconds passed. Screams, groans, and moans of men, women, and children filled the plaza; the sickening odor of burning human flesh permeated the air.

Carlos, slowly raised himself to his feet. Looking toward where the speaker's platform once stood, he could see only a wall of flames and smoke. A few survivors from the crowd were rushing in the direction of the flames to assist the injured people, the ones who had camped out the whole night to ensure that they got a front-row look at the new Miss Colombia. Fragments—just fragments—

was all that was left of the new Miss Colombia now. Her front-row fans fared not much better; burned, scorched, some totally cremated, others with their bodies riddled with pieces of lumber and metal as if they had been mercilessly gunned down with a machine gun. Babies and children lay dead, all of them burned beyond recognition; some firmly clutching their mothers' breasts as a last futile attempt for protection and sustenance. All sacrificed in the name of Bodega. And Julio—the ultimate martyr. Loyalty beyond life. Raoul would be saddened, but pleased. (Time: 1:38).

Over the din of police and ambulance sirens, Carlos was able to hear the screams of a plump, middle-aged woman running toward him. "Father! . . . Father!" she screamed to Carlos as tears streamed down her face. "You must come! You must come! People are dying! They need the last rites!"

In the shock and confusion of the situation, Carlos had momentarily forgotten that he was dressed as a priest. To walk away at this time might compromise his disguise and jeopardize the mission of rescuing Hector. Instantly, Carlos responded. "*Si, Señora.* I will follow you." (Time: 1:39).

Carlos followed the plump lady, passing row after row of scorched, perforated semblances of humanity—blackened, writhing, screeching, stinking, limbless, dying creatures—a veritable cemetery. Staying within his priestly role, he made the sign of the cross over as many of them as possible while he proceeded to a destination known only to the plump lady. She finally stopped in front of something that could be described only as a large mound of human flesh. The strength of the blast had stripped this thing of most of its clothing and had sheered off the left side of what was once probably a head. It was difficult to identify this object immediately as a head because it was one of several blunted, bloody extremities of this flesh mound. Remarkably, it twitched intermittently as if there was some faint vestige of life still remaining. (Time: 1:40).

The plump lady turned around abruptly and cried, "Father, this is my husband! You must bless him so he can go to heaven!"

Carlos wondered what good it would do to bless this bloody heap, even if he had the power to do so. Continuing to play the priest, he knelt down beside the twitching thing, and began to whisper over it, "*In nomine patris, et filii, et spiritu sancti ...*" Before he could complete the blessing, the bloody, massive half-head turned toward him. CHRIST!! Carlos gasped, IT'S ALIVE! he shouted to himself. Then, Pedro noticed something he had not seen before the movement began. On the thing's right ear was a large gold earring. Totally stunned, he suddenly realized that this was Goliath.

In garbled, gurgling sounds, the half-headed Goliath attempted to communicate. "Bless me, Father, for I . . . have . . . sinned," he struggled. "I . . . was . . . a . . . doub . . . double . . . agent. . . . For Bodega, I . . . killed . . . Pablo . . . Cordova . . . and his . . . child. For Th . . . rock. I . . . was . . . to . . . kill . . . Hector . . . this . . . morn . . . morning . . . but . . . the . . . police . . . moved . . . him . . . to a . . . diff . . . different . . . place. . . . Please . . . forgive . . . my . . . sins."

Carlos was astounded. He thought to himself, "Throckmiller! That gringo military scumbag! He ordered Hector's murder!" Carlos looked at his watch. One forty-one and thirty seconds. In thirty seconds the four-man guerrilla team would be leaving their van to conduct the rescue mission. Carlos had to warn them about Hector's change of location. Perfunctorily, Carlos sputtered, "You're forgiven, my son." He then quickly rose to his feet, and saying nothing to the plump lady, turned and ran as fast as he could in the direction of the fortress San Felipe de Borajas. His heart palpitating in anger, Carlos thought to himself as he ran, "I will personally disembowel Throckmiller and savor every second of it."

Goliath exhaled one last gasp while the plump lady knelt beside him crying hysterically.

5

From his bedroom high above the Plaza Bolivar, Guardina could see the flames and the thick black smoke rising in the distance.

Bedlam was the only word to describe it. There were no pigeons within a mile of the fortress now. No friends. No advisors. He felt unusually lonely. He reached for the telephone and dialed the office of his chief of staff.

A taped recording responded, "You have reached the office of the President's Chief of Staff. Due to the Independence Day celebration, there is no one here now to take your call. After the beep, please leave a message, stating the day and time of your call, the person with whom you wish to speak, your name and telephone number, and someone will get back to you as soon as possible. Have a happy Independence Day." Guardina slammed down the receiver.

"Christ, even the *Government* has shut down!" Guardina exclaimed audibly. He hastily dialed the citadel operator.

"Yes, Mr. President?"

(Hoarsely) "What the hell is happening in the Plaza?"

"Fireworks, Mr. President. It happens every Independence Day. You sound awful, sir. Are you feeling all right?"

"Forget how I'm feeling. . . . Fireworks? Have you looked outside?"

"Well, not really, Mr. President. I'm in a small room in the subbasement of the citadel. I just heard the fireworks go off a few minutes ago."

"Well, it's more than fireworks. Get me the Chief of Police of the fortress San Felipe de Borajas!"

"Certainly, Mr. President. . . . Ringing. . . . Ringing again. . . . Mr. President, there doesn't seem to be any answer."

"Keep trying, and call me back when you get someone to answer."

"Yes, sir. I will be happy to do so."

President Guardina stared out the window and viewed the spectacle of human carnage unfolding before him. Here he was, the President of Colombia, and he felt helpless . . . literally helpless.

0368-COOL

6

Practically galloping, Carlos rounded a corner just in time to see four uniformed police exiting a black van parked about one hundred feet away from the entrance to the detention area of the fortress. The van had large, circular Cartagena seals on the side panels. Carlos recognized these as a type of magnetized emblems that the Bodegas used to disguise all sorts of cartel vehicles, boats, and aircraft. He was relieved to have located the other members of the guerrilla team. Still running at top speed, he saw the foursome quickly make their way toward the detention area entrance. With all the voice he could muster, Carlos called to them, "Officers! Officers!"

The man bringing up the rear of the foursome turned around. "Yes, Father?" he inquired, immediately recognizing Carlos as a compatriot. "How can we help you?"

Breathlessly, Carlos uttered, "We need to talk."

The tailing member called to the other three, and all five men walked toward the black van. Once inside, Carlos blurted, "Fucking Throckmiller has put a contract out on Hector. The police have moved Hector to another location."

The senior man of the four, who was wearing lieutenant's bars, calmly stated, "That doesn't make sense. Why would Throckmiller do that? Where did you get this information?"

"From a double agent who was dying in the Plaza. No man lies when he is dying. Not even a double agent."

"Yes, but he could be mistaken."

"Not this guy. He's been involved with the cartels for a long time. He's experienced. Besides, he was so sure that Throckmiller ordered Hector's demise that he confessed to a *priest*—me—that he himself was the hit man for Throckmiller. I am convinced beyond all doubt that he is telling the truth."

"Okay, even if we agree that Hector may have been relocated, what do we do now?" the lieutenant asked pointedly to Carlos.

"Well, we can't go back to Raoul empty-handed. I think we

should first confirm somehow whether or not Hector is in the first floor detention center. If he is, we rescue him. If he is not, we take hostages."

"How do we confirm Hector's whereabouts within the next few minutes?" the lieutenant inquired impatiently.

Carlos rapidly retorted, "I have an idea. I will present myself to the desk sergeant as a priest who has been specifically designated by President Guardina, through Archbishop Spinoza, to administer the sacrament of penance to Hector Bodega. The sergeant will either allow me to see Hector, tell me he cannot let me see Hector, or confirm that Hector has been moved to another location."

"Well, the idea sounds okay to me," responded the lieutenant. "It's the only one we got, so you'd better execute it quickly."

Carlos left the van while adjusting his Roman collar and brushing some of the soot and ashes from the arms of his cassock. Walking briskly down the sidewalk toward the entrance to the detention center, he saw, in his left peripheral vision, a black Mercedes limousine with small flags perched on the front fenders pull up along the curb beside him. Through the smoked-glass windows, he glanced into the air-conditioned vehicle and saw, in addition to the driver, two women and a man sitting in the back. Looking more carefully at the flags, he noticed that they carried the American stars and stripes. He wondered what this vehicle was doing there and who its occupants were.

Upon entering the detention center office area, Carlos encountered a sergeant sitting at a telephone switchboard lit up like a Christmas tree. The switchboard was buzzing incessantly. Carlos mustered all of his composure to repress a smile. The sergeant would have been much more efficient had he been an octopus with several sets of ears. The plaza explosion, as planned, had created the type of pandemonium conducive to a prison break.

"Good afternoon, Father. Just a minute . . . " the sergeant greeted Carlos and quickly answered another call. Carlos waited while he wrote down the details of a request for police assistance.

Answering another call, the sergeant identified himself and told the caller to hold. Covering the mouthpiece of the telephone with his hand, he said to Carlos, "What can I do for you Father?"

"I am Father Gallega. Archbishop Spinoza requested that I administer the sacrament of penance to Hector Bodega this afternoon. I am a personal friend of President Guardina, and I suppose that is why I have been asked to do it. Apparently, Bodega made an official request through Government channels to see a priest."

"Playing government investigator, Father?" the sergeant asked wryly.

"No, nothing like that. You are certainly aware that priests who hear confession are bound to secrecy."

"Oh sure, Father. I was just kidding. But I'm sorry, I can't help you with your request. Just a minute . . . ." The sergeant began speaking into the telephone again and taking notes. Two minutes passed and the sergeant was still taking notes. Becoming increasingly anxious, Carlos began tapping a penknife on the counter. After a couple of more minutes, Carlos, exasperated, slammed the penknife down on the counter, clasped his hands behind his back, and walked in a continuous full circle in front of the counter, strutting like a rooster demanding a hen's attention. Another minute passed.

The sergeant finally hung up and looked up at Carlos. "You see, Father," he said, "Hector Bodega is not here. Actually, I'm the only person here. All of the prisoners including Hector Bodega were transported to another location this morning. Everybody in the police guard assigned to the detention area is over at the Plaza."

"Do you know where the prisoners were taken?"

"No, unfortunately, I don't, Father. I was called in to handle the telephones during this emergency. No one told me where the prisoners were taken. Perhaps you could call back or come back tomorrow."

"Yeah, yeah, I'll consider that," Carlos said in a way indicating that he was preoccupied with another thought. "Before you answer any more calls—perhaps you can tell me who is in that limo out here."

The sergeant rose from his chair, leaned over the desk, and craned his neck to see out the glass doors toward the street. "Oh, that limo? Those are U.S. dignitaries here for the Independence Day celebration. Two of them are U.S. legislators. I know because I was part of the police contingent providing security for them for the last few days. I'm going to have to get back to the switchboard, Father. Anything else you need?"

"No, No, . . . not really," Carlos said disconnectedly. "Thanks for the info, Sergeant."

"No problem, Father," adding with a slight grin, "just remember me in your prayers."

Carlos turned and proceeded toward the door, walking at a decidedly faster pace than when he entered. The limo was still sitting there with the same four occupants. The three people in the back seemed to be talking among themselves. Carlos made his way, half-running, to the black van, quickly slid back the side door, entered, and slammed the door behind him. "EUREKA!!!" he shouted with almost childish glee.

"What happened?" the lieutenant responded with feverish enthusiasm.

"Hector's not here, and I can't find out where he is," Carlos blurted.

"So what's so good about that?" queried the lieutenant.

"*Nothing's* good about that. . . . but there's something better." Turning toward the front of the van and pointing out the front window, Carlos continued. "See that limo?"—not waiting for a response—"it contains at least two gringo Congressmen. We've struck pay dirt. I think we have our hostages."

The lieutenant smiled evilly like a cat watching a canary. "So we have." Looking down at his watch and then back out the front window of the van, the lieutenant said authoritatively, "I'll take it from here."

Exiting the van, the uniformed lieutenant walked toward the black limousine in which the three back seat occupants were still

294 JOHN W. COOLEY

chatting. He walked around the front of the limo to the driver's side and tapped on the side window, motioning to the chauffeur to roll down his window. The chauffeur opened the powered window and volunteered, "Officer, these are U.S. dignitaries here to see President Guardina. They understand that he is ill, but they need to talk to him about the current chaos in the Plaza.

Do you want me to park the limousine someplace else until they leave?"

The lieutenant responded, "No, señor, that will not be necessary. I have been advised to inform you that President Guardina is not here. Late this morning he was helicoptered to his villa on one of the islands in *Islas del Rosario,* about thirteen miles off shore. His doctor thought that the villa's serenity would be more conducive to a speedy recovery. President Guardina left a message for the dignitaries, however."

"Yes, what is it?"

"He would like them to come to his villa, have dinner with him, and spend the night. There is a helicopter waiting for them a few blocks from here. We must hurry, though. The safety of the dignitaries is our highest priority now. All you need to do is follow my police van to the helipad and we will quickly have them on their way."

The chauffeur turned and with his left hand slid open the glass divider separating him from the back compartment. Before the chauffeur could speak, Carrington exclaimed, "What's going on?" In English, the chauffeur explained the situation.

Distressed, Lila interjected, "I can't leave right away. I don't have my makeup kit or curlers with me. I must pick up some things from my room before we go to the helipad."

"I'm sorry, señora," said the chauffeur. "The police officer has advised me that we must go directly to the helipad. It's a matter of your safety at this point."

"It'll only take fifteen or twenty minutes," Lila retorted.

Taking the chauffeur off the spot, Carrington mediated. "Lila, our safety is more important than hair curlers right now. We really don't have a choice. We must leave Cartagena immediately as the officer insists."

"Oh, all right. But you and Esther will be the losers on this deal. You will have to tolerate me all day tomorrow looking like some character from a horror movie."

Winking at Esther and smiling slightly, Carrington rejoined, "We'll manage."

The chauffeur turned quickly toward the lieutenant and breathily exclaimed, "Let's go!"

The lieutenant ran back to the black van and reentered it. The van zoomed away from the curb and the limousine screeched its wheels to keep close on the van's tail. No one in the van saw the desk sergeant standing at the glass entranceway to the detention center waving Carlos' penknife in the air, trying to get someone's attention.

7

After seemingly interminable twists and turns through a maze of narrow streets crowded with throngs of people spilling over from the Plaza, the two-vehicle caravan finally made its way to the thoroughfare which would take them to the helipad. Minutes later the caravan rounded a corner, permitting a view of two helicopters adorned with presidential seals with their rotors just beginning to turn. By the time the two vehicles moved closer to them, the rotors were at maximum spin. Stepping out of the vehicles, the occupants were greeted by a deafening sound and a gale-force downdraft. The lieutenant, accompanied by two guerrillas dressed as armed police officers, caught Carrington's eye and pointed toward the helicopter on the right. Carrington got the message and hustled Esther and Lila along to the helicopter door. They entered the helicopter with the lieutenant and the other two officers following close behind. Carlos, now in police garb, and the other two guerrillas dressed as police entered the second helicopter. The helicopters simultaneously took off, turning southeasterly, in the direction of their destination.

After being airborne for about fifteen minutes, Carrington began to become concerned. By all reasonable estimates, they should have been landing on the island by now. He looked out the window and all he could see were mountains, valleys, streams, and jungle canopy for miles and miles. No ocean in sight. Certainly no island. He tapped the shoulder of the lieutenant who was sitting in front of him. Attempting to communicate above the deafening roar of the rotors, Carrington yelled, "What's going on here? Where are you taking us?"

Mouthing the words slowly, the lieutenant responded "Be patient, señor. We'll be there soon."

"Yes—but *where* will we be?" Carrington shouted angrily.

Taking his revolver out of his polished leather holster and pointing it at Carrington's throat, the lieutenant again mouthed even more slowly, "Dead, Senator, . . . if you don't shut up."

Carrington looked over toward Esther and Lila who had been unable to hear the previous exchange but who appeared alarmed at the sight of the lieutenant pointing the revolver toward Carrington. The once-powerful Carrington now felt powerless. He was a captive. All of the cocktail parties, the tits-for-tats, the sweetheart deals, the winks and nods of his profession were of no help to him now. He was totally helpless in the hands of these savages. But he refused to take this subjugation without a fight.

Of all the votes of his career, the vote he was about to take was the most important. All the time realizing the risks involved, he voted to take action.

Abruptly, Carrington slammed his right fist into the lieutenant's jaw while grabbing the lieutenant's revolver with his left hand. In the scuffle, the gun fired, penetrating the inside wall of the helicopter a few inches above Esther's head. Esther and Lila were screaming, frantically attempting to move further back into the helicopter away from the wrestling twosome. One of the other two guerrillas drew his revolver and hit Carrington forcefully on the head from the rear, crushing his skull. Carrington fell to the floor of the helicopter bleeding profusely and groaning with pain. "A wounded prisoner is of no value to us!" the lieutenant yelled to the two guerrillas. "Get rid of him!!"

Amid the shrieks and screams of Esther and Lila who realized the seeming inevitability of what was about to happen, one guerrilla opened the helicopter's sliding door, and the other dragged Carrington's now limp body toward the opening. Carrington was gasping for breath and intermittently moaning in pain, and pleading for mercy. The guerrilla who had struck Carrington was now holding the revolver about an inch from the back of Carrington's head and beginning to squeeze the trigger.

The lieutenant, indicating the negative by shaking his head, pushed the guerrilla's hand away until the barrel of the gun was pointing outside the helicopter door. The lieutenant stood up, his eyes focused at all times on Carrington. Esther and Lila felt relieved, believing Carrington's life would be spared.

Then, without notice, the lieutenant began kicking Carrington repeatedly in the side, back, and abdomen as Carrington's body writhed in an attempt to avoid the blows. Writhing in pain, Carrington's body teetered on the threshold of the helicopter's side opening, two thousand feet above the jungle canopy. In a sarcastically diabolical voice, the lieutenant giving Carrington's thrashing torso one final powerful kick to its side, yelled "TOUCHDOWN!!!!!" The force of the kick moved Carrington's body three inches off the floor of the helicopter and propelled it through the side opening. Carrington's attenuating death scream could be heard for several seconds, as the lieutenant rushed to the opening to see a speck of humankind splatter on the jungle canopy below. The lieutenant turned to Esther and Lila and growled, "That's what happens when you're not patient."

Esther turned her head to her right side to interrupt the lieutenant's gaze and began to cry. Lila, with tears of fear and hate already streaming down her cheeks, slowly turned her head and stared out over the jungle canopy. Bits and pieces of the twenty-third Psalm, a cognitive remnant from her convent school days,

sprang into Lila's consciousness: "Because the Lord is my Shep-
herd, I have everything I need. He lets me rest in the meadow and
leads me beside the quiet stream. . . . Even when walking through
the dark valley of death, I will not be afraid, for he is close beside
me, guarding, guiding all the way . . . ."

Biting a quivering lower lip, Lila lowered her head, and sobbed
quietly.

<h1 style="text-align:center">8</h1>

Meanwhile, President Guardina was lying in bed wondering why
it was taking so long for the telephone operator to get through to
the citadel police desk. Just then, the phone rang.

Picking up the receiver, Guardina anxiously inquired, "Yes?"

"President Guardina, I have the citadel desk sergeant on the
line for you."

"Thank you. Put him through."

"President Guardina?" asked the voice on the other end of the line.

"Yes."

"This is Sergeant Fontana at the citadel police desk. The operator tells me you've been trying to get a hold of me."

"That's right, Sergeant—you or *anybody* in this government.
What in the world is going on out there in the Plaza?"

"Mr. President, a bomb has exploded in the Plaza.

"A *bomb*? Are you sure?"

"Yes, Mr. President. The initial reports from police on the
scene are that at least twenty people have been killed and about
five times that many have been injured, some critically. Every police vehicle, ambulance, and fire truck on Cartagena is at the Plaza,
and the hospital emergency rooms in the city are unable to cope
with the situation. The hospitals neither have the staff or the facilities to care for the injured. The Chief of Police fears that other
bombs may be detonated around the city, leaving the injured without any hope of emergency medical treatment. It is a true state of
pandemonium. That's why you haven't been able to get through

to me. For the past twenty minutes all fifteen lines on my switch-board have been ringing constantly. I am sorry if . . . "

Interrupting, President Guardina asked bluntly, "Did General Rojillo survive?"

The sergeant paused for a few seconds before he answered. "There is an unconfirmed report, Mr. President, that General Rojillo and both the former and the new Miss Colombia have been killed."

Realizing that Rojillo's fate could easily have been his own, Guardina exclaimed, "Oh, my God! . . . What a catastrophe! How soon will you know for sure?"

"I hope within the hour. However, if there are more bombings, I can't promise anything."

"I understand," said Guardina in a consoling voice. "It sounds like the police currently have their hands full."

"That's for sure, Mr. President. I'm just glad that the Chief of Police decided to move all the prisoners out of the citadel this morning. With all this confusion, it would be an ideal time for someone to try to stage a prison break and rescue Hector Bodega. Oh, speaking of him, . . . your friend Father Gallega was here a few minutes ago.

"Father Gallega? . . . *I* don't know any Father Gallega."

"You don't? He said he was your personal friend and that he was here, at your specific request, to hear Hector Bodega's confession."

"That's preposterous! Why would I send a priest to hear Bodega's confession?"

"Father Gallega told me that Bodega had requested, through official channels, permission to receive the sacrament of penance."

"Well, if he did, I know nothing about it."

"Then that may explain what I saw happen after Father Gallega left the citadel."

"What do you mean, Sergeant?"

"When he left the citadel office, he accidentally left his pen knife on the counter. As soon as I discovered it, I left the switchboard and ran to the glass doors to see if I could catch up with him to return his knife. Then I witnessed something very strange. I saw Father Gallega get into a black van bearing the Cartagena seal—a type of vehicle that is not part of our police fleet. The van then sped away from the curb. The dignitaries' limousine—you know the American legislators' car—roared away right behind the van and both vehicles disappeared down the street. I now think I know what happened."

"What?" President Guardina asked, seeming confused by the sergeant's narration.

"The American dignitaries have been kidnapped!"

"I certainly hope you're wrong, Sergeant."

"I'm beginning to put two and two together. I just noticed that this penknife has a figure carved on it. The figure is a skull superimposed on crossed machetes. That is the Bodega cartel emblem."

"How r . . . r . . . revolting," President Guardina sputtered.

"Notify your chief of police of the situation right away and start tracking them down. Time is of the essence!"

"Yes, Mr. President. This will take priority over all calls. I'll get right on it."

"Good. Keep me updated on this."

"Certainly, Mr. President."

Stunned by the news of the possible kidnapping, President Guardina slowly placed the receiver back into its cradle. In a few seconds, he picked it up again and dialed the operator.

"Yes, Mr. President?"

"Get me General Throckmiller."

FAIR MARKET VALUE

From a bird's-eye view, the camouflaged canvas tent was barely visible on the edge of a jungle clearing carved, craftsmanlike, to accommodate four helicopters. Two helicopters already occupied part of the clearing. Two other choppers engaged in the assassination/rescue operation would soon be arriving from Cartagena to take their places beside them.

Inside the tent, Raoul, sweat beading on his brow and stinging his eyes, moved a white pawn one square forward—the square diagonally adjacent to Federico's black pawn. The rules of the game allowed Federico either to move his black pawn diagonally and "capture" Raoul's white pawn; or to move one square forward taking the black pawn out of jeopardy; or to move some other black piece and surrender his black pawn to Raoul.

"*Your* move," Raoul announced, stating the obvious.

For a few moments, Federico studied the pieces on the chess board like a field commander analyzing a battlefield mock-up. His eyes fixed on the pawns, he finally said slowly and contemplatively, "I need some time, Commandante, . . . planning time. . . . Victory results from strategy, not serendipity."

Raoul smiled. He appreciated Federico's way with words. Some of Federico's insights over the years had been so profound that Raoul often wanted to keep a journal of them. Of course, like many good intentions people have in life, this one also got sidetracked. Not content to leave Federico's remark unanswered, Raoul retorted in a jovial way, "But Federico, if a commander waits too long to make a decision, the dust may settle and all his troops may be either slaughtered or captured."

"That assumes that the commander has no *intelligence!*" Federico shot back with a devilish grin. With that, he briskly moved his black pawn diagonally to capture Raoul's white pawn, simultaneously declaring, "Check!"

Now it was Raoul's turn to study the battlefield. By capturing Raoul's white pawn, Federico had contemporaneously created a situation where Raoul's well-surrounded, but imperfectly defended, white king was directly in the diagonal path of a black bishop where it was clearly in check. Raoul had been taken by surprise. Angered by this development, he was careful not to let his face show it. He had been broad sided because he had not noticed the black bishop ensconced on his pompous throne way over on the other side of the chess board, imposing his authority on everyone—even from afar—even on a *king* no less.

Raoul despised the Catholic Church and everything it represented. Being placed in jeopardy by a *bishop* was repulsive to him. Instinctively, he surveyed the field for options. His white king only had one square available. He noted that alternative and then looked for other options. He carefully scrutinized the combat zone to see if he had any warrior who could capture the black bishop. That would have been his preference. He would love to capture the black bishop in a guerrilla sting operation and *castrate* him if that were possible. It wasn't.

Raoul moved the white pawn one space forward, inevitably signaling a strategy that was wholly defensive. "I hope this doesn't mess up your plans *too* much," Raoul said sarcastically.

Federico, his jaw now resting on his clenched fist, gave no immediate response. He was too busy relishing Raoul's strategic error. Raoul had not fully appreciated was the devastating force of Federico's horse cavalry—his black knight. In a flash, Federico moved his cavalry into action. With lightning speed, Federico's cavalry knocked-out Raoul's white castle—a move that Raoul had not anticipated.

Raoul was mentally reeling as if had just been punched by a roundhouse left hook. There was nothing Raoul could do about Federico's cavalry. Raoul's only hope now was to make some ingenious move that would thoroughly disrupt Federico's offensive momentum. He studied the battlefield for a few moments but was unable to identify some miracle troop movement that would save him from defeat. Biding time, he finally moved a white pawn on the far right side of the battlefield one square forward and hoped for the best. Federico pressed on with the momentum of his attack. With dispatch, Federico moved his black bishop to overtake the single white pawn which had been blocking its dominance over the white king.

"Checkmate!!" shouted Federico.

Raoul was initially dubious. His white king was being threatened by a black bishop. That was certain. But surely his king could move one square diagonally, thereby removing it from the clutches of the black bishop. He studied the situation for a few more seconds. Then reality struck. Oh god! That fucking black knight! he thought to himself. That god damned fucking black knight is dominating the only square piece of battlefield available to my king! He had no alternatives left. He couldn't move his king, he couldn't block the black bishop's line of fire, and he couldn't overtake either the black bishop or the black knight. There was one more thing he couldn't do. He couldn't help relating the figure of the black knight to the "Black Knights of the Hudson," those fucking West Pointers. The Ulysses S. Grants, the Robert E. Lees, the George Armstrong Custers, the Jeb Stuarts. He despised them all, with a twisted sort of respect. The Douglas MacArthurs, the Dwight Eisenhowers, the Omar Bradleys, the George Pattons. Hated them—all of them. The William Westmorelands, the Norman Schwartzkopfs, the Maxwell Throckmillers. He abhorred the thought of them, but he had read every historical account of their battlefield successes that he could get his hands on. Throckmiller . . . that god damn fucking son-of-a-bitch black knight Throckmiller! he thought to himself. . . . And that falsely pious Vatican-kissing, cock sucking hypocrite Bishop Spinoza! He was trapped by these two shitheads. Humiliated, all he could think about was that he had been forced to capitulate, simultaneously, to both the Church and to a foreign cavalry. This was insult added to injury. Suddenly, his fury having reached a crescendo, Raoul rose to his feet, picked up the chessboard, and with all the force he could marshal, hurled the battlefield and all its warriors against the wall of the tent.

Federico, still seated, began laughing uncontrollably.

"Shut the fuck up," Raoul yelled.

"But Commandante, you are so funny."

"Funny? Fuck funny! What's so funny about it?"

"It's funny, Commandante, that you take losing so seriously . . . and personally."

"Losing *is* serious. Bodegas don't lose . . . anything. Yeah, Federico. Go ahead. *Keep* laughing. I hope you *die* laughing, Federico . . . *now!*"

No sooner were those last words out of his mouth, Raoul had already regretted uttering them. He knew that Federico was right. He knew that he had a tendency to make rash assumptions and that Federico often helped him to be more rational and realistic in competitive situations. Raoul also knew that he needed Federico. He needed Federico's level-headedness in the heat of conflict. As he watched Federico pick up the chessboard and pieces now laying everywhere on the floor of the tent, Raoul had an impulse to apologize. But he couldn't. Leaders just don't apologize. That's a sign of weakness. And leaders should *never* appear weak in the eyes of their subordinates. Raoul turned and stormed out of the tent, intending to remind Federico who was still in command.

As he was leaving the tent, Raoul could hear the faint humming of helicopter rotors somewhere in the distance. Forgetting what had just occurred inside the tent, Raoul shouted excitedly, "Federico, they're coming! The choppers are coming, Federico!"

Federico rushed outside the tent and called to eight or so fatigue-clad men sitting and kibitzing in the jungle shade near the clearing. "Take your positions!" he shouted. The men, bearing AK-47s and other automatic weapons, proceeded to predesignated positions around the periphery of the clearing. This was a defensive measure to protect against the possibility of some unexpected event—like the helicopters being filled with Government police. Federico thought of everything. He never left anything to chance. For him, it was always strategy, never serendipity.

2

Lila felt her head getting light as the lead helicopter in which she was riding began descending rapidly. She felt nauseous. The same way she felt when General Throckmiller was describing the slaughter of Pablo Cordova and his small son during the briefing at Cartagena. Then it was the brutality, the gore, the blood. This time it was the fumes. The sickening noxious odor of technological advancement. She had endured more than three hours of it. "If it *smells* this bad, what is it doing to my brain cells?" she thought, trying to keep her mind off of her current predicament. The sensation of the helicopter's descent stimulated mixed feelings of relief from the effects of the fume capsule and of fear as to what would happen next.

Lila looked over at Esther. She was either sleeping or had passed out from fear and exhaustion. Her chic tan suit was now wrinkled and stained with perspiration. The once puffed royal blue scarf knotted, gardenialike, under her chin and resting on her impeccably tailored silk blouse, now resembled a three-day-old cut gladiola which had dropped onto a smudged and discolored table cloth. Her usual 1960 in-place hairdo, now looked more like Tiny Tim's undisciplined tresses on a bad hair day. For a second, Lila felt like laughing. But she didn't get the chance. A substantial jolt distracted her, shook the whole helicopter, and awakened Esther. They had finally landed.

Near the edge of the clearing just behind two of his uniformed soldiers, Raoul stood with his hands on his hips, sporting a broad smile with a huge smoldering Cuban cigar protruding from the side of his mouth. He couldn't wait to see the figure of his brother Hector stepping out of one of the helicopters. Equally expectant,

Federico was standing beside him. But, being a pragmatist, Federico was very cautious about his optimism. His expectations had been dashed many times in the past. Raoul and Federico continued watching as the lieutenant exited the nearer helicopter first and motioned to others inside to disembark. Meanwhile, four men in Government police uniforms exited the farther helicopter. This startled Federico. He almost shouted to the peripheral guards to open fire. Luckily, he contained that impulse, remembering that police uniforms were part of the guerrillas' planned disguise.

Raoul had not even notice them. He was too intent on seeing his brother emerge from the lieutenant's helicopter. He watched carefully as three disguised men stepped down from the near helicopter in succession and stood next to the lieutenant. But no Hector. Then, as the dust was clearing more rapidly, he watched the lieutenant reach his arm inside the helicopter door. *This* would be Hector . . . *surely*.

Then saw the figure of a woman in a tan suit, her hands cuffed behind her, standing in the open doorframe. "Who the fuck is that?" he thought to himself amid the din and dust caused by the slowing helicopter rotors. He turned and glanced at Federico incredulously. Once again he riveted his attention on the closer helicopter; Federico did the same.

When the woman was standing on the ground, two of the police-dressed men approached her, one on each side, and began to escort her toward Raoul and Federico.

They continued to watch as the lieutenant reached his arm inside the helicopter door again. "*This* must be Hector," Raoul thought. In the doorframe appeared another handcuffed female figure. When she jumped down from the helicopter, the other two guards steered her toward Raoul and Federico. The lieutenant trailed behind. Raoul finally realized that Hector was not with them. "TWO BITCHES AND NO HECTOR," Raoul yelled in Federico's ear. "THAT LIEUTENANT OF YOURS HAS SOME EXPLAINING TO DO!"

The lieutenant caught up with the guerrillas escorting Lila

and Esther when they were a few feet from Raoul and Hector. "Raoul, this is Lieutenant Bolero," said Federico. "He was in charge of the Cartagena operation."

The lieutenant reached out his hand toward Raoul in an attempted handshake. Raoul did not respond. His hands still on his hips, and looking directly into the lieutenant's eyes, Raoul shouted at him with audible contempt, "Where the hell is my brother?"

"We don't know, Commandante," the lieutenant answered with trepidation, Carlos coming to his side.

"What do you mean 'you don't know', lieutenant? It's your job to know!" Raoul shouted.

Moving his head and nodding toward the two women being held by the guerrillas, the lieutenant said, "We need to talk, Commandante . . . in private."

"*Vamanos*!" Raoul said turning and heading in the direction of his tent, which by now had sections of the sides rolled up to allow in fresh air. Federico, the lieutenant, and Carlos followed Raoul in single file. While following Federico, the lieutenant turned and motioned to his men to take the two women to a shaded area under the jungle canopy a few hundred feet from Raoul's tent.

"Give them some water and keep them alive. . . . Torture them, if you like. But whatever you do, keep them alive," the lieutenant ordered.

Half-delirious, Lila and Esther only tuned in the word "water", which by now they craved.

Once inside the tent, Raoul, still harboring anger and contempt, growled at the lieutenant, "So what happened to my brother?"

"Tell us everything, and start from the beginning," Federico added.

"Commandante, perhaps Carlos should tell the story. He was closest to what occurred in the Plaza, and he spoke to the police about Hector's whereabouts."

Carlos began to relate the details of the operation beginning with the fishermen cover, through the incidents connected with the Plaza bombing, including the sacrifice of Julio, the death of General Rojillo and the two Miss Colombias; the disclosure of the Goliath-figure about General Throckmiller's order to annihilate Hector; the police sergeant's information that Hector had been moved from the citadel; the taking of the dignitaries as hostages; and Carrington's death, describing his fall from the helicopter as an accident.

When Carlos concluded, Federico asked, "Why would Throckmiller order Hector's death? Wouldn't he rather have him as a live war trophy?"

"All we know," replied Carlos, "is that the Goliath-figure said that `Throck' ordered him to kill Hector."

"Throck? . . . Throck?" bellowed Raoul. "You idiot! Goliath was referring to that bastard Pedro "The Rock"—Bishop Spinoza!" Raoul looked at Federico and said blankly, "What a sorry fucking state of affairs. The President's alive, a Congressman is dead, a bishop's ordered Hector's death, Julio's committed suicide, Hector is lost, and we have two whiny fucking bitches to contend with. What could be worse?"

In his usual, soothing manner, Federico helped Raoul visualize a more optimistic scene. "Commandante, look at the positive aspects of what happened. These men did the best they could in very difficult circumstances. What we really have here is a dead chief of staff, which should make the President fearful, a dead Congressman, which should let the Americans know that we mean business, and two hostages whose fair market value is equal to, or greater than, Hector's. We can trade them for Hector and just about anything else we want. Think of it as sacrificing two pawns to place the king in check. Checkmate is sure to follow."

"Perhaps, so." Raoul conceded. "But what's our next move?"

Federico motioned for the lieutenant and Carlos to leave the tent. After they had departed, Federico said to Raoul, "This is what I suggest we do, Commandante. We should get word to President Guardina that we have captured the two American women and that we are willing to trade them for Hector at an agreed location. We should also require that Hector be transported safely and that his escorts be unarmed. We should warn the President that if there are any foul-ups, the hostages will be killed."

"Plan sounds fine to me," said Raoul. "When do we execute it?"

"It is four-thirty now. I suggest we get a message to Guardina by ten tomorrow morning. We don't want to give him too much time to think about this. We'll specify four p.m. tomorrow as the exchange time and this location as the exchange point. We'll spend tonight and pretty much of tomorrow at the caves having the men seal off and conceal our equipment and munitions. Does that meet with your approval, Commandante?"

"Yes, but two things."

"What, Commandante?"

"First, I want to meet with Spinoza tonight."

"No problem, Commandante. I'll arrange it immediately."

"And second, before we leave Colombia tomorrow, I want Throckmiller's head on a platter."

"My pleasure, Commandante" Federico said grinning. "Béarnaise or teriyaki?"

STAGED ASSAULT

Within minutes after Raoul and Federico had left the encampment that afternoon, Carlos and Lieutenant Bolero were busy plotting how the two female captives could provide them entertainment. Raoul's only instructions were to keep them alive. They were fair game for any kind of torture the guerrillas' twisted minds could concoct.

"Why don't we soak their hands and feet with gasoline, and set them on fire," said Carlos within earshot of the two women. "That way we won't have to worry about them trying to escape into the jungle."

"Not a bad idea, Carlos" the lieutenant replied, "but I'd hate to waste a scarce resource like that."

Esther and Lila listened intently, separately concluding that the two were just playing mind games.

"You have a point there," said Carlos. "I suppose we could hang them by their feet over a fire and watch their hair burn and their makeup melt and run. Fire's cheap and there's plenty of it."

He had to be kidding, Esther thought. Just too outrageous.

"Yes, but the torture isn't slow enough." said Bolero. "How about a good old fashioned gangbang. That could take an hour or so. Why don't you start, first, Carlos."

Carlos bounded to his feet and went over and stood in front of Lila who was lying on the ground with her hands cuffed behind her back. Both women sensed the two men now weren't kidding.

He pulled Lila up by her hair and leaned her against a tree. "Tell me why Esther should be raped and not you," he sneered.

Lila blanked. "I . . . I . . . can't think of any reason why Esther should be raped at all."

"Then you want to be raped, instead."

"No . . . No . . . " stammered Lila. "Neither of us wants to be raped."

"Well, let's try this approach," said Carlos. "Do you find me attractive."

Choosing her words carefully, Lila replied weakly, "I don't find you unattractive."

"Then you wouldn't mind making love with me. Right?"

"I didn't say that."

"Then what *did* you say?"

"It's not what I said, it's what I meant. I don't want to be raped; I don't want to make love."

"Give me your best argument why I shouldn't rape you."

Lila hesitated, afraid to play her only ace in the hole.

Finally, she blurted loudly, "Because I'm Emilio's girlfriend, that's why."

Hearing this, Esther was dumbfounded.

"Oh, so *you're* Emilio's girlfriend, are you?"

"Yes, and if you lay a hand on me, I know he'll kill you."

"Don't be too sure, cupcake. Emilio has many girlfriends. You're just one member of his harem in the States. Lucky for you, I never mess with a main squeeze of a close friend."

Lieutenant Bolero piped up, "You must be the bitch he's working with to bump off women West Pointers."

Lila didn't respond. Esther's eyes widened.

Pushing for an answer, Bolero continued, "He told me he paid big money to U.S. soldiers to kill or incapacitate these women during their training. I hear he nailed three of the five women targets. Sixty percent success rate ain't bad, is it cupcake?"

Still, Lila refused to respond.

"One of the two left is a general's daughter, right?" Bolero pried. "She escaped her deathtrap someplace in Florida—got cold feet goin' outta chopper. You know exactly who that is, don't you bitch. You planned it didn't you?"

Lila looked away sharply.

Stroking Lila's cheek, Carlos urged cynically, "You were part of that little conspiracy, weren't you, dear heart?" Carlos looked toward Esther to make sure she was listening, then refocused on Lila. "You supplied Emilio with critical information about their training, didn't you?"

Still no response.

"Say yes, honeybun, so I'll know you're one of us!" Carlos screeched, beginning to lose his cool.

Carlos brought his right arm around in a wide arc and slapped Lila hard in the face, forcibly moving her off the ground, away from the tree, and a couple feet farther from Esther. "Answer me, bitch !!" Carlos yelled.

"Yes, Yes, Yes, I did it! I'm one of you. Please don't hurt me!" Lila bawled, using the heels on her shoes to scoot farther away from Carlos.

"Why didn't you just say so in the first place," said Carlos. "Coulda saved me a lot of energy on this hot afternoon."

Lila laid back on the leaf-strewn jungle floor sobbing and rocking from side to side.

Esther was not sure what to make of what just happened. Was Lila lying about her role in thwarting the Minerva Experiment to avoid further abuse? No matter what, it seemed clear that Emilio was involved in the conspiracy up to his neck.

Carlos turned his attention to Esther who shrank away as he approached. "I suppose, cunt, you're gonna tell us you're one of us too," Carlos said sarcastically. "What's *your* story?"

"I don't have one."

"Everyone has a story, chick-a-dee."

"Well, I don't."

"I bet you're a friend of Emilio, too."

"Actually, we have a business arrangement."

Lila's ears perked up.

"What—he fucks you for nuthin'?"

"No, not exactly. He pays me for giving him information instead of giving it to someone else."

"In Colombia, we call that blackmail. So *you're* the fuckin' wench who's pressuring Emilio for bucks . . . big bucks ."

"No, No," Esther screamed. "That's not true."

"It's true, bitch. Everything points to you."

"No! You got the wrong person!"

"Don't think so. My good friend Emilio would love to be here to see what we're gonna do to you. I bet he'd pay seventy-five grand to watch it."

Instantly, Carlos roughly shoved Esther over on her stomach, looped a piece of rawhide around her feet, and started dragging her, chest down, across the encampment area and into Raoul's tent. In a few seconds, he emerged, and announced to four young guerrillas standing nearby smoking cigarettes, "Gents, she's all yours for the taking. Just clean up the place when you're finished." The four guerrillas immediately laid down their rifles and entered the tent together.

Esther's horrifying, shrill screams sliced the steaming jungle air for the next hour. About half-way through the ordeal, Lila, no longer able to tolerate the sounds or the thought of Esther's ghastly fate, passed out.

2

Late that same afternoon, Archbishop Spinoza sat quietly reading his book of vespers under a flickering light in the dreary rectory of Our Lady of Sorrows parish in Santa Rosas de Osos, a small town located north and west of Medellín. Monsignor Montero had invited him to stay the night, and he had accepted. The bishop, quite active and youthful for his sixty-two years, often visited the parishes in his diocese, sometimes spending days with his "flocks" as he referred to them. He loved being with the common people and he missed the days of his own parish ministry. He could easily do without the pomp and circumstance of the Catholic hierarchy. It was phony, arrogant—as were the drug lords whom he also despised. He was one of the few prelates who had stood his ground against the cartels and clergy that cooperated with them. It hadn't been easy. His recent edict to excommunicate Catholics convicted of assisting the drug cartels drew criticism from all levels of the Catholic clergy. Some critics believed the bishop's action was too harsh; others objected out of a justifiable fear for their lives. "The Rock" didn't budge; the edict was to be enforced.

He looked up from his prayer book just in time to see through the window, a jeep pulling up the gravel road. It parked near the front door of the rectory, and two men in fatigue clothing got out. He watched as Monsignor Montero approached them and shook their hands in what appeared to be a warm greeting. One of them resembled Raoul Bodega. Why would the monsignor be welcoming a noted drug lord? The bishop concluded he must be mistaken about the man's identity.

Spinoza moved away from the window and started toward the door of the study. He wanted to find out what was going on. Just as he reached for the door knob, the door opened into him and forced him to backstep a few feet. Montero entered, closed the door quickly behind him, and spoke in a whisper.

"Your eminence," he began, his face conveying extreme terror. "Raoul Bodega's here. He wants to talk to you immediately. His lieutenant's holding my housekeeper at knifepoint in the kitchen. He'll kill her if . . . "

Before Spinoza could react, Raoul forced the door open and instructed Spinoza to sit down and Montero to leave. Montero wasted no time departing.

Walking toward Spinoza and removing a folded-up straight razor from his pocket, Raoul got right to the point. "What's all this about you putting a contract out on my brother?"

"I, I d . . . don't know what you . . . " Spinoza stuttered, noticing the object in Raoul's hand.

"Don't lie to me!" Raoul bellowed. "You ordered my brother killed. I know you did!"

The bishop remained silent.

Raoul opened the razor in front of Spinoza and then walked

behind his chair.

"That was a big mistake, your eminence," Raoul said mockingly, seizing the prelate by the hair and running the cold, dull side of the razor's blade briskly across his neck."

Spinoza closed his eyes tightly, waiting to feel blood trickle down his neck.

Seconds of silence intervened. "Surprise!!" Raoul mocked, now standing in front of Spinoza. "You've been saved and I'm your savior. I'm your personal Christ."

Spinoza opened his eyes to the sight of Raoul glaring at him contemptibly.

"Remember this, Rocky—or whatever they call you. I can snuff you out in a second."

Spinoza collapsed the blade of the razor into its wooden handle and began walking back and forth in front of Spinoza, holding the folded razor in one hand and tapping it in the palm of the other."

"How's your mother?" Raoul asked.

"My mother? What do you mean?"

"She lives on Punta Norte street in Bogotá, correct?"

"Yes, so what?"

"Lives by herself?"

"Yes, . . . and she's doing quite well for her eighty years."

"See her often?"

"About once a week."

"Good. Now picture her in your mind—her ears sliced off, her eyeballs gouged out, and a rail spike sticking out of her forehead."

Spinoza, becoming nauseous, looked down at the floor.

"Not a pretty sight, huh, Rocky? Not a pretty sight at all."

Raoul still pacing back and forth, put the straight razor back into his pocket. "The good news is that none of this has to happen," he continued. "You have the complete power to stop it. It's simple. All you have to do is retract your edict."

Spinoza felt castrated. The pressure was overwhelming. As much as he hated it, he had no choice but to make the move.

"Well? What do you say, your eminence?" Raoul taunted.

Spinoza lowered his chin to his chest and rocked his head up and down in begrudging acceptance.

"Good, your eminence," said Raoul. "Then we have a deal."

Raoul again removed the razor from his pocket and opened it slowly. He turned around and started toward the door. On the wall next to the door hung a large religious painting set in an elegant gold frame. The scene was similar to Michaelangelo's *Pieta* sculpture—the Blessed Virgin Mary seated in front of a wooden cross cradling her battered, bleeding dead son in her arms. Using the razor, Raoul slashed the picture diagonally as he passed through the doorway and slammed the door behind him.

Spinoza broke into tears, thanking God that he was still breathing.

Raoul and Federico quickly left the rectory and jumped into the jeep. The jeep's rear tires threw gravel against the building as Federico gunned the engine and sped toward the main road. Once outside town, Federico got Raoul's attention, saying. "See, Commandante. In real life, if you're king, there's more than one way to get out of check. You can force a bishop to move!"

Raoul laughed heartily. "Yes . . . and you can also *kill* the black knight!"

They were still laughing and joking when they arrived back at the encampment, a couple of hours before dusk. Carlos greeted them with a salute. Still sitting in the jeep, Raoul saluted back and asked, "Everything okay?"

"Everything's just fine, Commandante. We've taken good care of our two guests. . . . They're alive anyway."

Raoul smiled his approval.

3

That same evening, Kate, Bryan and the others were finishing up a training exercise for Operation Athena at Fort Sherman, Panama, on the west side of the Canal. The Rangers had been there since about the middle of September undergoing advanced jungle training. They were all getting antsy for real combat. Kate, relaxing in a T-shirt and loose khaki shorts, sat in the side doorway of a Huey. The uniform was unauthorized and Kate knew it. It was no big deal. Things had become a little lax in the last couple of weeks. The Rangers had expected the operation to start sooner, and they were becoming bored with training that seemed repetitive and rote.

As Kate swung her legs back and forth, shoots of jungle groundcover reached up through the chopper's skids and caressed the sides of her exposed thighs. Patiently, she watched Bryan through the thicket, his head frequently bobbing up and down.

"Watcha doin?" Kate asked.

"Just killin' time," Bryan responded.

For another minute or two, Bryan quickly moved around the thick foliage, visible from only the shoulders up. Then, without warning, he burst into the clearing a few meters in front of Kate. "Ta Da!" he intoned as if he had just performed a magic act. In his arms he carried a neatly stacked pile of pink, white, and yellow orchids.

"They're gorgeous!" Kate exclaimed, scooting off the door ledge and moving toward him. Picking one of the posies out of his arms, Kate held it up to the side of her head as if to model it.

"I asked for dozen red roses," Bryan quipped, "but I had to settle for a dozen of these."

"Tsk, Tsk," replied Kate, now modeling the orchid on the other side of her head. "I'd rather have orchids any day."

"You would?"

"Sure. For a woman, they have a special meaning," Kate said in a silky voice.

"Yeah—you mean proms, weddings and Mother's Days, I guess."

"Actually, more than that. "Orchid" derives from a Greek word meaning testicles."

"You must be kidding."

"No, I'm not, Bryan. I had this course on Greek mythology in high school and . . . "

"So?"

"So when a man gives a woman an orchid, he's really making a statement."

"Yeah, and when he gives her a dozen orchids?" Bryan asked, turning his smile up a notch.

"It could mean a couple things. Either the man is confident about his masculinity, or—"

"Or—maybe I don't want to know the `or'," Bryan interjected.

"Maybe not," she grinned, turning to catch the reflection of her orchid-adorned hair in the shiny metal skin of the helicopter. Pushing her hair back from her face and still looking at her reflection, she asked devilishly, "aren't you afraid of getting caught out here alone with a subordinate officer?"

"Why should I be. We're on an official training assignment, aren't we?"

"Yeah, but the rest of the Rangers returned to the barracks an hour ago."

"They did? I guess I didn't notice."

"You're in charge aren't you?"

"Yeah, that's right. I'm in charge and I say we're still official."

"Then let's *make* it official," Kate said, taking Bryan by the hand and leading him up into the helicopter.

"I've never done it in a *cock*pit," Bryan teased.

"I'd wonder about you if you had."

"Guess there's always a first time for everything."

Kate quickly removed her shorts and shirt, dropped down into the pilot's seat, and motioned for Bryan to sit next to her as co-pilot. There was no question in his mind who was in charge this time. Quite a change from that little tryst they had in jungle training in Florida. When he was in place next to her, she climbed onto his lap, and facing him, began unbuttoning his fatigue shirt. Soon, her tongue was traversing the contours of his ears and she could feel his hardness growing and quaking beneath her.

Reaching behind her back and unhooking her bra, he buried his face in her heaving breasts, and began running his hands indiscriminately over her warm, pulsating body. Coming up for air, he babbled breathily, "What about Throckmiller?"

"Oh, please," moaned Kate, as she stiffened in a twinge of erotic pleasure and pulled Bryan's T-shirt up over his head.

"We're supposed to meet him in an hour . . . ," he groaned, pushing her gently back against the controls and quickly unzipping his trousers. " . . . Across the Canal . . . at Fort Clayton . . . " Feverishly manipulating her way through his hairy jungle in search of orchids, she hushed, "Do we have enough time?".

"Not to worry," Bryan gasped. "We'll take the chopper!"

)368-COOL

SALT AND PEPPER

Throckmiller was in his office at SIXCOM headquarters at Fort Clayton, Panama going over some routine paperwork. It was 6:00 p.m., and he was about to wrap things up and go over to the Quarry Heights Officers' Club to have his usual two martinis before dinner. Tonight was special. He was going to dine with Second Lieutenant Kathryn McKeane and Captain Bryan Flanagan and discuss Operation Athena. They were coming from Fort Sherman on the west side of the Canal. He had never met either of them before, but he felt like he knew Kate all of his life just from the descriptions given him by her father, Major General Charles McKeane. Now *there* was a soldier. USMA '65. Top of his class. Most decorated field grade officer in the Gulf War. Brilliant, honorable, resourceful, and a dozen more superlatives. Kate had some big shoes to fill. Her dad had a superb reputation for accomplishing any mission. Throckmiller was anxious to see how she measured up.

As for Captain Flanagan?—Throckmiller didn't know much about him, except that he was now commanding one of the Ranger companies for Operation Athena. Aside from that, he only knew what Chuck McKeane shared with him briefly at a cocktail party in D.C. a few weeks previously. Bryan—as Chuck referred to him— came from a good family, did well in his class at West Point, excelled in Ranger School and was actually kept on as an instructor after he completed it. He was a natural expert in survival and guerrilla warfare. Apparently, he had spent his summers in high school and college guiding fishing and hunting expeditions in Canada, Colorado, and the Florida Everglades. He was a certified civilian helicopter pilot. Kate had apparently met Bryan right before she started Ranger School. Chuck McKeane had said Bryan really gave her hell in Ranger School—really brought out her animal instincts and made a tough combat fighter out of her. Chuck had thought there might be a romantic interest there as well, but he couldn't be sure.

Throckmiller signed the last piece of routine correspondence and leaned back in his executive's swivel chair, clasping his hands behind his head and looking up at the ceiling. "U.S. women in ground combat," he thought to himself. "I never thought it would happen in my lifetime—not even in an experiment." When Throckmiller had initially heard about Operation Athena, he was opposed to it, as were most all the generals. However, the military needed something to balance the terrible publicity that the Navy had received from the Tailhook scandal, so Throckmiller went along with it—even came out in support of it.

A telephone's buzzing sound broke the silence of Throckmiller's office and ended his philosophical musings.

He pushed the button on his speaker phone. "General Throckmiller," he said in an intentionally deepened voice.

"General, I have President Guardina on the line," said the military operator.

"Please put him right through, Corporal," said Throckmiller picking up the receiver. Hearing a click and a static background rush, Throckmiller queried, "President Guardina?"

"Yes, this is President Guardina."

"Mr. President, we have a pretty bad connection. How well can you hear me?"

"Pretty well. Just exercise your command voice into that damned military walkie-talkie, General," Guardina said in an effort to smooth the way for the bad news he was about to deliver.

Throckmiller was surprised to receive a telephone call directly from Guardina. This had never occurred before. Something important must have happened. "What's new, Mr. President?" Throckmiller blared into his receiver, trying awkwardly to find a balance between deference and nonchalance.

"I have some bad news. I thought you should know as soon as I had an opportunity to confirm it."

"What's happened?"

"First of all, General Rojillo, my chief of staff, has been killed in an explosion in the Plaza along with several other people."

"Oh my God!"

"Not only that, General, we have now confirmed that Senator Carrington, Representative Grant, and Lila Davis-Whitfield, have been kidnapped by a faction operating at the direction of the Bodega brothers. We have no information as to where they are except that witnesses saw two helicopters carrying the hostages leaving Cartagena this afternoon heading in a southeasterly direction toward Medellín. We have reported the incident to the U.S. State Department and they requested that we notify you immediately. Needless to say, General, this is a diplomatically sensitive situation that requires handling with kid gloves."

"I understand. Perhaps we should think about launching Operation Athena sooner than we had planned. Of course it would have to be conducted more quietly and delicately than we originally anticipated.

"Would you be able to get your Ranger units into the Medellín area *tonight*?" Guardina asked.

"Certainly. The Rangers are on a one-hour alert—meaning they can be suited up, fully equipped, and ready to be dispatched from Howard Air Force Base on one hour's notice. I just need to know precisely where the Bodegas and the hostages are, and I can have Rangers there in a matter of a few hours."

"Terrific!" Guardina replied, sounding relieved to know that the Americans would be sharing the responsibility to rescue some of their own. "I'll get back to you later on this evening as soon as our intelligence units get a precise fix on the location of the hostages."

"Fine," said Throckmiller. "I'll let the base telephone operator know where I'll be at all times, so he can get a hold of me immediately when you call."

"I hope to get back to you within the next hour or two, General. So long for now."

After hanging up the receiver, Throckmiller swiveled his chair and looked out his office window, now bathed in several shades of orange and gold emanating from a giant red solar disc, half submerged in the infinite blueness of ocean. Night would come soon. And with it, perhaps, Operation Athena.

2

It was a short jeep ride from Throckmiller's office to the officers' club, and this evening the General was enjoying the rush of cool air beating against his face as he conversed casually with his driver, Corporal Baxter. Over the six months they had been together, the General and Baxter had become fast friends. Mostly out of mutual loneliness. Also, there were some personal things that the General felt he could not discuss with his subordinate officers and still maintain professional distance. In many ways, Baxter had been able to fill that void and had become Throckmiller's confidant. Someone he could bounce ideas off of; discuss his feelings and frustrations; on whom to test his theories. A channel to the soul of his troops—like Napoleon's stable boy.

"Hot date tonight, General?" winked Baxter, as he swung his jeep into the driveway in front of the officers club, exquisitely Spanish in design.

"You might say that, Corporal" joked Throckmiller, knowing all the while that they both knew that there were no females at SIXCOM headquarters or in the Ranger compound. Well, save a few. But Baxter didn't know about them.

"Now, you'd better be in by midnight, General" Baxter said. "You have to be up bright and early to lead us all tomorrow morning."

Throckmiller mused to himself, "If Baxter only knew the truth of what he just said." Getting out of the jeep, Throckmiller turned to Baxter and said, "You can pick me up in an hour and a half. In the meantime, get me a seventy-two-hour weather forecast for the Cartagena, Medellín, and Bogotá areas. We might be going on a trip tomorrow."

"Sure, General." Baxter replied while executing a sharp half-salute. "See you at eight-thirty."

Throckmiller listened to the jeep speed away as he started up the white marble steps toward the massive mahogany doors of the officers' club. When he reached the top, he turned around to take one last look at the spectacular sunset. The 0-Club, resembling an ancient Franciscan monastery, was situated on a high promontory of land near the bay. The vistas from the club were unparalleled in their depiction of the sensual intermingling of sea and jungle. Only a sliver of a yellowish-orange crescent was visible on the horizon; long and layered cumulus clouds exuded a gentle purplish haze. Throckmiller wondered if all the Rangers under his command would live to see another sunset—like this or any other. Sensing Throckmiller's approach through a slitted window in the massive portal, a native Panamanian in a black tuxedo opened the door wide and greeted the General. Throckmiller smiled and returned the greeting as he entered.

The lavishly furnished entry hall of the O-Club was flanked on each side by ornately decorated rooms which competed with it and each other in luxuriant splendor. On the left was the grand dining room with a forty-foot bay window at the far end framing a dramatic view of the ocean. On the right was what was once called "the gentlemen's parlor," now referred to as the officers' lounge, with its solid oak, geometric paneled twenty-foot high walls and its fifty-foot birds-eye maple bar. In decades past, it serviced liter-ally brigades of officers, raucously telling jokes and riddles before dinner, or more quietly exchanging war stories of all types over liqueurs and cigars, after. Now, with the decreased U.S. military presence in Panama, the officers' lounge was only a shadow of its former self, typically uninhabited and quiet. Ghostly quiet.

Throckmiller stuck his head in the officers' lounge and looked around to see if he could spot Kate and Bryan. The only person

visible in the lounge was a chief warrant officer reading a newspaper in a distant corner of the room. Throckmiller did not know
him; it didn't matter either way, because the CWO was so absorbed that he didn't notice the general.

"May I help you, General?" boomed a voice from the left, out
of Throckmiller's line of vision, coming from behind the bar.
Startled, Throckmiller saw a Panamanian bartender, decked
out in a white waistcoat and a black bow tie, polishing a crystal
champagne glass, alternately holding it up to the light to view it,
breathing a cloud of vapor on it, and gently massaging the vapor
away. So unexpected was the voice, it brought back memories of
accidental activation of trip flares in the nocturnal Vietnam jungle.

"Yes, you c-c-can," stammered Throckmiller. "Have you seen
a couple of young army officers around here recently?"

"Not really, General. It's been pretty quiet around here the
last hour or so, in fact, the last year or so. There are a few people in
the dining room—Colonel types. Oh yeah, I did see a young officer in civies and his wife head toward the dining room about
fifteen minutes ago. I haven't seen two young officers, though."

"Thanks, pardner," Throckmiller said, realizing that it was still
the sign of the times that "women" and "officers" were mutually
exclusive terms. Throckmiller made a beeline to the officers dining
room. At the entrance he looked around for a table with a female
seated at it. Spying only one such table in the room, Throckmiller
nodded in the direction of it to the head waiter, who led
Throckmiller towards it. When he approached the table, Kate and
Bryan abruptly broke off their conversation and stood up, practically at braced attention.

"Good evening, General," said Kate extending her hand to
give Throckmiller a firm handshake. "It's a pleasure finally to meet
you. My dad has said such wonderful things about you."

"That's very kind of you to say," said Throckmiller noticing
Kate's slender, yet well endowed figure. He hadn't seen a woman
with a build like that in years. "If your dad said that I walk on
water, don't believe him," Throckmiller added with a wide grin.

368-COOL

Quickly extending his hand towards Kate's companion, Throckmiller said, "Flanagan, I suppose."

"That's right, General. It's a real pleasure."

The head waiter seated Throckmiller next to Kate and across from Bryan; then clicked his fingers to get the attention of a subordinate. Throckmiller said apologetically, "I'm sorry I'm late. Had some unexpected business to take care of right before I left the office. Have you ordered yet?"

"No, we haven't, sir. We just got here ourselves, sir. Anyway, sir, we wouldn't start without the guest of honor, sir,"

Bryan alliterated.

In a stern, yet fatherly voice, Throckmiller advised, "Look, folks, I want you to relax tonight. Cut the `sir' stuff. I want to get to know you both personally. We have a lot of ground to cover. Call me Throck, if you like. Practically everyone else does."

Kate expected Throckmiller to be gracious, but she hadn't anticipated that he would invite them to call him by his nickname.

Groping for right words, Kate said cautiously, "I think we can cut the `sir' stuff, but I'd be more comfortable just calling you General.

"Oh, all right. . . . But I want you both to relax." Throckmiller insisted. "We have to talk turkey about Operation Athena."

Kate looked up to see Sandy Rothman walking toward the table.

"Oh General," said Kate, "I hope you don't mind. I invited Lieutenant Sandy Rothman to join us this evening. She is one of the Ranger platoon leaders also."

Throckmiller stood up, greeted Sandy, and cordially requested that she join them for dinner.

The waiter distributed menus and took drink orders while the four shared highly animated stories of West Point. Cadet days were always on the agenda for discussion when two or more ring-knockers congregated. By the second martini, Throckmiller was living up to his reputation of being a grand yarn spinner.

A few minutes later when the waiter returned, the four dinner companions were laughing and talking. "And your father, Kate . . . your father never lived that one down," said Throckmiller noticing the waiter's presence. "Are you ready to order, General?" the waiter inquired. Throckmiller's smile quickly faded as he picked up the menu. In a self-important tone, he said to the waiter, "We'll have châteaubriand with all the trimmings for everyone," and scooting forward and putting his elbows on the table with his clasped hands under his chin, "and of course the same vintage Rothschild that I ordered last week when I entertained General Winterfield, the Army Chief of Staff." The waiter nodded and smiled, indicating obvious recognition of the General's preferences. Looking at the three young officers, Throckmiller said with an air of determination, "Just so there is no misunderstanding, you three are *my* guests this evening."

"That's very kind of you, General. But there is one thing."

"Yes?"

"I *don't eat* red meat," Kate said with a slight smile, but pointedly enough to communicate to Throckmiller that she did not appreciate his preempting her right to order her own meal.

"Oh, I'm sorry," Throckmiller said, not fully realizing until now how independent and assertive Kate was. Kate was definitely a woman with her own mind and it showed. "I just assumed that everyone would want the Club's most expensive item on the menu. Please forgive me for being so presumptuous."

"Think nothing of it," Kate said matter-of-factly to Throckmiller, and then turned to the waiter to consult with him privately about the menu. Breaking off their consultation abruptly and pointing to the middle of the menu page, Kate announced "I'll have the red snapper."

"How appropriate," Throckmiller mused to himself.

"I'll have châteaubriand with the General," Bryan said to the waiter, though he would have much preferred the medallions of veal. Discretion, Bryan felt in this instance, was the better part of valor. The General's ego perhaps could not endure back-to-back rejections.

Sandy said to the waiter, "the châteaubriand is fine."

Bryan piped up, "General, something happened to one of my classmates in airborne training at Fort Benning that I thought was quite humorous. Jake, my classmate, was one of those cadets whose physical aptitude was barely sufficient to get him into West Point.

He had more political pull than an ability to do pull-ups. Throughout his time at West Point, he was one of those egghead academic types—wore academic stars on his collars at the Point and all that—but had trouble with any athletics beyond tying his shoes. Well, he made it through—all four years, with a lot of help from his classmates. I remember another cadet and myself using the firemen's carry several times to get him through the morning runs and forced marches at Camp Buckner during our second summer at the Point. He really screwed up on the "slide for life" when he didn't let go of the pulley mechanism and followed the cable right to the embankment. He broke a couple of bones, but he could have killed himself."

"Anyway, after we graduated and were in Airborne School, "Genius Jake," as we called him, was still living up to his reputation as an athletic bumbler. He did pretty well on his first three jumps, but the fourth one—with full field gear—was quite memorable. Apparently, out of fear, he froze in the doorway of the C-130, and it was only the momentum of the column of paratroopers behind him that forced him out the door. A tight body position he didn't have. His arms and legs were flailing in the backwash of the aircraft like a rag doll's. After his chute opened, a gush of updraft pushed his legs up above is head and his feet got entangled in his chute's risers so that he was descending in an inverted position.

"I never heard of such a thing," interjected Throckmiller.

"Neither had anyone else," replied Bryan continuing his story, "but the best was yet to come. Twenty-five of us or so had already landed and were getting out of our parachute harnesses. We heard a scream, `MEDIC!! . . . MEDIC!! . . . MEDIC!!' and looked up to see upside-down Jake, hurtling head first about a hundred feet in the air, coming in for a landing. Several of us rushed over, buffered his fall, and kept him from breaking his neck."

"Was he okay? Did he finish Airborne training?" asked Throckmiller.

"Well, he managed to get through his last night jump and graduate from Airborne School, but he decided to take a rain check on Ranger School. And as expected, he never redeemed it. He transferred into the Finance Corps shortly afterwards."

"Good for him!" exclaimed Throckmiller.

"Good for *him*?" replied Bryan. "Good for *us*, General! Can you imagine having someone like Genius Jake on a Ranger mission as important as Operation Athena? It could be a disaster!"

Just at that moment, the waiter came toward their table with a large tray of food, and set it down on a nearby table. After removing the silver warming tops from the plates and placing them before the foursome, the waiter asked them if there was anything else he could get for them. Throckmiller began to say, "No, I think . . . " but quickly bit his lip and changed his response to, "I don't need anything," and then to the others he said, "how about you folks?"

"Oh yes," Kate quickly replied, "do you have some lemon?"

"Certainly, madam, I'll fetch it," said the waiter as he flitted away.

General Throckmiller's eyes widened as he looked down with pleasure at the steaming feast before him. "Could you please pass the salt, Kate?" Throckmiller asked, impatient to start eating. Kate passed it to him and he proceeded to douse his food liberally with it. "Can't get enough salt in this hot climate," Throckmiller said with an air the wisdom which reportedly comes from experience. With both hands, he gently moved the plate a centimeter to the left and a centimeter closer to him, as if precisely calibrating an artillery piece before attack. He slid his chair a little closer to the table, picked up his steak knife and fork, and dug in. Leaning slightly over his food while attempting to cut off a succulent-looking corner of the châteaubriand, Throckmiller looked up long enough to say, "I think we'd better get to the subject of Operation Athena." .

368-COOL

"I'm for that, General," Kate said quickly.

The waiter returned to the table with Kate's lemon and a basket of dinner rolls. He then encircled the table with a pepper mill. He cranked pepper on Kate's food for what seemed an eternity before she gave him a signal. Kate, mirroring the General's previous comment, remarked, "Can't get enough pepper in this Panamanian climate." Throckmiller caught the irony and smirked.

As the waiter left, Throckmiller leaned closer to the other two and said in a quiet tone, "From now on we have to keep our voices low. The walls may have ears—even waiters cannot be trusted."

"No problem, General," Bryan said in a hushed voice.

"I have just received information," Throckmiller whispered, "which may require us to kick Operation Athena off tonight. The Bodegas have kidnapped three American dignitaries and are believed to be holding them in one of four abandoned gold mines near Envigado, a suburb of Medellín."

"What dignitaries?" Kate interjected.

"Representative Grant, Senator Carrington, and a Lila Davis-Whitfield," replied Throckmiller.

"I know Representative Grant—quite well," said Kate. "I hope she's all right."

"All three are believed to be still alive," said Throckmiller. "But, as you can imagine, there is a great deal of pressure to accelerate Operation Athena."

"We're ready, sir," said Bryan.

"As you have learned in your previous briefings," Throckmiller continued, "four Ranger companies will be inserted at night in the vicinity of the gold mines. At daybreak they will separately and simultaneously attack each of the objectives, designated `A', `B', `C', and `D'. Two Ranger companies will be held in reserve about six miles south of the location `A'. Bryan, as you know, you will be commanding one of the two reserve Ranger companies and Kate will be one of your platoon leaders.

"So is Sandy," Bryan interjected.

"Yes, that's right," Throckmiller acknowledged and then continued. "Four helicopter gunships will provide cover for each of the advancing Ranger companies at each of the four objectives. We will also soften up the area surrounding the four targets a few minutes before the attacks with synchronized precision bombing executed by low-flying, stealth fighter-bombers. I will be in a helicopter following the operation's progress and directing the assault from the air. You may get word to move out in the next couple of hours. Do any of you have any questions about your specific mission?" Throckmiller paused and looked around, intentionally failing to mention anything about the tactical nuclear warheads that may be buried in or near the mines.

"Yes, I have one, General," Bryan said. "Throughout our training for this operation, I've asked repeatedly why my Ranger company—undisputably the best in the battalion—is being held in reserve. I haven't gotten a good response." Looking toward Kate, he continued, "I know that Kate is puzzled by this too."

Nodding affirmatively, Kate chimed, "Yes General, we want to be where the action is."

Smiling, Throckmiller replied, "Don't worry, you will be. The reason your company is being held in reserve is for maximum flexibility. And your platoon, Kate, will be the strike platoon no matter what happens. Bear with me and I'll explain."

"General," Kate asked, "when you explain that, will you also please explain the implications of the hostage development in the overall plan? We've rehearsed this operation several times here in Panama but none of these drills envisioned a hostage situation. How do the hostages alter our mission?"

"Good question, Kate," Throckmiller said, moving closer to them. "As I think you've already surmised, I may have to change the overall game plan at the last moment, depending on what our intelligence sources turn up on the location of the hostages. You may be required to follow specific, new instructions without knowing the reasons why the instructions are being given. This is where that unquestioning obedience to orders you learned at the Point will come in handy."

With both hands, Throckmiller reached to the center of the table, retrieved the tall sterling silver salt and pepper shakers, and set them down, about a foot apart. He picked up the salt shaker again and set it down deliberately, and said, "assume these are the four goldmines." Handling the pepper shaker similarly, he said, "assume this is where the hostages are being held." Continuing, "I may, at the last moment, learn that the hostages are located here," he said as he lightly touched the pepper shaker. "In that event, I will order the attack on the four gold mines to proceed, and simultaneously I will dispatch your Ranger company, Bryan, to rescue the hostages," Throckmiller said, again touching the pepper shaker.

"If I confirm, however," Throckmiller continued, "that the hostages are being held in one of the four gold mines, I will launch the attack against the other three mines, and at the same time, I will quickly dispatch your company, Bryan, to the vicinity of the gold mine where the hostages are. The jungle is pretty thick around the mines, so it is likely that your troops will be dropped by helicopter-rappel.

Bryan glanced briefly toward Kate.

"We will then have to play it by ear," Throckmiller continued. "I will have three highly skilled Spanish-speaking crisis negotiators—PhD psychologist types—with me in case we need them. We may be engaged in a stand off for hours or even days. In that event, the safety of the hostages will be our highest priority. We don't want to precipitate a fiasco like the Branch Davidian massacre in Waco, Texas in the Spring of 1993 or a botched swat-team operation like the Rangers pulled off in Mogadishu Somalia in September of that same year. Operation Athena *must* be a success and I'm counting on you two to make it one."

"Don't worry, General," said Bryan. "We'll give it our absolute best. And Kate, here, will command the lead platoon no matter which plan you ultimately direct us to implement."

Kate added, "And remember, although we did not rehearse a hostage rescue scenario in our training for Operation Athena, we did have a segment on hostage rescue during our Ranger training."

"Great! That's good news. I wasn't aware of that," said Throckmiller. "They didn't teach hostage rescue when I went through Ranger training thirty years or so ago." Looking at his watch, Throckmiller continued, "It's getting late and you two need to get some shut-eye if this thing is really going to kick off sometime after midnight. Any more questions before we call it a night?"

"Yes, I have one," Kate said hurriedly. "How are we going to get these troops into the vicinity of these mines at night without being detected? Helicopters and trucks make a heck of a lot of noise."

"I'm glad you asked, Kate," said Throckmiller. "I've got a little surprise for you both. Not only are we testing the mettle of women in combat with our Operation Athena, but we are also testing prototypes of a new battery-powered, light-armored personnel carrier for the Department of Defense. Using these vehicles, we will be able to helicopter our troops to a point several miles from the mines and then transport them silently along the jungle roads to a dispersal point closer to the mines. The vehicles are equipped with infra-red lighting so that they can maneuver over the roads, but cannot be seen. They are the latest innovation in overland stealth vehicles."

"Sounds exciting!" Kate shrieked, quickly covering her mouth with her hand.

Putting his index finger to his lips, Throckmiller whispered, "Remember all this is top secret. Treat it as such. There's one more thing I want to cover with you. It's about the Palladium. Do any of you know what that is?"

"Yes, General," said Kate. "I know the whole history of it. I can fill in Bryan and Sandy back at the barracks. But what does that have to do with Operation Athena?"

"Well, actually it was one of the reasons the operation got its name. Intelligence sources have advised me that the Bodega brothers have the golden statue of Pallas Athena. They move it from place to place. Strangely, they keep it in a coffin-shaped box. I am under direct orders from General Winterfield to find it and bring it back to the United States."

"But won't the Colombian Government object to that?" asked Kate.

"Apparently, the Colombian Government knows nothing about it," Throckmiller replied. "The State Department's view is that if Rangers acquire it during the operation, it would be considered part of the spoils of war and the U.S. would have legal title to it. It's worth many tens of millions of dollars."

"Some war trophy," mused Sandy.

Looking at his watch, Throckmiller felt it was time to call it an evening. "Well, my fine warriors," he said, "we must bid adieu for now. You will get word through the chain of command if I decide to launch this thing tonight. In the meantime, you both better get some sleep."

Still talking quietly, the four officers rose from the table and walked together out of the dining room and toward the front door of the officers' club where the tuxedoed doorman was standing statue-like near the reception desk. When they reached the front door, the general's jeep driver, who had been waiting in the reception area, approached to a point where the General could perceive his presence. Just then, from the vicinity of the dining room, the tuxedoed head waiter walked briskly toward Throckmiller and said breathlessly, "General, I'm glad I caught you. You have a telephone call in the dining room. The caller said its important. I can have it transferred out here to the reception desk."

"Please do," Throckmiller responded.

The head waiter picked up the telephone at the reception desk and dialed three numbers and, extending the receiver toward Throckmiller, said, "Here's your call, General."

Throckmiller looked directly at the head waiter and said, "Thank you very much. Could we have some privacy?"

"Certainly, sir," the head waiter replied, motioning to the tuxedoed doorman and walking away with him back toward the dining room.

Throckmiller put the receiver to his ear and said, "This is General Throckmiller."

"General, this is President Guardina. We have confirmed that the two female hostages are being held at one of the four locations we previously discussed. We have not yet confirmed the whereabouts of Congressman Carrington. We need to take action right away to rescue the two women. We'll deal with the Carrington problem later."

"Just one second, Mr. President," Throckmiller said as he covered the transmitting end of the receiver and looked toward Baxter. "What's the forecast, Corporal?"

Saying nothing, Baxter gave the General a circular "okay" hand signal and winked.

Throckmiller knew exactly what that meant. He put the receiver back up to his mouth. "Mr. President, I will give the order to execute the plan tonight." Throckmiller said in an intentionally vague way, conscious of the possibility of a wiretap. "Good, General. We need to keep in close communication over the next twenty-four hours. Be sure to keep me and my staff informed of the progress."

"Don't worry, Mr. President. I will."

"Okay. Good luck, and so long for now, General."

"So long, Mr. President," said Throckmiller hanging up the receiver.

Turning to the others, Throckmiller asked with a leprechaunish look, "How's your night vision?" Laughing, the four officers and Baxter left the O-Club, walked slowly down the marble steps, and made their way to the driveway. The sounds of their final parting words blended with the cacophony of the crickets, cicadas, and tree toads.

NIGHT VISION

After descending the slippery metal ladder leading from the command cupola of the shifting personnel carrier, Kate managed to maintain her balance by plopping down in one of the molded fiber-glass seats along the interior wall. Having reached this stable island of safety, she adjusted the chin strap on her jungle-matted helmet and made a final visual and functional check of her M16 rifle.

She checked the rifle with great care. In the dim light of the troop-filled hulk, she tugged and pushed on the forward bolt assist and the charging handle and inspected the rear sight adjustor to ensure that it was ready for action. Her M16 was her "baby" and she cared for it like one. She knew its characteristics and capabilities like the back of her hand: slightly over six pounds in weight, a little over three feet in length, firing 5.56 millimeter rounds at a velocity of 3,282 feet per second, up to an effective target range of 440 yards. Her M16A2 model was vastly improved over the Vietnam-era A1 version which was widely criticized for constantly jamming. Equipped with a special setting to permit firing three-round bursts on each pull of the trigger, the A2 provided a good compromise between accuracy and firepower. The flash hider on the A2 was newly designed to overcome the tendency of the A1's muzzle blast to kick up dust when fired from the prone position. With all its improvements, the M16A2 came to be known as one of the best fighting rifles in the world. Kate's weapon was additionally fitted with an M203 forty-millimeter grenade launcher clipped underneath the ribbed foregrip and barrel, giving her weapon enhanced high-explosive fire capability.

After giving her weapon a final check, she placed it across her lap, stroking its barrel for a few moments like a hunter might pet a bloodhound to inspire a successful hunt. Through force of habit, she next felt along her beltline to see if her bayonet was properly sheathed. She always thought the bayonet was an unnecessary anachronism. She was of the mind that if the enemy gets close enough to make the bayonet useful, the chances are real good that you will be pushing up daisies. But, being a good soldier, she followed the regulations to the "T" and always carried it with her; she required her subordinates to do the same. Besides, it was sometimes useful in opening C-ration tins.

Kate and the other Rangers had been riding in one of the ten electric vehicles—the experimental prototypes General Throckmiller had described—for about an hour and fifteen minutes. Prototype or not, these were cramped quarters and she was anxious to get to the reserves staging area. This caravan of Electric Energy-Efficient Lorries (Electric EELs for short) had been formed at a Colombian military compound northwest of Envigado where the vehicles had been stored by the U.S. for the past month in anticipation of Operation Athena. The EELs were now slowly making their way along the sinewy mountain roads toward the gold mines. Bryan was in the lead command vehicle, and Kate was in the fifth. Baxter's weather forecast had been more than slightly off. It was raining when they took off from Howard Air Force Base near Panama City, and a steady downpour greeted them when their C-5A transport plane finally touched down at the specially designed airstrip outside of Medellín. The rain had continued during the troop transfer to the overland transport vehicles. At some points along the road, the big rubber tires of the EELs became half-buried in mud, but somehow, like bulldogs, the electric prototypes managed to develop enough power to pull themselves out of the mire. About a half an hour before, Bryan's vehicle had skidded down a steep grade on a curve in the road and wound up balanced precariously on the edge of a hundred-foot precipice. After freeing his vehicle from danger with a winch, Bryan, on foot, guided the convoy along an alternate, more level donkey-cart trail higher on the ridge. Every passing second brought the convoy closer to the rear staging area designated for the two reserve Ranger companies.

Hearing the rain pounding against the surrounding metal, Kate began to feel apprehensive about the events about to unfold in the next few hours. A knot was forming in her stomach, she had a lump in her throat, and her palms itched. She had felt like this a couple of times before in Airborne and Ranger Schools, but somehow, this was different. This was *real*. These weren't war games. She was equipped with *real* bullets. So were the Bodegas. The mission was *real*. So were the hostages.

Death was a *real* possibility.

Attempting to distract herself from such thinking, Kate pulled Operation's passwords and codewords out of her fatigue jacket pocket and began a fervent reading of them with the help of a pen flashlight. "Flintlock" meant to ready the reserves; "scamper" meant to move the reserves; "cocksure" was the order to launch the attack; "flipside" was a request for troop extraction by helicopter; "gestalt" indicated a change in plans; the radio call sign for the operation was "Brazen Boot"; and on and on. Reading under these lighting conditions reminded Kate of one of her father's many stories about studying after lights out in a dim-lit hallway during his plebe year at the Point. She could now tell him that his squinting experience had a practical training aspect. That is, if she ever saw him again. She was beginning to wonder about that. Here she was in the middle of the jungle, about to step out of a vehicle into God knows what, and her father was busy planning a secret mission into the former Yugoslavia. Even if each of them had a ninety percent probability of surviving another year, the combined probability of both of them surviving was just over eighty percent. Not a really pleasant thought, considering what Kate had already been through in life.

In her youth, Kate had suffered through constant separation from her father because of his hardship tours over the years; her mother dying of breast cancer by the time Kate was the tender age of thirteen, studying her ass off to get into West Point and then studying her ass off to stay there; having to prove that she was as physically strong as and athletically equal to the male cadets when she was not; striving to excel in Airborne and Ranger Schools; her best friend, Tina, getting seriously injured and having a miscarriage; and being asked to represent all of womanhood in Operation Athena. Just a few minor details. Jesus Christ! How much could they expect of a 23-year-old?

Just then she felt the EEL make a sharp turn to the left slamming her backbone flat and erect against the inside right wall and causing her to lose her balance momentarily. The other Rangers, strapped in, were unaffected by the unexpected sensation of centrifugal forces. Regaining her composure after the turn, her face flushed, she saw two Rangers across the way smiling broadly at her and then looking at each other and shaking their heads from side to side as if saying, "What a stupid bitch." Of course, she wasn't *sure* that's what they were thinking. She had seen those looks from men before when she had screwed up but she had never noticed them when a male had done similar things. Maybe she was just supersensitive. . . . Maybe.

The vehicle came to an abrupt halt, forcing Kate's right shoulder against the front partition of the vehicle behind the control panel. This time she didn't lose her balance. Through a small opening in the partition, Kate called to the driver in an authoritative tone, "What's the situation, Private?"

The driver, a Private-First-Class wearing infrared goggles and specially trained for this night operation, responded, "I think we've reached our destination, Lieutenant. I see troops getting out of vehicles ahead. That's a pretty good sign. Because of the radio blackout, we only have visual cues."

Hearing that, Kate gave a series of commands to the other Rangers. "Prepare to disembark. Check your equipment—yours and your buddy's. Double-check your nuclear protective gear and your gas masks. Check and adjust your infrared goggles. It's pitch-black out there. Without operational goggles, you might as well be blind."

While the Rangers were doing their final checks, Kate tightened her goggles, grabbed her M16, and in a half-squatting position made her way crab-like to the rear of the vehicle. Pushing the green "Rear Exit" button, the EEL's rear doors opened wide exposing the thick rain forest whose canopy protected them from the downpour.

"Take your positions", Kate commanded in a voice that even surprised her for its bravura. The Rangers exited the vehicle as they had rehearsed many times in their maneuvers, taking up positions to the right side of the vehicle a half-circle with a hundred-foot radius. Kate was at the half-circle's center with her radioman at her side.

As soon as they were all in place, Kate heard a voice over the radio transmitter: "Brazen Boot One, this is Brazen Boot Five, over". Kate recognized the voice as Bryan's.

"This is Brazen Boot One. Over." she responded anxiously.

"This is Brazen Boot Five. Come to the head of the column for a briefing. Over," the voice said.

"Roger," Kate responded.

After putting her platoon sergeant in charge, Kate laboriously thrashed her way through the jungle vegetation in the direction of what she believed to be the head of the column. By this time the electric vehicles were turning around and making their way back in the direction of the main road. As long as she kept the returning vehicles on her left, she felt she would be heading in the direction of Bryan. She was right. Through the dense jungle foliage, she soon spotted a clearing and a vague outline of people milling around. As she approached closer, she saw Bryan, sitting on an upturned log with a radioman by his side.

"Kate!" exclaimed Bryan. "We're waiting for an important radio transmission from General Throckmiller. I think there's been a change in plans."

"What d'ya mean?"

"Throck sent a `gestalt' message a few minutes ago with a `standby,' responded Bryan with knowing irreverence in his voice.

Kate looked down at Bryan's paratrooper boots. They were caked in mud up to the top eyelet—a tacit tribute to his leadership in getting the Ranger column to its present location on time. "What d'ya think's in the wind?" "Don't know," said Bryan. "Maybe the hostages evaporated." Extending an opened granola bar toward her, Bryan said "Here, Kate, make yourself at home." Declining the snack, Kate sat down next to Bryan on the unstable log. "Whooooops!" said Kate as the log made a rocking motion. Pausing and smiling, "maybe the *Bodegas* evaporated" Kate added, hoping against hope that her day of reckoning was being postponed.

By this time, the rain had stopped completely; the large-billed toucans squawked their dissonant calls throughout the rainforest.

"Brazen Boot Five, this is Brazen Boot Six," came the voice of Throckmiller over the radio, in direct competition with the toucans.

"This is Brazen Boot, Five," said Bryan.

"This is Brazen Boot Six. Urgent. Meet me at coordinates 65308640 with Brazen Boot One immediately. LRP spotted in your vicinity. Take necessary precautions. Over."

"This is Brazen Boot Five. . . . Roger."

Bryan plugged the numbers Throckmiller had uttered into a handheld computer and he saw the numbers 32647314 come up on the small screen, with a map showing his own location and the location of the deciphered coordinates.

"Oh Christ!" said Bryan throwing the last of the granola bar forcefully against his command vehicle and watching it splatter in all directions. "Bodega has one of his long-range patrols out here someplace and Throckmiller is in a cave a mile and a half from here across a river and in the direction of the mines. He couldn't have picked a more hard-to-reach place even if he had tried . . . ."

"Maybe he *did* try," replied Kate. "If it's hard for us to reach, likewise for the Bodegas."

"Perhaps. Let's get going."

0368-COOL

With that, Bryan tugged on Kate's arm and pulled her off the log toward his command vehicle. "Kate, you stay down below; I'll be up in the cupola. We'll try to get as close to Throckmiller's location by vehicle and then go the rest of the way on foot."

"Sounds good to me," Kate said, quickly entering the rear of the command vehicle.

Bryan turned and, in a stage whisper, ordered his company executive officer to take charge in his absence. Completely drenched, Bryan climbed the vehicle's exterior up into the command cupola and yelled down to the driver, "Head for the main road and turn left. Go down the main road until I give you further directions."

"Aye, aye, sir" said the driver mimmicking a submariner's response.

"We're *landlubbers*, Private, and don't you forget it," Bryan shot back in faked anger.

Within minutes, the electric command vehicle had negotiated its way back to the main road and was proceeding in a generally northwesterly direction. The weather had lifted and the full moon provided Bryan clear view of the road from his position in the cupola. In the distance he could just make out what appeared to be a large branch of a banana tree lying in the road. The driver, who slowed down, had seen it too. Over the intercom, Bryan said to the driver, "What do you make of that, Private?"

"Can't quite tell, sir. Do you want me to illuminate it with a spotlight?"

"No, we can't risk it. Why don't you stop here and I'll get out and take a closer look."

Bryan climbed down into the interior of the vehicle, and headed for the rear exit. As he passed Kate, she asked nervously, "What is it?"

"Not sure. Keep an extra magazine of bullets handy just in case."

"Be careful, Bryan," Kate managed to say before got completely out of earshot.

The object was about ten yards away positioned across the

road, and Bryan slowly approached it. He now perceived it be a little wider than the road itself. The closer he got to it, the more he became satisfied that it was a big log. Preparing to remove it, he walked back to the front of the command vehicle and motioned to the driver to release the brake on the winch. He unreeled the cable as walked to the side of the road taking the cable around a banana tree and then back again toward the log. When the winch was activated, the cable would then pull the log to the side of the road, out of the path of the command vehicle. Bryan approached within about three feet of the log, pulled about four extra feet of cable toward him, then turned toward the driver and gave him a signal to reactivate the winch brake before the reeling-in operation on a subsequent command. Still facing the vehicle, Bryan reached deep into his fatigue jacket pocket and felt around for a turnbuckle to fasten onto the looped end of the cable in order to form a noose to slip around the log. WHAAAAAAAAAAAAAAAAAAAAAAAP!!! Bryan suddenly found himself lying on the ground a few feet in front of the command vehicle, completely dazed as if Godzilla had given him a rabbit punch from the back. Every bone in his body ached. For a few moments he felt totally paralyzed. Slowly, he raised his head and peered in the direction of the log. Then he saw them. Oh my God, he saw them. Those two huge shining emerald-colored lights at one end of the "log". It began to raise up off the ground—two inches—four inches—then six inches. It started to move toward him. A strange hissing noise filled the air.

Oh my God, a caiman, thought Bryan to himself. A huge, hissing, stinking, fucking bull croc coming directly at me.

Suddenly he realized what had happened. They had arrived at the river. The river had risen far above the overflow bridge and was up to the top of the roadway. The croc had been lying on the river bank which now happened to be part of the roadway. He had as much right to be on the river bank as the vehicle had a right to be on the road. And the croc was intent on protecting his turf. Bryan had to think of something . . . fast. The caiman continued to move awkwardly but steadfastly toward Bryan, its gaping mouth half open in a jagged-tooth smile, before moving in for the kill. The driver, seeing Bryan's predicament through the parapet window, screeched into the intercom, "Lieutenant!!! Lieutenant!! The Captain's in trouble . . . A HUGE CROC!!"

Instinctively, Kate flung herself to the rear of the vehicle and pushed the yellow "Open Bottom" button which instantaneously caused a three-by-four foot watertight door in the bottom of the vehicle to slide open. This feature had been specially designed for the prototype vehicle to facilitate the movement of troops into and out of foxholes and trenches. A similar sliding door was located in the top of the vehicle to permit interchange of troops between vehicles, when they were stacked piggy-back on a C-5A transport plane. The specs hadn't anticipated the doors' advantage of saving troops from crocodiles. Kate stuck her head down through the bottom door, now wide open, to see what Bryan had gotten himself into.

Upside down, Kate's view was initially disorienting. All she could see from between the vehicle's front wheels was the outline of the back of Bryan's head raised three inches above the ground, his face pointed away from the vehicle. Perched above Bryan's head was an object resembling a volcano with two emerald-green lights at its base. The volcano was stationary, for the moment at least. The caiman was apparently also disoriented, confused by the shape of the electric vehicle and the infrared lighting.

"Bryan!" Kate yelled in a hushed voice, conscious that the Bodega patrol might be close by. "Crawl under the EEL!!" Bryan, still dazed by the blow he just endured, whispered back as loudly as he dared, "I can't. One slight move and I'm breakfast for this beast!"

"Stay where you are," Kate said, reassuringly. "I'm going to try to distract him."

Kate left the rear of the EEL and ran along the road on the right-side of the vehicle, beyond its front end, until she was even with the caiman and about six feet from it. Startled, the reptile turned crosswise in the road again, and faced her directly. Hissing, it slowly moving toward her.

"Get under the EEL, Bryan!" Kate exclaimed hysterically.

Bryan, still lying on his back, drew his knees up to dig his heels into the muddy roadbed; they slipped twice, affording no traction. The movement caught the caiman's eye. It lunged toward Bryan and snapped at him barely missing his raised knee. Energized by fear, Bryan rolled over on his stomach and, using his hands and his legs, pushed himself along the soaked ground, finally managing to get the bulk of his body under the EEL. The caiman made another lurch for Bryan, this time succeeding in catching the reinforced heel of Bryan's left boot in the tip of his steel-trap snout. Horrified, Kate impulsively pulled her bayonet from its sheath, flung herself headlong onto the back of the caiman, and effected an adrenalized pendulumlike swing of the bayonet, plunging it deep into the top of the caiman's head between its eyes. The caiman thrashed from side to side, in a snakelike motion, releasing Bryan's foot; bronco-style, it threw Kate off to the side. Kate intentionally rolled over three times toward the right side of the road to increase her distance from the beast.

Meanwhile, Bryan managed to get his whole body, including his boots, under the EEL. Enraged, the skewered bull caiman charged after Kate, who by this time was in a crouched position by the side of the road facing the rear of the vehicle. Catching a glimpse of the croc's unorthodox crown ornament moving swiftly in her direction, Kate sprang toward the rear of the EEL as if coming off the blocks in a hundred-yard dash. The audible snap of the caiman's jaws missed her by inches.

Kate entered the rear of the EEL, and with both arms, reached down through the floor opening and began frantically to grasp the back of Bryan's fatigue jacket in an attempt to pull him into the vehicle. Bryan, his body still racked with pain, attempted to help by doing a half push-up, the modified exercise for female cadets at the Point.

While Bryan had his back straight, supporting himself on his hands and knees, the enraged bayoneted beast made one last massive lunge toward the right underside of the vehicle, wedging its long, bloodied snout under Bryan's inclined body. Snapping open its powerful jaws, the frustrated crocodile unwittingly catapulted Bryan's limp torso up into the vehicle where Kate was able to get a good grip and drag him the rest of the way inside. The reptile's open jaws jabbed the air inside the vehicle toward Kate. Maintaining her cool, Kate bounded for the red button at the rear of the vehicle to close the bottom door. She hit the button with the palm of her hand and simultaneously clicked the safety override switch with her index finger. The bottom door slid shut with the force of a guillotine, just as the beast was momentarily recoiling, catching half of the croc's long, bloodied and mud-caked snout. The heavy steel door rattled up and down in sympathetic rhythm with the reptile's erratic calisthenics. The EEL shook dramatically as if caught in an earthquake.

Thinking fast, Kate yelled to the driver, "MOVE OUT, PRIVATE!!!" Kate could hear the whirring sound of the electric motors being revved to their top capacity; then came the sudden jolt of the transmission locking into gear. The motors were straining audibly. At the same time the right side of the vehicle raised two-and-a-half feet, throwing Bryan and Kate against the left inside wall. As the rear tractor-type wheels of the EEL rolled over the torso of the reptile, Kate and Bryan heard loud popping and cracking sounds inside the EEL as the beast's snout slowly twisted, detaching from the rest of its head and spurting blood in several directions.

Kate stepped quickly to the rear door view slit and looked out. In the moonlight, she saw the partially mutilated, former "king-of-the-road" writhing, contorting, and rolling over continuously.

"Couldn't have done better with an alarm clock and stick of dynamite," Kate thought to herself, conjuring up childhood memories of, Peter Pan. They had yet to conquer the chief obstacle, however—the river.

The EEL traveled a couple hundred feet and came to an abrupt halt when its front tires moved into the shallow edge of the rapidly moving current. Over the intercom, the driver announced, "Lieutenant, we're at the river and the current seems quite swift due to the heavy rains. It's moving from the left of the vehicle to the right. You can open the bottom door and take a look for yourself. How's Captain Flanagan doing?"

Activating the button to open the bottom door, Kate watched the crocodile's ripped-off snout fall into water. It was swept away in a split second. Looking down at the torrent of water speeding by, Kate replied over the intercom, "The Captain's moving . . . but not nearly as fast as this river. By the way, that was a great driving job, Private. What's your name?"

"Russett, Lieutenant, but most people call me "Rusty.""

"Well, Rusty, you ought to enter the Indy Five Hundred after that display of ability."

"I'll give it some thought. . . . But for the time being, what do you want me to do about this river, Lieutenant?"

"This may sound like a stupid question, Rusty, but is this thing we're riding in amphibious?"

"It's supposed to be, Lieutenant. In training at the Aberdeen Proving Ground, I drove one of these things through lakes and stuff, and it stayed afloat. I want to remind you, though, that this is a prototype, and maybe there are still a few bugs to be worked out. And after that croc attack, it may have just lost its "float warranty.""

"Hear ya, Rusty. By the way, how wide is this river, anyhow?"

"From what I can tell by reading my electronic map on the control panel, the river's normally only about seventy-five feet wide. But in this flooded condition, it's probably double that. Wait a minute, ma'am, I can use the laser rangefinder here to find out its width to the nearest half inch." Placing his hand on the pistol grip molded into the side of the control panel, the driver squeezed the trigger. In a microsecond, the laser beam struck an object on the other side of the river and reflected back. The electronic map on the control panel registered a series of numbers. Lieutenant . . . my screen here shows one hundred seventy-three feet, three and one-half inches. Do you want that in meters?"

"Naw. I'd like to try a crossing. How do we waterproof this thing?"

"There's a feature here on the control panel, Lieutenant, that electronically checks all of the doors on the vehicle to ensure they're watertight. I'll activate it. . . . The message on the screen indicates "ALL SYSTEMS GO." Looks like we're tight as a tick."

"Okay, Rusty, let's move out."

"May I make a suggestion, Lieutenant?"

"Sure."

"This river is so swift, we won't be able to go directly across and reach the roadbed on the other side. The EEL will drift quite a distance downstream. I think we should put the EEL into the river a few hundred yards upstream to make sure we marry up with the roadbed on the other side.

"Good idea. Is there a way to do it?"

"I see a donkey-cart trail off to the left over here along the side of the river. What d'ya say we try it?"

"Fine. Have at it, Rusty"

Rusty put the EEL in reverse and backed up about fifty feet. He then turned the vehicle sharply to the left and proceeded down the rutted trail into the ever-deepening blackness. When his odometer registered five hundred meters, Rusty activated the intercom.

"Lieutenant, I think we're far enough upstream now to go into the water. I have limited visibility off to my right, but if I can find an opening in the trees wide enough to move this thing through, I'd like to try it."

"Go ahead, Rusty. I'm leaving the driving to you. I hate to be a backseat driver."

Rusty saw a break in the thick jungle foliage and made a sharp right turn toward the river. Almost immediately, the front of the EEL pointed forty-five degrees downward and slid about thirty feet down a steep embankment nosing into stagnant backwaters of the river. When the vehicle came to a rest in a canted orientation, Kate yelled into the intercom, "What in Christ's name happened?"

"Can't say for sure, Lieutenant. The road must have angled

some away from the river and here we sit in a motionless pool. OH, MY GOD! OH, MY GOD!"

"What's wrong, Rusty? What's wrong?"

"The fucking EEL is punctured!" Rusty yelled. Water's leaking in all around me!! I CAN'T GET MY SEATBELT UNLOCKED!! GET UP TO THE AUXILIARY CONTROLS IN THE CUPOLA AND BACK US OUT OF THIS MESS!!"

Kate scrambled up the ladder to the auxiliary control panel in the command cupola. She impulsively moved a lever on the panel to the "reverse" position. Immediately she could hear the EEL's rear tires spinning on the embankment.

Rusty was shrieking now. "FASTER, LIEUTENANT, FASTER! THE WATER IS POURING IN! HELP! SOMETHING'S BITING ME! RIPPING ME!

Kate knew exactly what was happening. The dreaded piranha. There's nothing she could do for Rusty now. His flesh would be stripped from his bones in a matter of seconds.

"Rusty! Rusty!" she screamed into the intercom. There was no response.

Then she heard a loud noise below like a door slamming shut. She looked down the ladder and saw a double door between the driver's compartment and the rear hull that wasn't there before. She realized the significance. Rusty's dying gesture was to seal himself off and save the lives of herself and Bryan.

Sealing off of the driver's compartment had an additional unplanned effect. Kate sensed the front end of the vehicle slowly rising, buoyed up by the air trapped in the sealed driver's compartment. The EEL was soon floating upright, heading out to the rapidly flowing river. Bryan was still in a semi-dazed condition. If she was to get to the other side and reach the roadbed, she would have to do it on her own. From her position high in the command cupola, she captained her vessel slowly through the flooded mangrove swamp and into a slow moving stream. Looking down from the glass enclosure she spotted a twenty-foot anaconda wending its way through the tangled tree roots, half-submerged in the stand-

368-COOL

ing water. When she arrived at the river proper, she steered the vehicle hard to the left to compensate for the water's rapid movement to the right. The vehicle turned in a full circle once, but afterwards moved to left of center of the river. Kate wondered how she would know where the roadbed on the other side of the river was located. Then in the distance, she spotted the outline of the carcass of the dead caiman on the right side of the river. Looking directly across to the other side, she knew exactly where the roadbed was. She accelerated the EEL to its full speed and turned the rudder to the left. The EEL crashed with a jolt into the riverbank, twenty meters or so above the roadbed. Kate had made it across the river.

The impact had shaken Bryan out of his numbed condition.

"Where are we, Kate?" Bryan shouted up to Kate in the cupola.

"We're on vacation in the Caribbean," Kate yelled back.

"Great! Bring me a piña colada."

"You must be feeling better," Kate retorted.

"Yeah, a little bit."

"What's the situation, Kate?"

"It'll take too long to explain. I'm going to get on the horn to Throckmiller, and tell him we're still on the way. Do you feel well enough to travel?"

"Yeah, if I can continue on in the EEL for a while."

"All right, I'll see if Throckmiller can clue us in on a shortcut."

"Brazen Boot Six, this is Brazen Boot One. Over" Kate said into the radio transmitter.

"Brazen Boot One, this is Brazen Boot Six. Over." came the response over the receiver.

"Brazen Boot Six, we've had a few complications, but we are still proceeding to your location." Giving him the coded coordinates of their present location, she then asked, "Any route recommendations? Over."

"This is Brazen Boot Six. Suggest you move southwest along H-2-0 to coordinates 87346520. Then look up."

"This is Brazen Boot One. Roger and out."

"Roger!" shouted Bryan up to Kate. "How'd you understand that?"

"I think I can figure it out, Bryan. Southwest along H-2-0 means move along this side of the river—H_2O—to the decoded coordinates. Should be easy. Let's try it."

"Whatever you say, Kate. But what does 'then look up' mean?

"Maybe just what it says. Let's get going."

From the controls in the command cupola, Kate maneuvered the EEL onto the riverbank and eventually to the roadbed. Driving the EEL was a lot easier than driving a five-ton truck, which she had done many times before in her training at West Point. She proceeded down the roadbed looking for a trail again off to the left. Finally, she spied one. She gave it a sharp left and drove down the trail for approximately a thousand meters, the jungle undergrowth scratching against the vehicle all the way. Ahead she could see the trail enter a deep ravine, with sheer granite cliffs shooting upwards on both sides. She drove about another five hundred meters into the center of the ravine, and rechecked the decoded coordinates of her destination.

"Well, we're here," she yelled down to Bryan.

"The good Lord wasn't willin', the creek rose, and we still made it," responded Bryan. "Seems like a miracle."

Kate climbed down out of the command cupola, pushed the button opening the sliding door above the main compartment, and climbed out on top of the EEL. She looked up. What she saw amazed her.

About half-way up the two-hundred-foot precipice was a twelve-foot circular opening of what appeared to be a cave. A rope with a harness was being lowered from the cave, and the harness abruptly stopped dangling about three feet in front of her. "How about a ride up the jump tower?" Kate whispered to Bryan in the well of the vehicle, recalling her Airborne School experience.

Having no idea what she was talking about, Bryan replied, "No, I think I'll take a pass this time."

"No, I'm serious, Bryan. There's a harness with a hoist out here to take us up to the General."

"Either the General died and went to heaven, or you're hallucinating, Kate."

"Take a look for yourself, smarty."

Bryan moved to the opening and looked up. There it was, the elevator to the stars, waiting for them. "Okay, you go first, Kate."

"Oh no, you don't, Bryan. I want to make sure you can even climb out of the EEL, much less get yourself into the harness."

With a lot of effort, Bryan pulled himself out of the EEL and, with Kate's help, got himself into the harness. He tugged on the rope, and up he went. Kate watched from below. When he reached the top, he was eased out of the harness, and it was lowered again for Kate who climbed into it. She gave two tugs on the rope and began moving slowly up the side of the cliff.

In the distance, she heard a noise like a firecracker exploding. Instantly, chips of rocks from the side of the cliff splattered in her face. HOLY SHIT! THEY'RE USING ME FOR TARGET PRACTICE, thought Kate to herself. She heard three more explosions. This time, three rounds struck the cliff, one above her head and one on either side of her, causing a hail of stones to tumble on her. Bodega's sharpshooters were having their fun at Kate's expense. Finally, the rope hoisted her into the mouth of the cave and a sergeant major escorted her downhill inside to where Throckmiller and Bryan were warming themselves around a low campfire. Throckmiller reached out his hand to greet her. "Bryan's been telling me about how exciting your trip to Colombia has already been."

"You might say that, General." Kate replied with a half-smile.

"Well, I'm glad you both made it here safely. I'm sorry to hear about your driver, Private Russett. I have already dispatched soldiers to evacuate his remains and notify his next of kin. We must, however, proceed with our mission. I warned you that there might be a change in plans, and there is. Take a look at this. President Guardina received this from Raoul Bodega a short while ago."

Throckmiller handed Kate a piece of paper with a typed message on it. Bryan moved just behind her and read over her shoulder in the flickering light:

Wimpering American bitches will be exchanged for Hector in helicopter rendezvous on November 12 at 4:00 P.M. at coordinates 95847321. If Hector is not safely transported, or if there is any armed escort, bitches will be immediately decapitated.

"Sounds like Raoul means business, General." volunteered Bryan.

"Not only that, Bryan, it looks like Bodega has figured out our map coordinate code," observed Kate. "It kinda explains why I was being used for target practice a few minutes ago."

"I think you're both right," said Throckmiller. "There have been some new developments you two should know about. I want to get your reactions. I may have to ask you to take on a disguise, Kate."

"Sounds interesting," Kate mused. "Right out of Greek mythology."

The three talked beside the campfire while their shadows danced on the side of the cave. In another twenty minutes the sun would be rising.

HIGH-TECH JUSTICE

The following afternoon, Raoul sat alone at a workbench in a hollowed out chamber off the principal mineshaft. Craftsmanlike, with his straight razor he was carving female figures from huge carrots Federico had provided. After sculpting five or so, he began surgically removing their heads one by one. Just as he started to decapitate the fourth, Federico approached and handed him a one-line message. Raoul's mouth spread into a thin-lipped smile as he read it. "Emilio will accompany Hector during transfer."

Raoul slapped the message against his leg. "Finally, some good news," he rasped. "Those gringos won't know what hit 'em."

Federico walked across the earthen floor of the chamber and stroked the top of the pine coffin sensuously. "The copter will be here soon. Should we load it aboard?"

"No," replied Raoul. "Just you, me, and the two American bitches will be traveling. Leave the Greek here. We'll come back for it later. But just in case, prepare for the worst."

"Yes, Commandante," said Federico. Opening the lid of the coffin and the top of a thick plexiglass liner, he raised the contents slightly to wedge in a small package. He closed the coffin and patted it gently. "Everything's ready, Commandante."

2

Meanwhile, Throckmiller, in a chopper hovering near the attack zone, watched a Bodega helicopter move toward mine D and land near the opening. Two male figures, he assumed to be Raoul and a cartel lieutenant, and two female figures, apparently Lila and Esther, boarded the helicopter which raised off the ground and flew away in a cloud of dust. Throckmiller relayed the "move out" order to Bryan's pilot.

"Brazen Boot Six gave us the go!" the pilot shouted to Bryan. Instantly, Bryan told Kate, dressed as a nurse, to get her "patient" ready. Without delay, Kate grabbed some gauze and tape from the helicopter floor and ran toward the Rangers who were guarding Hector. She wrapped Hector's head in gauze, mummylike, and then put a wide swatch of tape over his mouth. Emilio watched, speechless. Kate then pointed to a stretcher and told the Rangers to strap Hector on it and carry him to the chopper, whose rotors were beginning to turn. Bryan was standing next to the helicopter, assisting with the stretcher. He got in last and signaled to the pilot to take off. Within twenty minutes they would be at the hostage exchange site.

Meanwhile, when Hector's helicopter was out of sight for ten minutes, Throckmiller issued orders for the four forward Ranger companies to move within a couple kilometers of the four mines. He ensured they were far enough away to be safe from any detonations of tactical nuclear warheads that may have been buried by the Bodegas. After those Ranger companies were in place, he ordered jet air strikes to soften up the four objectives. Low-flying Stealth fighter bombers zoomed in on the four mines dropping bombs which ripped thick vegetation away from the mine openings creating avenues of approach for the four Ranger companies. Eddies of uniformed cartel soldiers formed at the mine openings and swarmed out into the clearings like armies of ants whose safe habitat was disturbed unexpectedly by a brash interloper. Watching the rifle-bearing cartel soldiers fan out into the thick jungle terrain, Throckmiller gave the command for a second air strike, this time slightly farther away from the mine openings. The jets cut another swath out of the jungle, this time taking fifty or so cartel soldiers with them. Whole bodies and body parts sailed through the air in the swirling black smoke as the jets roared up and clear of the mountainous backdrop. Hundreds of cartel soldiers pushed deeper into the jungle, and Throckmiller immedi-

ately gave the command for the four forward Ranger companies
to close in on several pockets of resistance organized by cartel
soldiers struggling to reorient themselves after the surprise attack.
The Rangers closed in on the pockets of resistance, one by one,
and neutralized them. Within a few minutes, they had moved
toward their four objectives and had formed a perimeter around
each of the mine entrances. One of the reserve companies was
ordered to fly in and conduct a sweep of their targets. They were
to capture any stray cartel soldiers and recover any weapons or
equipment from inside the mines. Sandy's platoon headed for
mine 'D'.

Kate, manipulating a grenade-sized plastic object, looked back
curiously at Hector strapped in the stretcher. He lay motionless
looking up at the ceiling of the chopper, incongruously serene for
the murderous animal that he was. She wondered what was going
through his diabolical mind. Emilio sat across from her twiddling
his thumbs, his dark face set in a uncharacteristic blank expression. She looked over Bryan's shoulder and caught a glimpse of
another chopper approaching. For a few seconds the two choppers
shared a swaying dance and then simultaneously descended onto a
plateau which jutted out of the dense jungle terrain.

Bryan, unarmed like the rest, was first out of the Ranger chopper, his eyes immediately locking onto the hulk of Federico outside the other chopper. Running toward Federico under the whirring blades of the two aircraft, Bryan could discern, but barely, the
profiles of Lila and Esther still inside the craft. He stopped, turned,
and gave a hand signal to Kate to have Hector moved out of the
their chopper. Kate responded quickly, and within seconds, the
two Rangers carrying Hector on the stretcher were shuffling toward Raoul's craft. Kate, as a dutiful nurse, walked alongside the
stretcher, and then watched as Bryan supervised the Rangers load-
ing Hector onto the chopper.

Lila and Esther then appeared in the chopper's doorway. Kate
walked backward a few steps, giving the impression that she wanted
to get out of the Rangers' way. She lowered her left hand and

placed the plastic object next to the fuselage of the chopper. Magnetized and olive in color, it adhered to the aircraft and blended perfectly with its exterior.

Fifty yards away, Emilio stood outside the Ranger chopper, gauging the progress of the hostage exchange. Seeing Hector already aboard the chopper and Lila and Esther in the doorway, Emilio drew a small pistol from inside his shirt, and at point blank range, shot the Ranger chopper pilot in the head twice. The pilot slumped over his controls and then slipped out of his seat onto the cockpit floor.

Emilio ran toward Raoul's helicopter. Pointing the gun toward Lila and Esther, Emilio loudly yelled at them, "Move back into that chopper!" When they complied, he himself jumped on board, extended his hand to pull Federico inside, and the chopper began its ascent. Emilio grabbed Esther by the hair and pulled her face next to his and said, "Forty-eight hours, huh? I ought to blow your fucking brains out." He then shoved her forcefully away from him. Kneeling in the doorway, he glared back at her in contempt and pointed his pistol toward the two Rangers still on the ground. "Watch this, Esther!" he yelled. "This could be you!" He then fired two shots at each of Rangers. Both dropped instantly, blood gushing from their temples.

Undaunted, Kate ran and knelt beside the downed Rangers. Neither was breathing. She felt their wrists. Pulseless.

"Get in the chopper!" Bryan yelled to her.

"We can't just leave them!" she screamed back.

"The dead have few needs. Let's get moving."

Bryan took Kate's hand, and pulled her at a run toward the other chopper, as Kate stared back toward the two corpses. Once aboard the aircraft, Bryan was the first to see more evidence of Emilio's homicidal handiwork. He dragged the dead pilot out of the cockpit by the armpits. Kate viewed the morbid scene, angered by the senseless slaughter which had just occurred.

Bryan jumped into the pilot's seat and grabbed the controls. They were a little different than those of civilian choppers he had flown before. While Kate was climbing in the co-pilot's seat, Bryan raised the craft slowly off the ground, taking a few extra seconds to familiarize himself with the sensitivity of the controls. He gave it half throttle in the direction of Raoul's departure route.

Once above the tree line, Bryan saw a speck of something in the distance. It had to be Raoul. No other aircraft would be traveling over that godforsaken jungle terrain. Bryan gave it full throttle and watched as the speck became progressively larger; finally, Raoul's craft came into full view. It seemed to be following a sinewy ribbon of river through the jungle in a southwesterly direction.

Meanwhile on Raoul's craft, emotions were running high.

"You fucking two-faced Colombian asshole!" Lila screamed into Emilio's face.

For Esther, shock yielded quickly to fury. "I second that!" she screamed, unable to think of a more piercingly fitting epithet. Raoul whirled to stare at the two women, quick anger rising in his eyes. In a low voice, taut with rage, Raoul said to Emilio, "Dispose of them. Now!"

"Are you sure, Commandante?" Emilio said tentatively. "Shouldn't we torture them first?"

Raoul tightened his jaw and glared at Emilio for a few seconds. Emilio needed no translator.

Raoul signaled the pilot to descend to the river level. Soon, the chopper was skimming about ten meters above water. Caimans lined the banks basking in the late afternoon sun. Raoul nodded abruptly to Emilio.

Reacting instantly, Emilio backed out of the chopper and standing on the craft's skid, he by chance looked to the rear. The Rangers' copter—he saw it trailing behind them. Waving vigorously to get Raoul's attention, Emilio pointed to the rear of the craft. Raoul looked out of the other side and spotted it. He looked back toward Emilio, then toward the two women, and ran his index finger across his neck.

Emilio grabbed Lila by the arm and roughly pulled her toward him until her nose practically touched his. "You were a good lay," he screeched in her face, "but cunts like you are a dime a dozen." Lila's expression darkened in terror. Emilio yanked her arm again forcefully and jettisoned her past him and out of the craft. He then gave Esther an unexpected tug toward the door, screaming at her as she passed by, "happy trails, you black-mailing bitch mother fucker." The two women shrieked in unison as they streaked toward the water below. After a few seconds, their cries faded into silence.

Emilio, still standing on the skid, glanced again at the trailing craft now descending toward the river. When it disappeared out of his line of vision, he noticed the grenade-sized object on his own craft. He began to sidestep down the skid which terminated just beyond the chopper's door. He leaned as far as he could, stretching the entire length of his body, and attempted to dislodge it. Just as he got it in his grasp, the craft suddenly lurched, the pilot staying true to the course of the river's twists and turns. Emilio lost his balance and fell backward, his screams abruptly muted when his body finally hit the water. Alerted by Emilio's screaming and thrashing, several caimans slithered into the water from the riverbank. Within seconds, the caimans took him under. Emilio's arms and legs were ripped from him in a revolving turmoil. His head unscathed, broke through the water's surface momentarily; he awaited the second attack, his lower torso submerged in a rippling tide of his own blood. Then, he disappeared.

Raoul motioned to the pilot to circle around so that he could catch a perverse glimpse of Emilio in his final death throes. The former shoeshine boy from Medellín meant nothing to Raoul. Emilio had matured into just another expendable, bungling bureaucrat. Raoul was pleased that he was now off the payroll—for good.

It was no use. There were no signs of Emilio. What remained of his agony was just the occasional blood-dyed swirls and eddies on a slow-moving river.

Raoul ordered the pilot to move back upriver toward Bryan's chopper, now hovering low over the water. Raoul could see three ropes descending out of the chopper, one of them carrying a nurse wearing a life vest, the other two with orange doughnut-shaped tubes tied to the ends. Below the tubes, Raoul could see two heads bobbing up and down in the murky water. Raoul yelled at his pilot, "make a close pass!"

The pilot quickly obliged, steering the craft on a downward course below the level of Bryan's chopper, leveling off a few feet above water level. Raoul put out his hand, and Federico placed a .357 magnum in it. On the first pass, Raoul sized up the situation. At eyelevel with Kate, he drew a bead on her but did not pull the trigger, trying to get a feel for the lead time he would have to give his target on the next pass. He also didn't want to scare off the four caimans that had moved off the bank a few seconds previously and were heading straight towards them. Raoul's chopper went a few hundred meters upstream to make its loop back.

Meanwhile, Kate managed to get Esther, who was fully conscious, into one of the tubes, and Bryan activated the hoist to bring her slowly up. With considerable effort, Esther scrambled inside.

The four crocs continued to move toward Lila, now semiconscious, despite the deafening roar of the rotors. Kate had no choice. She gave Bryan a hand signal and he released more of the rope, causing her to splash into the water next to Lila. Kate grabbed hold of her around her chest and yanked on the rope for Bryan to pull her up. Still half in the water, Kate saw two huge topaz-colored eyes coming directly toward them at seemingly breakneck speed. Random teeth protruding from the beast's half-opened mouth created a chaotic wake of horror. The hinged saw-tooth trap opened wide, preparing to slam shut on Lila's half-submerged torso. Holding Lila firmly under her armpits, Kate kicked the orange lifebuoy in the direction of the caiman, throwing it temporarily off course. Its jaws crushed the lifebuoy flat and it circled beneath the two terrorized women clinging to the rope just slightly above the water. The rotors of Raoul's returning chopper clapped thunderously a short distance upriver.

For a few seconds, Raoul reveled in the spectacle of two defense-less women dangling at the end of a rope. As his chopper made its low-level approach, Raoul raised his handgun, rested the barrel on his arm, and waited for the target to come within his sights. There it was! He squeezed twice and looked back. Both bullets missed. A mechanical winch was rapidly drawing the two women up to the chopper door. With no time for another attempt, Raoul signaled his pilot to head toward the ocean and points south.

In the Ranger copter, Lila and Esther, slouched in the opening to the cockpit, looked like drenched rats. They mustered all strength possible to scan the horizon for any sign of Raoul's craft. Bryan attempted to talk to them for a few seconds, but that proved ineffectual. He then resumed the chase. But in the meantime, Raoul's chopper had disappeared from view.

Kate, sitting in the copilot seat next to Bryan pulled a small square plastic object from her pocket and slid back the top, exposing two buttons and a small screen. She pushed the button on the left. Immediately, a faint light began blinking on the radar screen at an angle of about ten o'clock. She showed the screen to Bryan who immediately adjusted his course slightly. As they proceeded, the blinking became faster and the light brighter. The radio-activated grenade planted on Raoul's craft was working.

Within a few minutes, Raoul's craft was in full view, a couple clicks in front of them and two hundred meters below. The pursued craft could have landed and was just taking off again; or, it could have merely descended to a lower level to fly under jungle cover. Bryan couldn't be sure.

Through the din of the cockpit noise, Kate turned to Lila and placed the small black box on the floor next to where Lila was sitting. Kate pointed to the red button on the right and pretended to push it. Then, with both hands together and slightly cupped, her fingers slightly spread apart, she made a grating sound and moved her hands slowly outward. Then she pointed to Raoul's helicopter. A perverse thrill surged through Lila whose mood instantly veered toward sweet revenge. There was nothing she wanted more than to kill

Emilio—the man who had used her, abused her, and, literally, tossed her away. She held all the power now. With one press of a button she could execute his death warrant—and wipe out the Bodegas at the same time. She was Supreme Commander of Women in Combat. Emilio was already dead.

Lila's index finger boldly for its target and hovered directly over it. Looking up, Lila's eyes caught Kate's and they shared the moment. Then, with a deliberate movement, she looked down and compressed the button.

Triumph flooded through Lila as she beheld the blast's vaporizing finality.

3

"Brazen Boot Five, this is Brazen Boot Six. Over," Throckmiller's voice boomed over Bryan's chopper radio.

"Brazen Boot Six, this is Brazen Boot Five. I'm reading you loud and clear. Over," Bryan replied.

"Brazen Boot Five, I need a progress report. May have another mission for you. Over."

"This is Brazen Boot Five. Mission accomplished, sir. We're awaiting orders."

"This is Brazen Boot Six. Report directly, then, to mineshaft `D'. The lieutenant in charge there needs assistance. Over. She's found something unusual and she doesn't know quite what to do with it."

"Roger, sir. We're on our way."

Within thirty minutes, Bryan was landing his chopper near the entrance to mineshaft 'D'. Sandy ran from the mine entrance and up to the chopper with the rotors still spinning. Bryan could tell from the cockpit that she was unusually agitated.

"Bryan!" Sandy screamed. "Wait till you see what we discovered in that mineshaft! I never saw anything like it!"

Lila, disheveled and battered, but seemingly having gained a second wind, stepped down from the chopper and moved close to Sandy to hear what she was about to say.

Kate disembarked with Esther on the other side of the chopper. Esther was extremely pale, and appeared to be in a state of shock from the mental, physical, and sexual abuse she had endured. While Bryan was talking to Sandy, Kate caught his arm and told him that she was going to get Esther transported to a hospital immediately. She would catch up with him in a few minutes. He waved her on.

Lila listened intently a few feet away as Sandy and Bryan spoke.

"It looks to be solid gold," said Sandy.

Lila moved closer.

"What does?" asked Bryan.

"The statue. Of some lady. It's huge."

"Where is it?" Bryan asked.

"Inside a little grotto off the mineshaft. Strangely, it's packed in a coffin. Come on, I'll show you."

Sandy, pistol drawn, took out her flashlight and headed for the entrance. Bryan followed Sandy into the mineshaft with Lila trailing behind.

Noticing that Lila was following them, Bryan turned to her and said, "This might be dangerous. I don't know what's inside. Could be some armed Bodega soldiers. Maybe you should go join Kate and the others."

"Don't be silly, Captain. I can take care of myself. If I lived through the last couple of hours, I can live through anything."

"You're at your own risk, ma'am."

The trio walked about a hundred meters into the mineshaft, and entered the grotto. On the floor in one darkened corner, there it was. The coffin's lid was off.

"Here it is," said Sandy. "One of my squads found this about an hour ago. I sent them on deeper into the shaft to see if they could turn up anything else."

Bryan and Lila walked over to the coffin and peered inside as Sandy held the flashlight.

"It's gorgeous," Bryan whispered almost reverently.

"It looks to be a Greek goddess, or something," Sandy replied.

Lila's eyes widened. This was the wealth she had dreamed of. This would be her true celebrity. The statue must have some historical significance. She would be ensconced in history. These two people with her—expendable, both of them. No one would know.

Meanwhile, Kate had found a flashlight in the chopper, and was halfway down the mineshaft coming toward the grotto. She heard two shots. She screamed, "Bryan! Bryan!"

Hearing Kate's screams, Lila checked to see if there was another bullet available in the clip. There was—just one.

She took two steps toward the coffin to take a closer look. She yearned to touch the statute, to feel the satin texture of its golden folds. She reached out her hand, and lifted the plexiglass covering.

By the time Throckmiller arrived, gray smoke was billowing out of the mine entrance and sounds of hideously mocking recorded voices crackled down the long cavity of the mineshaft up to the now completely caved-in grotto.

NEW HORIZONS

General McKeane was the last to arrive at the parade ground that beautiful afternoon in May. His plane was late getting out of D.C. He had a million things going on at the Pentagon, but he wasn't about to miss this. His daughter, along with thirty five enlisted men and women who had served in Operation Athena, were going to be honored in an awards ceremony on the West Point Plain, after which the Corps of Cadets was to pass in review. Walking to the reviewing stand from his military sedan, he noticed TV video vans and members of the press corps all around the bleacher area. This event was sure to be a great boon to his career as well as his daughter's.

Kate, positioned in front of the Rangers and facing the reviewing stand, nodded recognition as her father joined the others on the platform. An unusual array of people filled the reviewing section, many of them at her request. In the front row, Captain Martin, now a high-priced Wall Street lawyer in civilian clothes stood alongside his wife, Sharon, looking happily civilian; Sergeant "Hardtack" Davidson was next in line, polished and spit-shined to the hilt; next came the Generals—Throckmiller, Chandler, and McKeane; then, her sister, Karen, in that same gaudy, flowered dress she had worn graduation weekend; next to her, Esther Grant; and next to Esther, Todd and Emma Lou, soon to celebrate their first year of marriage. At the very end of the reviewing stand near the ramp, was Tina, in civilian clothes and sitting in a wheelchair. Alongside was Lori, who was in military uniform.

Three spaces had been intentionally reserved at the end of the line—one for Charmaine, one for Sandy, and one for Bryan. They were occupied by three large wreaths of Colombian orchids bearing their names. Bryan's wreath bore a wide ribbon sash emblazoned with an enlarged image of a Ranger tab. That had been Kate's wish—a symbolic return of the tab he had given her in Ranger School. There was no Lila. She was dead, killed in the mineshaft explosion along with Bryan and Sandy. General Winterfield—the chief of staff—had been invited, but he had a conflicting engagement. Kate was relieved he couldn't make it. The Academy's Superintendent was in Washington testifying before Congress on budget matters, so he also would not be present. Kate was pleased by that also, because that meant General Chandler, the Commandant, would be conducting the ceremony.

General Chandler stepped up to the microphone and welcomed the throngs of well-wishers and representatives of the press who had come to honor the heroes and heroines of Operation Athena. After giving a short speech highlighting women's involvement in the ground combat operations in Colombia, he left the reviewing stand and moved down the rows of Rangers, pinning combat medals over the breast pockets of both men and women. Kate about-faced and looked out across the Plain toward MacArthur Barracks when she saw the general approaching her. Kate had not felt this kind of sense of pride, this sense of accomplishment, since that day in May at the end of her plebe year when, standing in formation with hordes of her classmates in Central Area, the upperclassman in her company walked the ranks and shook each plebe's hand, one by one, in a congratulatory spirit of recognition.

As the general came nearer, Kate's left hand instinctively touched her lower coat pocket containing the gold Pallas Athena charm, in recognition of the good luck it had brought her in surviving Operation Athena.

General Chandler appeared before her. "You started this thing you know," he whispered while pinning a purple heart, a silver star, and a Colombian Campaign medal on her chest. "It was your speech before Congress that got this thing rolling." The general took a step backward and gave Kate a sharp hand salute. "Congratulations, Lieutenant, on a job well done."

Kate did not return the salute. The general did not appear offended.

"If it hadn't been me, sir, it would have been someone else. It was just a matter of time. Freedom takes time."

"Yes, the Colombians are sure thankful for their freedom."

"I wasn't referring to—"

"Bless you, Kate, and good luck in the infantry."

"The infantry?" Kate asked, surprised.

"Yes, the infantry. This morning President Benton, with the blessing of Congressional leaders, signed an Executive Order as Commander in Chief, directing the Army to permit qualified women access to all five combat branches of the army. I will be announcing this to the crowd when I go back up on the reviewing stand. But I wanted you to know first."

"Thank you, sir," Kate replied somewhat perplexed. "But you are aware of my disability, aren't you? My right arm is immobile from the explosion. It's useless. I can't even hold a rifle."

"But the doctors say that you have a fifty-fifty chance of regaining use of your arm within a year or two, don't they?. I wouldn't worry about it too much if I were you. The Queen of Battle's worth waiting for, Lieutenant."

"If you say so, sir," Kate replied.

General Chandler turned and walked quickly back to the reviewing stand. In a dramatic tone, he announced to crowd the news about the President's Executive Order. Kate heard the crowd roar approval. Esther, appearing more gray and wrinkled as a result of her Colombian ordeal, was grinning from ear to ear.

The cadet brigade commander then gave the order for the cadet corps to pass in review. The U.S. Military Academy Band immediately struck up a rousing rendition of the "West Point March" and more than four thousand West Point cadets began marching down the Plain to honor the Rangers' victory in Colombia. Four cadets carrying the colors passed and all the officers in the reviewing stand saluted. Kate couldn't. Her right arm couldn't move. It was humiliating. Countering more than two hundred

years of army tradition, she slowly raised her *left* arm and held a
rigid salute until the colors had moved completely out of her line
of sight. A tear trembled in her eye and cascaded down her cheek.
As company after company passed by, Kate recalled the lyrics of
the music the band was playing:

> *West Point, at the call,*
> *Thy Sons arise in honor to thee,*
> *May thy light shine ever bright,*
> *Guide thy sons aright,*
> *In far-off lands or distant seas.*
> *Thy name first above all,*
> *Through all the years thy motto we will bear:*
> *We, thy sons as we fight,*
> *May we strike for the right,*
> *Alma Mater, ever for thee.*

Reflecting on these words, Kate knew that what was happening on the Plain that day was merely a beginning, a very early
beginning for women. The Army's history was male, the traditions
were male, the songs were male. It would take decades to change
all that. Freedom takes time. She felt angry about the length of
time. Yet, she knew that the Army had taken an important first
step. It wasn't merely symbolic.

Kate looked over her left shoulder at the stone relief above the
entrance to the Academy Library. What happened that day on the
Plain would lend new significance to the figure of Athena—the
warrior and nurturer—the modern day example for "the total man".
As the last company passed in review, General McKeane left the
reviewing stand and rushed over to Kate. He hugged her tightly
and said, "Kate, you can't imagine how proud I am of you. You
can soon join the ranks of the combat infantry. Well—as soon as
you completely recover." Framing Kate between his extended arms,
he added, "I knew that making you tough it out when you were
young would make a difference someday."

Kate, momentarily stunned, replied pointedly, "Dad, how can you possibly take credit for this? I didn't do this for you, or because of you."

"Don't get bitchy, pumpkin. I just wanted to . . . "

"You just want to what? Tell me what a lousy father you've been? How you loved the military more than me? How you deserted Karen? Shirked your family responsibilities? What you did, Dad, was sick . . . sick. Maybe you can live with your guilt. But I'm not sure I can any longer."

"Shhhh—Kate. Somebody will hear you . . . "

"No, Dad. It's time you listen,—listen with your heart. What I accomplished, I did in spite of you. I did it for *me* Dad, for *me* and for countless women who are out there now in a man's world struggling not only to be recognized but also accepted as leaders."

"But Kate, I didn't mean to sound . . . "

"It may surprise you Dad, but at this moment I don't care about being in the infantry—or, even about being in the Army. I'm disabled; I can be discharged. I met the challenge. I proved myself to myself and to the skeptics. I just realized a few minutes ago, that's all I ever really wanted to do."

"Kate, you can't be . . . "

Her right arm hanging limply at her side, Kate turned and walked away from her father, stiffened as if at attention, looking glassy-eyed off into the distance, up the Hudson River well beyond Trophy Point and Battle Monument. Deep down, she pitied him. There he was—a man, who as an impressionable plebe, had witnessed MacArthur's stirring "Duty, Honor, Country" farewell-to-the-corps speech in May of 1962 and who, at that instant, made a commitment to do whatever was necessary to become a general officer someday; a man, who over his years in the military, had become imprisoned by the values of right, wrong, and responsibility of another generation; values wrought by a ramrod school of thought in which relationships were secondary to military priorities. There he stood, looking at the horizon. Somewhere beyond his comprehension. She pitied him, but she could not forgive him. Not today, anyway.

Across the Plain, Kate could vaguely make out the figure of Colin Martin, talking to some people in front of the MacArthur Memorial. She waved fondly. He smiled and waved back.

Kate turned back toward the reviewing stand and noticed her sister standing alone. Fixing on this scene for a few seconds, she empathized with the pain and loneliness of Karen's mental illness, the ridicule Karen had suffered over the years, her limited life experiences and potential, and her continuing bravery in a tough fight, day to day, to deal with all of these things. A true queen of battle.

Kate walked slowly toward her and, as she approached, she watched her sister's face fill with the pride of recognition. Extending her left hand toward her, Kate said quietly, "Come, Karen, it's time for us soldiers to take that next hill."